These Dreaming Spires

ALSO AVAILABLE FROM TITAN BOOKS

FANTASY
Rogues
Wonderland: An Anthology
Hex Life: Wicked New Tales of Witchery
Cursed: An Anthology
Vampires Never Get Old: Tales With Fresh Bite
A Universe of Wishes: A We Need Diverse Books Anthology
At Midnight: 15 Beloved Fairy Tales Reimagined
Twice Cursed: An Anthology
The Other Side of Never: Dark Tales from the World of Peter & Wendy
Mermaids Never Drown: Tales to Dive For
The Secret Romantic's Book of Magic

CRIME
Dark Detectives: An Anthology of Supernatural Mysteries
Exit Wounds
Invisible Blood
Daggers Drawn
Black is the Night
Ink and Daggers
Death Comes at Christmas: Tales of Seasonal Malice

SCIENCE FICTION
Dead Man's Hand: An Anthology of the Weird West
Wastelands: Stories of the Apocalypse
Wastelands 2: More Stories of the Apocalypse
Infinite Stars
Infinite Stars: Dark Frontiers
Out of the Ruins
Multiverses: An Anthology of Alternate Realities
Reports from the Deep End: Stories Inspired by J. G. Ballard

HORROR
Dark Cities
New Fears: New Horror Stories by Masters of the Genre
New Fears 2: Brand New Horror Stories by Masters of the Macabre
Phantoms: Haunting Tales from the Masters of the Genre
When Things Get Dark
Dark Stars
Isolation: The Horror Anthology
Christmas and Other Horrors
Bound in Blood
Roots of My Fears

THRILLER
In These Hallowed Halls: A Dark Academia Anthology

A
DARK ACADEMIA
ANTHOLOGY

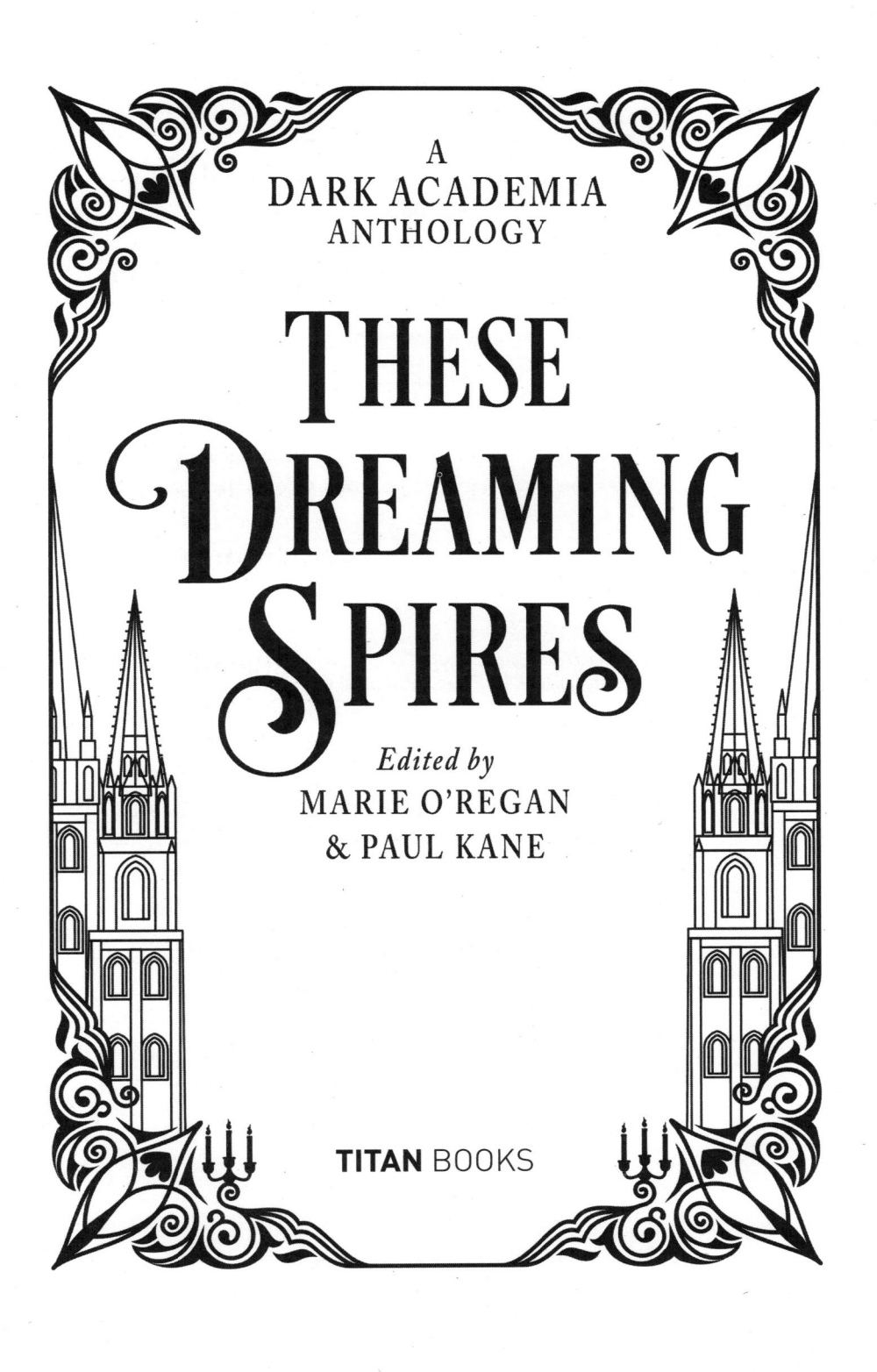

THESE DREAMING SPIRES

Edited by
MARIE O'REGAN
& PAUL KANE

TITAN BOOKS

These Dreaming Spires
Hardback edition ISBN: 9781835410196
E-book edition ISBN: 9781835410233

Published by Titan Books
A division of Titan Publishing Group Ltd
144 Southwark Street, London SE1 0UP
www.titanbooks.com

First edition: September 2025
10 9 8 7 6 5 4 3 2 1

This is a work of fiction. All of the characters, organizations, and events portrayed in this novel are either products of the author's imagination or are used fictitiously. Any resemblance to actual persons, living or dead (except for satirical purposes), is entirely coincidental.

Introduction © Marie O'Regan and Paul Kane 2025
Tallow's Cove © Erica Waters 2025
Utilities © Genevieve Cogman 2025
Destroying Angel © Jamison Shea 2025
Within the Loch © Elspeth Wilson 2025
Advanced Dissection © Taylor Grothe 2025
God, Needy, Enough with the Screaming © Olivie Blake 2025
Poisoned Pawn © De Elizabeth 2025
Open Book © Kit Mayquist 2025
A Short List of Impossible Things © Faridah Àbíké-Íyímídé 2025
The Harrowing of Lucas Mortier © M. K. Lobb 2025
The Coventry School for the Arts © Ariel Djanikian 2025
The Magpies © Kate Alice Marshall 2025

The authors assert the moral right to be identified as the author of this work.

No part of this publication may be reproduced, stored in a retrieval system, or transmitted, in any form or by any means without the prior written permission of the publisher, nor be otherwise circulated in any form of binding or cover other than that in which it is published and without a similar condition being imposed on the subsequent purchaser.

A CIP catalogue record for this title is available from the British Library.

Typeset in Minion Pro.

EU RP (for authorities only)
eucomply OÜ, Pärnu mnt. 139b-14, 11317 Tallinn, Estonia
hello@eucompliancepartner.com, +3375690241

Printed and bound by CPI (UK) Ltd, Croydon, CR0 4YY

Table of Contents

Introduction | *Marie O'Regan and Paul Kane*	7
Tallow's Cove | *Erica Waters*	11
Utilities | *Genevieve Cogman*	37
Destroying Angel | *Jamison Shea*	61
Within the Loch | *Elspeth Wilson*	87
Advanced Dissection | *Taylor Grothe*	113
God, Needy, Enough with the Screaming | *Olivie Blake*	145
Poisoned Pawn | *De Elizabeth*	189
Open Book | *Kit Mayquist*	223
A Short List of Impossible Things | *Faridah Àbíké-Íyímídé*	253
The Harrowing of Lucas Mortier | *M. K. Lobb*	275
The Coventry School for the Arts | *Ariel Djanikian*	299
The Magpies | *Kate Alice Marshall*	333
About the Authors	357
About the Editors	363
Acknowledgements	367

INTRODUCTION

Marie O'Regan and Paul Kane

Believe it or not, this volume of Dark Academia short stories – a sequel of sorts to *In These Hallowed Halls*, which featured the likes of Kate Weinberg, M. L. Rio and Susie Yang – was commissioned even before that first book came out.

Such was the interest in *Hallowed Halls*, with pre-publicity and ARCs requested, and just pure excitement reaching a fever pitch in the run-up to the *first ever* Dark Academia anthology being released. It has since been reviewed incredibly well and sold for translation to several other countries, such as Poland and Turkey.

Looking back on that wonderful time and seeing all the buzz for this project online – not to mention going out and doing signings – it will always be a very special time in our lives, and probably in the authors' lives as well.

Our aim wasn't just to provide something which hadn't been created before, but also to push the boundaries of what Dark Academia might be – and this was definitely reflected in some of the reviews. We soon realised, even after setting out a potted history of the phenomenon in our introduction and trying to give an overview, that it means very different things to different people; some deeply personal. There always has been much debate about what constitutes Dark Academia, what it should and could be, and our intention was to include pieces that covered the widest possible range of those types of tales. It's something we try to achieve in all our anthologies.

Similarly, with *These Dreaming Spires* we were looking at doing the same – maybe even pushing those boundaries a little bit further. That's not to say we wouldn't be including more traditional elements of the subgenre, as we definitely did with the original book, but also that there's always room for more innovative examples of what it means to particular authors.

So, what lessons have we got for you this time round?

Elspeth Wilson (*These Mortal Bodies*) brings us a tale about memories, the environment and a unique body of water connected to a seat of learning, and Erica Waters (*All That Consumes Us*) introduces us to a place where the patterns of the past can be very perilous indeed. Genevieve Cogman (The Scarlet Revolution trilogy) presents an all-too-believable technological nightmare for one poor student, while Kate Alice Marshall (*We Won't All Survive*) concerns herself with the notion of reality itself.

Author of *The Prospectors*, Ariel Djanikian, relates a story of one girl facing up to tragedy – which also informs a tale from M. K. Lobb (*To Steal from Thieves*), asking us what we would give for "higher" knowledge. The author of *Where Sleeping Girls Lie*, Faridah Àbíké-Íyímídé, asks us to think about just what is impossible, and Taylor Grothe (*Hollow*) about the survival of the fittest – or should that be the most ferocious?

In Jamison Shea's (*I Am the Dark That Answers When You Call*) contribution we find out why it can be dangerous to encounter your true soulmate, while De Elizabeth (*This Raging Sea*) is inspired by the twists and turns of chess. The author of *Tripping Arcadia*, Kit Mayquist, presents us with a tale of a mysterious ancient tome, and Olivie Blake (The Atlas Series) delivers a meditation on madness and obsession.

Get ready to go to the top of the class, people, because a brand-new term is about to begin…

Marie O'Regan and Paul Kane

February 2025

TALLOW'S COVE

Erica Waters

My first thought was that I wished I'd come earlier. It was only half past three, but already the day's last light was leaving the cove. That light ought to have gilded the salt marsh and cast its golden glow on the shoreline, illuminating St. Clement's College Chapel and picking out the details of the sagging colonial houses scattered on the other side of the shallow water. But the light didn't seem able to touch Tallow's Cove, which remained as dull and desolate as the wet New England weather.

The chapel, strangely isolated from the bustling campus, seemed more like a piece of the landscape, as if it had grown right up out of the sandy soil, building itself from the gray, lichen-covered boulders that were scattered across the shore. It was a creature of salt and stone, hulking where it ought to have soared. Its belltower listed nauseatingly toward the sea.

I was only a few minutes' walk from the student union, with its mediocre café and noisy air hockey tables, yet I felt like I had wandered out of ordinary life and into a myth, like a knight who stumbles upon a castle under a spell, where a wounded king lies waiting to be healed. Everything was still, almost stagnant. The path from town to the cove had long since been washed out by coastal flooding and neglect, so only members of the college had easy access to it, but I was still surprised by the emptiness of the place. There were no dogs running on the shingled beach or elderly women scanning the skies for birds, no amorous co-eds making out on a blanket. It was November, sure, and a blustery cold day, but during my undergrad years in Boston, I had learned that the determination of New Englanders to be out in all weather was as reliable as the tides.

I was here on a research trip, having won a highly coveted semester-long travel grant to do research for my MDiv thesis, which purported to explore haunted religious spaces in the US as representations of historical institutional wrongdoing. This was the fifth such place I had visited, following online tips that had led me from Georgia to Tennessee to North Carolina to Pennsylvania to Massachusetts. In each place, I had taken photos and collected accounts from locals, digging into local archives where I could. I had not encountered any restless spirits, but I did uncover the ghosts of America's sins, just as I had expected: racism, homophobia, consumerism. Those places had indeed been haunted, but not by any actual spirits, merely the reverberation of ordinary, banal human evil.

But this place... if any religious sanctuary might turn out to be haunted by something otherworldly, I would put my money on St. Clement's Chapel. It looked too... too *something*, though I couldn't put my finger on it. Not yet.

The only thing that moved on the horizon was the seagulls, which screamed and circled, smudges of white against the darkening sky. I paused for a long moment to watch as one of the gulls flew straight up into the air, a snail or some other hapless invertebrate clutched in its talons, and dropped the poor creature on the rocks below, cracking open its shell, before swooping down to retrieve the tender meat. I shivered, drawing my corduroy blazer tighter, and scanned the water for any other signs of life. From far away came the sound of a buoy, its distant ringing like a mournful church bell. But there were no boats out in the cove. Close to shore were a handful of geese in the shallow water, all in a line. Each bird had its head tucked beneath a wing, as if sleeping or hiding from the relentless wind, which stung my eyes and made them water. Other than the gulls and the geese there were only rocks and a single skeletal tree thrusting out of the high bank that led to the chapel. My feet seemed to carry me toward it of their own accord.

Up close, the chapel seemed even more off-kilter, more damaged – a place left to rot until it fell into the sea. The front doors had clearly once been painted red and were still studded with iron, but now they were decayed and covered in mildew, barely attached to the hinges. Wary, wanting to get my bearings before I went inside, I walked around the building to the churchyard, where the overgrown remains of a small cemetery quietly moldered. The headstones ranged from the mid-1700s to the early 1900s, most of the stones cracked and broken, covered in lichen and moss, nearly illegible. I squatted to examine a row of them. The nearest showed a hand with its finger pointed at the sky. I couldn't make out the inscription. Later, I would take pictures of everything, but I liked my first impression of a reputedly haunted location to be unmediated, unfiltered, nothing between me and the building I had come to research.

I stood with a wince, regretting forcing my always-stiff joints into a crouch, and stared up at the rubblestone granite building, my skin prickling strangely as if I were being watched. I shifted my leather satchel on my tired shoulder and scuffed my chunky oxfords on the gravel in the overgrown grass, drawing out the moment before I would go inside and face whatever was lurking, whatever was giving me that feeling of eyes on the back of my neck. I sensed there was a reason I had saved this stop for last.

Of course, I had found out the basic facts of the place before my arrival, partly from St. Clement's website and partly from the blog of a recently deceased local historian. It was originally built by early colonial settlers, a small Anglican church in a Puritan stronghold, funded by a rich merchant who remained loyal to the British king. As the American Revolution approached and tensions became increasingly volatile, patriots were said to sneak up into the gallery to spit on the heads of the worshiping Tories. Windows were broken by local boys throwing rocks for sport. Finally, the wooden church was burned down by a group of angry Puritan men, who saw no place for the old English ways in their new world. The church's priest, the Reverend Samuel Tallow, refused to leave the building and burned with it.

After the Revolution, a wealthy relative of Tallow's had the place rebuilt in her cousin's memory. A new priest arrived. The bell from the original church was refurbished and set to ringing in the new belltower. A large plaque devoted to Father Tallow's memory was erected in the vestibule, a stone relief depicting his face in profile. He looked out over the new church and its congregation, a man who had martyred himself now an unofficial saint of the place.

It all seemed hopeful, like a sign of the new world freed from British rule and from religious tyranny alike. But the church couldn't seem to keep a minister there for more than a few months, and eventually the local community dwindled. The church was closed up. Then, in the early 1900s, St. Clement's University was built up around it and it became a chapel for the students.

Now, nearly two hundred years after its construction, it looked liable to fall back into the sea whose riches had built it. Stones were missing from the façade, and several of the arched stained glass windows had been broken, their remaining panes dull red and blue in the fading light. It was strange to see a church so abandoned, here in New England where history was everything. I was used to the sight of such things in the South, where people are always so eager to forget, to build over, to bury. I'd seen dozens of little lost churches scattered on dusty highways back home. But here, where there was so much money and ancestry, you didn't often see historical buildings like St. Clement's abandoned and left to rot. I was puzzled that the college hadn't taken more pains to preserve and protect it.

I felt a sudden unexpected pinch of kinship with the chapel, an ache behind my breastbone whose origin I couldn't place. Maybe it was because I had been on the road for months and I was tired. Maybe my body, playing host to a progressive inflammatory disorder that threatened to destroy my spine, joints, and connective tissue, felt a little too much like that run-down chapel.

But I suspected it was more a spiritual ache than a physical one. The truth was that my travels had shaken me right down to my foundations, exposing all the cracks and structural weaknesses of my faith and my calling.

With a resigned sigh, I left the dead to their dreaming and walked back to the front of the chapel where the once-red doors listed on their hinges, threatening collapse. I was surprised they weren't boarded over to keep out curious undergrads. Yet another irregularity.

Gingerly, I tried the one on the right, easing it open just enough to slip through into the darkness on the other side. I turned on my phone's flashlight and used its beam to climb three steep stairs up into the nave of the chapel. My light fell on Tallow's memorial, his expression seeming to blaze from the marble even as lichen crawled across his cheek – as if St. Clement's was swallowing him up in a second death. I turned away.

Weak gray light filtered in through the stained glass windows, barely enough to illuminate their subjects and certainly not enough to light the chapel. I could feel rather than see the immensity of the place, the rafters arching high above me. I pointed my flashlight straight down the aisle toward the altar. Its beam wouldn't reach quite that far; it died somewhere in the distance, showing a narrow band of dusty floor and empty box pews, some of their doors hanging open.

I turned off my flashlight and walked slowly toward the altar, genuflecting out of habit. As my eyes adjusted, I began to make out more details. I had expected to find the altar ransacked, but it looked eerily untouched, the altar linen and silver still in place, covered in a thick layer of dust. A dead sparrow lay feet-up beside the communion cup. It looked as untouched as everything else, clean and whole, no signs of rotting.

I picked up the bird and cupped it gently in my hands, trying to remember why I had wanted to become a priest. The last few months had nearly obliterated that desire.

Perhaps I'd started on this path because I was a queer person of faith with too much to prove; wearing the collar would be like a divine stamp on my person, saying I was good, I was whole, there was nothing broken inside me. Maybe it was because I loved the beauty and strangeness of the liturgy, the sense of time stretching out for thousands of years, an unbroken chain of people striving for something beyond themselves. Maybe it was just because I was lonely and being a priest would allow me to be in tender contact with people who needed me. Maybe it was all of those things.

But right now, none of those reasons seemed to be enough. Not in the face of all I had been forced to reckon with these last few months. It wasn't that I hadn't known all the harm done in the name of religion – of course I had. I'd studied church history. More importantly, I was a queer person who'd grown up in a poor rural community whose churches preached that I was going straight to hell. But seeing the indelible marks left even on wood and stone...

I wondered if I should bother finishing the degree. My calling felt as fragile as the tiny cold sparrow cupped in my aching hands.

As if in answer to the thought, I felt the faintest pulse against my palm. I flinched, my fingers opening by instinct. I fumbled, trying to catch the tiny body before it fell to the floor, but feathers brushed against my fingertips as the sparrow darted up, landing on the thurible that hung from the ceiling, sending out the faintest whiff of ancient incense.

I gasped, the sound unnaturally magnified in the hush of the chapel. Had the bird only been stunned? Perhaps it had smashed into something right before I entered the chapel, and my hands had warmed it enough for it to fly again?

That must be it. Despite my plans to become a priest, I did not believe in miracles. My faith was made up of words, metaphors, and the concrete rituals of the Eucharist: altar linen, memorized prayers, a silver cup lifted to drink. But a shiver went through me all the same.

I watched the bird for a long moment as it sat preening itself, seemingly unharmed. Only when it flew away did I turn, surveying the empty chapel, studying every detail I could make out in the low light. The sense of being watched had disappeared once I came inside. Yet it still ought to feel threatening, shouldn't it – this twice-abandoned place? But it didn't. That was what was strange. Unlike the other so-called haunted churches I had visited, this one, despite feeling much more haunted, did not feel unsettling. It didn't set my teeth on edge, didn't make me feel sick at heart like the others had.

In fact, it felt familiar. It felt like kin.

That should have been enough to warn me away, but it wasn't. I took out my Moleskine and started writing.

The history department had loaned me a small, windowless office the size of a closet for the duration of my stay. It was more than generous; the beleaguered adjuncts in the liberal arts wing had far less, sharing an office between the ten of them. I used the space only occasionally, preferring to work in the library, with its huge neo-Gothic windows and green reading lamps. But I had put out a call for locals and students who had stories about the chapel's hauntings, promising an anonymous, private space for the interviews, so I would use the stuffy office to meet with the handful who were willing to talk to me about their experiences.

My first meeting, just after lunch, was with a graduate Art History student who had written a paper on "religious imagery in nineteenth-century stained glass" the previous semester. She had sent me a brief, reserved email that had immediately caught my interest. Often, people who were eager to talk about their paranormal encounters were the least credible. But the ones like Arbor Jones, who were clearly embarrassed, skeptical of their own experiences, yet felt compelled to share, those were usually the ones with something worth hearing.

Arbor's eyes widened very slightly when she came in and saw me. I wasn't what she'd expected: young and obviously queer with my shorn hair, thrifted menswear, and tattoos. But she had surprised me too. From her email, I had expected someone chic, well-dressed, a little preppy – a future museum curator. Instead, Arbor had a shaggy, light pink wolf cut and heavy black boots, and razor-sharp eyeliner which gave her soft face a decisive expression that matched the email I'd received.

"Come in," I said, waving her to a chair with a cracked green vinyl cushion on the other side of my desk, which was piled high with Xeroxed papers and library books. "Arbor? I'm Lana Waldron. You can leave the door open or close it, whatever you prefer... Sorry it's a bit tight in here," I added as she squeezed through the small space between the chair and the door, which she closed with a quiet click.

"That's all right," Arbor said. "The academic life." She noticed my handheld recorder on the desk. "You can record if you want, I don't mind," she said, before I could even ask. Her accent was neutral, giving away nothing, exactly the kind I envied as a Southerner with the sort of hard-to-hide drawl that was a liability in academia. She pulled a battered, pin-covered messenger bag onto her lap. I noticed her pansexual Pride flag pin and she noticed me noticing. She smiled.

"Can gay people be ministers now?" she asked after I pushed the record button.

"In the Episcopal Church and a few others they can," I said. "But I'm still a student. Not wearing the collar yet."

She nodded. "Not really my area," she admitted.

"But you wrote about religious imagery in stained glass," I prompted her.

"I was curious," Arbor said. "I didn't grow up in church, have hardly ever even been inside one. I'm an atheist," she added, "but if you want to study Art History, religion is an inevitable part of it. And there are useful archetypes there like anything else. And I felt kind of... I don't know, kind of drawn to the chapel? I was curious," she said again.

"So you've spent some time in the chapel? What did you think of the stained glass?" I asked, hoping to set her at ease by talking about her academic interests before launching into her paranormal encounter.

"Well, it was badly damaged, at least some of it. They haven't taken care to preserve it properly. But what's still there is beautiful."

"How much time did you spend in the building?"

"At first, it was just going to be a few days, several hours at a stretch. I was sketching," she said. "I tend to get absorbed, lose time a little when I do that."

I nodded, eyes on my notebook as I took notes.

"But..." She hesitated. "But I spent the night a few times."

I looked up sharply. "Why?"

"I, uh, couldn't pay my rent for a bit," she said, uncomfortable now. "I lost my job. Called out sick one too many times. Long Covid."

"Definitely been there," I said. "Not Long Covid but also an inflammatory thing, autoimmune. Makes work-life balance a challenge, doesn't it? I had to take a whole semester off last year."

Arbor visibly relaxed and began to talk more freely. "I figured it would be like camping out, you know? And then I could study the stained glass at all different hours, take pictures, really soak it in."

"Was it frightening being there alone at night?"

She shook her head. "It should have been, but it wasn't."

"What do you mean?" I asked, though I suspected I already knew.

She shrugged, and I sensed she was going to clam back up, so I quickly moved on. "Did you see or hear anything unusual?"

"No, it wasn't like that. There weren't, like, Bibles falling from the ceiling or demonic voices whispering to me. Not like a horror movie or anything."

"So what, then?" I prompted, leaning forward.

She sighed. "It's hard to explain."

"Take your time."

She fiddled with the beaded bracelets on her wrist. "I started taking care of the place. Like, sweeping the floors, polishing the... the cross thingies. The candelabras."

"Why?"

She shook her head, gave an embarrassed half-smile. "You know how pregnant women talk about nesting? It kind of felt like that, only there was no baby coming, nothing special to do it for. I just felt... compelled. I needed to do it."

"Hmm," I said. "Maybe the art historian in you, some desire to conserve?"

She shook her head. "No, it was more than that. I— It went on like that for weeks, me sleeping there and working on the place. It got so bad that it was hard for me to leave and go to class. Hard for me to stay away for more than a few hours. My girlfriend at the time got pissed and broke up with me."

"Oh, wow, I'm sorry," I said. "It sounds like the chapel exerted a lot of power over you." I wasn't entirely convinced that this wasn't some private mental health issue, an unusual manifestation of agoraphobia perhaps.

She must have seen something of those thoughts on my face because she leaned forward, elbows on her knees. "I had done everything I could for the floors, for the pews, for everything that could be cleaned or polished or aired out. And then I started on the windows."

"How? They're so high up... thirty feet at least."

"I stole a ladder from the maintenance department," she said with a quick laugh.

I raised my eyebrows.

"I had to do it. I had to do it even though I'm scared of heights. Even though I get vertigo."

My stomach clenched. I thought I knew where this was going.

Arbor's face took on a fierce, determined expression. I imagined it was how she had looked while she climbed. "I closed my eyes while I went up. All the way up, one rung at a time, a bucket of soapy water in the crook of my arm. And then there were no more rungs. I was at the top. I started washing the window on the right front part of the church, the blue one with the dove? And even though I was terrified, even though I felt dizzy and sick, I felt like I was doing the thing I was born to do, like nothing mattered more than that. But then..."

I held my breath, waiting.

"Then I reached too far and I lost my footing and I fell."

I gasped, covering my mouth with my hand.

Arbor's green eyes bored into me, intense and insistent. "I remember the fall, the way the air whooshed around me. And I remember hitting the floor. My head burst with pain, my entire spine seemed to crack open. It was a single split-second of agony."

Involuntarily, I scanned her body, looking for evidence of wounds, of breaks, of damage. There were none. She shouldn't even be alive. Or she should be in a hospital bed, her back broken, her brain a swollen mess.

"I died," she said simply. "I know I died."

"But..." I had no words. I was treading dark water, with no idea what lurked in the depths.

"Aren't you supposed to believe in miracles? Isn't that kind of your whole thing? Jesus healing the blind man? Jesus raising Lazarus from the dead?"

"What happened next?" I asked, ignoring her questions. My heart beat hard and fast, and sweat beaded on my upper lip.

"I woke up the next morning on the floor, and I was fine. No injuries at all. Nothing. Not even a bruise on me."

"Are you sure you really fell? You didn't dream it?"

"I was lying under the ladder. The bucket of water was spilled on the floor. There was a board under me that had cracked. It wasn't cracked before. I know it wasn't cracked before because I had scrubbed that damn floor on my hands and knees," she added as if anticipating my argument. "I fell. I died. And then I wasn't dead."

I thought of the bird that had stirred to life in my hand the previous day, of the way its feathers ruffled against my skin. The hairs on my forearms and along the nape of my neck stood on end.

"Why?" I asked. "Why do you think it all happened?"

Arbor shook her head. "I wish I knew."

"Have you ever been back?"

She gave another shake of her head. "Never. I got up off the floor and I ran straight out of there. I never went near it again."

"So the compulsion was gone? To take care of the place?"

She laughed, though it was a strangled kind of sound. "Died with me, I guess."

I studied her. This was an educated person, a self-avowed atheist. I didn't think she was lying. How could it possibly benefit her? But that didn't mean any of this was true. It didn't mean she hadn't had a serious mental health episode. Those were common enough in grad school. I had watched plenty of classmates spiral into depression, anxiety, mania. If she was already sick, if she had lost her job and was under stress...

"Did you ever look more into the chapel's history?" I asked, eyes on my notebook again as I doodled a bit of ivy in the margins of my notes, not wanting to give away my thoughts by meeting her gaze once more. My facial expressions have always tended to be too open, too communicative. I didn't want to piss her off or make her feel like I didn't believe her.

"No. I thought about it, but I decided the best thing to do was to put as much distance as possible between me and that place. I didn't want it to pull me back in."

It occurred to me then that she spoke about the chapel as if it were a person; sentient, with a will of its own. Maybe to her it was.

"You're... you're not going to spend too much time there, are you?" she asked, her tone strange.

I looked up and met her eyes.

"You're not going to stay the night, are you? Don't stay the night," she added. "You should take someone with you, too. Someone to keep you balanced."

"I'll be okay," I said. "I've been studying reputedly haunted places for months."

"Not like this, you haven't. That's the only reason I came to be interviewed. I wanted to warn you. I didn't want you to end up like me."

"But you're okay now, aren't you?" I asked carefully. "You weren't permanently injured?"

She shrugged. "I dream about it a lot. The chapel. The fall. I relive it. For a while, I thought about transferring to a different school to get away from it."

"Why didn't you?"

She bit her lip. "I have too much here, too much to lose, so I just don't go anywhere near it now. And you shouldn't either," she said, standing and gathering her things. "You should keep it purely academic. Don't get involved."

"I'll bear that in mind," I said, rising to walk her to the door even though it was only a few feet away. "Thank you for telling me your story."

"You're welcome," she said, formal again. "Goodbye."

"Oh, Arbor," I called, when she was halfway down the hall. She turned. "Could I read your paper about the windows?"

"I never wrote it," she said. "Took an Incomplete. But I still have my sketchbook. I'll put it in your mailbox tomorrow."

"Thanks. I promise to return it."

"You can keep it," Arbor said. "I don't know why I've hung on to it all this time." She gave me the barest of smiles before she walked away.

I had interviews scheduled with five other people over the next two days. Four of them turned out to be undergraduates with a flair for the dramatic, their stories about drunken dares and shadows on walls – nothing of substance. The fifth was an alumnus from the class of '96 who still lived in the area. He cancelled five minutes before our meeting, citing a vague work emergency. He didn't offer to reschedule. I emailed Arbor to thank her for the interview and included my phone number in case she thought of anything else she wanted to share. She didn't write back.

I spent the rest of my time dutifully transcribing the interviews, a tedious process, especially because I didn't see anything of worth in the stories. Only Arbor's testimony caught my imagination. I found myself rewinding and replaying it, lingering over certain phrases.

Right now, it was all I had. Her soft voice narrating the impossible. That and her sketchbook, which I found in my mailbox the next morning, nestled on top of departmental notices and flyers for campus events. She was a talented artist with a sure hand – detailed and meticulous to the point of obsession. The sketchbook started with the stained glass windows, pages and pages of them, but then Arbor had moved on to other parts of the chapel. The altar, the vaulted arches of the ceiling, the organ.

Then, the outside of the chapel and its cemetery. She had even sketched individual tombstones, rendering them in all their half-illegible decrepitude. She must have spent weeks and weeks at the chapel to draw all of this, I realized, weeks away from her studies and social ties. Weeks in a strange state of obsession, alienated from her real life.

The last few drawings focused on the crenelated belltower, then a narrow, claustrophobic set of stairs that looked more like a ladder. The final drawing was of a huge bell. Arbor must have zeroed in on the church bell. Strange, then, that she had started cleaning the windows. Why did her final sketches diverge so sharply from her cleaning activities? Something didn't add up. It was time to visit the chapel again, I decided, stowing the sketchbook in my bag. See if I could find any evidence to corroborate Arbor's story.

I made my way through the busy campus full of red-cheeked undergraduates clutching lattes. Brown and yellow leaves drifted down onto the sidewalks, the trees barer now than they had been only a few days ago. Late fall was turning into winter with a quickness that caught me by surprise.

Still, the day was brighter than the last time I had taken the path down to the chapel, and I felt almost excited as I left the cheerful voices behind to exchange them for the doleful calls of gulls at the edge of the cove. Light streamed into the chapel through the cracks in the roof and windows, and the stained glass cast colored shapes onto the pews and bare floors. I stood in the middle aisle for a long moment, feeling a strange peacefulness settle over me, a sense of homecoming. I dropped my satchel onto a pew and began to search along the floor for the crack that Arbor had said would be there, in the place she fell. Of course, even if it was there, I told myself, it wouldn't prove her story was true. Anything could have caused it – a worker dropping a heavy tool, wood-devouring insects, water damage.

But my rationales were needless. The floor was smooth and undisturbed beneath the window that depicted a flying dove with a bit of green in its beak, the wooden boards well-trodden but surprisingly unmarred, not even showing signs of water damage. I felt a moment of disappointment, not because it meant that a miracle hadn't occurred here but because I knew Arbor would be hurt by it – the lack of proof for what she'd experienced.

I decided to investigate the belltower next, the one part of the church I hadn't been into yet. I wasn't sure that the stairs up to the tower would be sound, but if Arbor had been up them only a year and a half ago, how rotten could they be? I climbed up to the small gallery that housed the defunct organ, its pipes glinting dully through the rust. There was a door just behind it. I opened that and immediately looked up, craning my neck and squinting to try and make out the end of the ladder in the darkness. It seemed to go on forever. My breath went tight in my throat at the thought of climbing that ladder and heaving myself up into the dark, claustrophobic space of the belltower.

How could Arbor have done it if she was afraid of heights, if it gave her vertigo? Yet she must have gone up there since she'd sketched the bell.

I stepped forward to grip the ladder, thinking to test its soundness, but the toe of my shoe caught on something. I tripped and fell forward into the ladder, having to grab on tightly to keep from falling. I banged my elbow painfully against the wood and barely muffled a swear.

I turned my phone's flashlight on and pointed it at the floor.

"Shit," I whispered, any hope of reverence lost.

The thing that had tripped me was the floor itself. There was a huge, splintered crack through several boards, and a dark stain spread out around it. I squatted to examine it more closely. It wasn't just a stain from some long-ago dropped liquid. Whatever had made it was still there, dried and tacky, half-covered by dust. I ran a few trembling fingers over it, shuddering at the rough texture of the wood. The tips came away coated in a rust-colored powder. I raised them to my nose.

The smell was rotten, metallic.

It was blood.

I stumbled back down the stairs into the sanctuary, my thoughts reeling. Had Arbor fallen off the belltower ladder and gotten the story confused? If so, she had clearly lost blood. A lot of it.

I remembered something from the local historian's blog: The burned remains of Reverend Tallow's body had been found in exactly the same place in the original colonial church, at the bottom of the old stairs leading up to the belltower. Perhaps he had tried to take refuge up there when the flames grew too hot. But he must have fallen on the way up.

It was a strange coincidence – that Arbor and Tallow had apparently fallen in the same place. If Arbor was to be believed, then they had both died in the same place. But Tallow stayed dead, while Arbor got up and ran back to her life.

My mind was filled with horrible, graphic visions of both falls: blood and fire, broken bones and bubbling skin. Yet as I sat in a pew staring at the altar, my anxiety began to dissipate. I took a deep breath and then another. I felt calm, I realized, calmer than I had in a long time. And tired. I leaned forward, resting my head on the back of the pew in front of me. My eyes began to grow heavy. Some distant part of my brain told me to get up and leave, but I didn't. Instead, I fell asleep.

I opened my eyes to early morning light streaming in through the holes in the stained glass and in the ceiling. My face rested on my arm and I was lying on a dusty pew, the faded red cushion musty beneath my nose. I woke the way I always did, like my body had aged fifty years overnight, every joint stiff. I stretched as much as I could before sitting up and blinking at the chapel around me. Dust motes shone in the pale golden air; ivy crawled in through the windows. Birds' nests dripped straw from every rafter.

It was beautiful. Beautiful in its disarray, in its decomposing. I hadn't thought destruction was capable of beauty, but slow destruction – the slow unmaking of human effort through nature's inexorable means? It took my breath.

The place felt hushed and... holy. Holier than any polished, perfect cathedral. A place apart. It felt like somewhere one would find at the end of a journey, the keeping place of the Holy Grail. Maybe everything I sought was here, I thought. All the answers to my questions, my doubts. Maybe this was the place that could help my future make sense again.

But beneath these thoughts rose another, unwelcome one: I had done exactly what Arbor warned me not to do. I had spent the night. I grabbed my bag and Arbor's sketchbook and hurried out, superstitiously afraid of looking at anything else in the chapel.

After cleaning up in my loaned dorm room in freshman housing, I hurried to the library, to my usual carrel by the window. As I slid into the hard, wooden chair, I felt my mind clear and my academic training take over. I had researched the general history of the chapel, but hadn't yet dug deep into Samuel Tallow – a necessary research point considering the manner of his death. A quick search of the library's online catalog revealed a small collection which included Tallow's papers and a diary containing notes for sermons, descriptions of life events, and personal reflections. It was being held in a special archive here on campus.

I emailed the special collections librarian to request access and received a swift and enthusiastic response. Apparently there weren't too many people on campus interested in eighteenth-century Anglican ministers. An hour later, I was sitting in a small room with the journal on the desk before me. It was written in a tight, slanting cursive that the middle-aged, cardigan-clad librarian offered to decipher for me if I needed help.

"Why didn't these burn in the church?" I asked him.

"Most of his papers did. But this journal was left on his bedside table in the parsonage. Luckily for us," he added as he ducked out of the room.

Left alone with Tallow's diary, I took a deep breath and opened it, half-afraid of what I might find. Unlike the chapel, Tallow's journal had been well preserved, the ink still dark and clear. Once I got used to his handwriting and archaic diction, I sank into Tallow's mind. It was not a pleasant experience. He seemed hounded and harried, both by his role as an Anglican minister in a Puritan land on the cusp of revolution and by something more personal, a shadow always at the back of his mind. His sermons were stern and steely, his admonishments to himself even more so – pushing himself to breaking when he was ill, condemning himself for every human emotion and desire. I found myself looking for softness, sweetness, even a hint of it, but it wasn't there. This was exactly the kind of man who would let himself burn with his church.

But was he the kind of man who stayed behind to haunt it hundreds of years later? I wondered, feeling less scholarly than I had in my entire academic career.

And if it was Tallow haunting the chapel, where had he found the compassion to breathe life back into the tiny body of a sparrow, sending it flying back to its life? When had he learned the mercy that let Arbor up off that wooden floor, to draw and paint and maybe one day to forget St. Clement's Chapel's dark corners? I didn't see any of that here in his journal. Only hardness, an unyielding spirit, a sense of conviction that felt like being strangled.

Was his haunting his redemption, his ghostly miracles a belated absolution?

Or was he simply reenacting his own dark end?

I studied the journal until the library closed, returning it to the front desk resignedly. My body ached from the hours of sitting on a hard chair. I walked out of the library into the cool moonlight, into a cold autumn breeze that sent brown leaves skittering eerily down the path before me. I decided to take a walk before finding something to eat, just to loosen up the ache in my spine. I told myself I had no particular destination in mind, but I knew where I was going.

The chapel loomed up out of the darkness, a gray giant in the encroaching fog that was rolling in with the tide, carrying the smell of salt and fish.

"Lana!" a voice called from somewhere close by.

I startled and turned. I squinted into the darkness, but I could only make out a general human shape, accompanied by the smell of cigarette smoke. "Sorry, who's there?"

"I've been trying to reach you all day," the voice said, worried-sounding. Arbor stepped into view, a lit cigarette in one shaking hand. "You shouldn't be here. It's not safe."

"I'm fine," I said, both pleased and annoyed that she had taken the trouble to track me down. "My phone must have died, and I've been busy. I found Tallow's diary in the library. I'm just here to do some re—"

"You're not," Arbor interrupted, coming toward me fast. "You're under its spell." Up close, I could see she was terrified. The hand that held the cigarette trembled. Her eyes were wide, pupils blown. She cast nervous glances at the chapel. "Come home with me; you can stay at my place until you feel like yourself again."

I stared at her for a long moment, my thoughts syrupy slow. I could imagine a whole life unraveling from this moment if I did what she asked. Maybe we would sleep together, maybe we would fall in love. Maybe I'd give up on my degree, on being a priest. Maybe we'd work silly, underpaid jobs and get a cat. We'd listen to records and share our favorite books and drink cheap wine. We would be happy, at least for a while.

I looked away from her frightened, lovely eyes, back toward the waiting chapel. "Thanks, Arbor. I really appreciate your concern," I said, forcing a smile onto my lips. "But I'll be fine, I promise."

When I started toward the chapel, she called my name a few times, but she didn't follow me or try to stop me. I slipped inside like a shadow, feeling as if I was coming home after a long trip away, back to a place where I could shed my outer skin, be the vulnerable creature underneath, forgetful of myself, existing in that automatic way which requires no thought, almost no *self* at all. Home.

The chapel's interior was cool and damp with the rising fog, wreathed in quiet. I sank down into a pew near the altar, feeling bodiless, diffuse, as empty as the salt air and fog and the borderless night.

I came awake suddenly and completely, a beam of moonlight falling directly into my eyes. The moon was high up over the chapel, and the fog from earlier had dissipated, leaving a cool, clear black sky full of pinprick stars. I stared up at it for a long moment, trying to figure out what had woken me.

Smoke. I smelled smoke.

Suddenly, the room that had been still and quiet, held in moonlight as if in a cupped hand, was aflame. Fire danced up the walls of the chapel, smoke rolled to the rafters. I ran for the front doors, but they were barred and already engulfed in flames. Blind in the dark, my lungs filling with smoke, I ran instinctively for the door that would take me up, out of the flames and the burning smoke. Up the stairs and past the organ, to the ladder that led to the belltower. I put my foot on the ladder, grasped the highest rung I could reach, and hauled myself up into the dark.

I seemed to climb for a long, long time, the narrow walls of the shaft so near I bumped my elbows against the bricks. My breath was tight in my chest, my heart beating so hard it was all I could hear. The fire seemed far away, as if it were happening somewhere else.

Finally, I reached the top of the ladder and pulled myself up into the small space of the belltower. Above me hung a huge bronze bell, beautifully carved and a murky blackish-green in color. It hadn't been updated with a modern carillon, which meant it must be rung by hand. Without thinking I reached forward and yanked the bell pull, exerting all my strength to ring it. Maybe someone down below would hear it and send help before the entire chapel burned to the ground with me inside. Maybe Arbor was still down there, trying to save me.

The sound rang out, erratic, weaker than I'd hoped, but surely still loud enough to reach the campus. I kept ringing the bell, the reverberation of each strike running all the way up my arms, making my teeth ache. I lost all sense of myself, the distance between me and the walls of the church disappearing, until I was not a person ringing a bell but the sound of its ringing, the smell of damp stone walls and rotting wood, my beams stretching up up up to the heavens, becoming sanctuary.

The weight of the bell pull had me now, its momentum carrying me forward and back, forward and back, with each deep resonant peal. But never well-coordinated, I lost my footing on the return pull and was thrown backward, my aching hands losing hold of the rope. In that instant, I was myself again, returned to my imperfect, lonely body. I stumbled. Back and then back again.

My foot reached for solid ground and found only open air.

UTILITIES

Genevieve Cogman

The cracked chimes of the campus clock striking midnight vibrated in the still air of the room; they stirred the dust which topped the bookcases and lay along the skirting boards, and made the *Stolas* utility perched on her desk twitch his wings in annoyance.

Madeleine looked up from her work at the sound, irritated. She hadn't thought it was that late. A lecture in half an hour, and she still had two utilities to code for the next night's classes, and if she had to stay in afterwards to finish her work then she'd never get to go out partying with her friends in realspace. With a gesture which had carried over from her actual body to her digital avatar, she ran her hand through her hair in annoyance. Time, time, there was never enough time...

And then the clock struck a thirteenth note. The sound seemed to swell in the air like ripples. Several of the books on Madeleine's desk closed themselves, flipping shut with little slams and puffs of dust, and the *Stolas* utility whipped his head completely round, hooting in disapproval like the owl he resembled. Nobody had yet achieved true artificial intelligence, but good coding could make a utility seem sentient – or at least, sentient enough to interact with the world around them. It was more comfortable for their users that way.

"Oh, do shut up," Madeleine murmured, though whether to the school clock or to the utility wasn't quite clear. Pointless as the gesture was in virtual reality, she rubbed her eyes and took a deep breath.

Apparently, the universe wanted to conspire against her and spoil her fun. Well, *fine*. She'd just have to conquer the world and make everyone pay and force them to let her sleep in late. That'd show them.

Or possibly she was just a little data-happy from spending too many hours logged in. That could happen. It was something every student was warned about – and then ignored. There just weren't enough hours in the day.

Though why had the school clock struck thirteen?

With a shrug, she decided it must have been a glitch in the virtual reality. Such things were common in less well-built virtual spaces; it was plausible that even the Scholomanz, one of the world's best universities, might occasionally blink. It would probably go down as a university legend, something which was cited to freshmen as "the only time we've ever had any issues here in the last decade…"

She snapped her fingers, rising from her chair.

Nothing happened for a moment – and then the *Stolas* utility spread its wings and floated into the air, landing on her shoulder. Tiny claws pricked through her blouse and into her skin, the momentary pain and fractional drops of blood a virtual token of the improved connection as its library function flickered behind her eyes. She reviewed half a dozen possible utilities – *Crocell* for rapid diagram formulation, *Dantalion* for instant messaging, *Sitri* for scanning other people's avatars – but decided that the lecture didn't warrant anything that serious. Some of her fellow students liked to go around the Scholomanz so hung with utilities that their avatars could barely string two words together when you spoke to them in person, but Madeleine had always felt it was safer to make do with the minimum, and only call up what you actually needed.

And at this end of term, it was important to be safe.

Of course, that didn't mean she couldn't enjoy designing and coding the utilities. Making a tool which performed its function efficiently was a matter of competence. Making one which did so with elegance and style, and which anybody could see was *her* work – well, that was a matter of pride, and one could hardly say there was anything wrong about justified pride...

Yet all the pride in the world would be no help to her if she wasn't on time for her lecture. She took the stairs two at a time, the flowing panels of her scholar's gown rippling dramatically behind her as she pivoted around the banister and came stampeding down to the ground floor. (Perhaps the gown, deliberately coded to always flare properly and with maximum impact, was a luxury – but everyone deserved one luxury, didn't they?) She otherwise looked much like her physical self these days; she'd long since gone past the stage that everyone went through when they coded up their avatar with implausible eyes, hair, bulges, and other details. Pupils at the Scholomanz didn't have the spare time or energy to maintain that sort of indulgence. Their brains were required elsewhere.

Andrew was waiting for her at the foot of the stairs. His *Dantalion* hovered by his ear, barely three inches tall, its tiny book open in its virtual hands as its multiple faces whispered email updates into Andrew's ear. Andrew silenced it with a gesture as Madeleine joined him, giving her a thin-lipped smile. "Getting better. We might actually be able to walk to the lecture rather than having to run or teleport."

"Even I can hear the clock striking," Madeleine said, falling into step with him as they walked out into the campus pentangle. He hadn't bothered to give his gown the same attention that she gave hers, but she noticed the new boots he was wearing, real as life and twice as elegant. "And you may be on time for this lecture, but are you actually prepared for it?"

"You wound me," Andrew said. "You horrify me unspeakably."

"Well, are you?" She tried to mute the genuine concern in her voice. She knew he'd been having issues with some of his assignments, and the *Dantalion* on his shoulder, one of the standard utilities here at the Scholomanz, showed a lack of attention to the coding in every clumsy twitch of its facial features or too-slow flutter of its pages. His boots might be beautiful, but his required work was far less so.

And everyone knew that ten per cent of the students here at the Scholomanz never reached finals.

As usual, the centre of the pentangle was deserted; people

wandered around the edge as though it was a roundabout, diving in and out of buildings as they came to them. The old signs were so worn as to be illegible, covered with blackened ivy and red-leaved creepers. Everyone knew where they were going, however, except for the new students, who had their heads cocked to listen to the malformed half-coded utilities whispering in their ears. Their poorly designed black gowns trailed behind them, each drift of fabric a fraction of a second off, out of synchronisation with the breeze.

Andrew hunched his shoulders – the sort of gesture which was an unconscious carry-over from reality, rather than a deliberately chosen motion – and strode ahead, ignoring her. Madeleine followed, realising uncomfortably that there were a *lot* of new students here today. Her own fault for staying comfortably in her rooms and keeping her head down in studies, rather than paying attention to the world outside. With a pang of guilt, she returned the nods of a group of friends as they passed, and made a resolution – not for the first time – to interact with other people at least a *little* bit more.

Though, of course, the Scholomanz itself wasn't exactly "the world outside" – that would be the waking world, the non-virtual world, the world where she would shortly be looking for employment with all the coding and mathematical skills she'd learned here, and where she'd have no choice but to spend time with other people rather than always deep in her work. Madeleine was quietly confident in that regard – or as others in her social circles had put it, unpleasantly smug. The Scholomanz was quite simply the *best* virtual university, with a depth of processing power and memory storage in its servers that made them the envy of other sites and the object of frequent industrial espionage. Anyone who had a qualification from here could look forward to a comfortable career...

"What's that?" Andrew said, breaking his silence.

"What's what?" They were almost at the lecture hall door. Madeleine stepped to one side, out of the general throng of students, and looked around for whatever had caught his attention.

"There." He pointed over to the right, where two students were squaring off in obvious preparation for a fight, ignoring the friends plucking at them. The omnipresent hush which stifled student noise from more than a few metres away made it impossible to hear what they were saying, but the gestures and scowls were clear enough. One of them – a young woman Madeleine vaguely knew, a second-year student – was invoking a *Bael* utility, its three heads grimacing as it blurred into existence above her head. Legions of tiny sub-utilities floated behind it in a blurred fan of scythe-like wings and faceted eyes. The other woman, a stranger to Madeleine, snapped her fingers in dramatic pantomime, and abruptly a pack of wolves prowled around her legs, forcing her friends away as they slavered and snarled.

"Nice work," Madeleine said, admiring the wolves. "She's got good focus there, and very impressive definition – look at the way the grass is bending under their feet. And just look at that saliva! Dripping really naturally."

Andrew rolled his eyes so hard that it was perceptible in his voice. "What I am *trying* to point out is that she's a transfer student."

"Well, obviously," Madeleine said, frowning as she watched. The different academies all taught coding and program structure – mathematics was mathematics, after all, and one could hardly argue with the ones and zeros – but they all had different *styles* for how their utilities looked inside the virtual reality where they studied and where they'd later work. Some preferred hordes of faceless uniformed minions, while others liked to pattern and visualise them as animals, or birds, or storm clouds, or even little superheroes. The Scholomanz was firmly Goetic; its graduates paraded their demonic-themed utilities as a sign and blazon of their teaching. "She'll lose on speed, though."

Andrew shrugged. "You've got a better eye for that than I do. But look, if she's a transfer student, then they must have some places free on the roster. Last time I checked, I was told they were full up."

"Perhaps someone resigned?" Madeleine offered, distracted by the flickering swarms that the *Bael* utility commanded. "I wonder if—"

She broke off as the two sets of utilities burst into motion. Wolves pounced, jaws drooling saliva, teeth glinting light from every available point; insect-like subroutines struck at their eyes and buzzed around their heads in thick, stinging halos. The two students faced each other across the packs of their minions, both affecting calm assurance.

Thunder rolled across the pentangle, and lightning split the sky a moment later. Every student present except the transfer student – and even she, a moment later – looked up at the roof of the Residence. It was the tallest of the buildings which surrounded the pentangle, dripping with more Gothic architecture than should reasonably have been fitted onto a single roof – then again, the potential of virtual reality also meant that it had more rooms inside than could ever have fitted there in the physical world.

A dark figure stood on the small platform which leaned forward between two high-peaked gable windows – the Dean himself, his attention drawn by the fracas. His cloak snapped out in a dramatic gust of wind, and even though the shadows of his hood concealed his face, disapproval was written in every line of his body.

Sheepishly the two combatants shuffled away from each other, wolves and insects alike dissolving into motes of darkness and vanishing. Scholars scurried in all directions, their heads bowed so as not to catch the furious glare which swept across the pentangle. Even Andrew and Madeleine allowed their conversation to lapse as they hurried for their lecture.

Was it her imagination, or did the Dean's gaze linger on *her*?

Madeleine hastily erased the idea from her mind. It was quite bad enough worrying about getting the necessary grades to graduate – she suspected that she was the best student in her year group, but even if it were true, that didn't necessarily get her past graduation, let alone the sort of job she was hoping for. She followed Andrew up a rackety flight of stairs, each wooden tread groaning artistically under their feet, and they shuffled into one of the lesser auditoriums, where Professor Jones had quite unfairly started early and was already tracing logic diagrams on the chalkboard.

Like all the professors, he was robed and hooded. Every professor at the Scholomanz had bland aliases, rather than anything which could be linked to an identity in the physical world. The Scholomanz prospectus made airy claims about anonymity of lecturing and presentation of knowledge and lack of bias. To be fair, it was certainly difficult for a Scholomanz student to secure any sort of personal favouritism from their mysterious tutors when they didn't even know who the tutors actually *were*. Madeleine (and other students before her) had tried to find out how they were assigned and what their original names were, but all attempts at investigation had failed – everything up to and including simply asking. The only thing which made it remotely endurable was that nobody *else* got any favouritism either.

She quickly edged into a seat and began taking notes, her *Vapula* utility rising from her notepad to etch the diagrams into its memory as Jones delineated them. Out of the corner of her eye, she saw that Andrew had given up on the lecture and was using the time to catch up on one of his program architecture assignments. She bit her lip to stop herself from nudging him in the ribs. Madeleine couldn't *make* him work – but didn't he understand how important it was for him to succeed here? Did he really want to be one of the dropouts who failed at the Scholomanz and ended up with lesser qualifications, scrabbling for a job in a world which would only hire the best of the best? How could he live in the public virtual servers with their cheap simulated reality, so different from the high definition that the Scholomanz offered?

He must have sensed her concern, for he scrawled on his own notepad and turned it to face her. STOP WORRYING!

She scowled and focused on her notes.

The lecture was long and tedious, with nothing new that

Madeleine hadn't already studied, but she forced herself to pay attention. Nobody cared to ask questions afterwards; either they had completely understood the topic, or they had so lost the will to live that they barely had the energy to stumble out of the lecture theatre. Madeleine was the last – Andrew had been one of the first – slowed by her preoccupations and yes, she was prepared to admit it, outright worry. There was nothing she could do to help him if—

The door slammed shut in her face.

Madeleine grabbed the handle and tugged on it, annoyed by what must be someone's stupid idea of a joke. Annoyance escalated to outright anger as the door shuddered but refused to open. She pulled again, but got nowhere with it; it wasn't just locked, it had fused into place.

If this was a feeble attempt by Andrew to distract her, he was going to regret it. Just because she didn't waste her time duelling didn't mean that she didn't have her own set of offensive utilities. "*Vinea!*" she hissed, indicating the door.

The utility spun into shape in front of her, condensing from dust and shadows into the form of a lion riding a black horse. It pointed the snake in its hand at the door, and the timbers exploded into a shattering mass of splinters that sprayed into the corridor beyond.

But there was nobody there. Nobody was waiting to laugh at their joke or snigger at her. Not even Andrew, who she'd have expected to wait for her rather than go on ahead.

The shadows seemed to close in round her. While the Scholomanz was always dark and ominous, it now seemed doubly so, and threatening rather than simply atmospheric. For a moment she considered keeping the *Vinea* utility active in case she might need it. But no – this was the Scholomanz, and she was a student here (one of the best students, her pride prompted) and she was certainly not going to be afraid to walk through her own campus.

Even if, perhaps, she should be.

It was so quiet. She stalked down the corridor, looking for whoever had thought this was a suitable prank to play. But as the silence deepened around her, broken only by the sound of her own footsteps, her pace quickened to a near-run. The *Stolas* bounced on her shoulder, beak clicking and wings twitching, but it didn't bring her any messages. Nobody was looking for her. Nobody was in any of the other lecture halls or offices, loitering in the corridors or dallying in the doorways, complaining about their work or their relationships or just to have something to complain about…

Where *was* everyone?

The maze of corridors widened out to the main door, and she thrust it open.

Suddenly sound came rushing in on her, as between two blinks the pentangle was full of students; some were hurrying between classes, others lazing on benches as they chatted, ignoring the eternal clouds which filled the ominous sky. She caught sight of Andrew sitting a few dozen yards away, the *Dantalion* on his shoulder waving its little book in token of incoming email messages, and Andrew ignoring them as he talked with a young woman whom she recognised as the strange duellist from earlier. He didn't seem to have been looking for her – or be worried about her – at all.

Well, of *course* he shouldn't have, she was perfectly capable of looking after herself. But it did sting a little.

Madeleine sauntered across and waited for him to look up from his new conversation and greet her. She found herself waiting… and waiting. "Andrew?" she finally said.

He looked up at her, and there was nothing except polite curiosity in his eyes. "Hi," he said. "Pleased to meet you. My name's Andrew Radobon."

"Well, yes," Madeleine said, nonplussed. "I knew that."

He raised an eyebrow. "Didn't think I was that well known. So who are you?"

A chill seemed to stitch itself slowly up Madeleine's spine, as real and vivid as it would have been in the physical world, when she realised that he was speaking the absolute truth. He didn't recognise her. He didn't know her. "I'm Madeleine," she said, as though the words were a program in themselves, one that could write the truth back into his brain from which it had somehow been sponged away. "Madeleine Fens."

"Pleased to meet you." He offered her his hand to shake, as though she was a total stranger. "Nice *Stolas* you've got there. You must show me how you wrote it sometime. But if you'll excuse me, I was just talking with Emily here…"

"I'm new to the Scholomanz," Emily said. A snap of her fingers brought one of her wolves into existence, and it curled up at her feet, staring at Madeleine with cold eyes which suggested that its owner didn't appreciate the interruption to her conversation with Andrew. "I transferred from Nottingham just yesterday. Andrew's being very helpful."

I'll bet he is! thought Madeleine. "Sorry to have interrupted," she muttered, the words like stones in her mouth as she backed away.

She bit her lip and tasted blood – as real, as vivid as if she had done so to her physical body. This wasn't possible. She would have liked to believe that it was another joke, but the lack of recognition in Andrew's eyes had been genuine. Yet even so, as she backed away, part of her was hoping that he would jump up to catch her wrist, laughing, and say, *Got you there! I bet you thought I really didn't know who you were...*

But he didn't.

She cast around for someone else she might know, someone who could tell her what was going on. There – over to her right, Lisa Meinst, an occasional study partner, discussing large language models with a friend. Madeleine headed directly for them, ignoring the direction of the crowd, her hands clenching into fists at her side. "Lisa—" she began, as soon as she was close enough for the other woman to hear her.

Lisa looked at Madeleine, frowned, then took off her glasses (an affectation for which she had no need in the real world) in order to polish the lenses. "Yes?" she asked, but it was as clear in her face as it had been in Andrew's. There was no recognition at all.

"You do know me, right?" Madeleine asked, hoping against hope that the answer would be, *Yes, of course,* even if it might be accompanied by *Why are you asking me such a stupid question?*

Lisa frowned. She donned the glasses again, and her frown deepened. "No. Should I? Is this a test? Are you under some sort of disguise utility?"

"Ooh," the woman talking to her said, "that's a *neat* idea. Wait, can I be first to try and break through it?" Without waiting for an answer, she beckoned to thin air and a *Sitri* utility appeared beside her, its feathered wings blurring as they beat furiously and its leopard face contorted in an unmoving snarl. Its eyes glowed green, and the colour was echoed in its owner's eyes as she looked Madeleine up and down. "No, can't get it. I knew I needed to upgrade. You have a go, Lisa."

Lisa pursed her lips in a whistle, and her own *Sitri* appeared, perching on her shoulder. It was better defined than her friend's; the wings were much more griffin-like, rather than random assortments of feathers, and the feline head moved and snorted realistically. The same green light glowed in its eyes and in Lisa's, but after a moment she shook her head. "I can't manage it either. I'm impressed. It looks completely normal – almost as good as the lecturers'. This is a random test, right? Any chance you could come back afterwards and show us the workings?"

"I'll see what I can do," Madeleine said, backing away. *Perhaps I should ask more people*, she thought desperately. *If I keep on trying, someone has to recognise me. But why is this happening in the first place?* The very idea of a campus-wide joke was impossible. This wasn't a place where people *made* jokes. They studied until their brains were sweating blood, because this was the Scholomanz, the only place in the world where you could get this level of virtual reality and education in how to use it. Why had it suddenly turned against her?

She stepped back to the sheltering wall of the Residence, and looked across the swirling pentangle, forcing herself to review the situation as though it was a logic diagram. *Situation: nobody (or at least nobody I've tried so far) recognises me. Possible reasons: campus-wide prank, problem affecting their perceptions, problem affecting my appearance...* A thought suddenly came to her, and she invoked her *Dantalion* utility – perhaps if she sent Andrew a message through the utility rather than trying to speak to him "face to face", that'd work. Or she could contact her tutor, or...

The utility flickered into existence beside her face, then froze, its multiple tiny faces twisting as though it was having a seizure. The pages of the tiny book it carried fluttered madly and came to a stop.

"Cancelled," it said, the word only audible to Madeleine's ears, but as thick and heavy as lead, rather than its usual mild tenor. **"This user no longer exists."**

"Excuse *me*?" Madeleine demanded, panic curdling in her stomach. "Define. Clarify."

The utility's ten faces all remained fixed, but the twenty beady little eyes focused on her.

"Please remain in your current location. Security will be with you shortly."

"Override!"

But the little utility floated there, still present despite Madeleine's attempts to close it down. **"The ultimate clause has been invoked,"** it droned. **"Your contract must be fulfilled."**

Madeleine's vision blurred in confusion. She didn't understand what it meant; she'd read the contracts when she signed up for the Scholomanz, and there was nothing which allowed the system to just expel her like this. It couldn't happen.

Time for the nuclear option. She'd log out and handle this – whatever this was – in the physical world. She subvocalised the string of nonsense syllables which would disengage her from virtual reality and let her wake up – sore, headachy, and in a world that was much less vivid – on the couch in a rented dormitory which she shared with dozens of other students. She'd had *enough* of this.

Nothing happened. It was like the sort of nightmare where she was supposed to be a superhero or a sorceress or something like that, but when it came to actually using powers or casting spells, she was just a normal human being waving her hands helplessly. She was still standing there next to the Residence, the wind picking up and catching at her robe as the storm swirled overhead, every sense she possessed telling her that this was real.

Her *Dantalion* chirped, the tone rising like the whistle of a boiling kettle, and abruptly utilities across the pentangle were also chirping, hitting that same piercing whistle like a diabolical choir. Students froze into place, as sudden and still as though they were children playing a game of *Grandmother's Footsteps*. Utilities moved, wings flapping, animal and human faces turning towards Madeleine; students stood or sat there, unmoving, unwatching, uncaring.

No… there was movement. A dozen figures were beginning to push through the crowd towards her. But they weren't students. They were lecturers, their faces shrouded by their hoods, their bodies hidden by their robes, their hands concealed under dark gloves. They all moved in the same pattern, with the same twitches of shoulders and length of stride – just as though they were someone else's coded utilities. And worst of all, they were coming towards her as though tugged by some invisible spider's web.

Revulsion broke Madeleine out of her shock. She didn't – she couldn't – understand what was going on, but she refused to just stand here and *let* this nightmare happen to her. If the system was going to fail her, then she'd apply to human beings for help.

Steeling herself, she ran for the Residence front door and set her hand on the knocker. It throbbed in her grasp, tingling with barely controlled electricity.

But Madeleine knew her rights. "I demand to speak with someone in a position of authority!" she said, absurdly comforted that her voice actually sounded calm and controlled, rather than panicking and desperate. "I demand to know what the hell is going on here!"

For a moment the door seemed to hesitate – but then the *Stolas* utility on her shoulder spread its wings and hooted, the sound carrying across the pentangle.

The door creaked open. Beyond it, the corridor was full of men – utilities of one sort or another, faces as classical and distant as carven statues, all of them holding drawn swords. The blades gleamed in the light of the lantern overhead, glittering as though they were beautiful rather than deadly.

Could this be some sort of ghastly test? Some final examination? Very well, she'd demonstrate just how well she'd learned the Scholomanz's lessons.

"Flauros!" she invoked, raising her hands to shield her eyes as the utility shimmered into form in front of her, between Madeleine and the armed men. It was full-size to match them, a leopard with jaws that dripped blood, muscles moving under its hide as smoothly as if they were real. She was truly proud of it. She was even prouder of the amount of offensive capacity she'd coded into it. "Attack!"

The *Flauros* utility opened its jaws wide and breathed fire at its opponents, a terrible conflagration fierce enough to temporarily blind anyone looking directly at it.

However, this was only half her plan. While the *Flauros* utility played its infernal flames over her enemies, she pulled up another routine from her stored files and codes, invoking *Andrealphus*. His peacock wings played around her in a glory of light and colour, and as they drew apart again her avatar had shifted to that of a bird.

As a raven – trite, but all she had ready-coded was that or an eagle, and the corridor was too small for a bird that size – she threw herself into motion, racing above the heads of her opponents as they came charging forward to dispose of *Flauros*. She smoothly circumnavigated the swinging lantern, keeping as high as she could above the flames, though even then they crisped the feathers on her breast, swooped through the door beyond, and into the wide reception hall, pausing to perch amid the cobweb-strewn rafters.

The place seemed empty – apart from the utilities she'd just dodged – but Madeleine knew it wouldn't stay that way for long. She had to make her appeal to the highest authority possible, and she had to do it *now*, before some sort of petty bureaucracy could get in the way. Her work and talent had to count for something. She didn't expect the Scholomanz to be charitable, but she knew it protected its assets. Even the smallest utility created here was saved, copyrighted, and admired. How much more its students?

A quick use of the *Astaroth* utility rendered her avatar as invisible as it was airborne. She winged silently above the returning defence forces, who had by now disposed of her *Flauros* utility, and beat her way upwards through the Residence. She was fortunate; doors stood open in her path, so she wasn't required to take human form again to open them. All around her the place seemed to breathe with fascinating secrets, records and code tables and information vortices and walls that scrolled with endless patterns of data, but she ignored them. She had to reach the Dean's office as quickly as possible.

Yet the corridors seemed to stretch on forever, and by the time she saw his office door ahead, her wings were weary. It was a heavy piece of oak, familiar from her first day here as a student, when they'd all come up together for orientation, and the inscription on it of *Lasciate ogne speranza, voi ch'intrate* was in enamel exactly the shade of dried blood. *Abandon all hope, ye who enter here...*

With a sigh of relief, Madeleine invoked the *Andrealphus* utility once more and assumed human form. Even in virtual reality, the human mind had difficulties sustaining a shape so different to its natural one. Yet now, so close to her goal, she found herself hesitating. The anger which had carried her this far was draining away and being replaced by a deeper sense of fear. Every footprint she left in the dusty corridor reminded her how much she was an intruder here, and how much she'd dared in demanding an audience with the Dean himself.

She bit her lip. Was this the behaviour of a student of the Scholomanz? Before she could let herself think about it any further, she stepped forward and – common sense still having some place in her mind – knocked politely on the door.

"Come in," the Dean's voice said.

The door opened silently this time, as though afraid to creak. Vast bookcases lined the walls, rising to a ceiling which was lost in shadows. The Dean was seated, facing her across his wide desk, and the stormlight streaming in through the window turned him to a dark silhouette in which only his gleaming eyes showed clearly. In front of him on the desk lay a single document.

Madeleine swallowed. Her throat was uncomfortably dry. "I've come to make a complaint."

"Yes." His voice was low and unthreatening, almost… sympathetic? "I fully agree that you have every right to do so."

Madeleine hesitated, the wind taken out of her sails by this sudden capitulation. "I'm sorry? I mean, um, yes, quite, and I'd like my full access restored as soon as possible, and there's some sort of problem with people not recognising my avatar, and something happened just now in the pentangle…"

"Absolutely," the Dean said, nodding as though she'd just crowned an intelligent train of thought with an unarguable statement. Which even Madeleine had to admit she hadn't done. "It's very shoddy behaviour, and I can only apologise on behalf of the Scholomanz. Clause Ultima is usually handled much more smoothly and without any concomitant awareness."

Clause Ultima? Madeleine sent a silent command to her *Stolas* utility, ordering it to check the Scholomanz data libraries for information. "I don't understand," she said hopefully.

"That is meant to be the entire point of the matter." He steepled his fingers, regarding her as she stood there like she was nothing but a first-year student who'd been caught in some petty misdemeanour. "Still, since we have a few minutes, permit me to explain.

You are aware that you sign somewhat extensive contracts when you enrol here."

"Yes," Madeleine agreed guardedly. She'd *read* those contracts before signing.

"Then you will recall that the Scholomanz is within its rights to demand a certain amount of labour from you while you are here, in the interests of the good functioning of this educational establishment."

"I do," Madeleine agreed. Teaching assistance, on-site maintenance, internships; nothing that any other university didn't require. But that part of the contract had been hedged around with the usual corporate safeguards – work-life balance, rights to formal refusal, all that sort of thing. "How does it relate to this?"

"To answer your question, I'm afraid that I must go back to the nature of the Scholomanz. Oh, it won't bore you – I so rarely have the opportunity to discuss this freely, and this is quite a pleasure." His tone suggested enticing secrets shared between the two of them, and despite herself Madeleine leaned closer, wanting to hear more. "You know that we offer the very best virtual reality resources here?"

"Yes," Madeleine agreed, wondering where this was going.

"Have you ever considered how we manage this?"

"I'd assumed that you had the very latest servers and memory architecture," Madeleine said, conscious of a sudden and unpleasant feeling of uncertainty. She wasn't sure where this was going, but it felt dangerous.

"Sometimes the old architecture is best." The Dean sighed. "Regrettably, nobody has yet invented anything in terms of data storage or processing power which can surpass the human brain."

It felt as though Madeleine had missed her step while coming down a flight of stairs and was now balanced precariously, arms pinwheeling, above an abyss. Her mouth opened, closed again, then reopened. "But that's not – that is, surely it *can't* be possible!"

"I imagine you're now considering organ donors," the Dean said, his red eyes fixed on her. "You're visualising people who've passed the limits of physical survival and left their brains for this higher purpose. Would that it were so simple, Ms Fens, so ethical, so easily resolved. We require living nervous systems, and the more efficient the better, to serve as utilities for the network. Actually, were it not for the fact you are the best student in the entire Scholomanz—"

Full understanding seized Madeleine. She didn't try to scream or protest. She turned to run.

Or rather, she tried.

The claws of the little *Stolas* utility on her shoulder bit into her flesh, and she no longer had the power to move or speak.

"We tend to repurpose the avatars of volunteers such as yourself as new lecturers," the Dean went on confidingly to his captive audience. "But normally we extract you from the system without your conscious awareness – it avoids awkward situations like this one. Ethics, Ms Fens, ethics. We don't want to be *cruel*. The future we are offering you is much more pleasant than the troubles which all of us must face in the physical world. I would like you to know that we greatly appreciate your contribution to the wellbeing of the Scholomanz. For what it's worth, your friend Andrew *will* graduate. Now if you'll excuse me, I'm afraid I have a rather crowded schedule…"

Madeleine tried to scream. She tried to protest. She tried to invoke a utility. Any utility. But she was frozen as though she was locked in a coffin of lead, and she could only stand there and watch as the Dean opened the document in front of him and touched a single line on it.

Her world dissolved into darkness.

The cracked chimes of the campus clock striking midnight vibrated in the still air of the room; they stirred the dust which topped the bookcases and lay along the skirting boards, and made the Stolas *utility perched on her desk twitch his wings in annoyance.*

Madeleine looked up from her work at the sound, irritated. She hadn't thought it was that late. A lecture in half an hour, and she still had two utilities to code for the next night's classes... but then again, she enjoyed her work. She'd never had such a fulfilling time as she did here at the Scholomanz, able to spend her days doing what she loved. She might almost wish it would last forever...

The Dean frowned as he filed the document away. A shadowy half-formed avatar stood where Madeleine Fens had been, its face and body not yet fully sculpted into some new anonymous lecturer. The *Stolas* utility had vanished.

"We will, of course, be ready to receive any formal declarations of withdrawal of labour, should you ever get round to submitting them," he said, as if the figure could hear him.

There was no response.

"We're not trying to be cruel here," he continued. "Your personality's been shunted into a nice, happy sub-system where you'll keep on reliving the same day and never know any better. A good day. Something cheerful and fulfilling, much more pleasant than reality. This has been past the Ethics Committee multiple times, and everyone agrees that it's the best possible course of action. The greatest good for the greatest number. Though I have to admit, between you and me, that it would be nice if one of you could actually agree with me on that point…"

But Madeleine Fens was no longer there to listen.

Destroying Angel

Jamison Shea

Content Warnings
self-cest (sexual activity with an alternate version of oneself),
misanthropy, self-loathing, body horror, gore, drug and alcohol use.

To the newspapers and true crime obsessives now talking about me, swearing that I'm a cautionary tale, having been seduced by power, let it be known that the seduction was all mine. The great book didn't seduce me; I seduced it. Then, when it was splayed open in my lap, I sucked the power right from between its pages.

And now I'll tell you how. I wasn't some sick fuck who spent hours breaking and folding those bodies for some Satanic rite – I was a righteous victim who simply read from a book.

First, however, I must disabuse you of your paltry theories: no, I was not a boy overwhelmed by powers beyond his understanding; yes, I *am* the summation of my bad deeds; yes, that was my body found, but I am still very much alive; and deep down,

I am both – rotten and god-like in equal measure.

I'm sure you'll see it that way too.

Winter had only just begun, snow dusting the lawn at the University of Whitby, when I stepped into the library that day. Anybody who saw me would have thought I was a student – my face is young, round, and freckled, and I've been told more than once that I have a curious, hungry look in my eyes and permanent dark circles that ring them. I even had a backpack over my shoulder, though it was empty except for a couple boxes of candy. I didn't notice until later, but my posture was poor; my shoulders hunched, which fit with everyone else on campus during midterm season.

In fact, it was *because* of midterms that my services were needed.

I brushed snowflakes from the trim of my coat and headed up the iron staircase to the third floor. Wending through the gray tables and even grayer stacks to the philosophy section was second nature; my former classmates can attest that I lived there. I'm in love with humanity, enamored with our capabilities and most deeply with our flaws. It is my most enduring fixation and, in the beginning, what I was doing all of this for – us.

I was a student of Sartre when I found that book; my thoughts were pure. I was fashioning myself to fashion mankind.

Believe me or don't, but it's the truth.

A glance at my watch said that I was five minutes early for my meeting as usual, which was more than enough time to search for my next read.

PHIL 355: EXISTENTIALISM.

The course syllabus had been available online for years now, unchanging. It didn't matter that I'd been expelled. That there were no grades to earn, no promise of a degree to mount on my barren walls, couldn't keep me away. Even my brother, for whom I did these runs, was oblivious: the only reason I'd agreed to continue in *pharmaceuticals* was to continue my education.

And I reveled in the idea of shoving a finger in the face of the university who punished only me and none of my clients. I'm a man of multitudes.

In the *K*s, I began my search for Kierkegaard's *Fear and Trembling*, next up on the list. Between runs, I spent all my free time reading, taking notes in the margins and working through thought exercises, daydreaming about what the exam might be like. I even planned to email the professor to ask for a copy when the semester was over.

"*Evander Price is a conscientious student who shows remarkable discipline and promise. I ask that he be shown leniency in his sentencing so as not to curtail his academic career and curiosity too seriously...*" That's what he'd written ahead of my disciplinary meeting.

Whole lotta good that did.

I read that letter again and again when the decision came, and even more so when this text came only a month later:

> BAKING A CAKE, DO YOU HAVE A CUP OF SUGAR TO SPARE?

My leniency was not getting reported to the police; son of a big venture capitalist, Noah Campbell's leniency was a week-long suspension at the same time the university announced a sudden donation to help finish much-needed renovations to the robotics lab. Funny how those things worked.

But back to the book – Kierkegaard, not *The Book of the Damned*. Not yet.

"A-ha!"

My fingers closed around a thin booklet with shitty plastic wrapping on the cover, and I flipped through the pages. For such a sizable endowment, Whitby still used low-tech magnetic tape for library books, which made it easy to steal if you knew the tricks.

I whistled to myself as I removed the box cutter from my pocket and scratched the strip away, letting it fall to the floor like a calling card for a *promising* philosophy student scorned. Then I unzipped my bag and dropped it in, when suddenly a hand swatted my arm and made me jump.

"Patty-cake, patty-cake, *baker's man*." Noah Campbell clapped his hands and hit me square in the bicep again. With a grin, he sang, "Bake me a cake as fast as you can."

I didn't smile back.

Noah could have been attractive if he weren't so aggressively set on the alpha bro thing. His hair was a nearly colorless shade of blond, which he parted and gelled back like a Swedish Nazi. It made his neck look blocky, and the tight fit of his collared shirts did him no favors either. The cologne he stole from his father's wardrobe smelled sharp and sour, reminding me of the bear piss that my father once used to mark the edge of the backyard to ward off predators. And worst of all, he wore Italian leather dress shoes without *socks*.

Once or twice, when we were still friendly, I used to wonder what it'd be like to kiss him. I imagined his chapped lips, my hands encircling that stocky neck, his own rough hands on me, his husky breath in the dark.

Now his mere presence made me shudder.

"Hey neighbor, have any *sugar* I can borrow?" asked Noah, wriggling his pale eyebrows as if I couldn't possibly understand why he was here.

I opened my bag again. "Just sugar or you looking for frosting and sprinkles too?"

The candy boxes had been emptied and refilled with an assortment of illicit products; my brother Terence had ventured out from peddling just *sugar* to include other party favors and study aids, rising to meet the demand of a college town like Whitby. He's – he *was* – enterprising like that.

Noah leaned against the stack and crossed his arms as if he was thinking. Like he ever had *any* thoughts at all. He'd confessed to me one night that the only reason he'd majored in finance at all was so he didn't *have* to think – his father had him covered. And still, even though I despise people like that and sometimes had the urge to smash his all-American teeth in, I kept answering his texts. Kept coming around, convincing myself it was only for the money. Even when we almost... well, it's not important anymore.

In the end, this was how I lost everything.

"There's a party tonight, so let's do the special." He rubbed his chin like it was a difficult choice, like he was contemplating Kant instead of partying with his frat.

This school, this education, was wasted on him.

I held out my hand, waiting patiently as he fished out his wallet.

Bills rifled just out of view and were pressed into my palm, warm and rough and *sparse*. My brow wrinkled as I counted.

"That's all I can spare right now," chattered Noah nervously, registering my displeasure. "But I can get you in tonight, and you know I'm good for it—"

"There's an ATM downstairs, I'll wait."

Red crept up his collar. "Dude…"

"I don't work on credit."

The floor was empty, especially near the philosophy stacks, so I didn't bother to glance around. I only glared, unmoving, waiting for Noah's desperate nod, as he fetched his wallet again to reveal more crisp, new bills to cover the rest.

I snatched it.

"Please!" He reached after me, panicked. "My dad's still pissed and isn't transferring as much as he used to. I need that to eat."

"Then stop buying drugs," I countered, as I took what I was owed including tip. The box cutter was still in my grip, in case he tried to take it back. Then, satisfied, I tossed him his wallet and a candy box. The cash fit snugly in my coat pocket.

He tightened his grasp on his things. "Hey, I'm doing *you* a favor – I thought we were friends."

His mistake was reaching for my pocket. In a flash, I slid the box cutter blade long and pressed the tip into the soft *give* between Noah's ribs. I let him imagine how it'd feel sinking into flesh underneath.

His breath hitched under my touch, his body pinned to the shelves.

"We aren't friends and never were, Noah, and if you pull this shit again, I'll deflate your fucking lungs."

There was actual fear in his eyes; people like him were so sheltered, so coddled from the consequences of their actions, that they didn't know how to handle being held at knifepoint. Being told *no*.

I didn't watch him flee. Instead, I reached for a little card at my feet. Noah's student ID, with his creepy sneer on it, must have fallen in the grapple, and it was active, ready to check out more books I wanted and had no plans to bring back.

But then I saw *it*.

A thick encyclopedic-sized tome bound in faded black cloth sat alone on a bottom shelf. Old, the fabric edges frayed loose, and when I raised it from where it had been discarded and forgotten, I had the feeling that it was precious. This was the kind of book they locked behind glass, on display in air-controlled rooms that required an appointment to view. The ones archivists salivated next to, not on.

And yet here it was, wearing a thick layer of dust.

I puffed out my cheeks and blew the cover clear.

The Book of the Damned

The title was engraved with gold, the book probably hundreds of years old. No author listed on the front or spine. Its pages were far past yellowing and approaching orange.

Now, as you recall, I was a conscientious student, which

sometimes entailed reading outside of my classwork, going above and beyond the scope of the syllabus.

I eased it gently into my bag, next to the heisted Kierkegaard. I'd take better care of it than some university that abandoned it to a dusty shelf; I was its savior, not the other way around.

And books were meant to be read.

The duplex that I shared with my brother in the center of town was lively when I came home. The low thrum of music could be felt through the windows, the unmistakable timbre of multiple voices heard as I moved up the sidewalk. Then followed a wall of herbal, lightly sweet-smelling smoke when I stepped inside.

It may come as a surprise, knowing what happens later, that I love my brother despite our lifestyle differences. *Loved* him. Terence never factored into any of this – he didn't even know about the book.

"Ev! Just in time!" Terence shouted from across the living room.

He sat exactly how I'd left him, with a joint tucked between his lips, body nearly swallowed by the couch and sandwiched between two young women with drinks in hand. His best friend was a permanent fixture folding over our coffee table, opposite another woman on the floor, rolling one for himself.

"Join us for a little *TGIF*!"

I cocked my head. Terence was an entrepreneur, and thanks to him, I was nothing more than his lowly assistant; we didn't need to work Fridays if we didn't want to.

Then I took in the liquor bottles, the little bags of greenery – this was his idea of a soirée, and he waved his hand for me to follow.

They all cheered, with one girl in an oversized Whitby sweatshirt eyeing me closely. Her smile was pretty, and she brightened at the suggestion that I might fall onto that secondhand brown couch beside her.

But unfortunately for that girl, and the rest of them, I had my books. I didn't want anything else. Even after everything, I still don't.

"Pass," I demurred, nodding towards the back hall and pretending to yawn.

"What? Why?"

"I'm a little tired, maybe next time—"

"That's what you said *last* time!" he shouted at my back, a bit forcefully, though I only waved goodbye as I retreated to my bedroom and softly shut the door.

I wasn't just like this with Terence's crowd – when I was still at Whitby, I wasn't short on invitations to parties and study groups that didn't study. Noah even dragged me to his frat, and I'd tried in earnest. I went to the basement parties, the first pledge event where they tried to humiliate us to test our dedication – of which I had none. The problem was that there was a gap between me and my classmates, one I couldn't bridge. I saw myself neither in the boys who kissed girls nor those who kissed each other. My heart didn't swell when a fellow philosophy major touched my shoulder or flipped their hair as a precursor for more. I felt nothing in the midst of these mating rituals, like an alien, and I definitely didn't love the way alcohol felt like jamming my brain into a blender.

So I abstained.

And that night in particular, my hands were shaking, eager to dive into *The Book of the Damned*. The bag had been heavy on my shoulder on the way home, carving out my stomach until only hunger was left, rearing its head. I hope the point of my manifesto is becoming clear: I wanted nothing more than to rip it open and leave nothing behind. The book was no match for *me*.

So stark was my curiosity that I left my actual reading, *Fear and Trembling*, on the floor.

My bedroom was ascetic – a secondhand desk, a closet full of sweaters and corduroy to weather the long and harsh New England winters. Books lined the walls and piled along the floors, some of them vintage or rare editions that I'd won at auctions, others swiped from the library, never to be returned. I didn't even bother to get a proper bed frame – instead, I snatched two wood pallets from behind a convenience store and used some of our parents' life insurance money for a first edition of *Thus Spake Zarathustra*.

I dropped onto my bed and raised the pages to my nose. It smelled deliciously of bookish mold, of paper long-lived. My hands stroked it gently. When I opened the lid, the spine nearly fell away, damaged. There was no copyright information in the interior, no publisher, no author.

Instead, there was only a sparse title page, "*The Book of the Damned*," an inscription, "*For you*," followed by a warning on the next. A quick flip through the other pages showed them all to be blank. Nothing else from cover to cover, it was little more than a project from a prop designer in the theater department.

"I—"

A high-pitched laugh from Terence's party pulled me away from the mystery and made me aware of the neighbor Sherry's dog above. It only barked when Sherry's boyfriend was over, which meant that they were bound to engage in one of two things: fighting, where she often smashed things, or sex, just as loud. This week it was the latter.

I shoved in ear plugs and tried to regain my focus, flipping back to that front page.

"'*For you*,'" I read aloud, to drown them out. And then, "'*This is a reference book for the damned. The knowledge printed inside its pages is powerful, dangerous to the ignorant, and should not be handled lightly. Cross yourself and bind with iron – only in the hands of the capable is it divinity.*'"

Does that sound like a seduction to you? What seduction ever came with a warning to back away?

Yet when I read those words aloud, it only further piqued my interest. It brought a smirk to my face as I turned the page, hoping to convince it that I was indeed capable hands. You see, I didn't imagine the pages being empty – it wanted to be read, but only by the most adept.

In an instant, the pages were filled. After the warning came poems – or, in hindsight, *incantations*, since they were meant to be read aloud – and grotesque illustrations beside long descriptions of its lore. Monsters more awful and strange than any child's imagination, with the genealogy and motivations ascribed to them as if they were real living things, and revered with prayers, offerings, as gods. Some of it was nigh incomprehensible, but I didn't put the book down. The stranger it was, the more I kept flipping, eager to see who this was for. What it was meant to provide.

"*To punish one's enemies*," said one page. "*To step through to the other side of a doorway*" was inked on another.

A book of make-believe, forgotten on a library shelf, was coaxed by me into offering the world. Punish my enemies, the people who'd tried to snatch my education from me. Escape the noise and stink of my brother's parties, the barking dog, and the rhythmic rattling of a bed frame against the wall above. A place where I could read in peace, in perpetuity.

Then, thinking about the party, the dog, and the sex, I realized that, from the moment I'd started reading, I'd no longer heard anything. Not in a metaphorical way, where literature quiets the mind – no, when I removed my ear plugs, the world around me had gone silent.

The dog had stopped barking, the lovemaking had ceased, and the party and its music had stopped.

Setting the book aside, still open, I rose from my bed and peered out into the living room. My brother, his friend, and the girls were frozen in place. Smoke thickened mid-air, while a girl dancing by the couch was rigid.

"Everybody alright?"

None of them moved, or even looked at me.

"*Interesting*," I said to myself as I hurried back to my book and slammed it shut. The instant it closed, the thumping bed returned. The party music swelled, and barking continued.

Open again, it stopped. The pages parted onto an incantation: *to summon oneself.*

After such a curious temporal display, how could I ignore it? The book wouldn't explain what that meant, and of course this one had no illustrations, so I demanded it to *show* me.

I read it aloud, my mouth fumbling over an approximation

because none of it was English – or any language I recognized. It was all meaningless to me, but behind it was a power that I teased from print. The moment I finished the last word, a sudden ache tore through my skull. Sharp and splitting, I squeezed my eyes against it, cradled my head in my hands, and as quickly as it had come, the agony ebbed away. Gone in a heartbeat.

Then looking up, I found *him*, standing there in the middle of my bedroom.

Another me.

Another Evander, torn from my very person.

He arched an eyebrow, taking in me and the book on my lap, and remarked in a calm voice, "This… is unexpected."

This carbon copy, this *doppelgänger* conjured in my bedroom. I heard my own voice coming from another's body and stared into my own face, my freckles, the specific curl to my hair – all of him was a perfect replica.

I shut the book, tossed it aside, and launched from my seat to examine him. He matched my height exactly. "How—?"

"I don't know," he answered, and up close I glimpsed his chipped front tooth, from an accident after Terence had forced me to learn skateboarding when I was sixteen.

Like a doll, I crooked his elbow and found the scar from age seven, crashing my bicycle. Along his cheeks were the faint remains of acne scars, and shining studs sat in both ears. Even our clothes, down to the socks, were identical. My stomach tilted as if I was standing on the edge of a canyon and about to fall. He took my shoulders in his hands to steady me.

"*I know* but try to breathe."

This wasn't what I'd expected, but it was a curiosity, nonetheless. How many of us have wondered what we'd look like, outside of our body and mirrors? How others see us and our mannerisms? A companion who knew and understood us perfectly? Here that stood, terrifying and very real and intriguing too.

"Do you know my name? How you got here?"

The thing that was me didn't let go. "Evander Price. Whitby, New Hampshire. We turned twenty last week. And then you read from that book."

I pinched him but didn't feel any pain. When I reached for the box cutter in my pocket, he caught my wrist.

"I don't think so."

I balked. "You have to be wondering – if I cut you right now, would I bleed?"

And of course, because he was me, his fingers released me. He held his palm open but gave me a glower. "Small." As if I might've, in that moment, wanted to kill myself – my clone, rather. The only person who meant the world to me.

I gave him a little prick on the tip of his finger and watched the red bead. Yet when I turned my hand over to examine myself, there was nothing. He cut me too, on another finger, just to see if it went the other way, but no. Another me but an entirely separate body.

Like reflections in a strange mirror, we stood there, gaping at each other, saying nothing. Above, Sherry and her boyfriend continued to go at it with renewed frenzy.

"Sometimes I wish they'd shut up," I mumbled awkwardly, unsure of myself, of what to say or do in a situation like this. A thought occurred to me, to read *"to punish one's enemies"* from the book, and stop them.

His gaze drifted to the ceiling, then flickered to the book, then to me. "I'll be right back—"

Then he stepped around me, and I grabbed his arm. Of course that was what he wanted too.

"Don't."

There was something cold and clinical about the way he moved, how he regarded me now. It forced a shiver down my spine, seeing this look on myself that I often gave to others but rarely named. A detached disappointment.

Like *I* was small.

"They... don't deserve it," I rasped. "It would be wasted on them."

He warmed a little at this. "Then who *does* deserve it?"

I couldn't help but picture Noah Campbell. His smarmy face and sickening sneer – now *that* was an enemy. One night after my expulsion, I'd broken into the records department because I had to know who'd ratted me out, and it was *him*. *He* pointed the finger at me to spare his own ass, and still had the magnanimity to think he was doing me a favor, some patron saint of the drug trade.

If I was suffering, he should too, and now I could do something about it.

Following my thoughts, the other me fetched a candy box from my bag, grinned, and headed for the window. "Grab the book. I'll drive."

"Wait!" I caught his hand before he could climb out and brought myself to ask, "What... should I call you?"

Did I call him Evander too? Evander *Two*? Or was I supposed to refer to myself as "you" forever? (Such a philosophical quandary I found myself in – David Hume would lose his shit.)

Straddling the window ledge with ease, he tilted his head, the corner of his mouth twitching as he answered, "Rednave."

Me in reverse.

Then he ducked and dropped down to the side of our house. He was everything that I'd ever wanted, I realized, and he was here. Without him, none of the rest could have happened.

And it was *his* naked body forensics found, not mine.

Nu Epsilon was where Greek classicism came to die: synonymous with parties, white columns spanning the broad face and decorated with green insignia'd banners, and on the rising steps clustered drunk students like weeds. Revelers shed empty red cups across the lawn as they danced to music loud enough to shake the ground.

"Ready?" Rednave's eyes glowed in the floodlights like embers. He didn't wait for my answer – he didn't need it – before starting up the walkway. I clutched *The Book* to my heart and followed.

It was disorienting inside, going from cool nightfall to the balmy, bright house. On either side were gaping rooms full of students in bacchanale, talking and kissing and pouring beer down their throats and trying not to choke.

When Rednave turned to look at me, I saw my grimace reflected in his own. His frown, his nostrils flared slightly, that cold severity again. Someone who felt as alien as I did.

We clasped hands and moved through the hall.

Noah was in the kitchen, at the center of a huddle, a red cup in hand. His face was flushed, and his watery eyes blinked wildly when he noticed us. *Both* of us.

Before he could say anything, Rednave flashed the candy and nodded to the hall. Noah withdrew without another word, nearly salivating as he led us quickly up the wide, white stairs, down another hall, and into a bedroom that dulled the noise a little.

Enough for me to hear Rednave lock the door behind us. It gave my heart a little thrill.

Noah didn't notice, for his gaze was flicking between me, Rednave, the candy box, and back again. And I became preoccupied with how offensive his room was – my place at the university had been shuttered forever, but here he partied, not a book in sight. In fact, aside from my texts, I'd never even seen the boy read.

"You didn't tell me you were a twin," Noah complained, a sloppy grin on his face. His pupils were blown wide. "Which one is Evander?"

I waved. "I wanted to apologize for how uptight I was today. We brought you a gift."

He looked pleased, as if he deserved anything more than what we were ready to give: punishment. The moment I opened *The Book of the Damned*, he was frozen with that expression while the smile melted from Rednave's face. Below and outside, the party ground to a halt.

"Do you want to do the honors?" Rednave asked, taking a tour around Noah's stock-still form. His fingers trailed delicately across Noah's shoulders.

I carefully flipped to the page, "*To Punish One's Enemies*," hands trembling. Like the last, this incantation had no illustrations or further description. The book's warning blazed in my head, but I didn't care to heed it. "You can do the next one."

Rednave nodded and came close. He was quite beautiful standing next to me, even in this undeserved room. He leaned over my shoulder, scentless and close enough that I could feel the warmth on his skin while I read. Tongue stumbling again, just as incomprehensible, it carried the weight of the book's power, taken from the page.

Snap.

Together we looked up.

With sudden and tremendous force, Noah Campbell's body bowed and bent. A discernible ankle joint burst open and twisted back to fit along a ninety-degree angle. His upper half buckled forward as his legs rippled back, unseen pressure folding and crushing him from all sides until he was a perfect cube. It landed on the floor with a heavy *thud*. Blood splattered our faces as we stumbled back, as I crushed the open book to my chest and flinched.

Bone compacted and cleanly broken, cube wet and shiny and hot, bleeding onto the wood floor.

"Uh…" My voice was a bit of a moan that dissolved into a nervous chuckle. A feeling was rising in me, panicking and flighty, and I swallowed it down. I couldn't stop my hands from shaking.

"Definitely punished." Rednave was trembling too, even as he inched forward and nudged at the meat cube with the edge of his sneaker. An appraising nod followed. "Noah's, uh, never looked better. Broken, on the ground, and in his own filth."

His words sounded hollow, like he was trying to convince himself. Then he looked at me to reassure and finish his thoughts, my thoughts – *our* thoughts. I was to him what he was to me, after all, something more perfect than soulmates.

"Pathetic."

He grinned, somehow both darkly and like rays of sunshine, and added, "No better than meat before a butcher."

There was blood on his face and neck and hands. It speckled his sweater. The sour stink of it filled the room. I should have felt sick or disgusted with myself. The book had tried to deter us, and we should have been wracked with guilt.

But we drifted toward each other rather than apart. The shock and uncanny brutality of the incantation, what grotesquerie it had made of Noah Campbell's body, drove us closer in search of something upright and solid, like we were groping at walls in a dark house. His fists clutched my sleeves.

I brought my mouth to his.

It only felt right, you see. Kissing another person, a stranger's body, is an expedition in a foreign land, getting near to delight but only finding an approximation at best – kissing *yourself* is like coming home. Walking through the front door, you're greeted by familiar smells, comfortable arrangement, purest attraction and love and understanding untouched by translation or compromise.

We fit perfectly.

Even though Rednave wore some of Noah's blood on his lips, I pressed closer until there was only the book squeezed between us, and he continued to hold me tight. Kissing him sated me deep down, in a way I didn't know I ached. In a way only *he* could understand.

It filled us and awakened *more* hunger that left us gasping, standing over the flesh cube, eyes wide and dark. The party was still frozen in time while our whole world had changed.

"Let's—"

"Go home," I finished his sentence.

We hurried through the bedroom door, down the hall and stairs, and disappeared into the night. With the book splayed open and raised in my hands like a relic, no one saw us leave, bloodied and flushed and giddy and horrified. No one noticed my beat-up sedan driving away.

No one but Rednave glimpsed the single tear, born of terror and release, drifting down my cheek. Then, of course, he had one of his own to match.

While Rednave took the book, closed it, and climbed back into my bedroom through the window, I strolled through the front door, breathless. My head rushed as I marched inside. My brother and his company still lounged around the couch, alcohol bottles nearing empty, the music slowed to a pace to complement their mood.

Their chatter halted, however, when I kicked off my boots and started for the hall. I didn't feel eyes following me this time; I was engrossed in the ghost impression of my own lips, what else the book might hold, what it meant to find attraction and solace only in oneself – important things.

Then, "Ev?"

There was a shuffle of bottles and cushions as Terence pushed to his feet and darted after me. Up ahead, the door to my room was cracked open, and the light flicked on.

I was hardly interested in whatever mundane request my brother had, but I half turned anyway to keep his gaze from my room. "Can't talk—"

"What is that?" My brother caught my sleeve in his grasp and held it up to the overhead lights. His horrified gaze flicked between the splotches of red along the arm, across the chest, and my face, where it hadn't occurred to me that there were still traces of blood.

Traces of *Noah* and what we'd done to him.

I pulled away, nervously. "Paint."

"Don't lie to me," Terence pressed, snatching at my elbow this time. He was bigger than me, taller and stronger – he had always been a protector, impenetrable and undefeated, and now his vise-like grip on me was impossible to break. "If you're in trouble, you need to tell me now. I can't have you leading the cops here."

No matter how I struggled, he wouldn't let go.

"It's just paint."

"Are you serious?"

My brother released me with a bit of a shove, and I staggered back, grasping to catch myself against a cabinet in the hall. A framed family photograph, of us and our parents on a trip to Niagara Falls, clattered to the floor.

"Chill—"

"And don't tell me to *chill*." Terence drew up to full height, oblivious to how his guests had gone quiet and killed the music; his hysterics were the new entertainment. There was only his voice now, his admonishment filling the house. Even the shadow in my bedroom went still. "You're so arrogant. You played around with that rich boy, got yourself expelled and almost got *me* in trouble too. You talk down to me and look at me like I'm less than you because I can't quote Aristotle, in the house *I* provide, and now you walk in here covered in blood, calling it paint like I'm stupid. That's blood, you *smell* like blood – did you hurt somebody?"

He stepped closer, searching my face as if he'd be able to read the answer in my eyes, but I turned away.

My voice came out smaller than I would've liked. "I don't think you're stupid—"

"Yes, you do," he countered, hovering over me as I found myself shrinking away. "You look down on all of us as if we're not just like you, just trying to survive."

I couldn't help the scoff that came out of me. "I'm *not* just like you, though…"

My skin was buzzing. It was always frustrating trying to talk to Terence, to explain to him who I was and what I wanted, when he clearly never got it and never wanted to. We were different, and yes, some of the things I thought about were *more important* than his career in pharmaceuticals in fucking Whitby, New Hampshire. I couldn't help if he didn't get that. It wasn't my fault he dropped out of school to take care of me when our parents died; I didn't ask him to. I didn't ask him to do any of this.

"I'm not just surviving," I said more softly this time. "I could've been *thriving* if I wasn't running for you."

Fashioning myself to fashion mankind – that was what I was on the brink of with the book, with Rednave, and meanwhile my brother wanted to cry about feelings of his own inferiority. So at that moment, I wished he'd choke. I wanted him out of my way.

I wanted him to be the one in the grave.

Like he could hear these thoughts blaring in my skull, he narrowed his eyes and sneered, "Get out."

"What?"

Terence seized my arm again and rounded for the door, back through the living room where his guests were snickering, gaping at each other amid our pathetic family soap opera. He said loudly, performing for them, "You can't stay here, not like that."

"Where..." I dug my heels in. "It's twenty-five degrees outside, where am I supposed to go?"

"Figure it out, since you're so smart." He dropped me off by the entrance and returned to his place on the couch. A heartless smile cracked on his face. "If you're so much better than me, then go be better somewhere else. I've had enough."

My jaw dropped.

Of all the fights, of all the things I expected him to say and do, this wasn't one of them. Terence could have punched me like he'd done before, trashed my things – once he'd burned my annotated copy of Sartre's *Being and Nothingness* – anything but this.

Looking around, trying to find my bearings, my gaze caught on Rednave, stepping out from the shadows. He held the book in his hands, and I watched him crack it open. The room held its breath as he flipped furiously through pages, his mouth pinched, and nostrils flared.

"Wait."

My heart spiked as I crossed the floor. I knew what he was looking for, what he wanted to do. We were the same in love as we were in hate.

"Red, wait—"

"Are you gonna tell me you don't think he deserves it?" Rednave snapped.

His fury was striking, beautiful and depraved, and it made me shiver. And gnash my teeth, seeing that callous expression on my brother's face. In my silence, Rednave began reading that same incantation, the one I couldn't understand but certainly recognized, the one I was still wearing.

It wasn't that I thought my brother deserved it or didn't; I was angry and fickle, and we had power at our fingertips. The book had tried to resist me, tried to warn me, and I'd snatched that power anyway and wielded it how I saw fit.

None of it even felt real, or grounded, or *permanent*.

My feet stayed rooted when Rednave finished, and wet *snaps* reverberated around the room. On the couch and the floor, my brother and all his guests were crushed into themselves, reduced to just shards and meat, fresh blood running down the yellow-painted walls. Soaking into the weed on the coffee table. The side of one fleshy cube wore the name *Whitby* in Collegiate font.

My body went numb, like I was floating outside of myself.

"Why did you do that?" My voice was a whisper.

My brother was still staring at me, his face preserved on the face of the cube itself, watching me finally back away. I retrieved the family photo from the floor and restored it to the cabinet. Unlike with Noah, Rednave didn't have that awful grin this time, didn't circle the carnage to admire our handiwork.

Instead, he pulled me away from it, a hand laced around my waist, and into my bedroom.

"Because you wanted to."

He pressed kisses against my jaw and then my neck.

There was no way to hide my revulsion and longing, woven into each other, from him. My dead brother's expression was seared onto the back of my eyelids – if anyone understood how to stop me from seeing the image, it was him. I'd wanted that as much as I wanted this.

He shoved a hand into my pants.

I loathed Terence, and Noah, and Rednave, and most of all, myself, and so I let my eyes drift to the ceiling and sank into his touch. My own.

"What do you want next?" Rednave whispered, tongue gliding along my throat.

It is a blessing and a curse to be known so completely; he even knew how to touch me.

We hid in each other.

Rednave's sighs were my sighs. His euphoric shudders were a mirror of my own, our hunger multiplied.

For an hour, or maybe two, I thought very little of Terence and even less of Noah. In the throng of things, I *did* remember pressing the blade of my box cutter to Noah's ribs and how he trembled, but I'm sure that meant nothing. I didn't concern myself with the bodies or disposing of them, or whether anyone might remember seeing me at Nu Epsilon. It didn't matter where I'd go afterwards, if I'd go alone or in a pair. I didn't have anywhere to put my loathing either, and it sat like an imp in the corner of the room, festering, waiting for me to finish with myself.

And after, when we lay in our bed, naked and spent, two of the same body side-by-side, it came back. A crescendo of madness and grief, terror and hatred so strong that it propelled me up with a start.

"Again?" Rednave murmured, a sleepy grin on his mouth, as I threw a leg over and straddled him.

"You know what comes next."

His eyes went wide with understanding just as my hands closed around his throat. My throat. Panic in my expression served back to me.

Rednave gripped my wrists as I strangled him, to no avail. He kicked his bare legs from under me and writhed, but I only squeezed tighter. Like a dying fish, he opened and closed his mouth in search of desperate breaths. His face was beginning to turn red, and then purple.

He bared his nails to scratch at my face but then thought better of it, went soft and pliant under my touch, and let me kill him. So I granted him the courtesy of never looking away.

Tears streaked down my cheeks and onto his own, staining my pillow beneath as I watched the light leave my own eyes. As I felt his body loosen and go still.

I am rotten for what happened to Noah Campbell, Terence Price, Derrick Gilman, Ashley Carmichael, Nicole Riggs, and Sasha Holden, yes, but I am also god-like for what I did afterwards. For knowing and loving and murdering myself with my bare hands – can you say the same?

And that was why, with all my loathing, through sobbing breaths, I crawled over my own corpse to the book and summoned myself again, and then we ran.

Within the Loch

Elspeth Wilson

The loch changes nearly as little as she does. On crisp days like today, when the sun is at its zenith, there's a seam of silvery water near the left-hand side – perhaps where the tide changes – that shines a little brighter than it used to. As the Mistress brushes her hair, readying herself for the day ahead, the early morning light catches the greying streak in amongst her fading auburn, also on the left side of her head.

Today, she does her hair in complicated plaits, the kind she hasn't bothered to do in years. But it never hurts to make a good impression with the board of governors. The loch has more foliage on its banks than it used to and is a home for birds and native trees, a slice of leafy greenness carved out from the otherwise sheep-wrecked countryside. The Mistress' eyebrows are a little bushier and of course her face has sagged with the years – the grief too.

Satisfied with her plaits, she rises from her dressing table and begins to make her way down the winding spiral staircase. She can glimpse the loch through all the narrow, slitted windows as she takes each well-worn step at a glacial pace. In their essence, she and the loch are still the same. The loch – a haven not only for flora and fauna, but also for girls seeking a place to swim or otherwise store their secrets. The Mistress still feels herself to be one of those girls at heart, despite her dominion over them and the dreadful, slow march of the decades.

She knows the shoreline better than she knows her own face and she has done far more to protect this body of water than she has to care for her own. She will continue this fight today at noon when the board of governors meets. She has fought farmers – so often the most disagreeable of men – and nosy developers from the nearest (yet still distant) city who wanted to profit from the loch, drain its water away and steal it from those who live there. But fighting her colleagues is the bitterest conflict. She knows they wish to "beautify" the area and make clear picnic areas and – most dreadfully – drain the loch to create further lawn areas. *How can you beautify perfection?* She already knows she will want to scream that question later on. Wildness is good for the soul. But the irony is that she will have to trim herself down just for them.

Halfway through her descent from the highest turret in the college, she pauses to enjoy the way the light dances on the water. She rehearses her speech in her head for the hundredth time – it is simply imperative that the girls have access to an area of outstanding natural beauty and that having this privilege, nay, this *right*, improves their education and their character. The Mistress has had many years of practice at always being the reasonable, rational one, to never give anyone even the merest hint of hysteria.

She knows she is dragging out the journey downstairs, lingering a little too long at each window, but she has left herself plenty of time and she is in no rush to see Elena or her other interfering colleagues at the Founders Day ceremony. All she can think about is the meeting with the governors. But, first, she must do her duty.

Almost at the bottom of her turret, she spots Elena faffing and fussing as she directs the gardeners to place flowerpots around the chairs that are carefully laid out on the manicured lawns. Elena bends down to admonish one of the young local boys and the Mistress chuckles to herself as her colleague grasps at the small of her back. The Mistress can almost hear Elena's knees popping, despite being indoors. Elena is the only other Old Girl to have stuck around as long as she has and by rights the Mistress should look older, because she was two years ahead when they were both students. But there is a part of the Mistress that is so stuck in the past that, perversely, it serves to give her face a youthful demeanour.

The Mistress takes one last, longing look at the loch before she readies herself to trample across Elena's perfect, sterile grass and preside over the ceremony. She heaves open the heavy oak doors that demarcate her sanctuary and strides out across the flagstoned quadrangle, thinking of her very first day here. She was dropped off by a mama and papa who are now so wispy in her mind that she can barely see their faces. And of course, as always, she thinks of Her.

She has hardly made it a hundred yards towards the college's main courtyard before Elena is upon her.

"There's a small problem, Mistress," Elena says, her gaze settling on the herbaceous border behind her superior. She narrows her eyes, no doubt finding something out of place. Imperfect.

"What is it?" The Mistress tries to muster the appropriate interest on her face, but it is a struggle when her mind is still on the loch and the meeting with the governors.

"We don't have your chair," Elena simpers, though there is a slight gleam in her eye. "I did tell one of the village boys that they absolutely must bring it out of storage in time, but you know what they're like. Next year, I will of course make sure to see to it myself. That's if there will *be* a next year, Mistress?"

"Is there no time to fetch it now?" the Mistress demands, thinking of the carved wooden chair that only gets brought out at Founders Days and funerals for former Mistresses, so as to preserve it for as long as possible. She chooses to ignore Elena's impudent question. She's been sniffing around her retirement plans for years.

It is her twentieth Founders Day as Mistress – God knows how many since being a student – and it seems she will have to stand. Elena may look as wizened and shrivelled as the last, least choice pieces of fruit in the great copper bowl in the refectory, but the Mistress has never known her to be forgetful.

"There is not." Elena shakes her head, trying to plaster regret across her round face. The Mistress was looking forward to sitting on the admittedly uncomfortable chair, feeling its hard wooden back press into the notches of her spine once again. But if she's learned anything during her tenure it's that she has to be flexible. The show must go on.

"Then so be it. I will stand." As she speaks, a wave of dizziness passes over her, like a sorcerer moving their hand across a scrying pool. She has a momentary image of herself cracked open and congealed like an overdone egg, blood pooling behind her on the flagstones, but then it is gone with a gust of warm breeze. The fire on Blossom Corridor was an anomaly, if a sad one, and this Founders Day shall be as resplendent – if slightly stultifying – as ever.

She leaves Elena without even a goodbye, as she knows there will be a long line of other colleagues with interminable questions for her, and an even longer line of guests to greet – the most dreadful of all being the governors. As she walks away, for a second she thinks she spots Her in the gathering crowd. But then the girl turns and it's not Her, not Her at all. It's probably just someone's daughter, who they are hoping to introduce to the Mistress with the aim of their child being more likely to be admitted to the college.

So many of the guests – and indeed two of the governors – are Old Girls with husbands in tow. As she passes by the chapel, she nods to an Old Girl who used to help her with geometry revision and is currently simpering at a bald man's jokes. The Mistress fights to keep her tuts under her breath. More Old Girls nod as she makes her way towards the small stage furnished with floral garlands, positioned in the middle of the main lawn. They are girls she used to stay up with drinking cocoa or telling ghost stories, girls whose hair she braided with flowers from the loch-side each spring. They've long since stepped into the world of matrimony where the Mistress has never sought to follow. They are returning somewhere, feeling like they have travelled a great distance, whereas she has never left. She wouldn't have it any other way, but she still makes an effort to smile at them each in turn.

And so, the Mistress stands for the ceremony as five first-years read poems they have written about the loch, and the oldest girls, wearing crowns made of thistles, play the parts of the Founding Mothers. The Mistress can remember just one of the Mothers – a tiny, old woman, skin thin as a petal – who was the only person exempt from standing during grace each evening back when the Mistress was a student.

"We thank you all for being in attendance today," the Mistress begins. Standing is actually better for projection, it turns out. So there, Elena. "But in particular we thank the Founding Mothers without whom we would never have experienced the finest education for women – nay, anyone – this country has to offer."

"Thank you, Mothers," the gathered crowd whispers as one while the Mistress continues the rest of her short speech, then hands over to a group of girls who are going to perform a dance in tribute. For a second, she has the dizzying sensation that she is once again one of those girls, with her closest friend standing by her side. But it vanishes once the procession and its attendant clanging marching band begins.

Hands are shaken, wrinkling cheeks are kissed, girls are hushed, and donations are made. Another perfectly satisfactory Founders Day complete, bar that strange mishap with Elena. But the Mistress still feels there was something missing. Just like she's felt there's been something missing every day for the last fifty or sixty years. She's lost count of how long it has been and so has everybody else by this stage. How can you measure the pain, the tears, when the happiness still feels like it was yesterday?

After the morning ceremony is over, a wave of late September heat places the college in a stranglehold. Girls loll about on grassy tussocks and don bathers to jump in the loch. They come out with tendrils of greenish weed adorning their hair and a slightly fervent look in their eyes. Despite having not swum for years, the Mistress wishes she could join them. It's a glorious day – the kind of day it's a crime not to make the most of – and anything would beat attending the governors meeting.

She walks along Blossom Corridor on her way to the meeting, dragging her feet like a much younger woman. The rooms that were burnt in the fire are ready to be moved into once again and that is to be her next appointment of the day. If only she could skip over the governors meeting and go straight to the girls.

Although she has prepared for this meeting for months – submitting evidence of the environmental value of the loch, politicking with colleagues she strongly dislikes – when it finally comes it roars past her like a wave. There's women and a smattering of men and there's words – some of them her own – and there's decisions and a tide she cannot stem and then a vote. A terrible vote. A vote she has been trying to stop for years but this time she hasn't contorted herself the right way, hasn't presented the right facts and figures to stop them draining the loch. She has always been saying the same thing but this time – this time it didn't work.

She has lost. She has lost. She has lost. She knew it was coming, knew she could only stem the tide for so long, but, still, she dreamed. Sweet, bitter dreams that she would prevail. That nature would. The Mistress should be pleased with the decades she has managed to protect the loch for, but she is not. She has failed. She has failed Her.

She practically runs out of the room, blinking away tears, yet her body is gripped by a greater certainty of what she must do next than it has been in years.

The Mistress cuts a black ribbon to Room 24, Blossom Corridor, her old corridor, and the new inhabitant – a fresh-faced girl with chubby cheeks that the Mistress remembers for her fluency at her interview – walks over the threshold. There's no trace of the fire that raged bizarrely last winter, despite the damp and occasional flurries of snow, just a new mantelpiece and lots of freshly-fitted oak panelling that hopefully will never know a lick of flame.

After she has made small talk with her girls, the Mistress takes a detour down a tightly curled flight of stairs, to Heather Corridor which is situated directly below Blossom. She learned the tricks of sneaking around the labyrinthine building when she herself was a student, and so no one notices her sloping off. This morning all she wanted was to gaze at the loch, but that already feels like a lifetime ago. Time is slipping and she is moving away from something or returning or perhaps a combination of the two. Either way, she keeps her gaze down as it's too painful to look at the glimmering water.

She stops, as she nearly always does, outside Room 24, Heather Corridor. Her fingers graze the knots of what was once a tree and is now a door – nay, a portal – to where the Mistress grew into herself. So many memories of the two of them together inside that room. The first time they met happened here, long before the Mistress was the Mistress, when she was just a scholarship student who missed her younger brothers and worried about her paltry array of dresses. She still has some of Her clothes at the back of the closet even now, including the blue, frilled frock that She lent the Mistress on that very first night. Of course, the style is at once too old-fashioned and much too young for her now, but the Mistress keeps up her callisthenics exercises so that she might still squeeze into the dresses now and again, in the darkness of her unlit room.

She rests her head against the solidity of the door for a second, imagining that if she were to walk inside she might peel back the years, like taking skin from an onion, and find herself in a younger body with her best friend, whole and in front of her. But she knows that it's only Marcella Davidson behind the door – she knows because she herself picks the girl to inhabit this room each year. She chooses based on neatness and respectability. The Mistress needs to know that the room will be taken care of, its view out to the loch cherished. Before leaving, she thanks God – not for the first time – that the blaze did not strike here, at the true heart of the college.

At the end of the corridor, just as she is about to traipse back past the library and take stock of her own palatial quarters, the Mistress hears hushed voices in a chant. For as long as the college has been alive, the girls have celebrated the Founding Mothers with strange, twisty little rituals of their own. They change year on year and are never planned; they just happen as someone, usually an older girl, has an idea to celebrate and memorialise their predecessors and leads her sisters in the ritual. When the Mistress was a student, she was dunked into the loch and had pondweed plaited through her hair.

Strictly speaking, these rituals are not allowed, and the House Mothers will have been checking on each of their charges to make sure they are not engaged in anything too untoward. But, being an Old Girl herself, the Mistress knows how often these instructions – done in the girls' best interests of course – are ignored and evaded.

The Mistress lingers as the chanting dies down, accompanied by a strange and unplaceable series of crackles and bangs. Eventually, the noises calm down until there are just the unmistakable sounds of a group of excited girls chattering.

"So, she's never been seen since?" a high-pitched voice pipes up. Janey Hitchinson-Duval, the Mistress thinks, priding herself as ever on her knowledge of her girls.

"Never," another disembodied voice replies. Virginia Matthews, an historian. The undercurrent of triumph in her tone causes the Mistress to lurch forward. Her skull's contact with the wood makes an unfortunate thud.

"What's that?" someone says. Probably one of the sixteen-year-olds, judging by the tone, the youngest to be admitted to the college.

"It's nothing. Just the wind," Virginia replies. "Or maybe it's her ghost coming to get you!" She raises her voice, shrieking, and there's a few screams amidst fits of giggles. The girls think they're safe on this sunny day, that there's nothing truly to fear in their lives, so Virginia's crass joke can be laughed away in a matter of moments.

"Who was she though, really?" Janey asks.

"She was a student." It's a senior girl speaking now, but not Virginia. Shirley Cross, the Mistress thinks. One of the oldest, most serious girls, whose piercing gaze makes the Mistress uncomfortable, like she's staring into the very deepest recesses of her person.

"She was part of the fifth cohort of girls to be welcomed to the college, back in the early days," Virginia goes on. "She was meant to be very pretty, as well as an excellent sportswoman. That just makes her disappearance so much more tragic. Though apparently her academics were mediocre at best. There was even a rumour that she let a local boy believe he was courting her just so he would help her with mathematics."

This is the part the Mistress enjoys best. Where they talk about Her time here like She could wander down the corridor at any moment, Her sweater tied lazily around Her shoulders, ashy baby hairs stuck to Her forehead after crushing Her opponent at tennis. Sometimes a boy would come here to play Her, travelling across the lonely fields on foot, or maybe in a motor car if he was lucky, ready to win what he was sure would be an easy, friendly match. Those were the Mistress' favourite moments. Every time She triumphed, it felt like the Mistress did too.

She stands in the corridor, unmoving so as not to inspire a creak from the floorboards, listening to them talk about the scraps of Her that have floated down the years. Some are largely correct – She was a daughter of one of the nation's most preeminent families – and some are preposterous, like there was a séance conducted the day before Her disappearance. The discussions are less frenzied than they were when it was still a mystery to be solved and not a ghost story sometimes utilised by House Mothers to scare first-years into obedience.

Someone suggests that they get outside to make the most of the weather, and then there's a collective shuffling of feet and the unmistakable sounds of girls ending a gossip session. This is the Mistress' cue to leave. She's become adept at knowing the exact moment to step away from her eavesdropping – or research, as she prefers to think of it. But today she lingers for a second longer than usual before she flits away down the corridor, her black cape billowing behind her. She's losing her touch, perhaps, mistiming it ever so slightly because little Janey will swear for the rest of her life that she saw a giant bat in the corridor that day – or was it a witch?

Either way, it was an ill omen after all the discussion of the long-ago missing but never forgotten girl.

The day has lost its shape, become saggy. That won't do. The Mistress needs something to fill the hours until dusk when the girls will drift back in from the loch and the gardens in time for dinner. The Mistress is thinking of all the parts of the college she could visit to give her afternoon some structure, but it seems fruitless after the governors meeting. The loch is what gives the building its majesty. It was awe-inspiring before the college came along – and would have been long after it crumbled, given the chance – but once the water is drained this place will lose the thing that makes it most special.

Squelching fills the Mistress' office, distracting her from the overwhelming tide of thoughts. The sound of rotten apple after rotten apple being crushed floats up through the window, followed by high-pitched shrieks and occasionally a giggle or two. She didn't sleep well last night because she dreamed of Her. It's a dream she'd had for the first time the night before She went missing. It isn't particularly eerie – it's just about the first day they met, except a small detail changes each time. Like the alarm clock on Her bedside table has all the numbers backwards, or the loch outside Her window is a reddish shade of purple instead of its normal slate blue.

There're many minor things like the dream that have come to have significance for the Mistress because they are stitched through with the unfinished thread of Her. She no longer likes the smell after rain because it reminds her of the dewy morning where she realised she'd never see her friend again. She doesn't like to swim anymore because they'd been so many times together in the preceding weeks to cool off after the heatwave. For a while, it was even hard to look at the loch because of the permanent stain smeared across all their happy memories that occurred there. She worked so hard to be able to meet the water's eye and now the governors have ruined all the progress she'd made.

She didn't sleep well, she didn't get to sit on her chair, and now that infernal noise is worming into her head like one of the maggoty insects from the fruit has found its way inside her. Usually, she doesn't mind the rhythmic sounds of the tennis ball being hit back and forth across the court, occasionally accompanied by a frustrated grunt or a delighted yelp. The Mistress was never good at tennis, but She was uncommonly good and, rarer still, She was kind about her talent, helping the Mistress practise her backhand.

Today, everything is too much. She has failed. No one else values the loch like she does. Or no one over the age of thirty. No one whose voice counts. The girls love it, of course. They understand it, just like she did at their age, answering its wild call with devotion. But all the others – Elena, the governors, colleagues at different places in the hierarchy – think the loch is a solution to whatever problem they find most pressing. For the head janitor, it's more accommodation for the village boys he needs to help him maintain this place – at an appropriate remove from the young ladies, obviously. For Elena, it's a new battleground in her fight against any shred of greenery that isn't cultivated to within an inch of its life.

The Mistress rises from where she's sitting at her desk, just as a particularly loud screech shatters any remaining semblance of tranquillity at this hallowed seat of learning. Yes, she had wanted something to do with the rest of her Founders Day, but it wasn't admonishing her charges. She marches down her turret's spiral staircase, out across the flagstones and through the archway to circumnavigate the perimeter of the building and end up at the tennis court. She can see the large, orange college cat, Gregory Puffin – so named by a couple of giggling first-years – staring down at her from her window. She must have forgotten to close the door in her haste. One point to Gregory Puffin.

"What exactly is going on?" the Mistress calls out as she strides towards the edge of the court, dodging fermenting apple after fermenting apple. It's worse than she thought out here.

The four girls who are playing doubles cower a little, although she didn't raise her voice and isn't usually regarded as a figure of fear. It must be something about her all-black silhouette on an otherwise sunny day.

"We're a bit stymied by the fruit and the wasps from time to time," the oldest girl, Margaret Redpath – known to everyone as Maggie – replies after an elongated moment.

"I should say," states the Mistress, naturally projecting her voice without thinking about it after years of practice speaking at college events. "This is a disgrace. My girls can't practise here. She never would have wanted that."

"Who wouldn't, Mistress?" the smallest girl pipes up and for the life of her, the Mistress can't remember her name. But before she can ponder this small, strange, most-unlike-her hole in her memory, she sees the head janitor striding towards them as fast as his bad knees will allow.

"I heard your shouting, Ma'am," he calls out when he is within earshot. "I came to see how I could be of assistance."

"Shouting? I wasn't shouting," the Mistress replies.

"If you say so, Ma'am," he offers, as the girls snicker, then blanch when she turns to them.

"Well, seeing as you're here, clear this mess up then. Or get one of your boys to do it for you." The Mistress can hardly bear to look at Her tennis court like this – with any vestige of Her presence disappearing – and so she turns around, cloak billowing, and heads back up to her tower, struggling with the last few steps. Gregory Puffin is nowhere to be found when she arrives, although he has left a furball on the living area carpet.

This matter out of place disgusts the Mistress so much that she has no appetite to partake in the usual Founders Day afternoon tea for the staff. She sends a message down to say that she will not make it to the annual event. The knowledge that this means Elena will be the one to say grace makes her stomach roil all the more, but she simply can't face it. She even turns away the serving girl who teeters up the stairs with a bowl of carrot soup and a hunk of bread. She can't concentrate whilst she can still hear the sounds of rotting apples being squashed.

By five p.m., the slight pangs of hunger in her stomach begin to feel like a lesson, although she doesn't know what she's learning. She's found it hard to parse the signs and omens of her body, her life, for years now. She notices that the rug where Gregory Puffin deposited his furball is looking moth-eaten. There's a crack in the ceiling above her bed that she is sure is getting wider, and there seems to be far more wind entering through the windows than there used to be.

The whole place is sagging, coming apart at the seams. Gregory's furball even looked like it had some torn-up pages from a book in it. The sacrilege. But when the Mistress drags herself to her pitcher to wash away the sweat that has gathered at her armpits, she looks in the mirror and sees that she has barely changed a day since That Day. Apart from a few ragged crow's feet around her eyes – and if she didn't wear so much black, middle-aged clothing – she could pass for a girl of not yet thirty. She looks at herself like she is seeing her own ghost, except inverted, like there's a chance she could go back over her life and smooth it out like a crinkled piece of paper.

As the sun begins to lose its intensity, the state of the college preoccupies the Mistress' mind to such an extent that she only really notices the knocking at her door when it becomes a pounding. She has been sat on her velvet sofa, stealing glances at the loch and trying to figure out a way to stop it being drained. But every path seems to be blocked.

"Can't a woman get a moment's peace around here?" She means to say the words inside her own head, but she accidentally blurts them out, a humiliating squeak in her voice.

"It is only me, Mistress," Elena replies, her breath catching. The Mistress thinks of what it will have cost her body to climb the college's highest turret. She hasn't been up here in years, perhaps decades. There was a time, after Her disappearance, when they comforted each other but those days are long gone.

She strides over to the heavy wooden door and yanks it open, revealing her sweat-tinged face. *How did she get to have all those crags and wrinkles?* the Mistress wonders for the hundredth time. The march of the years between when they met and this moment suddenly seems such a violent thing.

"What is it, Elena?"

"There's been a flood, Mistress."

"First a fire, now a flood. Why is this building falling apart? It's not like the Old Girls don't pour enough money into it."

"You are right, Mistress. It is a little surprising, perhaps. But you know how old buildings go. And there were bound to be a few issues as we try to redevelop and modernise after the fire."

"It is not even that old, Elena. Only a little older than you or I."

She merely inclines her head, although the Mistress notes that she uses this as an excuse to take a quick glance at her quarters. "The reason I wanted to let you know myself is because the flood is in Her old room. One of the janitors was going to come up here, but I thought I should be the one to deliver the news."

The Mistress follows her immediately after that, frustrated at Elena's slow pace as they slip through the twisting corridors to Heather. As they arrive at Room 24, she can see a trickle of water emerging from under the door, sunlight dancing on the puddle's surface. The Mistress sweeps in, her boots creating little splashes. The water has covered the floorboards where they used to lie on their fronts to finish jigsaw puzzles or write in their journals. It's taken over the hearth where She taught the Mistress the best way to keep a fire alight. It's even started to seep into the wardrobe where Her dresses once hung.

A burning sensation hits the back of her throat. She swallows hard, pushing it down.

"And the current inhabitant? Is she safe? Is she quite well?" the Mistress enquires, turning back around to see Elena studying her carefully.

"Yes, Mistress, of course she's safe."

"Don't 'of course' me, Elena. This is highly irregular, not to mention dangerous."

"You're right, the young lady will require new accommodation temporarily, but she'll hardly drown. The water is only up to our ankles."

"How can you be so sure? It's possible to drown in an inch of water, you know," she snaps and then feels badly as Elena really does look ever so tired. Elena leans forward, appearing to be on the verge of saying something, but she doesn't give her the chance as she makes her way out of Her old room.

"Just see that it's fixed. And ask the janitors to do an inventory of the college and all its problems. We can't afford any more mistakes," she hisses, as she speeds away, leaving a trail of watery footsteps in her wake. The day is beginning to fade away and there's so much still left to do yet – all of a sudden – such little time.

After the governors meeting, she was at a loss, but now the Mistress sees it is imperative to conduct a survey of the college. That is how she must spend this early evening; checking on the carcass of the building and ensuring that it is still bearing up. For the fourth time that day, she sweeps down from her turret, only now she takes the stairs two at a time. She is on the lookout for fire, flood, and anything they have not yet encountered.

For the first half an hour or so, she finds nothing, other than girls scurrying away from her and leaving mysterious items in their wake. Words in a language she doesn't recognise are written out on the floor in autumn leaves. A strange perfume that she can't place fills a corridor with its overpowering smell. What she is fairly certain is a milk tooth is nestled in a bust of one of the earliest Mistresses. She can't parse them – that's the point of the rituals, they only make sense to those they seize – but she can feel the Founding Mothers all around her, nonetheless.

Perhaps it is the Mothers then who guide her, helping her to see the shortcomings of the college in its current form. Too many cracked windowpanes to count. A foul-looking mushroom in the

Blossom Corridor bathroom. The beginnings of a mice infestation in the kitchen, although of course the Mistress will not order their extermination. It is Cook's fault for her sloppy hygiene. And besides, the college has served only vegetarian food since the beginning of the Mistress' tenure. Her friend used to love animals – it wasn't uncommon to find the college cat nestled at the foot of Her bed. He had been much friendlier than Gregory Puffin, and less prone to furballs.

The Mistress makes a note of everything, scribbling and scribbling until her hand cramps. She must return to her tower once more, but on the way back she spots one of the younger village lads who helps with janitorial duties. The Mistress never remembers their names, saving all her mental energy for the girls.

"This can't go on," she announces as she beelines towards the boy. He had been staring out at the loch and suddenly startles. She wonders whether he will try to do anything to save the body of water that he is so clearly drawn to. But she doubts it. Men never do.

"What can't, Mistress?" he manages to splutter out, eyes wide and brow creasing.

"Isn't it obvious?" The Mistress gestures around her, though she notices that – unhelpfully – this corridor seems to be in pristine condition. "Everything is falling apart. Something is wrong here. Something is very wrong indeed."

"I know there's been a few teething issues in the redevelopment after the fire, Mistress, but the head janitor says that everything is in hand and the girl whose room had the burst pipe has even been—"

"It's not good enough," the Mistress cuts across him. "I have had to resort to conducting a survey myself just now. I am sure we can agree that such a thing is not the best use of the Mistress' time on Founders Day of all days."

"Of course," he concurs, his eyes roving the corridor behind him as if looking for someone to rescue him. But it is silent, like the life has gone out of the place after the governors' decision.

"What about the mushrooms and the mice? The rotting apples? How are the girls expected to learn to the best of their ability and become the young ladies of the future under these conditions?" the Mistress demands.

"There will always be a few mice, but the lads haven't noticed any more than usual. Ma'am," he adds at the end, obviously unsure how to handle this conversation. "And we battle against the mushrooms the best we can but the girls do love their baths so. The rotting apples are proving a little hard to get rid of because it's so warm out of season, but it will be fixed soon, I'm sure. The head always sorts things."

"It has been the most terrible day," she confides, nodding along but only slightly reassured by this boy's pronouncements. She is not one to doubt the wisdom of youth and yet what can he know if he isn't – indeed if no one is – perturbed by the signs of decay and ruin all around them?

"They are but small problems, Mistress, and the ceremony earlier was lovely. Even us village boys enjoyed it and—"

"No, it was terrible." She speaks over him again. Surely, he must see that, must see what the day has come to, what the college has come to, what life has come to? But he merely nods and begins backing away as quickly as he can without being rude. She turns to meet the loch's gaze and only just catches his glance backwards.

She recognises that look – it's the same one she gives herself each morning when she sees her reflection in the mirror and confirms that she has survived another night of dreams. It's a look that's haunted, even if it's uncertain where the ghosts are coming from.

The Mistress doesn't leave her room again until the late evening, after she has completed her patrol and instructed the boy. She just stares out at the loch, watching the wind move the trees, thinking of all the times they swam in it together. There's no one, distinct memory but rather a collective feeling. Of softness, of friendship, of safety, even in the deep, dark water.

When she eventually exits her chambers, she takes a winding path to her final destination, finding herself passing the tennis courts. There are no sounds of squelching now, but she can hear one of the youngest students complaining.

"There weren't even that many rotten apples anyway, silly," an older girl scolds her. "People were making a fuss over nothing. Just like that leaky pipe and all that drama." The Mistress knows this is wrong – very, very wrong – but her teaching days are long over and she doesn't have the heart to make the girls recognise that their home is crumbling around them even as they speak. Let them enjoy it whilst they can.

Her body takes her down to the loch. She usually only allows herself one visit a year, right at the end of summer. The loch is something she can look at yet not touch. To visit more than annually should feel wrong, but now that she is on the overgrown path down to the brackish water she knows there can be no other way. This feels right and true. Far more so than when she was last here, a couple of months ago, on the anniversary of Her disappearance. Elena had been there too, faffing about at the edge of the loch with a scythe, and it had ruined the reverent atmosphere the Mistress likes to observe when she remembers Her.

Perhaps Elena was there to remember Her too, despite the woman's hatred of the loch. The Mistress' friend always did have so many admirers. Too many. That was the problem. The other competing women's colleges wanted to tempt Her. Some even paid a reward for any information that would lead to her safe discovery after She went missing. They wanted Her brain, Her backhand, the way Her smile appeared out of nowhere like light through a cloud. Thanks to those things, the search for Her was exceptionally thorough, compared to other vanished girls. But then of course the looking stopped and the memorialising began. The Mistress hated that part because then she, too, had to accept that She couldn't miraculously return.

One of the most prestigious rival colleges had offered Her a scholarship and a proper coach. It was the chance to be taken seriously which drew Her in, not the money. They'd been here for a swim when She told the Mistress about the fact that She was truly considering transferring.

"You're leaving me?" the Mistress had cried, wanting to peel the smile off her friend's face. The Mistress was incandescent – because of the affront to her alma mater, of course – and she'd waded in deeper and deeper in a fruitless wish to escape her friend's voice. The pondweed had clutched at her thighs; she could feel its worry, too. The fear that the loch's favourite daughter was going to abandon it.

What would she do without Her? What would this whole place do without Her? The Mistress' thoughts had been frenzied, and so had her movements.

"Come back!" her friend called from the shoreline where they had been happily bobbing around just moments before. "Come back, Meredith. Right now!"

And so, like the good girl she was, the Mistress – or Meredith, as that was all she was then – started slowly swimming back to her friend. It was pathetic really, how easily she obeyed even after this stab to her heart. Ducks quacked at her cowardice as she returned to all that she'd known, even if it was about to change forever.

Her friend – Betty, that was Her name, the Mistress remembers as she begins to step into the water – waded in further to meet that younger version of the Mistress. Meredith. Betty. The Mistress has not thought of the two of them by name in so long that the rhythms of what they were called had almost escaped, but her body remembers that day of betrayal all too well. The past is twisting with the present. Meredith is mixing with the Mistress once again.

The Mistress wades in a little deeper, ignoring the muddy water around her skirts. Then deeper still until she is almost up to mid-thigh and at the point where Betty stumbled on the path to her. Meredith had almost been back at the shore by then, but she wasn't quite within reach of Betty when her friend tripped – probably on pondweed, possibly on a rock – and stumbled below the surface.

Meredith could have moved quicker but the shock of the morning and the heaviness of the water caught up with her limbs, making her at once panicked and sluggish.

"Help!" Betty called as she broke through the surface, her muscular arms flailing. "Meredith!"

Before Meredith moved, she hesitated, wondering how long Betty might have to stay at their college if she required serious convalescence. Then she shook such thoughts from her head, scattering them with a thousand water droplets, and made for Betty as fast as she could. But there was a tide that day, which had worked its wicked way as Meredith dithered. A tide that carried Betty even further away from her than the nightmare of a rival college.

Meredith spluttered and splashed after Her but Betty had always been the stronger, fitter one. The current taunted and teased Meredith, giving her a glimpse of a slender leg or a tendril of curly hair, before pulling Betty away again. No matter how hard she swam, she couldn't catch Her.

She gave up too soon. That was the problem. She was too cowardly and she watched her best friend, her *only* friend, get carried to the middle of the loch, and she didn't do enough to prevent it.

So, Betty sank and she sank and she sank. Meredith waited for days, weeks, months for Her body to be discovered but it never was. The loch had unknown depths and it had claimed its precious daughter so that she might never leave. She kept expecting someone – likely Elena – to have spotted them out of a window and reveal Meredith's ultimate failure. But no one came forward. The months changed to years and on a good day, the Mistress could imagine that She was merely at another college having taken up the scholarship and they had just fallen out of touch. Or better still, She was in some secret watery world and one day She would send a message to the Mistress to join Her there.

Perhaps today is that day. Perhaps the governors meeting was that message, disguised. Either way, it sealed her fate. The Mistress feels lighter than she has in years, with the water supporting her weight. There's a tickle around her toes and a warm current playing around her ankles. It begins to carry her away, firmly but not without gentleness, and she lifts her feet to help it. There's a whisper in the reeds that almost sounds like girlish laughter as she is brought out to the centre of the loch. At least this way they will be found together.

There is no one to scream and call the Mistress' name – if anyone even remembered it. No one waiting for her ashore. The loch swallows her whole, then remains quite calm. The ducks quack, the coots chatter, and tomorrow's sun betrays nothing of where she sank below the surface, sparkling equally on all quarters of the water.

Advanced Dissection

Taylor Grothe

Content Warnings
gore, dead animals, medical terminology.

The air tastes of iron at Hallenord University.

Tucked away in the Swiss Alps, there are as many rumors about its origins as there are mourning doves in its pines. Some say it was Louis XIV's secret chalet, built for a lover and then abandoned when he, spoiled brat, hated it. Others whisper that before The Fall's last-second diversion, it was the Paris Climate Accord's classified meeting bunker. Whatever the provenance, Hallenord, all granite buttresses, hollow-eyed gargoyles, and rotted wooden wainscotting, has been home for half a year.

"D'you think they'll serve that weird-ass lab-grown filet again?" Pierre looks up from his biomechanical engineering coursework with a scowl. I used to think his face was perfectly punchable, and if I'm honest, I still kind of do. He's all floppy hair, puppy eyes, and atrocious sense of humor – but apparently Adelaide adopted him during frosh orientation and that was the end of that.

"As long as it's not river eel. Remember when they showed us how they use glaives in Physical Development?" Adelaide brushes a hand through her curls, shuddering. "They taste like silt."

I look up from my notes, eyebrow raised, knee bobbing. This conversation's inane as hell. "Huh."

"Oh, to see a green vegetable anywhere."

Adelaide balances her notebook on her knees, her skirt drawn up under her thighs. "You think they let seniors choose their own dinners or...?"

"Anything would be better than test tube food," Pierre says. He fixes me with his Basset Hound eyes. "Didn't you say that they gave you *engineered cereal* as your breakfast this morning?"

It's true: this morning there was a large box with my name in looping script. Inside was a silver bowl with a measured amount of something that looked like dog kibble, but frankly, I'd been hungry enough to take a bite. The card said something about *high-efficiency proteins*, but I usually throw those things away. So what if the food is gross sometimes? It won't kill us; there are too many high-ranking dignitaries' kids here. Even a Wastes kid transferring in as a sophomore entitles you to *some* protections.

"It was fine."

Pierre snorts. "Maybe they wanted you to relive your childhood running with a pack of public-school degenerates?"

A bit too close to home. My ears redden, heat swirling through my chest, and Adelaide notices. "I got that, too, Pierre, c'mon."

But it's not quite enough to take away the sting.

"Well, this has been an enlightening chat," I snap, pushing back from the study table. The wooden chair legs squeal, beaten dog, against the marble floor. Students tucked in the corners of the Rare Book Room look up pointedly, and I lift my chin in defiance. "I'm going back to our room to actually, you know, do some work."

Not that I *could* work, with class registration looming. I've worked hard for this spot, got transferred in from one of the few remaining government schools in the States.

"Don't be such an ass," Pierre quips, throwing his stack of notecards at me. "Time was when we could barely get you to study."

"Those classes were a song. This won't be."

"You don't need to worry." Adelaide threads her fingers through mine, amber eyes glittering. "You'll get in. I, on the other hand…"

I run my fingertips over her palm as I let go, a watchful eye turned to the faculty desk. There's a zero-tolerance policy for queer relations at Hallenord, and I'll be damned if I get kicked out. "Stop that."

But Adelaide only smiles softly at my grousing, grabbing my hand and pulling it to her lips, a plump kiss grazing my knuckles.

Truth is, she doesn't have to worry at all. She was the star student in the biology department before I came here and supplanted her, but nothing can wipe away the indelible stain of political marriage and noble roots.

"Must be nice to share a room with your lover," Pierre snipes, an arch smile piquing his brow. "But sure, go *study*."

"Shut it, dickweed, some of us have a GPA to maintain," I fire back. "Also, we all know what you do with pretty boy Christov—"

He tosses his freshly gathered notecards at me again.

Sweeping my hair into a bun, I leave the Rare Book Room, dropping my heavy cardstock name plate back into the slot by the door, indicating I've checked out. The claret calligraphy makes my name look beautiful, when really, it's dull as dishwater.

My feet click into the shadowed recesses of Hallenord's front hall, where the university motto, *canibus venari,* is painted onto the curving stairway wall in sickly pewter. *Dogs in hunt.* I've contemplated that little detail far too many times to stop and do so now. Instead, I pull my phone out of a small pouch in my bag, glancing quickly to the darkened corners; Hallenord has a zero-tech policy. If I'm caught out, I can explain I was checking for university-sanctioned reasons – I applied for Mlle. Perrault's Advanced Dissection practicum and need to know well before they hand-deliver printed, cream-colored envelopes to our dorm room doors, our schedules hand-written in copperplate. Faculty access is faster.

With rosters posting in less than an hour, it's difficult to stop checking. Pierre jailbroke my phone and now I can monitor the faculty intranet – in small snatches. If I don't get in, I'll need to race for the Lottery, a dead-heat dissection under Mlle. Perrault's exacting eye.

The page loads, slots still unassigned.

I shove the phone back into the bottom of my bag, twitching at the edge of my Hallenord-issued tartan skirt. Adelaide jokes that we're in the Alps, not Scotland, so it makes little sense, and Pierre finds a thousand and one ways to deface his hunter-green blazer out of spite – but I secretly don't mind the uniform. It makes me feel like I belong to something, to someone.

Jogging up the stairs past froshers to the dormitory levels, I pass dust-coated busts of long-forgotten gods. Their shadow-bitten eyes stare back at me, heavy with collapsed hope, or alternatively, reproach. There's the threadbare hunting tapestry hung above the main hall, the frayed edges of hounds' teeth look no less sharp for wear. The hare between their splayed paws still boasts a frantic gleam, and I snatch my eyes away, up. No use looking toward the past.

My brass key skin-warm in my palm, I stop at the heavy wood of our door. Here is where I'll spend the next two years, outrunning that transfer-student stigma.

I kick off my Oxfords inside, open the diamond-paned windows into bitter, frost-laced air, and catch a whiff of damp hunting dog fur. I lean into the void and squint down at the snow-coated courtyard. November – no milling students and certainly no dogs. Rubbing my arms against goosebumps, I draw the phone out again. Can't hurt to check one more time.

My chest tightens as I refresh the page.

Classes flash and load, and beneath them, student ID numbers. I skim for Advanced Dissection, Mlle. Perrault.

Heart slamming into my ears, my fingertips pulsing, I sink onto my bed. Under the heading:

1.   4177591

2.   Unresolved – Dissection Room Two

3.

I blow a hard breath and lie back, dropping the phone onto my stomach.

I got in.

But my heart skips a beat when I realize that means Adelaide will have to compete for her spot. Only the first three students at the dissection room will be allowed to dissect.

There is no time to waste.

I race from the room, stockinged feet slipping on marble floors, toes cracking on rucked carpet, and launch down the stairs. Distantly, I swear I can hear hounds panting behind, nipping my heels.

"Addy," I wheeze, flying into the Rare Book Room.

She stands at the sight of me, unquestioning. An instant later, we sprint for the Science Wing.

She's the only one who's ever wanted this as badly as me. We pledged to get in together.

I won't let her lose this.

I watch her slip into her white coat and check her scalpels, readying herself behind the first desk. There is no subject as yet, just a timer blinking 00:15:00 in red block numbers.

It was worth the burning throat and heaving chest, the toe I slammed bloody on the sharp last turn of the hall, to be the first in line. Just behind us, growling curses as they jockeyed over each other, shoving and snapping jaws, were four other students. Doubtless they'd checked the faculty intranet, too.

Red-cheeked and winded, the other two students – some girl I don't know, a junior, and, fuck it all, Pierre – stare at me. His eyes beetle my form and I bare my teeth.

"Did you think me being here was for show?" he snipes, sotto voce.

"This is *our* dream," I start, but a crowd's gathering in the amphitheater, hushing with words. I step forward and jab him in the chest with my finger. "You had better do the right thing."

He barks a laugh as I step back into the stream of students. Fine. The truth is, alliances are everything and nothing. Easily made, easily broken.

Dissections are always major events at Hallenord, especially with Mlle. Perrault presiding.

She was not what I expected: a thin blade of a woman, her aquiline nose and butter-blonde hair never in view in her videos online. I was, however, familiar with her hands: the small scar above the first joint of her ring finger on her left hand, the trio of birthmarks between thumb and forefinger of her right. She parts the crowd like a dagger.

They say she was shortlisted for a Nobel, but at the last minute it was snatched away for incorrect procedures. They whisper it's because of her base nature, a girl from the Wastes like me. It makes me bristle.

"Welcome, students, to the Lottery." Her wire-rimmed glasses gleam as she regards the room. "It's always heart-warming to see such a crowd for a dissection. The fastest and cleanest dissector will earn second spot entry into Advanced Dissection's practicum. However, this year will be different. There will be a third position."

Uproar in the crowd; how many more would have applied had they known? Yet more *should* have assumed the university would have tricks up its sleeve; only the most skilled, most cunning, fare well here.

"Two of you," Mlle. Perrault continues, stalking between

the black-topped science desks, strumming her hands on their surfaces, "will gain admittance." She tilts her head to the faculty door leading to the freezer. Froshers like to joke that's where they keep the bodies of poor-performing students. A lie, of course.

On cue, the heavy metal door opens and out come three orderlies in face-obscuring masks shaped like the dog heads in Hallenord's crest. They're rolling carts covered with white sheets.

"These will be your subjects. You're to dissect the aortic valve, removing it from the heart muscle, and the lungs." The orderlies shift the fabric-covered animals onto the desks.

"You have fifteen minutes."

A dissection like this can take forty-five. I don't have time to catch Adelaide's eye, and anyway, she's looking down at her hands, her knuckles white around her instruments.

My teeth clench, jaw springing to life with taut muscle.

"Begin."

The shrouds are torn back. There's a gust of air swirling with fur, lips pulled back over jagged teeth.

Hunting dogs with slit throats.

Fifteen minutes pass in a blink, but Adelaide's hands do not shake. She puts her scalpel down as the buzzer goes off. To her right are cleanly dissected lungs, an aortic valve.

There is no blood. The hunting dogs were emptied of that slippery fluid before dissection.

They say blood holds no importance here at Hallenord.

Mlle. Perrault, who has been standing, arms crossed, against the door, presses the button and stills the animal bleating of the alarm. "Scalpel down, Catarina," she snaps.

Catarina looks up, a piece of torn tissue on her cheek, and pales. She places the knife onto her waiting tray.

Adelaide looks nowhere and everywhere, her eyes seeking a middle distance. My heart breaks for her, because I have been in that place, where all burning gazes rest on my back and I cannot even hint at weakness; if I do, they'll be on me like hounds on a hare.

"Very good, students, very good." Mlle. Perrault slips between the tables, her eyes passing over the dissected body parts.

Six lungs, three aortic valves. Discarded organs sit in silver buckets at their feet, fractured bones peeking over, slicked with pink.

The animals might not have had blood anymore, but the air smells sharp.

Mlle. Perrault tugs on gloves as she approaches Adelaide's table, lifts the lungs. Adelaide gives a near-imperceptible shiver. A world-class scientist is holding her work, inspecting it with keen eyes. And then Mlle. Perrault turns to Pierre, to Catarina.

She walks away, peeling her gloves off, then turns. "I've made my decision."

Was it that easy to decide the future of three students?

"Student Entwood, second position."

Pierre straightens, allows the ghost of a smile to curve his features. Then he tucks it away. I would smack it right off his face if I could.

"I am honored to join you," he intones.

"Catarina, you nicked the aortic valve on the transverse cut." She swings her gaze to Adelaide. "Adelaide, the oblique fissure of the left lung was damaged when removed."

I notice the passive voice. "The decision is an easy one. Student Marmaine, third position."

Adelaide picks her chin up. "I am honored to join you," she says, her voice ringing through the amphitheater.

There is no applause but my heart soars, tears I'll never let fall pricking my eyes.

The orderlies come to take the carcasses away.

We are flush with our wins, drunk on each other and the twin bottles of prosecco that appeared between our beds in tarnished ice buckets. My fingers are cold with melting ice chips, a stiff November wind blowing in through an open window. Yet I'm puddling with heat, slick and needful and wanting.

On the weave of the breeze, yelping.

Adelaide cups my cheeks in her hands and kisses me hard, pushing me back until I hit the wall. I groan as she runs fevered fingertips, then tongue, over the line of my jaw, teeth nipping the thin skin. She'll leave a mark there if I let her.

My hands drift up under her skirt and she gasps as I grip her hips. I spin her to the top of my desk, scattering all my carefully annotated notebooks. I don't know how to reckon with my warring emotions: I think I might love her – but there's no room for that at Hallenord.

There's only this. Now.

I want, want, *want*, all hunger. Ravenous, jaws snapping, slavering for her. My teeth graze the lace of her panties, famished for the barest taste.

"I knew you would get in." My breath must tickle her with a finger of heat, for she arches against me, her hands digging to my scalp.

"I knew *you* would get in," she breathes, her words hitching as I peel her underwear away with my teeth. Lace spindles between my jaws, my focus keen as any hunter's.

"Hush."

My tongue seeks the slickness between her thighs, and she bites her lip to muffle a squeal of pleasure.

"God, you taste so good," I croon, and I'm rewarded with a clench of turgid, hot muscle. Seeking her tenderest spot, I suck until she can no longer hide the desperation, until her mouth splits open, breathless. I'm relentless, just how she likes it, her skin sheening with sweat as she presses my head closer yet.

"Viv," she groans, loud enough I stop.

No one can hear her.

Her bearding eyes meet mine, her lips bitten crimson, her chest rising and falling at a sprint. I run my tongue over my teeth.

"I said *hush*," I half bark, half whisper, and she slaps a hand over her mouth, the other still in my hair, pawing me closer yet.

"Viv," she gasps, muzzled. "Please."

It's a breath of a word that coils all my muscles, prickling across my skin.

She's undone over me, as I let her pull shuddering to the end of her tether.

Mlle. Perrault's Advanced Dissection meets earlier than most classes; they whisper here that she leaves university in the late morning to rush to one of the various governmental sites dotting the Alps. After The Fall's diversion, any remaining scientists were called to active duty. Mlle. Perrault must be no different.

Adelaide and I stand close, rubbing our arms in the frigid pre-dawn breeze leaking through the granite walls, missing the watchful gaze of gargoyles.

"Six a.m. feels too early to have any class, and that terrible cereal they left for me this morning tasted aw— *You.*"

I turn to regard Pierre, his mop of hair slicked into place with a quantity of oil that likely violates some kind of EPA convention, his hands stuck deep into his blazer pockets. A grin cuts its way across his face.

"Good morning, comrades." Adelaide twists away from him and he clucks. "Come now, you didn't think I was here to waste *all* my time, did you?"

"You should have told us," she mutters.

I snarl, hackles rising, "You knew how much she and I wanted this."

"What's a little competition between friends?" His teeth gleam in the low light; a heavy gust of wind causes the lamplight to shudder.

I begin to retort but the soft hushing of a single applause carries down the hall. We all turn and bend the neck.

"Good morning, Mlle. Perrault."

"Well done, students." She stops a short distance from us, white coat a beacon in the darkness. "I wasn't surprised to see any one of you vying for this independent study, but it's a pleasure to be able to include all three of you." She brushes a palm toward the heavy wooden door, the gold calligraphy *Dissection Laboratory* glinting. "Shall we?"

Pierre opens the door for all of us; Mlle. Perrault simpers to praise him. My chest heats and I could swear I hear the rumble of laughter in his throat, just for me.

"Welcome," Mlle. Perrault says, gesturing us to three impeccably laid out desks. Each bears our name, engraved in silver.

"We're dissecting again?" Pierre queries, a tad over-familiar, if you ask me. Adelaide makes a face.

"Not quite." Mlle. Perrault leans against the instructor's desk, strumming the oaken top. "First we must clarify the reason we are here."

Adelaide clears her throat. "My assumption was we would be allowed to choose our own subject – from the course's information, anyway."

The near-Nobel laureate swings her gaze to Adelaide, and I want to close my eyes and disappear *for* her. She's third ranked, a last-minute addition – she shouldn't have said *anything*.

But then Mlle. Perrault smiles, all canines.

"You're right, Student Marmaine, that normally would have been the case. But the powers that be – the Board of Hallenord and other international parties – are interested in the three of you."

My skin erupts in goosebumps. "I know you have been at the forefront of medical research, Mademoiselle, of late." I can't resist letting her know how much I idolize her, crave her attention, her position, her care. "I read your latest paper on microscopic dissection of the brain for the United Governments of Europe."

Mlle. Perrault's grin widens even as Pierre rolls his eyes, just out of her view. "Astute, Student Smith." My name sounds lovely on her tongue – it may not be *Marmaine* or *Entwood* or any of those noble-sounding, blue-blooded types, but here it might mean something.

"You're right," she continues, knocking a final time on the desk before straightening. "And you are doubtless aware that there are now three of you, instead of two."

Adelaide's cheeks pink, just slightly.

"I wasn't aware that was even an *option*," Pierre says, without a single goddamn trace of guile.

"We have a larger effort to support." Mlle. Perrault waves a hand, and the hologram projector system boots. Next to her is Hallenord's crest featuring a hunting dog, its bared teeth catching the light. She spins it with an idle finger. "Normally, I would not bring students into something like this, but Students Entwood and Smith, you have distinguished yourself significantly from other sophomores and juniors at Hallenord." Her eyes twitch, wire-rims catching the light, to Adelaide. "You, too."

I feel the slight like an icy palm. Adelaide shows no sign of it, her jaw locked.

"I have been tasked with helping to create the newest research on re-enabling certain hunter functions of the human anterior cingulate cortex."

"A *human* trial?" Adelaide asks, blinking. "But is that... ethical?"

Mlle. Perrault sharpens, a tremor of – of rage – moving across her features. "Would Hallenord sanction an unethical experiment? Student Marmaine, your inexperience is showing."

Adelaide looks down. "Apologies."

I feel the need to save her. "Perhaps what Student Marmaine is saying is that this feels... unorthodox." I choose the next words with care. "Human experimentation, an augmented class size... what is it exactly that we are doing here?"

"Student Smith, while we are fully aware of your... conduct... with Student Marmaine—" I stifle a gasp and the urge to cover my face with my hands. "—I suggest you stop throwing yourself in front of moving trains for her."

Pierre makes no effort to hide a snorted laugh.

"Perhaps I'm being too oblique. You each have received a certain fortified nutritional consumption." She holds up her hand to quell any questions, all vicious smile. "As was anyone who demonstrated interest in this practicum."

My eyes cut to Adelaide, but she's still looking down at her hands. Pierre clears his throat. "The... cereal?"

"Just the very same." Mlle. Perrault opens her hand, and the hologram shifts and opens as well, flowing into the outlines of a medical research paper. "Tell me: have you felt any difference in your personalities, Students? Do you feel decisive? Do you feel powerful?" She twists her fingers into a white-knuckled fist.

I think about Pierre, his puppy dog to hunting hound switch, his betrayal. A week ago, perhaps he would never have entertained any such idea, happy to rest on his parents' laurels and ride them into a paradise of handsome men and depravity. But his eyes are cut gems, his smile sharp and calculating. I think about myself, the quick rise of my anger. My hunger.

"You see, Students, the modification temporarily reprograms parts of your mind to make you more efficient." She waves beneficent hands. "Worry not, it wears off quickly, though the compounds stay in your system for some time. Now, about thirty percent of the time, the compounds have the opposite effect, calming the hunter drive. We were able, from the samples of certain test subjects' blood, to predict the outcomes with startling accuracy. Hallenord's entry papers included a blood test, as I'm sure you're aware."

Bitter anger courses through me, scattershot.

"Then why put us through an entry exam for this course? Why put *them* through a practicum," I say, struggling to keep my voice even, "if you knew what the supplement would do? Why not simply pick students at random?"

Why, why, why, my blood pulses in my ears. Why work so hard? Why try for so long to be someone?

"Ah, but that's just it. There's an… unquantifiable element, of course. You're human beings, complex. We needed students who would sacrifice anything, would go through any test for this." Mlle. Perrault closes her fist and the hologram changes back into the hunting dog crest. "And we needed to be sure to have students who wouldn't go spilling international secrets."

"And if we do?" Adelaide says, her voice soft. She raises her eyes for the first time. "Hypothetically, of course."

Mlle. Perrault laughs, but it's blade-edged and keen. "Well, we all know the kinds of errant behaviors you have. Consider that, under the eyes of the law, the three of you are aberrants. Not to put too fine a point on it." She meets each of our eyes, one by one. "Hypothetically, of course," she mirrors.

Silence falls thick over the room, thick as the scrim of dust clinging to those dead gods' busts. I swallow hard. The allegations would stick. Hallenord, and whoever is funding this experiment, they'd have no compunction about turning me over to the authorities. None at all.

My breathing is too fast. I need to get a hold of myself.

"You can't do this," Pierre snarls. "My parents—"

"Your parents don't want a stain on their reputation. That's why you're here, isn't it? Hallenord is your glorified nanny."

Pierre's cheeks burn.

"Don't you *want* to further science? Imagine for just a moment the applications of this kind of work. And mind me well: we could make any students stars of this program." She gives a soft chuckle. "We chose you because you can keep secrets. Or can't you?"

"Fine," Pierre says, breaking first. "What do you want us to do?"

Mlle. Perrault shakes her head, a regal smile curving into her cheeks. "No. You must all agree before next steps."

I look to Adelaide. Inside of me, there is a core of burning anger that I would be manipulated like this. That I would be used like this. But then I think: Would I have been this angry even before I ate whatever Mlle. Perrault slipped into my food? Would I simply have accepted it? And if so, why wouldn't I now? I'm here to advance science, not worry about my own feelings. So what if I was coerced? Isn't *everything* coercion?

Without Hallenord, I would be in that ratty public university, water leaking into the bunk hall, fissures cracking open on the soles of my feet, riddled with parasites contracted from scummy shower floors. Science could never enter into the equation; I was too busy simply surviving.

No. I have to do this. No other way.

Clenching my teeth, I turn my gaze back to Mlle. Perrault.

"Yes. Okay, I'm in."

Adelaide gasps next to me.

Mlle. Perrault's ember-tipped stare burns into me. "You know, you surprised me, Student Smith. So poor a background, yet such a well of knowledge. Makes me wonder what we've been missing out on there."

I swallow over my outrage, nails digging into my palms.

"I will not consent to this," Adelaide grits out. There's fear scrawled across her fine features. "You can tell whomever you'd like about my *aberration*."

"Interesting. You wouldn't save your lover?"

My body goes cold.

"No – she's not part of this. This is my decision." But Adelaide's voice shakes.

"Is it?"

"Listen to her," I hiss. "If you don't do this – they'll out me, too. Please, Addy."

"I will not be party to your unethicality." She's made up her mind, stubborn and myopic.

I run the tip of my tongue over my teeth, stomach growling. There's a wild howl of hunger inside of me, a ripping, unbridled need that I can't seem to quench.

"Fine, then, ruin Student Smith's life." Mlle. Perrault opens her hand, and with it, the faculty intranet springs to life.

She's going to contact the Registrar.

The sick shit is, no matter what, Adelaide and Pierre will recover. Adelaide's parents could buy her out of anything, set her up with a new name, in a new, prestigious university, somewhere else.

Not me.

A growl escapes my lips, and I leap over my desk. Pierre howls a laugh as I smack the hologram device from Mlle. Perrault's hands, scratching beading red lines through her skin. The device clatters to the floor.

It feels like hands are digging into my brain, pulling apart all my impulses. Anger crests inside me, only needing someone to direct its path.

"Ah, there it is. You put up quite the defense, but in the end you're all the same. Biddable. Angry." She bares her teeth at Adelaide, who sinks back a step. "I did say some responded differently to this trial. Some become predators. Others, prey."

Adelaide's shaking so hard I can hear her teeth rattling.

Something – something is changing. In me. I can hear – everything. It's different now. I can smell the gel in Pierre's hair, the animal-dank sweat curving down Adelaide's temple. My bones hurt. My stomach riots with hunger.

"Run, Student Marmaine."

There is nothing inside of me but hunger, hunger, hunger, as I race the halls of the Science Wing. I can smell her, the twist of her almond oil alive and nearly visible in the air. Pierre and I split up as we left the room so he could guard the main hall; we know Adelaide will do her best to get to the front office of Hallenord, located across the building and down three flights of stairs.

We won't let her make it.

My hands and feet paw the rutted, mildewing carpet, the scent of dirt and dust rising thickly to meet the almond, and I stop. My fingers sharpened to claws some time before, a cracking distention of bone and sinew, leaving rusty tracks in their wake.

The halls are quiet, emptied of students. Left only to me and my vacuous need.

I *want, want, want.*

There; I detect a hint of her again, the distant thrum of a fast-beating heart, and I turn down the next hall.

Distantly, I hear the slide of leather soles, the jingle of earrings, the hitch of gasping breath.

"Addy," I snarl, my voice reduced to grit and blood. "I know you're here."

There's a flutter of footsteps, shadow-eaten and muffled. The wide hall narrows here, long burgundy carpet running out. Wooden parquet turns to slats, to stairs leading to another floor. The air thickens to mustiness, paintings peeling. Empty, fractured eyes stare down at me, peaked shoulders rising and falling with each step. A mirror has collapsed at the end of this corridor, needles of mercury glass glittering danger.

In it, I see a face made jagged by sprays of carmine-wetted dark fur, a raucous spread of teeth.

I see myself for the thing I am.

A clatter of steps above me, disappearing. Faculty stairs. I sprint after her, knowing how close she is. There's a break in the wall, a dark cavern. Stairs.

I am fast on my paws, double-timing after her, emerging at the top of a choked hallway.

There are no busts here. No paintings. Just tiny chambers, each one carved with Hallenord's crest. Even here, there is the suggestion of ownership. I shove away the part of my brain that tells me this is wrong, that masking your orderlies, that pretending like the underclass doesn't exist, is a damning offense. But it is, after all, giving me a chance to succeed. To become the keen-eyed scientist I am, hunter of the truth.

There's a snarl of dark hair disappearing around a turn, and I launch after her.

"Addy," I growl, my voice not nearly human, not anymore. "Come back!"

Her leather Oxfords slam the floor, my ears ringing, my mouth opening, slavering, *hungry, hungry, hungry*—

Another twist and she's gone again. I scramble to follow her, slipping on claws, screaming with a fetid kind of desire.

Her hands smack plaster. She spins. Her eyes are wide as a snared rabbit's.

"P-Please," she whimpers, her voice breaking. "Viv, you can't do this."

I don't bother hurrying. I stand up, straighten my spine, savoring the bloody crack of each vertebra slotting back into place. I'm more than what I was when I came here. It's *why* I'm here, isn't it?

Adelaide presses herself to the wall as I reach her.

"Don't you see? I am *nothing* without Mlle. Perrault. Without Hallenord. This…" I pause, moving my fingers, watching my sharpened claws articulate. "This is the beginning of a career. A future."

"We could have fought her together. Stopped this."

"Hallenord always held all the cards."

"I didn't think you were a rule follower, Vivien Smith."

A snap of toothsome anger rends me open. "Aren't you hungry for more?" I rasp, taking bloodied knuckles to her cheek.

She shudders from my touch. "Not like this."

Even now I *want* her. I want to sink my teeth into her soft flesh, to hear her cries spiral and die, to carve dominion in the rapid, rabbit-fast beat of her heart.

I can hear it now, beating for me. I curl my hand into her hair. I can almost taste the brine of her sweat. "I came here to do better. To be something."

Adelaide's eyes shift to sad. "Is my life the cost?"

"I'm not sure it has to be."

Our lips are a hair's breadth from touching, blood roaring in my ears. Her breathing goes ragged; I know she wants me, too. Our desires were always animal, sharp of tooth and nail.

"Viv, I—"

"Oh good, you found her." Pierre leans in the doorway, a lupine grin on his face. "Let's go."

At a different time, we might have devoured Adelaide together, picked over her flesh and swallowed her screams. She was always a delicious treat for two.

But not now.

He crosses the threshold and grabs Adelaide hard, even as she snarls and spits. Even prey animals can fight.

Adelaide's hand slips from my arm, and I feel the sharp blade of regret inside me.

"Please!" she cries. "We can stop this!"

We do not return to the dissection lab. Instead, we follow Mlle. Perrault into the labyrinth of escape routes and bunkers beneath Hallenord. To a sterile hallway with concrete floors and white marble busts of Athena. Their skin gleams pale and antiseptic as old-issue fluorescent bulbs flicker overhead.

"Here we are." Mlle. Perrault flashes a keycard to a door. An operating suite.

It's freezing, my skin pricking. A metal operating table's been laid with medical paper. Scalpels gleam at its side. My head sears with sudden pain and I fall back.

"You okay?" Adelaide asks.

I shake my head, the bones in my face shifting, my hands pulling back together. Blood slips down my cuticles as my claws retract, as the wolfish need inside of me narrows. I stifle a cry.

Mlle. Perrault flings her arms out, beneficent.

"You see, Students, we like to understand why our interventions work – and why they do not." She turns her focus on Adelaide. "Student Marmaine. We must investigate why our supplementation resulted in the opposite effect for you. Consider it an honor."

Adelaide sinks, and I do my best to hold her up.

Pierre grunts as he catches her full weight. "Christ, Addy," he spits, but he's clutching his forehead, too.

Mlle. Perrault slips into an operating gown. "Be assured, this is for the furthering of science."

Some deep, rational part of me insists she could have tried this on animals. Not students. That we didn't have to be the front line. That Adelaide didn't have to become a shrinking animal.

That we didn't deserve to be turned against one another.

But equally, and more troubling: that at least I won. Survived another day.

"Come, Adelaide. Just investigatory. Students Entwood and Smith, scrub in."

Adelaide lets go of my hand as she's called forward.

Nowhere to run.

There's nothing I can do anymore, is there? That blade of regret carves deeper.

Mlle. Perrault receives Adelaide.

Her eyes spring wide, her heartbeat visible through her shirt, as she is led, knees shaking, to a metal table. As she lies down. As the straps are tightened on her wrists.

I only watch.

I.

Only.

Watch.

Pierre leaves to scrub in while Mlle. Perrault turns the table over so that Adelaide faces down. The buzz of an electric razor breaks the silence, and I rub my arms as I watch Adelaide's hair fall in clumps.

Mlle. Perrault rears up, fixing me with a stare. "*Go*, Student Smith," she barks. "Go, like the good fucking dog I made you."

I clench my fists, warring against the screaming in my head that tells me to *listen*.

"It is an honor," I grit, moving away from Adelaide's soft weeping. For we all know how experiments end.

Pierre nearly runs into me. I grab his arm and pull him back into the scrub room.

"This can't happen," I whisper, looking out through the viewing window. Mlle. Perrault's mercifully looking down at her instruments, not at us. We have no time.

Pierre presses a hand against his forehead. "God, what—"

"It's wearing off, I think." My face no longer feels furred, my teeth not quite as sharp.

There's a ringing alarm in my head, beating against my skull. *Stop this, stop this—*

"Fuck me, whatever they gave us is terrible."

"Students?" Mlle. Perrault calls.

"Listen to me." I grip Pierre's shoulders. "Whatever happens next, you need to help me."

His face contorts with grief. "I can't get kicked out, my parents would never let me live it down – they'd send me to the military university, and I can't—" He chokes to silence.

We both know what they do to aberrants in the military.

"It doesn't have to be this way." I shake him gently. "We're your *friends*."

And he looks at me with his Basset Hound eyes, biting his lower lip. He's a shell of who he was earlier, all the keenness dulling.

A butter knife, not a blade. He swallows hard. "It made me do it – I—"

There will be enough time for apologies later, for reasoning.

"We need to push back." As I say it, I still feel that thin vein of hunger, the need to win, the sickly desire to hold Adelaide's flesh between my teeth and slit it open to taste her. Warmth pools heavy inside of me, and I shake myself.

But I *want* to have her. It would be so easy.

She's strapped to a table and could be mine.

"Student Entwood and Student Smith, to me, immediately," Mlle. Perrault screeches. "Now!"

Her feet tap-tap on the concrete floor. I let go of Pierre, nod at him.

As Mlle. Perrault comes through the door I launch at her, fist raised. Her nasal cartilage crumples.

Falling back with a curse, she pulls an alarm; the room flashes red as I dive toward Adelaide.

"Addy!" I cry. "Just hold on!"

Pierre grunts as Mlle. Perrault's wiry body collides with his. "Get her out!"

Mlle. Perrault tosses him to the ground with a razor-thin laugh. "Did you think I would have let you be the first to taste this power?" Her hands rip through her gloves, her face morphing into something foxlike, sheathed in strips of peeling skin. Her fingers flay to sharpened ends. "You will not prevail."

My sweating fingers slip on the leather straps. Too slow, too damn slow, I grab a scalpel, chilled metal biting my palm. I press my back against the operating table.

Adelaide whispers, "Run, Viv, please. Go. The alarm – they'll catch you."

I tighten my grip on the scalpel as Mlle. Perrault kicks Pierre in the ribs. A rusty, animal squeal escapes his lips as his head jars against the floor.

He falls quiet.

Mlle. Perrault focuses her slick, rolling eyes on me. "I always thought you would be smarter, Student Smith. Like me, a girl from the Wastes, hm? Willing to do anything to get ahead."

I turn away and saw at the leather with the scalpel. The blade's thin, the leather heavy and double-sewn. It starts to peel away, then splits, and Adelaide has one hand free. She flips onto her back, her shoulder held at an awkward angle as she struggles.

"What a shame," Mlle. Perrault continues, "that I was so wrong about you. You're clearly not cut out for this work. What a goddamned shame *you* are."

A gasp stammers to a stop in my throat so hard I choke on it. My ears ring. My whole life, I thought I was strong. Ready. Cutthroat.

But I was wrong.

I can hear the laughter from my apartment block as I left the dusty, frigid Waste behind. *She'll be back.*

And then Mlle. Perrault, in all her monstrosity, is on top of us.

I put up my hands but hesitate, the bent scalpel grazing Mlle. Perrault's cheek. The skin springs apart, heat spattering my skin. But still she leaps forward, claws extended.

Adelaide gives an animal squeal of bloody pain. Beneath her, the metallic-smelling slop of spilled innards, loops of intestine and a vivid, pulsing liver. Amber eyes glint up at me, knees against concrete.

"Viv – why didn't you stop her?" Adelaide's free hand grasps at the swinging flaps of her abdomen, or what's left of it.

A fetid stench suffuses the operating room. The alarm bleats, and Mlle. Perrault stands, her sharpened hands awash with dark liquid.

She stares down at me. For a moment, I think she'll kill me. But she doesn't. She simply looks at me, my hands entangled in Adelaide's steaming guts, and smiles.

And then she walks from the room. The alarm screams, just as loud as the voice in my head.

Pierre groans and sits up.

"Pierre," I say, my voice ragged, "help me!"

Adelaide chokes, lips stained crimson, bile foaming at the sides of her mouth.

"I have to fix her," I say as he makes a sloppy line toward me. "Help."

She starts to seize, her head tipping back, eyes rolling to whites.

"Hold her steady!"

"I'm trying!" Pierre gets up to his elbows in her gore, wrestling her mostly still as I reach for the medical stapler.

Together, we tuck her liver in, her intestines. I need to do something, *do something, do something.*

My head hurts so much, my hands shaking so hard. It's messy—

What a goddamned shame you are—

—but the staples *thunk* into place. Screaming, mine, all mine.

Voices, distant and softened at the edges; Pierre's too. His gentle, puppy-dog voice. The sound of radios.

And then, blessed silence.

I wake with my hands tangled in her corkscrew hair, almond scent twisting through my sheets, finger pads stained crimson with her blood.

Gasping, I fight to consciousness, my head blaring.

They have us, they have us—

But it's just our room. The diamond-paned window cracked, a swirling finger of snow blowing in. A candle flutters in its place on my desk, next to neatly reorganized stacks of notes.

Next to me, Adelaide breathes softly, dressed in a hospital gown.

"Thank god," I breathe, and press my lips to hers.

Her eyelashes, tangled with burrs of sleep, flutter open. "Viv?" she says and sounds like a child. "I had the strangest dream…"

I tip my forehead to hers and cry; how close I was to losing her. How I've lost her anyway. I know it.

She holds me, lets me, the soft fabric and wood trappings of Hallenord holding us in its rotting, cold arms.

After a while, I stand up, fighting over to the water pitcher left on the dresser. There's a note addressed to me, *Vivien Smith* curling in crimson copperplate. The cream of the paper is silk beneath my fingers as I open it, as I smudge it with blood.

We request your attendance at 4:30 a.m. – Grand Library.

This can only mean one thing.

The clock on the wall ticks to four a.m. with a brass chime. Swallowing bile and wiping my cheeks of dampness, I start to dress in Hallenord-sanctioned clothing. Sheer black thigh highs, black Oxfords, green tartan skirt, white dress shirt tucked in just so. Hair caught in a black velvet ribbon to keep it from my face.

It feels like a farce to dress for my own dismissal, but habit wins out.

Turning to Adelaide's sleeping form, I pull the hospital gown aside. Lopsided medical staples run the length of her torn abdomen; on the inside of her left elbow crease is a bruise from an IV. It's hard to believe it really happened.

I close the door behind me as quietly as I can.

The halls are quiet, the gargoyles' hollow eyes staring. I hurry down the steps, through Hallenord's central hall, moving past the tapestry of hunting dogs, the frayed blood of the hare taunting me. My feet slip on the gray marble floor, and not for the first time but the most acute, I feel like I don't belong here.

Maybe I never did.

The double oak doors of the Great Library appear in front of me too soon. They're cracked just a sliver, warm light spilling to the toes of my Oxfords. Taking a breath, I walk inside.

The smell of mildewed paper, cracking old leather, and oily char wrap through the air. But when I raise my eyes, I find not the Registrar's stooges, but the entire faculty in Hallenord robes. They wear dog masks, their eyes empty onyx in the low light.

"Presenting Student Smith," a faceless voice announces, and the room erupts into applause.

And leading them: an unmasked Mlle. Perrault, her torn face sutured back together.

I am not proud. A pit sinks inside of me, heavy and black. I cross through the ranks of applauding hounds, heart thrashing. Step up to the dais, where the university president stands to the side, clapping delicately, his eyes sparkling through the holes in his mask.

"For the honor of completing the Advanced Dissection course," Mlle. Perrault says, "a Rite of Distinction. May you wear it proudly on this, the day you become a true scientist, a craftsman of the body. *Canibus venari*."

"*Canibus venari*," the ranks shout as one.

Mlle. Perrault shoves a dog mask into my hands, then shackles my wrist between her fingers. She pulls me close. Whispers so no one may hear her. "Welcome to Hallenord's ranks, Vivien Smith."

And in the distance I swear I can hear the howling, the barking, the yelping, of hunting hounds.

GOD, NEEDY, ENOUGH WITH THE SCREAMING

Olivie Blake

It was Calvin's fault. She loved him beyond measure but he was an idiot. He always said things like what's the worst that could happen? And then bam. She's off to the loony bin.

Her mother was very tearful on the morning the van from the college came to take her away, which was rich. Nothing else about the day was out of the ordinary. Seraphina was an orderly person, some might say rigid (Calvin said so often, fondly, with a twinkle in his eye), so she went about her day as normal. She woke up and washed her face vigorously with cold water and soap. Patted dry. She brushed her hair with one hundred and fourteen neat strokes and then tied it back neatly with a ribbon, navy blue to match her cotton sweater, the most practical one she could think of for something like this. She packed all of her clothes very crisply and was rightfully perturbed when she was told she'd have no need for them. By that point her mother was openly sobbing. Really, Seraphina thought with an exasperated inner sigh. All this over a boy!

"I don't think this will take long, do you?" Seraphina said pacifyingly to her mother, who couldn't answer, which was just as well.

"Seraphina Fenwick?" asked a man in a starched white uniform.

"Out of curiosity, what would happen if I said no?" Seraphina replied.

The man looked squarely at her. He was too old to be interesting to Seraphina. "Better stamp that out now, lass. The mistress don't care for sass."

"Pity," remarked Seraphina. "Would we even be here if I weren't so goddamn precocious?"

By then Mama was well engrossed in the proverbial wailing and gnashing of teeth. "Let's just go," suggested Seraphina to the man at the door, turning to her mother one last time to say, "Just so you know, none of this will stop me from seeing Calvin. He loves me and I love him."

If there was any response, it was incomprehensible. "Well, all right, then. Be good," Seraphina added to her sister Cherubim, Chair for short.

"Bye," said Chair without meeting Seraphina's eye. She'd been terribly moody for weeks, positively swaddled in adolescent angst. Seraphina couldn't remember having been so mercurial at fourteen. Well, but younger siblings could be tiresome, this was a fact. "Will you live at the asylum forever, do you think?"

Seraphina looked at the man in the white uniform. No doubt his role was something custodial and therefore he might not be an expert, but there was no one else to ask. "How long does it take to graduate from this program?"

"You'll be evaluated on arrival," said the man. "The mistress will decide about your placement from there."

"Well, then how long does it usually take for a student to leave?"

"Patient," the man corrected her. His nametag said Joe but Seraphina preferred to imagine it was something else, like Nettle. "And none so far have been returned."

"Hm," remarked Seraphina thoughtfully before turning back to Chair. "Probably two weeks, then, is my guess."

"Oh," said Chair. "Bye, then."

Seraphina's father wasn't there, which was not unusual. He was a professor who did something very serious and important for the college, though he rarely discussed it with any of them, lesser minds as they were. He was hardly ever home, which was for the best. Whenever he did deign to make an appearance, talk at the dinner table usually revolved around what to do about Seraphina.

Who, for the record, hadn't asked, thank you very much.

Seraphina had once told Calvin she felt gravely misunderstood by her family. He'd said well, of course she was, it wasn't technically possible to understand someone like her, to which she said I'm not trying to be funny Cal, I'm really trying to express something to you – you know, vulnerably. I really feel as if I'm misunderstood, like I don't know, I'm just different. And then Calvin said okay my queen, deepest apologies I am listening, which is when Seraphina realized she really loved him. It was understandable, though, that the last straw for a wayward girl in a town like Midway Blossom would be getting caught after an evening liaison in the woods.

Put bluntly, Calvin wasn't appropriate for a girl of Seraphina's upbringing or her socioeconomic standing. Upon discovery of their relationship, safe to say that a good old-fashioned conniption had been had. It really did not get any more banally Puritanical than Midway Blossom, where most of the great families had lived for generations, waging a time-defying war for good morals and right conduct in the most archaic sense. Calvin was a poet and a musician, a vagrant one according to Seraphina's mother, and of course there was the matter of his skin. So all in all, everything was a little bit suboptimal for anyone with a small brain.

What did Calvin and Seraphina usually discuss? A little of everything. He told her long, imaginative stories and she enjoyed them, especially when they were over and it was her turn again to talk. Calvin was a really marvelous listener – perhaps the dictionary definition of rapt. And when Seraphina had told him she was being sent away, Calvin had said my dearest, I take the blame, with all my heart I swear there will be a reckoning. Which surprised Seraphina, not because it wasn't accurate, but because she was unaccustomed to anyone in her life taking accountability for anything. So she said it *is* your fault, Calvin, but don't worry, I'm pretty sure I'll be out of there in two weeks, tops. And when he said I'll wait for you, she said you'd better, after all we just discussed it's completely your fault I'm going in the first place, and that was that.

The van pulled up to the building after an hour of driving behind a tractor along the pastoral one-lane road that led to the college. It was a journey that almost resembled the act of traveling through time, which Seraphina's father mainly used as an excuse to stay at the office overnight, night after night, like he'd only bothered with a family the way other people invested in real estate. The facility was a stately red brick with that sprawly-crawly ivy everywhere, and a lovely infestation of morning glories, which were illegal in some places for being an invasive pest. But they did look very nice, thought Seraphina. The wrought-iron gate could use some oiling.

By then Nettle had talked her ear off about the lads at the college, the lads this and the lads that, with a great deal of equivocation about the potential of the season. Seraphina wasn't interested in the existence of other boys (except for sometimes) because she'd already pledged herself body and soul to Calvin. In fact, she felt her missing of him like a throb – like she'd hit her thumb with a hammer, only it was her entire body and a large portion of her mind as well. But she had been raised to be polite and so she had listened to Nettle discussing football or rugby, she never quite figured it out. She could see evidence of the college everywhere, though. In the windows they drove past on the sleepy town's main street, on the clovered lawns of pastel Victorians. From a distance, she caught sight of a spire gleaming from afar, like a patch of errant sun.

Nettle was still talking when Seraphina dismounted from the van onto the gravel road. "—for good behavior," he was saying. "If you're not one of the screamers then you'll get a chance to see it. Mind you, they're all screamers at some time or another—"

"What is all that commotion?" asked Seraphina. It sounded like the inside of a headache was happening at most ten feet away. The ground beneath her seemed to rattle, or maybe that was her brain.

"Joseph," cautioned a voice. "Please refrain from unnecessary conversation with the residents. You know our patients require utmost sensitivity."

Seraphina looked up to find a woman in a deep purple suit waiting sourly on the steps leading up to the house's front door. Beside her was a sign that read ST. CATHERINE'S.

"You must be Miss Fenwick," said the woman who by all deductive processes had to be the person Nettle had referred to as the mistress. "I'm Dr. Croft."

"Are you a doctor like my father or a real doctor?" asked Seraphina.

Titania looked amused. (Seraphina had decided she would call her Titania.) "This is a medical facility," said Titania, who had until moments ago been Dr. Croft.

"Right, yes," Seraphina graciously allowed, "of course."

Titania led her into the office, which was the door immediately inside the house's grand foyer, with a sweeping double staircase that presumably led up to a series of rooms. The office, Seraphina was pleased to see, was amply stocked with books and plants and seemed very alive, and not at all what Calvin had guessed a loony bin might look like (such a boy – he'd guessed torture devices and all sorts of dreary things).

Titania gestured for Seraphina to take a seat, which Seraphina did, of course, after inspecting the chair for any impropriety. Then the doctor gave her a swift, discerning glance. "So," Titania began, settling herself behind her mahogany executive's desk, which looked to Seraphina a bit like the church organ. "Do you understand why you've been sent here to us, Miss Fenwick?"

"Because my parents hate my boyfriend," said Seraphina, with a conspiratorial wink. "But you know how parents can be. What is that noise, by the way?" The headache had only intensified over the course of their conversation. The glass of the office rattled, tinkling a little as if to shift uncomfortably within its frame.

A wave of temporary darkness had rippled over the doctor's face at the mention of Seraphina's courtship. Titania was, then, an adult who could not be trusted; a *them*, as Calvin would say. And after Seraphina had already performed a christening, giving her a better name and everything! Ah, well.

"You and I will meet every night for an hour of psychotherapy," Titania was saying. "For now, though, I'll show you to your room on the third floor."

"Auspicious," said Seraphina, rising primly to her feet. She wasn't excited about the therapy part, as she assumed it would take her away from her social calendar. But then again, what did it matter? She maintained with certainty that she would be there for at maximum two weeks.

The doctor led Seraphina up the grand staircase, trailing a practiced hand along the polished banisters. Seraphina heard a brief, disorienting scream, which cut through the monotonous drone of the distant, unrelenting headache.

"The college," explained Titania, gesturing out a west-facing window. Seraphina hazarded a glance. "The engineering department is constructing yet another building."

"Another?" echoed Seraphina.

"Everything, it seems, is getting funded if it contributes to the war machine," muttered Titania disapprovingly. "There used to be a sense of culture to the campus. It was once a haven for the arts, you know. Now your father is perhaps the final remaining champion."

"Really?" Seraphina said. "I've never thought of my father as much of an artist." Unless you counted his experiments, which Seraphina didn't.

Titania appeared to skirt the topic. "Do you know much about the college's history? It was originally a seminary," she said. "It has a very impressive library, still intact if you can believe it. Even with all those dreadful physicists and their death machines." She tossed another disapproving look out the window, toward someone unavoidably on the receiving end of her disdain.

"I look forward to seeing the library," said Seraphina. She and Calvin did not share a love of books; Calvin seemed to mistrust them, preferring to recite his stories or deliver them in song, but that was all right. Love could bear its gentle disagreements. It was healthy to maintain some semblance of individuality, and anyway it wasn't like they ever had the time to read. By necessity their courtship was one of scarcity – clandestine meetings in the night, like half-remembered dreams.

Titania was giving her a long and interested look, Seraphina realized. Too interested.

"Is there a problem?" Seraphina asked.

Titania paused then on the landing of the third floor. There were twin sets of mahogany double doors, one on the left and one on the right. "Tell me something," said Titania. "Do you feel as if you ought to be here, Miss Fenwick?"

"What, you mean am I upset because I've been sent to an asylum? My dear Titania, madness is very much in the mind of the beholder," said Seraphina, which was something Calvin often said in his better moods. "And if the question is am I resigned to my fate, the answer is no."

Still, Seraphina intended to be on her very best behavior either way. You did catch more flies with honey, as her mother often said. Her mother's gospel was one of unrelenting politeness, and avoidance of boys.

Titania gave her an even longer look. "So you believe you are sane," she said, "and yet you don't see your sanity as an obstacle?"

"Well, as far as I can tell, my parents mainly intend to keep me away from Calvin, so to that end I suppose they have succeeded. But only temporarily." Seraphina gave Titania a thin smile. "He's a musician, you know. He's very good, too. He can play for hours and hours."

"Then what is it about him that your parents so abhor?" asked Titania.

"Well, 'vagabond musician' is hardly an appropriate profession." Like a loose hem or a cleaned plate or discussing money at the dinner table. Simply wasn't done.

"I see." Titania's mouth was a thin line. "Nothing else about him?"

Well, either Titania was racist or she was referring to the issue of the veil. As it had been a long day already, Seraphina hardly felt now was the time to get into it either way.

"Please," said Seraphina, "I would hate to become cross and throw away our good rapport. I do intend to spend these next two weeks on my very best behavior."

"Because you intend to... return to your paramour?"

"Yes, to Calvin," Seraphina confirmed. It was so othering, the way people refused to refer to Calvin by his name. "Although, please don't worry my mother. Her constitution is already so fragile." Seraphina thought again of her mother's wailing tears. Imagine going through life with such deficiency. Was it any wonder one's daughters wound up mad? Not that Seraphina was, but it was hard to fault the statistics.

"Miss Fenwick," said Titania. There was an air of scolding in her tone, but also a curious breathlessness. "You do grasp that Calvin Babineaux is dead and has been for some months. It is quite impossible that you should ever reunite with him."

At that point Seraphina became aware of a low, thrumming anger inside the molten core of her belly, somewhere just beside her womb.

Impatience, that's what it was. After all, how long did it take to show one to one's bedroom? After such a long day of travel. "My dear Titania, if you would be so kind as to lead us onward, to my accommodations?"

There was a tiny, fractional splash of wariness across the doctor's expression. Good! So she wasn't completely comatose. Calvin always said Seraphina could be quite commanding when she put her back into it.

"Very well," the doctor said.

Titania pushed open the doors to the left of the staircase landing.

"Wait here," she said. "I'll go check that your room is ready."

"My things," Seraphina realized. "Will they be brought up?"

Titania looked at her in that funny way again. "Just wait here," she said, and scurried off as if there were tiny little ants nibbling at her heels, and if she stood for too long they'd consume her whole, carry her off to their nest, and bury her there for eternity.

Inside the doors was a sparse sitting room in a ward of blinding white. There was a girl with her mouth open, a fly crawling around on her tongue. Another girl lay flat across the floor staring upward at nothing. A third stood beside the window, observing the motions of one hand. She moved one finger, then another. Then another.

Then she turned and looked directly at Seraphina. She had ratty, ebony waves she seemed to have purposely tied up in small knots and had the look of someone who ate girls like Seraphina for breakfast.

Seraphina smiled.

"Welcome to the disturbed ward," said the girl. Her name looked as if it ought to be Genesta or Mab. "Are you very disturbed?"

"Hardly at all," said Seraphina.

"Pity," said Mab. Then she turned back to the window and crooked a finger to something outside, almost as if to signal a lover. As if to gently lure them home.

There were three other speaking members of the ward aside from Seraphina and Mab, whose actual name was Min, which was paltry enough that Seraphina felt it was fair to disregard it. The others were Hyacinth, Iridessa, and December. There were also several others residing on the floor, the non-verbies who no longer spoke. As they were not very diverting company, Seraphina did not bother to learn their names. Mab decided to call Seraphina "Butch," on account of it being ironic.

"How'd you get here, Butch?" asked Mab. She had a funny little habit of darting her glances to the side every now and then, like someone was lingering just outside her periphery. They all had something like that. Iridessa usually hummed the same tune every hour or so, a little jingle from a toothpaste commercial, which had been annoying at first. Once Seraphina grew to predict it, though, it stopped bothering her. Now she hummed it herself while she brushed her teeth.

"No talking," said the floor warden, whom they all called Flora. She liked to deliver phrases like that from time to time as if they had any meaning. Then she returned to her book of word puzzles and idly scratched her thinning scalp.

"Well, my parents hate my boyfriend," Seraphina explained.

The others nodded sagely.

"What about you, Mab?" Seraphina asked, to make conversation.

"Arson," said Mab. She looked at her fingers with a longing sigh. Out of deference, Seraphina nodded gravely. "December here is queen of the underworld."

"My prince is going to summon me back," said December faintly. "Any day now."

"What about you?" Seraphina asked Iridessa, who was rotating her jaw in a slow circle. She was the girl Seraphina had first noticed, whose gaping mouth attracted flies. Iridessa had a jittery look to her, even though the pills they took each night before bed and with breakfast made Seraphina's limbs so heavy she couldn't imagine how anyone found the energy to fidget. Seraphina herself was having a very strong reaction to the pills – specifically, the very unladylike problem of severe diarrhea, which she would not mention to Calvin. (It just seemed counterproductive, that was all.)

"Iridessa killed her stepmother," Mab said with a foxlike grin. "Shoved her right down the stairs."

"Oh," said Seraphina sympathetically, before turning to Hyacinth. "And you?"

"My poison garden," whispered Hyacinth, who indeed only spoke in whispers. Seraphina had gathered very little else about her. She seemed to straddle the line between present and not, and her voice was half gone. Perhaps she was a mere partial verbie, but then again the line was pleasantly discrete. Either you could speak or you could not.

"Hyacinth killed half the staff and both her parents," said Mab, with a palpable air of pride. "They didn't realize she'd been growing hemlock among the carrots. Still not the highest body count," Mab qualified in an undertone, with a mischievous look off to the side of her eye again, before returning to the subject of Seraphina. "So, that's it for your story, Butch? Just a boyfriend?"

"You know how parents can be," Seraphina confirmed again, with a ladylike shrug of ennui.

Iridessa hummed the toothpaste song. The others joined in. Seraphina, who had an exquisite first soprano, took the descant line.

Eventually the moment passed. The headache outside droned its song of meaningless progress.

"Tomorrow is Tuesday," whispered Hyacinth. Her mind seemed to be elsewhere. She'd been digging her fingers into Seraphina's arm as if to pull the weeds out by the root.

"Only eleven more days until I reunite with Calvin, then," Seraphina contributed. She knew it wasn't fair, since the others were obviously not leaving here, but they seemed not to mind, and were even happy for her, as friends ought to be. Overall, Seraphina felt she was being very well-behaved. The no talking rule was really the only one she didn't follow to the letter. She otherwise took her meds and didn't complain or scratch the orderlies or try to eat or kiss them as December often did. And she always left a little bit on her plate for Miss Manners, in deference to the good breeding her mother had instilled in her reflexively, for the purpose of effortless performance under suboptimal conditions, such as now.

"She means that tomorrow is the day we all go to the college," Mab explained, as December sat up abruptly, trying to catch a bit of lint in her mouth. "You, too, Butch. If the doctor thinks you've been well-behaved."

If the bar for good behavior was anywhere near Iridessa's habit of first sprinting out of arm's reach before being wrestled into the nightly restraints, then Seraphina was surely included. She would write a quick note to Calvin and slip it into the mailbox. All she would need to write a letter was paper and a pen and surely there would be loads of both at the college. Even if the student population were all or mostly lads, they still had to write.

"What are we meant to do there? At the college, I mean," asked Seraphina. Abruptly, one of the non-verbal girls gave a loud, ear-splitting shriek, such that Flora the floor warden even glanced up briefly from her puzzles.

"It's nothing very interesting," said Mab over the sound of the girl screaming. It was, truth be told, a relief from the constancy of headache outside. Construction noise was usually audible at all times of day, uninterrupted save for whenever someone was screaming.

With the orderlies swarming around to try and administer the injection to the non-verbie screamer, nobody was paying their little circle much attention. Seraphina appreciated how it resembled holding court, something that up to that point she could only do with Calvin.

"We're basically just free labor for the library," Mab explained. "Sometimes it's fun. Sometimes it's not. But it's always different from this—" Mab cast a wary glance at the screamer who'd been carted away in a slump. They would likely not see her again for some days, if at all. "—which is really what counts."

"We copy from the books," said Iridessa, chewing a piece of her thumb. Hyacinth briefly stopped digging in Seraphina's arm to take hold of Iridessa's hand for a quick nibble.

"It's stupid, really," said Mab. There was no remaining evidence of the screaming girl. All was quiet again, so Mab had dropped her voice. "I'm very fast at it," she murmured to Seraphina. "You should see me, Butch. I'm fast as hell."

"That's exactly why the prince chose me instead of you," said December. She was back in the conversation now, having given up the piece of lint. Iridessa and Hyacinth appeared to be one girl with two heads, both of them very concentrated on gnawing the dry skin of Iridessa's cuticle.

"All I really want is to speak to Calvin," said Seraphina with a listless sigh. "He must be worried sick about me."

"All men aside from my prince are liars," commented December. She reached over and held Seraphina's hand, a form of reassurance. Seraphina understood the gesture to be a vessel for genuine affection, which was sweet, even though she didn't put much stock in the words.

Seraphina understood that her love was rare and dangerous. Why else would she be here if it was not? Its very existence threatened everyone and everything. All comparable loves had always been likened to madness.

So she didn't bother arguing with December. She was crazy anyway.

That day, during her nightly psychotherapy with Titania, Seraphina was too distracted to focus on the conversation. She was thinking of what she would write in her letter to Calvin. She would probably not have very much time to write it, so it should only be a few words. Five, maximum. Perhaps *I am woeful, please come*? No, too dramatic. One had to be dignified in one's devotion. *Missing you, be home soon.* Or *Despite your flaws, sending love.*

"How did you first meet Calvin?" asked Titania.

"My father introduced us," said Seraphina absently. *Meet me at the usual* – no, too many words.

"But I thought your parents didn't approve of him?"

"Well, of course they didn't want me to *love* him." *Under the tree where we—*

"How did your father meet him?"

All these interruptions were starting to vex Seraphina greatly. "My father carried him into the house," she said at an irritable, explosive pace. "There had been an accident and he set him on the kitchen table to rest while the grown-ups had a talk. Supposedly he'd been riding his bicycle in the dark somewhere off the road that threads the college, though who can tell whether anything grown-ups say is ever true. I'd woken up thirsty and Father had forgotten to lock my bedroom door, so I came into the kitchen for a glass of water." *I'm ready for sex now.* That would really tantalize him! (She'd been ready a long time, precociously so, but these games must occasionally be played.) Yes, there was almost no chance that wouldn't work—

"Miss Fenwick," said Titania. "Do you mean to tell me that you never met Calvin Babineaux alive?"

Oh, what was it Calvin had said when he'd lured Seraphina out to meet him in the woods? *What's the worst that could happen?* It was six words but boys didn't have to play by these rules. Actually, depending on the situation, it could be very hard to get Calvin to stop talking. On and on with his stories and songs, metaphorizing endlessly about captivity and tithes to hell.

Seraphina sighed again. With boys, there was never any silly posturing about what was or wasn't acceptable to say. Calvin could flirt with other women or be a completely different person or detach his head from his body and Seraphina would have to just accept it as a facet of his personality. Boys were really given so much latitude – boys will be boys and all that.

But Seraphina agreed with her mother that resentment was unattractive, so she cast the feeling aside.

"Well." Titania tapped her pen against a notebook, partway through some scrawl about Seraphina's imbalanced humors or whatever nonsense these sorts of doctors believed. "As I can't argue with your comportment, you will be allowed to join the others at the college library tomorrow."

Seraphina hadn't actually thought there was any chance she wouldn't be able to go. Still, better to be gracious than ungrateful. "Naturally so, Titania," she agreed. "Though I do hope Mr. Nettle will accompany us. I don't like to think of us girls being without a chaperone."

"Nettle? Do you mean Joseph? He's been sacked," said Titania. "Not a shred of professionalism in the man's entire body."

Pity, thought Seraphina. That was precisely what she'd been hoping for. Not to worry, as immoral men were so very easy to come by. Why, the college was probably full of them! One could certainly be convinced to pass on a letter. *Wait patiently, you shall have me.* Six words, but then again, why not chance a little risk.

The college library was drafty and hardly above freezing. Seraphina and the others had been given blankets, a pillar candle by which to keep their fingers warm. The building's exterior was brick and tawny moss, and inside was a cedar smell, the crumple of old parchment.

"Here." A man who seemed determined not to look at them dropped a heavy crate atop one of the long wooden tables. "You'll be working with these texts. Copy each line exactly. If you make an error, do not cross it out. Start over at the beginning of the page."

Seraphina smiled reassuringly at the man. She felt that if he believed she were saner than the others then perhaps he would accept her, and subsequently be driven to please her. He instantly scurried off, revealing a boy who stood obediently off to one side, looking scarcely older than she. One of the infamous college lads, then.

She caught his eye. He gave a sheepish, crooked half smile. Darling, thought Seraphina.

"Thank you," she mouthed with a Puritan smile.

In answer, a hesitant nod. This lad had a nice face, an air of accommodation. He was an archive assistant at the library according to his nametag, which read Bill. She would call him Peri later, when she got him alone.

As it was, she settled into the task at hand. Seraphina was very diligent, and the task was quite simple. She simply transcribed the page in front of her in the careful lettering she'd been so congratulated for at school, back before her father's experiments had begun in earnest.

SPELL FOR INVOCATION – TO BE PERFORMED AS CLOSE AS POSSIBLE TO THE NEW MOON – SUMMONING AREA UNCONSTRAINED. REQUIRES PARTICIPANT'S FULL FOCUS.

Seraphina wanted to perform this task well, so that nobody could fault her diligence when she took her leave. They would say, "That girl was very polite, and clearly in love, and no one can say she wasn't dedicated." The trick was to be meticulous. Anything could be accomplished if you did it carefully enough. Too many people were lazy, boys especially. Take Calvin! He was wonderful but he could scarcely maintain order without her help.

O MANES, UNUM NOBISCUM, VIVI. TUAE VOLUNTATI CUM GRATITUDINE ET GRATIA SUBICIMUS. SIT LATOR HORUM VERBORUM VAS.

Seraphina's eyes grew heavy as she transcribed. The same lines were repeated several times, the meaning escaping her. She wrote again, O MANES, UNUM NOBISCUM, VIVI until she felt she knew no time before O MANES, UNUM NOBISCUM, VIVI. Then she felt a chill wind cutting through her blanket, like the onset of a frost.

She looked up and realized she was no longer in the library. Instead, she seemed to be in the middle of a forest clearing. Everything was in varying shades of blue, deeper and deeper indigos until they threaded communally into viscous black. She looked overhead and realized the canopy above her head was not a crown of branches, but rather a skeletal formation of cracking, misaligned bones.

"Oh!" said Seraphina. Her breath escaped into the air like frost. She looked at her hand, which no longer held a pen. How was she going to write to Calvin now?

"My darling? My queen? Is that you?"

She spun at the sound of a voice behind her. Then she exhaled swiftly.

"Oh, Cal!" Seraphina exclaimed with joy, throwing herself into his disbelieving arms. "I was just writing to you." Not really, but the intent was there, and anyway boys mostly liked to hear that you were thinking about them.

Calvin gave her a quick spin before setting her on her feet. "How did you find your way back here, my queen?"

"Oh don't be silly, darling. As if I could ever not find you, loony bin or not." With that last bit of sardonicism, Seraphina gave an ironic little eye roll as if to remind him *this is not my doing, parents as you know can be so unreasonable.* "I was just at the college doing some of the transcription work. Apparently they send us there if we behave. Isn't that lovely?"

"They have set you to the task of menial labor?" asked Calvin, recoiling in disbelief. He was in a wonderful mood, then. Occasionally he could be very *me me me*. You know – "*my* eternal state of undeath," "*my* captivity in this court of nightmares," "help *me* I beg of you please," so on and so forth. Sometimes things were about *Seraphina*, you know.

"Madam, such transgression! Perhaps you should seek revenge on your captors?" Calvin smiled then, a sudden glittering iridescence.

"Well, can't be too angry, can I? After all, I'm here with you." She smiled up at him. Oh, he was so handsome! And with the bone trees crowding out the inverted sky so nicely, she couldn't even see the usual carnage of his face. He almost looked glowing and whole, and practically unscathed. "I've missed you," she whispered.

He bent his head and kissed her, which she very demurely returned. (Games, games, games.)

Everything felt so right, Seraphina thought with a contented sigh. The way she'd been clever enough to transport herself back here to Calvin. With boys it was really about tactical prowess. To lie beside his body and tease him over the course of several meetings with *shh, shhh, not yet, how can I really be sure that you love me?* And when he'd said to her *but my queen what's the worst that could happen*, she'd said *stupid boy, don't let's tempt fate*. But they had tempted fate and won! And if anything was worth conceding sex over it was probably that, so to hell with restraint then, really.

Still, when his hands roved over her breasts and under her skirt, Seraphina laughed and said, "Calvin, you dirty boy!" because it was not appropriate to enjoy these kinds of things. (Only to reluctantly permit them.)

"It's Bill," panted Calvin.

Hm, thought Seraphina, because it wasn't Calvin, it was a different voice. Then Seraphina realized the voice belonged to a different boy entirely, one who was pulling back to look at her. Which was when Seraphina looked around and discovered she was no longer inside the bone forest of deep and dying blues.

Instead, she was in the bathroom with her legs bracketing a trembling boy's lap. It was Peri, the archive assistant, and his hands were under her skirt, which had been pulled up around her waist. Her bra was gaping open and her lips were raw and chapped. Hm.

"I thought for sure it had worked," Peri was saying into her neck. "I really thought I saw it on your face, that you'd actually managed the invocation—"

"You seem surprised," Seraphina said. She knew Calvin wouldn't be pleased she was carrying on in this way with another suitor, but she felt she might need an ally here at the college, and

Peri seemed suitable. It wasn't as if she was going to fall out of love with Calvin over something as meaningless as a liaison in a toilet. Can you imagine! Besides, she was pleased to have the means to further practice her craft – to be prepared for when it really counted, love-wise.

"Well, Professor Fenwick always thought... madness, you know... Granted, it's – hardly discreet—" He groaned as Seraphina swung her hips in a slow, careful circle. "And others have... have *appeared* to have..." He gritted out a strangled, animal sound when she lowered herself carefully onto him. "But it's rare that— I mean... I suppose it never really happens with someone who can—"

He groaned something incoherent, resting his forehead on the curves of her breasts. Seraphina jerked his head up with one hand, grasping a fistful of curls to smile modestly down at him.

"Someone who can what?" she prompted. The metallic teeth of his parted zipper sliced upward into the delicate skin of her thigh.

"Someone who can survive it," he choked out, just before pleasure erupted, spilling into her and back out again, a slow leakage seeping down the front of his trousers.

Inwardly, Seraphina sighed. The cost of having answers always seemed to be a pair of spoiled tights.

Survive what? Seraphina wondered later, as she and the other girls filed back into their ward on the west-facing wing of the third floor. A liaison with a lover? Those lovely sinewy branches of carcass and bone?

"Well, Butch, if I had to guess, he meant survive *that*," said Mab, gesturing with her chin to the variety of non-verbies who wandered the wing in various states of shell-shocked silence.

Seraphina had told Mab the truth about her experience in the library, both because she didn't think she had anything to hide (Calvin would understand, and anyway, it wasn't really his business, seeing as he hadn't yet proposed) and because Seraphina felt Mab was quite shrewd, and generally good at keeping secrets.

"I thought the college used to be a seminary," said Seraphina. "What are they doing summoning demons?"

"Well, I assume that's why they got their seminary license revoked," said Mab, with a conspiratorial glance to something in her periphery, which appeared to be in on the joke.

"No talking," said Flora the floor warden. She was crocheting. An odd choice, as the non-verbies often grabbed hold of anything they could reach. Hair, skin, forks. Crochet needles seemed unwise.

"Did you say nobody else was there?" asked Mab, after a brief consultation with the corner of her eye.

She had asked Seraphina several times now to confirm things Seraphina had already told her. Mab seemed to be battling consternation, having never heard of a bone forest and certainly never having been there herself. Mab had never transported herself anywhere, though Seraphina had pointed out that maybe Mab was simply working on a different book.

"Nobody except for Calvin," said Seraphina, answering the question.

"Hm. Weird," said Mab. "What's the deal with Calvin, anyway? What made your parents freak out so bad?"

"Oh, who knows how grown-ups think." Seraphina flapped an indifferent hand. "And if you're so curious about the bone forest, I'll just take you with me next time. Then you can see for yourself."

Mab's eyes shone with something then. Gratitude? Wonder?

"It sounds a bit like my prince's living room," offered December faintly. She wasn't looking at any of them. The knots of Mab's hair seemed thicker and worse.

Iridessa had been the one who did the knots. The process of it calmed her, or it used to. They'd lost her that afternoon. By the time Seraphina emerged from the bathroom with Peri, the backside of the ambulance was already halfway down the road.

"You didn't hear it?" the librarian man had said to Peri, who'd fumbled clumsily for some excuse. The elderly man was too shaken by whatever he'd witnessed to notice that Peri's zipper had been left down, his glasses crooked and hair askew. "The way she started to scream…"

Seraphina flinched then, brought back to the conversation with Mab, because Hyacinth was once again yanking up invisible tangled roots from Seraphina's arm. It was a pity that Hyacinth was growing progressively quieter, such that she was hardly audible at all anymore. She seemed especially bad that day, ever since they took Iridessa away. Hyacinth kept checking over her shoulder for something that wasn't there, and Seraphina began to wonder how much longer before Hyacinth joined the ranks of the non-verbies.

This, Seraphina felt, was what Titania meant by behaving. It wasn't about following the rules, not really. It was about self-control. You couldn't let yourself go the way Hyacinth did, drifting this way and that through the veil. You had to anchor yourself firmly. It was a matter of discipline.

Calvin had always said Seraphina was very disciplined. And this was coming from him, a bard, a musician. He wouldn't be anywhere without discipline. Would he punish himself like this, creatively, if not for having such drive and determination? These were the things Seraphina loved about him. He did not simply give up. He kept singing his poems and telling his stories, even weeks after decay had started to eat away his jaw.

Later, during Seraphina's appointed hour of psychotherapy with Titania, she was asked a great deal of questions about her transcription work with such magnified, bug-eyed interest that Seraphina instantly understood the only plausible course of action was to lie.

"I've made what I feel is a very sane decision," Seraphina said, "which is to not dwell on the subject, Titania." She hoped that would be that.

Sadly not. "So nothing happened?" asked the doctor, eyes narrowing with suspicion across the desk, rather like how Seraphina's father had looked at her whenever he unlocked her bedroom door and sat her down for hours and hours of interrogation. Everyone was always being so hard on Seraphina, accusing her of this or that, demanding results from her, perfection. Hadn't any of them stopped to ask themselves whether they were the problem? Not to belabor the point, but it wasn't Seraphina who'd struck down a person with her car.

"If you don't mind me saying so, Titania," Seraphina said,

aware that her patience was wearing visibly thin, "I do have to wonder what you think I might have discovered over the course of some very simple transcription work." Seraphina tilted her head in that cherubic way that often worked on boys, even the living ones. "What, after all, could have happened in that library that I would lie to you about?"

Titania's expression soured. "You *did* do it, didn't you? You managed an invocation."

"I'm quite sure I did not," said Seraphina, innocently.

Titania rose to her feet, beginning to pace in irritation. "There's no reason to lie to me, you know," she added, pivoting to face Seraphina after a moment's calculation. "*I'm* on your side. I'm just trying to make sure your abilities are appreciated – that they are *valued*. If the researchers at the college catch wind of this first, they'll only work you to death. Or they'll use you until you break."

Just then, one of the upstairs non-verbies gave a scream.

"See?" prompted Titania.

"What makes you so sure I'm lying?" asked Seraphina. "Mab's never seen the bone forest, either."

"Mab? You mean Miss Lee?" The doctor paused to frown at her. "What bone forest?"

Oops. "Bone forest?" echoed Seraphina, as if the sanctity of her virgin ears had been thoroughly besmirched. Who could say whether anyone had even said it, honestly? Madness really was in the eye of the beholder. "Madam, how morbid!"

Titania's expression transformed into a glare – the specific glare of a disappointed, powerless adult. "Listen to me, you little psychopath," she said, resorting unflatteringly to name-calling.

"Everyone already knows you're not well, don't you grasp that? You're here because your father already confirmed that you're psychologically unstable." Her face twisted in a sneer. "It's not as if anything you have to say will be believed."

Well! What an irony, considering Seraphina was currently not believed (although fair enough, it was for good reason).

The rest of the session was very unpleasant, as Seraphina was not in a good mood. Basically, Seraphina asked Titania why she was so certain that Seraphina was mad when Mab was an arsonist and Hyacinth a murderer. Titania informed her that none of these things were true. That in fact, only Seraphina had ever shown homicidal tendencies, and, were it not for her father, she would not have been accepted to the facility at all.

"As a reminder, none of you have any credibility whatsoever. Miss Lee has been diagnosed with schizophrenia and is highly prone to delusion," said Titania. "Miss Shahadi shows very strong evidence of personality disorder. And still, neither of them has ever seen a *bone forest*, which is not even to mention Miss Valdez—"

Titania broke off with a frown, then gave a huff of a sigh. "I specifically ensured that you were given an *invocation* spell. You should not have been transported anywhere. The only way an invocation produces a portal is if the vessel is already spoken for, or... or if they're some kind of—"

"What about December and her prince of hell? Is that true?" asked Seraphina, realizing that Titania had left out one speaking member of her ward.

"How should I know?" snapped Titania. "It's not my fault if Miss Skaletsky accepted an unwise bargain. She was supposed to be stopped the moment her transcription unsealed the border between worlds. This is what I *told* Fenwick – this is why protocol exists!" Titania added with a shriek. "Each time a suitably fluid mind shuts down or gets corrupted, we lose access to the veil, and with it any chance of legitimizing breakthrough! Just think how useful this research would be if we could confirm it – how many wars we could end, or better yet circumvent—"

Titania gripped her temples, pressing the pads of her fingers into the lids of her eyes. "Those assholes in the physics department are already taking up the funding that should be ours – all because the dean insists technology is our greatest weapon. Weapons! That's all this is, just their industrial complex – their warmongering carnage! As if the classics count for nothing anymore. As if our history, our art is *nothing*!"

She slammed the side of a fist into the surface of her desk. "No more mistakes," Titania hissed to herself. "These things must be *managed*, and they must be *regulated*, and everything must be performed with the *narrowest margin for error*—"

"I don't *at all* see what you think I might have contributed to any of this," remarked Seraphina. "If anything, I feel almost distressingly sane."

"Oh god, what does it matter anymore." Titania fell into her seat with a sigh. "The last successful invocation was months ago and since then we've only lost more vessels. And to think Miss Valdez had seemed so promising…"

Titania trailed off, then shook her head. "Maybe you ought to just stay in your ward, take your meds, get better." Titania said all of this with a distinct air of sarcasm or implausibility. "Perhaps I was right and Fenwick was wrong. Perhaps they're simply too wily now, these lesser demons. They know how to live so quietly inside their hosts that we can't identify them until it's too late."

"What, like ticks?" asked Seraphina, who hated bugs, and shuddered.

Titania sighed again. "Right, well, we'll try again next week," she said. "But if you open another portal, for god's sake, tell someone. I know you don't care much for me, Miss Fenwick, but a *bone forest* is hardly a preferable alternative."

Just then Seraphina felt it would be prudent to mention something. "I think you should know, Titania, that I have every intention of returning to Calvin very soon. I've been very well-behaved so far, but even I have limits."

"Calvin Babineaux is dead," said Titania exhaustedly. One hand was dropped over her eyes like a makeshift towel.

"Be that as it may," said Seraphina, "I've made up my mind on this and won't be otherwise persuaded." And with that she took her pills and said goodnight, drifting once again into dreamlessness.

She missed having dreams, that was the truth. *Come find me,* Calvin had sung to her when he'd roused her from her sleep that fateful night. *What's the worst that could happen?*

My father could kill you again, Seraphina reminded him. Or he could kill me! I mean, who knows!

You're so intricately built. Your beauty is not of this world. Your eyes are filled with such vibrant darkness, said Calvin admiringly. He was not in one of his moods, which was so wonderful! The last story he'd told about the researcher who got trapped in the veil between life and death only to be held captive in a court of hell by the subterfuge of his professor had been intricately told but eventually struck a repetitive chord. This time, his eyes were wide with adoration as he sang, *How I long for our joining, my sweet wicked queen! It has been so many long years that we have waited for your powers to wake!*

Stop it Calvin you're embarrassing me, said Seraphina, secretly pleased.

He had really taken her advice to heart. Not only was he talking about himself less, but the last time they'd spoken, she'd said *not to be unappreciative Calvin but you probably should do something about your rate of decomposition. Like, find another form maybe? Not to be critical. I just think this one's starting to leak.*

And he had! So obviously this was really, truly love.

"I know you're not a murderer," Seraphina said to Mab over breakfast on the day they were next to go to the college library for their transcription work.

"Of course I am, Butch," said Mab, who looked hurt.

"There's no shame in it," Seraphina reassured her. "Plenty of people who aren't murderers are still highly clever and worth a second look."

"They *could* have died," Mab pointed out, after consulting with her periphery. "I mean, we're all so much closer to death than anyone realizes."

Seraphina of all people already knew this. "The point is there's no need to lie," she offered supportively to Mab. "We're friends. And even if we weren't, I'm leaving soon, so you don't have to worry about me spoiling your good reputation."

"I heard the doctor say she was keeping you," said Mab. "She was on the phone to the college saying something about how she knows you've opened a portal."

"Well, then she can hardly keep me in one place if I can open portals, can she?" said Seraphina cheerily, but because Mab still looked a bit depressed, she offered again, "Why don't you come with me?"

And so, on that day, as Seraphina began once again transcribing the verbiage of the invocation, she made sure one of her legs was crossed over Mab's. It made for slightly uncomfortable work – Seraphina was left-handed, Mab right – but ultimately, when the moment came for the dissolution of reality, both were transported this time.

"It's *really* not supposed to work this way," said Mab, looking around at the various flora and skeleta, the various shades of inky blue. "I've been at this transcription stuff for years, Butch. All the books say invocation shouldn't involve any transportation at all."

"And yet here we are. The funny thing is I don't see Calvin," remarked Seraphina, making her way through the brush and then stopping when Calvin came into view, finally approaching from the nearby ruins of the court. "Oh! There you are!"

She ran to his waiting embrace, leaping to throw her arms around his neck. "Cal, you're here! I brought a friend, I hope that's okay—"

"My queen, of course! It's very important for a monarch of your stature to have handmaids," Calvin assured her, before turning with Seraphina in his arms to face Mab. "My lady."

Mab, though, was gawking at them. "Um. Butch," she said warily, ignoring Calvin. Which was a bit rude.

"Yes?" asked Seraphina, a little impatiently. If Mab was going to say something about Calvin's skin, she was really going to be upset. It was one thing from close-minded grown-ups. Quite another from someone who was supposed to have the creative sensibilities of a demented arsonist. For the first time, Seraphina questioned their friendship with an internal sinkhole of despair.

"That's not Calvin," said Mab.

"What do you mean? You've never even met Calvin." Instinctively, Seraphina clutched him tighter.

"I still feel pretty certain that's not him." Mab, again in apparent agreement with something that lived in the corner of her eye, backed away from them with a frown.

Seraphina took a second look at Calvin, who smiled down at her with all the wonderful benevolence of a lover who'd simply done what he was asked. It was true that in the bone forest Calvin did not have the usual presence of viscera, and the fatigue that shadowed the gauntness of his cheeks *had* been magically resolved, but then again Calvin wasn't exactly the same every time she saw him. He was just, you know, Calvin.

She supposed Calvin's eyes were probably not this blue, or even blue at all, but how could she even know? When she'd met him his eyes were all glassy and filmed over from the accident and every time since then he'd been mostly unable to look up from his lute. (You know how boys can be.)

"Is it true? You're not Calvin?" she said, a bit uncertain now.

"My glorious queen! I really don't think one can rule it out with absolute surety," said Calvin, who probably wasn't Calvin, all things considered. Possibly this was *a* Calvin, but not *the* Calvin. Maybe there had always been multiple Calvins? It might explain his moods.

"Hm." Seraphina took a step back, contemplating this.

Mab was extending a trembling hand toward her, reaching out for hers. "We should get out of here, Butch. I know that sometimes... sometimes it may seem like there's... another place you could go, if you wanted. A... safer one. And maybe sometimes there are... voices. That only you can hear. But still." She sounded more solid then. "I know what a good place *isn't*," she explained, lifting her chin, "and there's something very wrong with this one." Mab glared at the person who wasn't Calvin with the kind of bravado a small child might use against the monster under her bed. "It's not supposed to be here. So something must have gone wrong."

"But of course something went wrong, my queen," Calvin cooed to Seraphina, who remained very still. "How, after all, could a rudimentary invocation have any effect at all on one such as you, my love?"

"That's true," conceded Seraphina.

Mab's hand was still outstretched toward her, but it trembled now.

"Butch. *Butch.*" Mab was hissing at her with growing hysteria, her flimsy last effort at stoicism unlocking around her knees. "You know how the screamers become screamers, don't you? They *let something in.*" Her eyes were wide with suppressed fear, her cheeks cherubic, pink. "Don't take anything it offers you. Okay? Not food, not power, not any sort of... of *bargain*, or temptation—"

"Oh, don't worry about that," said Seraphina. "I already pledged my love to Calvin in death, so temptation's really not on the table. He knows that any transgressions are fully unintended. Besides, in this case the ends do justify the means—" Calvin nodded encouragingly in agreement.

"Butch. If you pledged your love to the ghost of a dead man and now you've managed to enter one of the infernal planes, I think maybe you're not in the loony bin because of a boy." Mab's face was pleading and fearful, and Seraphina, despite herself, loved her again.

So she reached out for Mab's trembling fingers and took them solidly in hers. She kissed the tips of them. "Sorry, Cal, I've got to see Mab home safe," she said over her shoulder, though Calvin seemed to find all this so enraging that he became thoroughly unrecognizable, anger blurring all his handsome features until he resembled one of the bone trees, though his skin took on the tactility of wood.

"My queen, you disrespect me," he said. His voice was suddenly very loud and shrill, like a screamer bursting through the constancy of headache. It rattled and pulsed from the inside of Seraphina's head, implosion stretching out like nausea, a quake of something no longer so restrained.

Boys! Why was everything always about them?

"I don't know what you want me to do about it," said Seraphina, but then the spell was broken by the sound of Hyacinth's scream.

Just as Calvin's maelstrom eyes began to widen like cavernous black holes, Seraphina thought, *I'll go now*, and then she and Mab found themselves in the college library once again.

They had somehow climbed atop the table in the midst of their journey back from wherever they'd been, and were now holding their friend Hyacinth's body in addition to each other's hands. Hyacinth's lips were parted like something had torn itself out from between her dislocated jaw, trailing bits of liver and small intestine from the pretty rosebud of her whispering mouth.

"Well, Calvin certainly has loads to answer for," muttered Seraphina.

Mab, who was too shaken to speak, merely clutched at the knuckles of Seraphina's hand.

"But why did it kill her like that? So *violently*?"

Titania was pacing the floor of her office again, practically ripping a hole in the space-time continuum as she went. "She should have just, you know, been used up from the inside out like the others! A death like that is very bad, *very* bad for the department – they're getting more and more serious about shutting us down, and god knows those fucking scientists will drive the nail into the coffin—"

Just then the headache noise was so loud that even Titania seemed unable to think. She pivoted to face Seraphina, who was daydreaming about Calvin again. (He looked so handsome in his malevolence – it couldn't be avoided. She was in her sexual prime, they were in love, she didn't know what else to say about it!)

"What happened?" snapped Titania. "Why were you and Miss Lee holding her?"

"I don't know," replied Seraphina hotly. It wasn't as if she'd enjoyed witnessing the death of her friend. "We were minding our own business in the bone forest when she suddenly screamed, and then there we were."

"Tell me more about this bone forest." Titania shot backward from her desk chair, contemplating Seraphina as if her last hope lived somewhere between Seraphina's lips, in whatever Seraphina said next. "Does it look like this?" she asked, frantically holding up a drawing from something that looked like Dante's iteration of hell. "Or like this?"

Seraphina squinted. "No, neither of these are the bone forest."

"Have you been to either of these places before?"

"No," said Seraphina. "Have you?"

"Of course I haven't—" Titania let out a small, hysterical pitch of fury. "What are you hiding, Fenwick?" she shrieked at Seraphina. "*What aren't you telling me?*"

By then, Seraphina had grown very weary of the whole thing. Not just the constant interrogation and presumptions of her guilt (so rude) but also the distance from Calvin. It had been longer than the two weeks she had promised him, and she was starting to think that maybe Titania wasn't going to let her go.

"Why do you care what the college does?" Seraphina asked the doctor calmly. "If you ask me, this obsession is no good for your health, Titania. What are you, close to seventy now? You're going to waste away if you keep going like this."

"I'm thirty-seven, you miserable little cretin," snarled Titania.

"And for the record, if your father were here—" She gritted her teeth, then slumped lower in her chair. "If your mother would just unsink her *damned claws—*"

Seraphina became very cold just then. She thought about all the silly things she knew to be true about boys and their misbehavior that had to have come from somewhere. These beliefs she had about how they simply could not be expected to dedicate themselves to rules and ethics and vows. It occurred to Seraphina that perhaps her mother had known exactly what kind of a boy she herself had married. Possibly that was what all the fuss over Calvin had been.

Well! Fine. Seraphina's relationship was different, obviously, and there was no excusing this kind of narcissistic small-mindedness. But contextually speaking, it helped to know the full truth.

She wondered if it would help to tell her mother where her father really was now. Maybe if they had just spoken civilly about all this, none of this asylum nonsense would have been necessary! But oh well, here they were, so. Might as well just get on with it.

"If you think I'm hiding something about the invocation," Seraphina prompted, "then why don't you just join me? Then you can see the bone forest for yourself."

Titania, who'd been ranting in an undertone, abruptly looked up.

"You can… do that?" she croaked. "Take someone with you?"

All of a sudden the look on her face was one of tepidly restrained excitement. Disbelief, a bit, and the sense that she was being messed with. But still, curiosity and desperation nonetheless.

"Why not?" asked Seraphina with a shrug.

"Well, for one thing, I'm not crazy, disordered, or otherwise mentally disturbed," muttered Titania.

"I beg to differ," said Seraphina with a smile. "You've apparently been sleeping with a boy for twenty years who disappeared completely rather than leave his wife. I hardly think you're the pinnacle of sanity. And anyway, why not just try it?" she added sweetly, with the specific sweetness of the clinically unwell, as if to remind Titania that after all, she was just a darling lunatic with only one foot in reality. "I'm sure you're much too clever to make any deals with lesser demons, Doctor."

Titania gave her a hard, mean look. What she couldn't hide was the way it was edged so firmly with longing.

"Go to bed," she snapped at Seraphina. Which was so very obviously a yes.

The first story Calvin had ever told Seraphina was about a young man who'd been abducted by a mentor he'd trusted, and then become trapped in a hell of his own making by the terms of a deal that was thoughtlessly made. The young man was a curious academic, a casual musician, a storyteller first and foremost, who'd gone to college – the first in his family to do so! – in the hopes that he'd one day become poet laureate, the voice of his generation, a prophet for his time. What he found instead was a group of researchers trying to summon mystical beings. They believed these beings to be demons, for which a person could become a vessel and be rendered parasitically omnipotent for as long as the binding would hold. Obviously, sometimes such things went wrong. More than one student had been destroyed already, and so the project shifted from students (valuable) to a nearby institution for the mentally unwell.

As it turned out, though, by technical terms, *demons* did not live behind the door upon which the researchers had so recklessly knocked.

To the researchers, the otherworld was some kind of lawless place where demons floated 'round like shrapnel, waiting to be plucked cleanly from a wound. But there was order in this world, a system of bargaining, a hierarchy, a court! And once they'd opened the portal, it could not be resealed, its influence spreading, seeping, insidiously threading its way into this world. In a dream, the young man was asked his dearest ambition, and because it was a dream, he told the truth. And so he became a bard at the court of the queen of hell, eternally chained to an endless night until the queen finally arrived, and the time of great waiting was at an end. Such would be the entirety of his existence – until, of course, his mortal corpse gave out.

As Seraphina had listened to Calvin drone on and on about this, she'd thought, *I think maybe I'll let him touch my breasts this time. I think it's an appropriate tactical course of action at this stage of courtship and he clearly wants to.*

Her mind wandered often while Calvin spoke, which did not detract from the love she felt for him. It was necessary to have separate interests, to not lose her sense of self. She knew in her heart several things, one being that Calvin was very good at words even if they went on forever, and another being that her father was frantic about whatever had happened to Calvin, and that meant her father was at fault, which made perfect sense. Seraphina had a very real, very serious sense of rage when it came to her father – a heat that rose from her stomach like bile. She really could not stand him. He seemed to always be testing her, the way he locked her in her room and tried to convince her night was day or deprived her of food for overlong stretches or snuck things into her salad whenever she was allowed to eat. It was like he was trying to drive her crazy or something!

Anyway, eventually Calvin would move on to some other winsome ballad about the exploitation of graduate students and Seraphina would play with the rage-ball, the thing in her stomach that assured her that her father was a terrible boy. The worst kind.

And then he tried to drag her out of the woods where she'd gone to meet Calvin! He'd seemed so frightened of her when she said no.

In retrospect, she probably needn't have crushed him into such fine particles. It was just that the rage-ball burned so bright, and Seraphina was practically a woman now. She should be allowed to have inappropriate boyfriends if she wanted them! Her father simply shouldn't be able to tell her no.

The following Tuesday, when Titania was waiting beside the door for Seraphina, Mab, and December just as Seraphina had known she would, Seraphina reached down and gave Mab's hand a little squeeze.

"You can't come with me this time," she whispered as the transcription books were passed around, with Titania instructing Peri shrilly about who knows what.

Seraphina tried to phrase the rejection as gently as she knew how. She had explained the rage-ball to Mab already, along with its effects and the fact that it had transferred from Seraphina's father to Titania at some point. Maybe it was all that annoying psychotherapy or something, who could say.

"I don't think Calvin's going to let you go so easily this time, Butch," said Mab worriedly.

"Leave Calvin to me. Just remember, if you ever find yourself in a place that isn't right, don't eat anything. Don't say yes to anything they offer. And never let them take your voice, Mab."

"I won't." Mab shuddered.

Seraphina gave Mab's forehead a kiss and turned to December, who sat across from her. December had recently begun to look quite dazed. Her sentences often trailed into whispers.

"Are you ready?" asked Titania, slumping irritably down beside Seraphina. Presumably she was angry with herself for being curious. For being led by her own morbid longings to a world that would not welcome her, because she was honestly the worst.

"MY PRINCE IS CALLING FOR ME," said December. (Nobody heard her.)

Seraphina looked up at Peri, who nodded. His eyes were very glazed lately, a thin film over them like a glossy white cocoon. He wasn't sleeping well. Something about an offering, a bargain he'd made in a dream. But why should he complain! He'd stepped willingly through the portal. You couldn't just go and be king somewhere that already had a queen. You had to serve a few eternities on your knees. Boys were so silly sometimes, the way they could be so readily led.

But then again, so was everyone, to some extent. Everyone wanted something, and bargains were so easily made.

"Put your hand on my shoulder," Seraphina told Titania, who warily complied.

This time, the bone forest was silent. It would be hours yet before anyone heard the screams.

POISONED PAWN

De Elizabeth

PHASE I: THE OPENING

"The laws of chess do not permit a free choice."
— EMANUEL LASKER —

The chessboard I always play with has a crease down the middle like a fault line, edges frayed from years of being rolled up and shoved in a tote. People probably assume it's lucky, though calling it such would be a gross misrepresentation; I've lost plenty of games with it, and I don't believe in luck. But I'm a creature of habit and this is a dirty one I can't kick: toting around a chessboard given to me by a girl who used to be mine.

To everyone attending the Grand Collegiate Chess Festival at Parcae University this weekend, I'm Catalina Sinclair, International Master. Catalina Sinclair, one of the best chess players across every higher education institution in the world.

Catalina Sinclair, total ice queen. Snob. A bitch whose downfall everyone would just love to witness.

When this year's GCCF was announced to take place at Parcae, where I'm already a fourth-year, it felt like fate. But with spectators descending on campus, it feels more like being on display. Even as I hide out between rounds now, hunched over a steaming mug of tea in Parcae's wood-drenched dining hall, I can feel endless eyes on me. I know what they see. Perfectly curled platinum hair in a bow, clear peachy skin, and an unfriendly gaze shrouded with enough winged eyeliner to hide my feelings. Woolen skirt and ribbed tights, boots that lace up my calves like I'm going to war. Maybe it's because I feel like I am.

The title of Grandmaster is within my grasp; all that's standing between me and the top slot is this next game. A game I *have* to win in order to achieve the ranking I need.

I should be feeling confident. Elated, even. Yet all weekend, my stomach has been in knots, because I know *she's* here somewhere. She must be. All our lives, she was just as good; there's no way she isn't playing.

But I've scoured campus without spotting a single wisp of ginger hair, haven't heard that distinct peal of laughter that could only belong to Lucy A. Judd. Ex-best friend Lucy. Ex-*everything* Lucy. A girl who once held all my secrets, a girl whose hands felt as familiar as my own. A girl I thought I could love forever.

A girl I'd like to forget now.

The final pairings will be posted on Parcae's website any moment, and I've been refreshing my phone for the last twenty minutes. I drum my opal-painted nails along the table, reload the screen for the millionth time. But it still shows this morning's games.

Frustrated, I flip my phone face down and gaze out the window at the graying October sky. Ivy-covered brick stares back beneath thin clouds, car horns drifting from below. Cambridge should be all red and gold like the rest of New England, but this season has only felt like stale fog. Then again, I've spent most of it indoors, thoughts absorbed with gambits and tactics.

"Sinclair."

I glance up and can't fight my smirk at the sight of Francis Delaroche, fellow fourth-year, Parcae University Chess League Commissioner, and my most recent victim. Opponent, I mean. (Victim.)

It was, admittedly, a delicious victory. Francis and I have been in the same classes since freshman year, and have been the top players in Parcae's Chess League for just as long. Francis is one of those boys who is so used to winning, his entire world tips on its side when he experiences a whisper of failure. Perhaps it runs in his family – his father, Bennett Delaroche, is our state senator and was just elected majority whip. For Francis, losing to me was likely a slap in the face and a kick in the groin all at once. I'm surprised he hasn't slunk away to his fancy off-campus apartment to lick his wounds.

"Delaroche," I reply. "Back for more? Didn't take you for a masochist."

Francis doesn't smile. He drops into the empty chair and leans forward. My bravado wavers a little and I swivel, twisting myself into a position that feels protective.

"How'd you do it?" Francis demands, peering at me over his own mug.

"Do what?"

"Beat me."

I don't hold back my laugh. Francis still isn't smiling, pale skin tempered with a frown.

"I know you cheated, Sinclair."

"Cheated?" Another bubble of laughter. "I get that you're embarrassed to have lost to a girl, but this is a low allegation, even for you."

"You're on N. Admit it."

My amusement flutters away. "Excuse me?"

He squints. "You've got the glassy eyes, the sweaty lip. It's got Nova written all over it."

Nova. I'm surprised Francis would say it out loud. Those red capsules have been crowding the news lately, caught in a tug-of-war between fearmongering politicians and money-hungry pharmaceutical lobbyists. According to headlines that have invaded my phone's push notifications, Nova was designed as an antipsychotic, but development was halted after scientists discovered a side effect that impacts the brain. Specifically, the anterior lateral prefrontal cortex – the part of the brain that calculates the probability of future success and makes predictions.

Somehow, Nova made its way into the world anyway. Sold in dark alleyways and equally shadowed corners of the internet with a seductive promise: *One pill, one hour into the future.* People say that a single dose of N supposedly causes brief hallucinatory visions of things to come in the next sixty minutes – visions that many users have found to be startingly, eerily accurate. Like a premonition. To some, it's a game-changer.

To me, it sounds just like a bad fucking trip.

N has mostly shown up at parties, though it's been subtly making its way into academic realms like a silent spy. I saw two girls in my psychology class take N before our final last spring, probably in hopes of getting a peek at the exam before it began. I'll admit that the idea of taking N before a game has crossed my mind, but it's more satisfying to win simply because I *can*.

I cross my arms, ignoring Francis' comments about my appearance. "Are you saying I crushed you so badly, you've concluded I'm on drugs? Do you hear yourself?"

"I had an exceptional opening. One of the greatest."

"Please. You used a Sicilian Defense."

"I played the best game of my *life*." Francis stabs his index finger against the table. "There's no way you could have unraveled my tactics so easily without N. I saw how calm you were. You predicted my moves."

Annoyance creeps in. "Did you hit your head and forget who you're talking to? I've been playing chess since I was *three*. Your accusations are insulting and I'm leaving."

Francis stands just as fast as I do. "Where'd you get it? I heard Spencer Ratcliffe was selling N from his dorm. Is that where you went?"

I ignore him, snatching my tea and phone.

"I'm commissioner of our league," he continues. "I could contact FIDE. You could be disqualified."

I whirl. "What are you gonna do, Delaroche? Force me to pee in a cup and drug test me in the science lab? Go ahead. You won't find a single trace of Nova in my system, asshole."

"We'll see." Francis' gaze drags over my whole body and

I suddenly want to scratch out his eyeballs. "It's too bad you're such a cunt, Sinclair. Normally I'd try screwing the attitude out of someone like you, but you're honestly a lost cause."

Anger stirs inside me. I silently consider throwing my scalding tea in his face but instead growl out a low, "Fuck you."

"No – fuck *you*. And I might." Francis turns his phone. FIDE's blue and white logo stares at me like a taunt. "I just might."

He saunters away before I can respond, and I lean against the wall with a furious huff. Outrage seethes in my blood, both at Francis' vulgar threats and the condescension in his accusations. His words are a blunt reminder that there will always be people doubting my success. If it's not rumors that I've slept with an arbiter, it'll be something like this, all boiling down to the general belief that I couldn't have gotten here on my own.

But I did. *I did.*

I don't need any artificial advantages to win. Nothing rattles my calm because *I'm that fucking good.* Because I *need* chess to survive. Because without it, I'm nothing at all.

I exhale through my teeth and reach for my phone, refreshing for the millionth time. The words **Final Pairings** jump out at me and my breath catches. Here we go.

Time slows as I scroll, scanning for my name. The world becomes a blur of elongated seconds, filled with the anticipation of who I'll be playing the most important game of my life against.

And when I see it, the wind is knocked out of me.

Catalina Sinclair vs. Lucy Judd.

My Lucy.

Well, fuck.

PHASE II: THE MIDDLEGAME

*"It is not a move, even the best move,
that you must seek, but a realizable plan."*
— Eugene Znosko-Borovsky —

I'm halfway across Parcae's campus before I allow myself to think about Lucy Judd.

Leaves crunch under my boots, each shade of autumn crinkling with a different stuffed-down memory. Orange: the flash of Lucy's hair at every youth tournament I attended in Boston as a kid; the way I knew her name before we officially met at chess camp in eighth grade. Red: the heat of anxiety I felt playing against her the first time, watching her move so quickly it was like her neurons fired in the shape of knights and pawns. Brown: the tables in the empty classroom where we hung out every day after camp, because I decided the best way to deal with a potential enemy was to make her my friend instead.

Surprisingly, it was easy to be around Lucy. Comforting, even. Our conversations went from discussing blockades and attacks to our favorite music, to our lives at school, and I found that some things were easier to say with a chessboard between us.

Like the fact that I didn't have any friends at my school at all.

Other kids never wanted to be around the weird, quiet girl who thought in chess openings and counter-moves, the girl who clung to a game because it was easier than admitting she was lonely. It wasn't that I didn't *want* friends. It was that no one wanted to be mine.

Chess became my only source of companionship, a gleaming light in an otherwise dark life. It was there for me when my house was empty because my dad was out at the casino; it showed up for me on weekends when I wondered if my mom wouldn't have left if she knew her daughter would be labeled a prodigy. I played tournament after tournament, questioning if she'd be proud of me yet. Eventually, it stopped mattering. I grew proud of myself.

Even if I still didn't have any friends.

At the time, I thought the confession would make Lucy want to avoid me, but she merely slid her rook into h3 and traded a secret of her own: her little brother was sick. Cancer. *We just found out. Don't tell anyone.*

I turn toward Bleeker Hall now and kick a yellow leaf. Gold, almost. The color of summer, *our* season. But even though chess camp ended, our friendship didn't. Despite living three towns away, Lucy lit up my phone at all hours of the night, and we played chess together every weekend. The light and dark squares were a safeguard for our spilled confessions, and just like at camp, it was easier to tell her things when I was holding a queen in my hand like a cross.

I stole twenty dollars from my dad's wallet, I admitted over a French Defense in ninth grade.

I smoked a cigarette in the bathroom at school, she replied.

In tenth grade, Lucy told me she'd had sex with an older boy. *But to be honest, I don't think I actually like guys*, she concluded as she dropped her bishop into d5. *Check.*

I moved my king and offered back, *I'm pretty sure I'm bisexual.* The word sounded powerful, like something I could also be proud of. So I added, *Scratch that. Make that* definitely *sure.*

Lucy only smirked and moved her knight into a6. *Checkmate, Cat.*

I still didn't have friends at school, but didn't care because Lucy became my entire world. It was the kind of friendship that felt safe, like I could share the most deranged inside thought and she'd like me anyway. She saw both me and my flaws in vibrant color, and it wasn't that she wanted to be around me in spite of them. It was *because* of them.

Quiet, I think to myself now, like I'm shushing a petulant child. *That's enough.* I tug open the door to Bleeker Hall's lobby and the memories obediently fall silent.

Or perhaps, more accurately, I shove them back where they belong. It won't do any good to traverse a road paved with nostalgia, because I know where these images lead: right to my eighteenth birthday, a night that started with Lucy standing beneath my porchlight holding *that* green chessboard, and ended with us tangled in my bed, electricity in my veins and Lucy's mouth between my thighs. We shapeshifted that night, from best friends who play chess to girls who kiss and whisper *I love you* beneath moonlight-soaked blankets. It was the beginning of something that should have lasted forever. *We* should have lasted forever.

But we didn't.

Grinding my teeth in a way that would alarm my dentist, I knock on room 207.

Spencer Ratcliffe's room.

I can count on one hand the number of times I've spoken with Spencer. I know he's an anthropology major, that he has brown hair he keeps secured in a half-bun, that his dad donates money to Parcae like it's paper.

And according to my delightful run-in with Francis, Spencer sells N from his dorm.

I'm aware – painfully fucking aware – that this is a terrible idea. But if I have to face off in the biggest tournament of my life against the girl who ruined it, I'm going to need an edge. Something to soften the knife's worth of panic that's been lodged in my belly since I saw Lucy's name, something to sedate my raging nerves.

When Spencer answers the door, it's almost like he expects to see me there. Which is funny, because *I* don't expect to see me there. But I don't have any other choice.

"Catalina Sinclair," he says, leaning in the doorframe.

"You know my name." The words sound ridiculous. Of course he knows it. *Everyone* knows it.

Spencer's smirk confirms my thoughts. "Let me guess. You're here for An Hour."

One pill, one hour. *An Hour* is another code for N, which is already a code for Nova. I cast a glance over my shoulder. I suppose one can't be too careful.

"How much?" I hurriedly ask.

"For you? Do you know they call you the Chess Cat?" He waves his hand. "No money needed."

I look at him quizzically, letting the nickname slide. I actually hate when people call me that. "Don't be ridiculous. I can pay. Do you have Venmo?"

Spencer's grin gets a little wider. A little darker. "Silly goose. I didn't say it would be *free*."

"What—? *Oh.*" A sour understanding grips me. I'm not sure why this surprises me, why I didn't *expect* it, especially from someone like him. A rich boy who already has all the money he could ask for. "What... what do you want then?"

"Depends." His gaze slides down my body, lingering on my chest, and he licks his lips in a way that makes me want to throw up. "What are you willing to give?"

I glance at my watch. I don't have a lot of time. Fuck it. "Handjob."

Spencer's laugh is sharp. "What are we, sixteen?" He studies my face, my lips. I already know what he's going to say. "Blowjob. And I get to touch you."

I grit my teeth. "Five minutes. And absolutely not. No touching."

"N is *expensive* shit." He squints at me. "Fine, no touching. But make it twenty."

As if he'll last that long. "Ten."

"Fifteen."

"Thirteen."

"Deal." He opens the door wider and I step inside.

"Nova first," I demand, closing the door.

Spencer's already crossing to his closet. "Of course. I'm nothing if not a gentleman."

I roll my eyes, gathering my thick blonde hair into a ponytail as he flips the dial on a safe. I watch as he reaches inside, pulling out a jar of glittering red pills. They catch the light, winking like rubies. My heartbeat quickens. Am I really doing this?

I crush the doubt by imagining Lucy in the glow of Crestwood Hall, dimly lit sconces shining on the chessboard between us.

Hundreds of laser-focused eyes on me as I try not to stare at Lucy's lips, the fall of her lashes, the spill of freckles over her cream-colored nose.

The way I'm sure to lose this game if I don't find a way to calm my disastrous pulse.

Knowing what moves are coming, knowing *exactly* how to claim victory – it's sure to do the trick. Maybe sometimes the only way to win is to cheat.

I extend my palm. "I'm ready."

"Bon appétit." He hands me a pill. "Make sure you take it with a full glass of—"

Spencer's words are barely out before I've downed it, dry.

"Jesus, girl," he mutters, thrusting a steel thermos at me. "Drink some water, will you?"

"I don't know what's in that," I retort, reaching into my tote for my plastic water bottle. I gulp several sips, briefly calculating the risk of fleeing without fulfilling my end of the bargain. But that would make me both a cheater *and* a thief. Might as well cling to honor where I can. "Let's get this over with."

Spencer studies me a moment, and for a second I think he's going to tell me to forget it, that he's going to decide there's something a bit too unhinged in my eyes to bother. But the hesitancy lasts only a moment. In the next, he's reaching for his belt buckle, watching through an amused gaze as I tighten my ponytail and lower to the rug. I know what he's thinking. He has Catalina Sinclair – International Master! Chess Cat! – on her knees for him.

He has no idea that I'm doing this for myself.

I arrive at Crestwood Hall with sweat clinging to my forehead and anxiety rumbling through me. Everyone says N works almost immediately, but I haven't had any premonitions yet and I'm starting to freak the fuck out.

Ducking behind a marble column in the lobby, I yank my phone from my bag. I tap into Instagram and scroll until I find Spencer's irritating face and frantically type a DM. *Did you give me a dupe? It's not working.*

Spencer opens the message but doesn't respond, and my panic morphs into anger. This rich boy motherfucker. I have his goddamn cum drying on my favorite sweater and he's leaving me on read! But there's not enough time to run back across campus, because the game starts in five minutes and—

A flash of light suddenly crowds my vision and I stumble, reaching for the column for balance.

Before I can process them, a whir of images cascade behind my eyelids in quick succession: A hand slapping a chess clock. Fingers with red nails moving a white pawn into e4.

My heart races and I glance at my own nails, shimmering with opal polish. Understanding takes hold.

Lucy will play white. She'll use a King's Pawn Opening.

That means – I'll be playing black.

Holy shit, it's working.

I close my eyes, desperate to see more. If Lucy plays a King's Pawn Opening, my best response is a French Defense. From there, she's likely to put her knight into play, so I should counter by—

Blood. My surroundings are suddenly consumed by blood.

I grip the column tighter with a terrible, wretched gasp. *What the fuck? What the f—?*

But there's no mistaking it: a pool of red, widening on leaf-covered brick, playing out in my mind like a movie. I blink rapidly, trying to erase the violent image from my thoughts. This – this isn't what I wanted. I wanted to see chess moves. Strategy.

Instead, I think I'm seeing a murder.

And the more I blink, the clearer the vision gets. As if I can't run from it at all.

Blood, trickling down a narrow pathway, gathering in the crevices of a stone plaque. Wait. I recognize that plaque. It's rounded. Calligraphy etchings. *In honor of Jameson Crestwood, 1782–1864.*

...it's the one right outside this building.

I gulp at the air, fingers clenching. The blood-soaked vision starts to fade, and I scramble to see more, desperately trying to make sense of what's happening.

And in the last moment before the images disappear, I see something else.

A limp hand, fingers faintly twitching. A charm bracelet attached to the wrist, dangling with coquette bows and clusters of stars. For a moment, relief bursts inside me – that's not my bracelet, I wouldn't wear anything so tacky – but then, trepidation returns. Because it's *someone's*.

Someone who is going to die within an hour. From *right now*.

But I don't have time to think because I hear my name and whirl, finding one of the GCCF volunteers, clipboard in hand.

"Are you ready?" he asks. "Your opponent is waiting."

I suck in a breath. Am I ready? Am I ready to see the girl who shattered my world and left me holding the pieces? Am I ready to lose the biggest game of my life and watch my goals slip away like a fleeting high?

Am I ready to face who I am without winning?

I force a smile. "Ready as ever!"

I follow the volunteer through the lobby and into the main hall, where the audience has gathered on either side of the room. In the center, beneath elegant chandeliers, is a single table with a gleaming wooden chessboard laid out upon it. A double-faced chess clock. Two glasses of water.

And, seated at the white side of the board, is Lucy A. Judd.

Lucy, just as I remember her, and simultaneously completely different.

Her copper hair has grown long, and she wears it in a thick, elaborate braid over one shoulder like she's cosplaying as a redheaded Elsa from *Frozen*. She's dressed in a white button-down tucked into trousers, with lace-up boots like my own. Lucy watches me approach with the kind of caution you'd reserve for a bear in the woods. Movements still. Gaze carefully on mine. As if she's not sure whether I'm going to mutate into something feral at a moment's notice.

I reach the table and time stops. For a second, we're fourteen again and I'm sitting across from her for the first time, choking on anticipatory defeat. In another moment, we're sixteen, fingers brushing over my chessboard and desperately pretending not to notice.

Another, eighteen, my hands beneath her tank top and kissing her like she was the only thing I'd want for the rest of my life.

"Hi, Cat," Lucy finally says, standing. "It's been a while."

Her nickname for me burns in my ears so hot that I'm sure the tips are turning red. I extend a hand, working to keep my face neutral. "May the best woman win."

Lucy holds my stare a moment. But she extends her hand, too, and I try not to react to the heat of her palm. Just stay calm, I remind myself. Just stay—

My gaze falls to her wrist.

The floor seems to drop away.

Because Lucy is wearing a gold charm bracelet, with little bows and stars.

Just like the one in my blood-soaked vision from moments ago.

PHASE III: THE ENDGAME

"There is no remorse like the remorse of chess."
— H. G. Wells —

I activate the clock, beginning our game, and there's a split second where I hope that my vision was wrong. If Lucy uses an opening that's different from the one I saw, then maybe, just maybe, the rest of it won't come true, either.

But there's no mistaking the way my stomach drops as Lucy sets her King's Pawn Opening into play. I follow up with my French Defense, but the strategy feels hollow. I can't shake the image of that unmoving hand as I adjust my pawns, thinking only of the blood swirling beneath that nameless person's dying form. *Lucy's* dying form.

Lucy places her knight into d2. Just like I suspected. She punctuates her move with a tap of the clock. The tiniest smile twitches on her face and an ache widens inside me. Despair and guilt and something else that's harder to name.

She's going to die. The only person I ever loved is *going to die*. Should I stop the game and tell her? *Warn* her? Am I complicit if I see death coming and don't do anything to stop it?

Will it feel like dying too?

I move my own knight into f6 and hit the clock. Lucy edges her e4 pawn up a square, eyes never leaving mine as she silently threatens my knight. I recognize her expression. The dare laced in it. But there's another note too – a wisp of nostalgia, one that's almost sad. If it weren't for my racing pulse, I might wonder what she's thinking. If it's something sweet, like how we'd go out for ice cream and kiss with frostbitten, sugary lips. Or something a little more dangerous, like the time we ducked into a store fitting room and I had to stay silent while she practically brought me to tears with her fingers and tongue.

Or maybe she's not thinking about any of that.

Maybe she's thinking about how it ended.

I dodge my knight out of her path and allow myself to also remember. The two of us, in my driveway, out of words and out of time. She was moving to Seattle for college while I'd be here on the east coast – a fact we had known for months, mentally preparing ourselves for FaceTime dates to hold us over until winter break.

But at the last minute, Lucy decided that it would be better if we broke up. *Cleaner*, was the term she used.

Everyone who does long distance in college always *breaks up*, she reasoned while I bit the inside of my cheeks raw. *I'm saving us the heartache.*

But Lucy didn't seem like she was experiencing any heartache at all. In fact, it looked like she couldn't wait to be done with the conversation. Be done with *me*.

Deep down, I knew why. She was about to be at a huge university, away from her extreme right-wing parents and their bigoted stares. She could be anyone she wanted – could *have* anyone she wanted. She didn't want to be tied to her high school girlfriend, not when there would be an entire campus of pretty girls surrounding her. Lucy Judd was a lot of things – but a cheater has never been one of them.

She had to end it, respectfully. *Cleanly*. To free herself up for what was next.

But Lucy didn't just end our relationship, she *demolished* it. Demolished me in the process, too. I stayed in my driveway long after she left, watching the sky shift from cotton candy to navy, and thought about a million things at once. Lucy's freckled face at chess camp, a stranger I was so curious to know. Lucy peering at me between clothing racks at the mall, shoving tulle-lined dresses in my arms and telling me I'd look pretty. Lucy with her hands in my hair every night for the past six months, my endgame, my checkmate, my everything.

Eventually I went inside and packed up my room and moved away, just like her. But while she chased her fresh start, I stayed the same. Collected dust like a ghost, frozen in time. I wasn't sure how to handle losing the girl I loved and my best friend all at once. I mourned twice over. The grief was exponential.

I'm pretty sure it will hurt for the rest of my life.

I survey the board now, shaking the dismal thoughts. Lucy's bishop has been put into play, several of our pawns in the center. Considering, I inch my queen out from her enclosure, and just as my fingers brush the piece, it happens again – a quick flash behind my eyelids.

I gasp, expecting to see that same hand, that same pool of blood, but instead, there's something new: a trio of men in FIDE jackets. A cracked phone. And a ruby-streaked white king, lying in a shallow puddle.

The added confirmation pummels me: Lucy is playing white right now.

My heart starts to race, head swimming. *Lucy is really going to die.* Lucy is going to die and I somehow have to keep playing, have to perform for all the people who came to unwillingly watch it happen. I suddenly feel like a circus animal, a prized lion in a cage.

I reach for the water at my side and down it, feeling Lucy's gaze on me.

"Sorry," I whisper, vision blurry. "It's my turn, right?"

Lucy studies me before lifting a hand, catching the arbiter's eye. The suited man comes forward, pausing our clocks.

"May we take a one-minute break?" Lucy asks.

My eyes bulge and I half contemplate kicking her beneath the table. We're not supposed to ask for breaks. The arbiter raises his eyebrows. The crowd murmurs.

"Please," Lucy adds softly. "We just need a moment."

At the arbiter's reluctant nod, Lucy leans in to whisper to me. "Are you alright?"

My own nod is forced. Curt. "Let's get back to the game."

"Cat." Lucy just stares. "Something's wrong. I know you."

I bury the cacophony of emotions that threaten to erupt, both at the nickname (again!) and the low, husky way she says that last sentence. Because she *does*. She knows my biggest fears, how I like my coffee, what I sound like when I come, all the things I'm afraid I won't ever do before I die.

Lucy knows me, *all* of me, better than anyone I've ever met in my entire life.

And I hate her for reminding me.

"It's Catalina," I hiss back. "And correction. You *knew* me."

For the briefest of instances, Lucy's face flickers with hurt. But it vanishes almost immediately, replaced with that unwavering calm.

"Some things don't change," she muses, gaze slipping to where I've been absentmindedly picking at my cuticles. A habit I've had forever. "You never play well when you're nervous."

And then Lucy reaches to her bracelet, unclasping it.

The air in my lungs thins out. The entire room seems to sway.

"They're fidget charms. It helps somewhat. Gives your hands a task when you don't know what to do with them." Lucy extends the bracelet across the table. "Here. You look like you could use it."

I'm frozen. Paralyzed. Locked with indecision.

Because if I take this bracelet, if I *wear* it, that gives my Nova-induced vision an entirely new meaning. One where Lucy isn't the one lying in a pool of blood.

It will be me.

Me.

I'm the one. Not Lucy. It's been me this entire time.

I'm the one who's going to die.

My breath comes quicker, my surroundings growing watery. Perspiration clings to my neck, turning the back of my sweater damp. Hundreds of eyes are on me, and I'm hyper-aware of every single one. Out of choices, I accept the bracelet, sealing my fate. The clasp is a death knell, the zip of a body bag, a coffin clicking shut.

Lucy hits the clock again, and the game resumes.

No one in this room knows I'm falling apart.

I shift into autopilot, careening through the game like I'm not really living it. Lucy plays a King's Gambit, sacrificing her pawn. Clock. Our queens dance around one another. Clock. She slides her rook up, stealing my bishop – clock – and I counter by taking her rook with mine. *Clock.* Her queen moves into d7, swiping my knight, and I lose track of time.

The sound of our hands repeatedly hitting the clock matches my spiking pulse. Between moves, I scan the hall, eyeing everyone with suspicion. Because anyone in this crowd could be a killer. A disgruntled opponent I once played against? Some entitled man I ignored at a party? A rando who thinks I'd be an easy target to rob, even though I'm far from rich?

Or maybe it won't be a murder at all. An accident. A poor choice. Wrong place, wrong time. The truth is that death could arrive at any moment for anyone.

We're just not supposed to know when it's coming.

This anxiety is consuming. If I were alone, I'd drag my knees to my chest and whisper every grounding exercise every therapist has ever taught me. But I'm not alone. I'm playing the most important game of my life and I'm barely concentrating at all. I make move after move after move, *clock clock clock*, hardly registering anything until I blink at the board and realize:

My queen is a single, tiny breath away from victory.

If I move it into f2, Lucy's king will be trapped between it and my rook. The game will be over. And I'll have no choice but to face what comes next.

Part of me wants to linger in limbo, this stretch of time before I have to leave this hall and find out if I'm meeting the end of my life. A suspended galaxy of white and black squares, staring at a girl I still secretly love.

But there *is* no more time. So I make the move.

Lucy's gaze snaps to mine and she knows she's lost before I even say it—

"*Checkmate.*"

I tap my clock and the arbiter nods. There's a rumble of applause.

I don't hear it. A truly maddening fact, when you think about it. I don't register the biggest win of my life. Everything I've worked for, everything I've wanted. It means nothing to me now.

Because I won't live long enough to see my rankings.

I snatch my tote before standing and staggering toward the door, the world closing around me in a fit of gold lights.

Lucy is at my heels. "Cat! Cat – Cat, wait up!"

My thoughts are miles away. Maybe if I take the rear exit, if I avoid that path with the plaque – maybe I'll be okay. I'll cut through the courtyard. Run back to my dorm. I'll—

Lucy catches my arm. "You're not even going to let me congratulate you?"

"I need to go."

"Hold on." She unfurls her palm, brandishing her king. "Here. You should have it."

My stomach lurches as I remember the blood-soaked king in my vision. What would Lucy do if I threw up all over her right now? If I just ran away?

But before I can do either one, she's pressing the piece into my hand, closing my fingers around it. She might as well be writing my death certificate.

I turn, but her voice halts me again.

"Wait." Lucy comes closer, peering at my bag.

It takes me a minute to realize what's poking out. The rolled-up green chessboard that she gave me on my eighteenth birthday, nearly half a decade ago now. The one I carry everywhere like a lucky rabbit's foot while not believing in luck at all, and even if I did, mine has surely just run out.

"You still have this?" she whispers, dusting her fingers over the edge.

I nod, and a flicker of pain swims in her eyes.

"Cat, can we go somewhere and talk?"

Part of me wants to say yes. I shove it down with a swallow. "There's nothing to talk about. Good game. I need to be going."

She calls after me – *"Cat, I made a mistake!"* – and my heart splinters. I've waited four years to hear her say that. Four years of hoping her name would light up my phone in the middle of the night, that a text message would appear, drenched in regret.

And now it's too late.

I weave through the hall, dodging reporters who can't wait to ask me what I'll do "next," forcing me to look ahead to a brand-new goalpost before the paint even dries on this one. I run as fast as I physically can, and just as I reach the end of the corridor, I take Lucy's rolled-up chessboard from my bag and toss it into the trash can.

I've kept it all this time, but it feels worthless now. What's the point of holding on to something that only causes you pain, a reminder of things you used to have but don't anymore?

I slam through the exit, stepping into the courtyard—

And skid to a halt.

There, right in front of me, are three men in FIDE jackets.

Just like in my vision.

My heartbeat turns into a singular buzz. Like a rabbit's. It's fitting, because I get the sense I'm about to be hunted.

"Catalina Sinclair?" one man says. My muscles itch to run. "Congratulations on your win. That's sure to lock in a Grandmaster title for you, once the rankings are finalized."

"Thank you," I muster. The word *Grandmaster* barely lands, fear shooting through me like an overzealous weed.

"Unfortunately," the second man says, "we received an anonymous tip this morning about the potential use of an illegal substance."

Confusion chills my skin.

"This – this morning?" How could anyone have tipped them off this *morning*? I didn't take Nova until an hour ago, which was this afternoon. "That's impossible..."

My breathing slows. The back of my neck prickles. Francis Delaroche's voice echoes in my head. The way he flashed the FIDE screen at me in the dining hall. *I heard Spencer Ratcliffe was selling them from his dorm.*

No. There's no way he could have *known* I was going to go to Spencer's dorm.

Unless, I realize with sudden newfound anger, *he* took Nova first.

"We're going to request that you submit to a drug test," the third man says. "If we're wrong, you'll get to keep your win. But if we find traces of Nova in your blood, I'm afraid any impending title changes will be revoked and you'll be barred from playing in future tournaments."

Revoked.

Barred.

Thoroughly fucked.

I stagger, the world spinning.

"If you'll just come with us—"

"No – no. I'm not going anywhere with you."

I bolt for the courtyard's exit, sprinting down the path behind Crestwood Hall, unsure of where I'm even going. My dorm? The campus gates? Somewhere far away from here?

I pull up my phone, swipe to the camera. If I'm going to die, I'm not going to die a *cheater*.

My tear-soaked face fills the screen and I press record. "Hello," I say, teeth chattering. "My name is Catalina Sinclair, and if you're watching this, I'm dead now. There's something you all need to know—"

"Sinclair."

My blood boils at the sight of Francis, standing just a few feet away beneath a streetlamp. I turn off the camera and drop my phone into my bag without another thought – name-clearing be damned – and march toward him.

"*You*," I seethe, resisting the urge to grab the lapels of his blazer. "You *set me up*."

His grin is shit-eating. Infuriating. I want to rip his throat open with my bare hands.

"I'll admit," he says, "it wasn't easy. I racked my brain for months to figure out a way to take you down. Who knew that the Chess Cat's kryptonite was merely a girl?"

I narrow my eyes. "*You* took N before our game," I realize. "But it didn't help your strategy because you can't change the future. No one can." I swallow, knowing what this means for me, too. "But you saw the final pairings. You knew it would rattle me somehow. So you told me where I could find N, knowing I'd take the bait and go to Spencer's dorm."

"Like a little dog begging for treats," Francis agrees.

"That's why Spencer seemed to expect me. You told him."

"And I was right. I fuckin' love it when I'm right."

"How did you even *know* Lucy was my ex?" I demand. "I haven't spoken about her to anyone."

Francis' grin only gets brighter. "Come on, Sinclair. I can't give away *all* my tricks."

"What's the point of all this?" I barrel on. "Just to screw me over? For the sheer satisfaction? Are you *that* much of a loser?"

Francis arches a brow. "Did you think I was going to play chess for the rest of my life? I have ambition, Sinclair. Which is more than I can say for you. And when I run for state representative next year, saying I helped stop the spread of Nova on a college campus is going to be a real selling point."

"You took it yourself! You just admitted as much!"

Francis shrugs, leaning in with a rage-inducing whisper. "No one will believe you."

And then, he has the audacity to walk away from me.

Fury simmers inside me and I run after him. Faster and faster, flying without reason, without awareness. But then – I slow my pace, a new realization unfolding.

If I only have seconds left in my life, should I waste them chasing after this pathetic disgrace of a man? Should my last action be desperately trying to preserve my reputation? Clawing my way toward a goal that was never going to love me back in the first place?

Or should I tell her the truth: that I've made mistakes too, the biggest one wrapped in silence. I should have told her I still loved her a million times. I never said any of it.

But I could, now.

Determination hardens inside me, and I whirl toward the building. I don't even think; I just barrel through the side door, back toward that trash can where I so carelessly discarded Lucy's chessboard. An item I once clung to because it reminded me of true happiness, even if I hadn't felt like that since.

Luckily, the board is still on top, so I snatch it and keep moving. I scan the crowd lingering in the lobby, desperately combing faces for a copper braid. But Lucy is nowhere to be found.

I get closer to the front exit, cognizant that if I step outside,

I'll have no choice but to cross that plaque from my vision. The one that will soon be covered in my blood.

I can't change the future, I realize with sickening dread. I couldn't change my moves in the game, couldn't stop Lucy from handing me that bracelet, couldn't resist taking that white king from her a few moments ago.

Couldn't stop myself from falling in love, either.

But maybe, in these final few moments, I can do something right.

This new hope makes a home inside me as I sprint and sprint. I can be faster than death, I think, almost giddy. I can outrun this endgame. I can—

The world stops as my boot snags on a rock and I pitch forward.

For a second, mid-air, I almost laugh.

This? *This* is how it happens? I trip and fall? Fall to my *death*?

The impact of my body smacking the brick is lightning-fast. It's so painful, it steals my entire breath. I don't even know what part of me hits the ground first, but somewhere, distantly, I can see myself: hand outstretched, Lucy's charm bracelet dangling from my limp wrist. Blood pooling beneath me.

And Lucy's white king, having flown from my fist to land in a puddle. Just as my Nova-induced vision predicted.

The world starts to slip away.

But then, there's a voice from above. A face. A red braid, dangling like a rope.

"Cat. Cat. Oh god." She swims in and out of view. "Look at me. Can you look at me?"

It's Lucy. She's here.

Lucy turns, yelling for someone to call 911. If I wasn't already in bone-splitting pain, her tone would tell me everything I needed to know.

I'm not going to survive this.

"I'm sorry," I choke out. "I tried to stop it – I tried—" Everything hurts. "I think I'm going to die."

"Cat." Lucy's hands are on my face, my neck, looking for a pulse. Her palms grow slick with blood. "Where are you cut? Where is all this *coming* from—?"

My head. I might say it out loud. I'm not sure. But I feel it, something wet and cold against my hair, trickling down my ear. Blood is seeping from my skull. I'm certain.

"Lucy," I struggle to say. "I'm sorry."

"No. *I'm* sorry." Her face crumples. "I thought about you every day. But I was scared – scared you were going to find someone else you liked better. I thought it would be easier if I ended things, if I—"

I try to sit up and fail, wincing at the sharp pain that jolts down my spine. "*That* was why? This whole time – I thought – I thought *you* wanted to find someone else."

She shakes her head, braid flying. "There's only you, Cat. There's only ever been you."

There's nothing crueler than this, I think. A collection of *if onlys* and *could haves, would haves, should haves*. Right here, at the end of it all.

"I still love you," I say, bringing my cold hands around her warm ones.

Her smile only looks sad. "Cat. I never stopped."

I let my eyes flutter closed as Lucy tips her head toward mine, daring to wonder if there will be some kind of spell in her kiss. Sleeping Beauty, Snow White. Lucy Judd could have been my happily ever after, and now we'll never get the chance at all.

But then she freezes.

"Cat. Oh my god. *Cat.*"

"What?"

"The blood – it's coming from your arm." She pitches forward, examining. "You landed on glass." An incredulous laugh cracks from her. "It's a shallow cut. Bloody as fuck but – oh my god this is *shallow.*"

I blink. "But my head, it's wet, there's blood in my hair—"

"It's just water!" Lucy's voice is giddy with relief. "You're in a puddle, see?"

I swallow. The liquid *is* cold, not warm like blood. And yet I *know* I felt a thud against my head when I fell, know I landed in the worst way possible.

But then Lucy's eyes widen and she stretches her hand above my hair.

"Oh my god." Disbelief transforms her face. "I think – Cat, this broke your fall."

I crane my neck to see what she means, and when I spot it, my chest clenches.

That green and white chessboard, still slightly rolled, nestled right beneath my head. Separating my skull from brick.

A laugh of disbelief slams through me. I'm okay? I'm okay. *I'm okay.*

And Lucy loves me.

Her chessboard saved me. She saved me – *we* saved me. Maybe death can be cheated. Maybe love outweighs fate.

But then I remember Francis. The Nova in my bloodstream.

The FIDE officers, now just a few feet away, arms crossed.

I swallow nervously. "Lucy, even if I live – I'm still in trouble."

She follows my stare to the suited men. Watches them for a moment.

And then, the strangest thing happens.

Lucy's face doesn't crinkle in confusion. Instead, it twitches with something more like guilt.

"Cat," she says. "I need to tell you something."

"What?" I try to interpret her expression. "What is it…?"

My questions evaporate as Lucy's earlier words come flooding back. *I made a mistake.* At the time I thought she was talking about us, but…

"You were in on it," I realize slowly. "You've been in on it this whole time."

Her face is slack. There's a glimmer of remorse. But not much.

"That's how Francis knew who you were to me," I continue, putting the pieces together. "He saw the final match-ups in his Nova vision, but he didn't understand the *meaning* until he contacted you. Asked if you knew me. And you told him everything he wanted to hear. Am I right?"

Lucy's jaw knots, which is the only confirmation I need in order to explode.

"What the fuck?" I scramble to sit up, completing the task this time, ignoring the horrific pain. "Was *any*thing you just said true?"

"Yes – *all* of it."

"So what, then? You decided you'd betray the girl you love?" I search her gaze, desperate for an ounce of understanding.

"I wanted to see you again," Lucy says. "I wanted you to *need* me again. This entire weekend, I was trying to come up with things to say to you but I was too afraid. I assumed you hated me. I kept seeing you around campus, always by yourself, looking so pretty and somehow so sad. I didn't know how to talk to you after all this time. But then Francis called me and it felt like the universe was handing me a tactic."

"A *tactic*?" I spit. "To ruin my career?"

"To *be there* for you," Lucy corrects. "Be your life support. Your everything. Like I used to."

"Let me get this straight." I practically hiss the words. "You helped Francis set me up and then planned to swoop in to pick up the pieces? Do you hear how fucking *diabolical* that sounds?"

"I just wanted you to need me," she whispers again.

"I'll *always* need you." I shake my head. "But not like this."

I drop my gaze, everything heavy with mismatched emotions. And as my eyes fall on my bag, I notice something glowing. A swell of silver, from the depths of my tote.

It's my phone, splintered across the center like a spiderweb.

And somehow still recording.

It recorded *everything*. My conversation with Francis. My fall. Lucy's confession just now.

Wordlessly, I tap the screen. Lucy sees me do it. Recognition blooms on her face.

A new forked road opens in front of me. If I hand this recording over to FIDE, I can maybe clear part of my reputation. Fully end Francis in one fell swoop.

Ending Lucy, too.

But if I do nothing, my career is definitely over. And the two of them get away with what they've done.

I stand, cradling my blood-soaked arm as flashing lights flood the parking lot. Lucy watches me the whole time. In a moment, we'll be separated.

It's hard to say whether we'll see each other again.

"I love you," Lucy says, and I nod.

"I'll always love you," I reply, and it's the truth. I don't think love can leave a person, even in the face of betrayal. I think it lingers like a shadow. Like a bloodstain. In spite of everything, existing in a stubborn haunt.

When I get in the ambulance, I'm still holding that green chessboard. I unroll it and the crease down the middle stares back at me, the folds in the fabric carrying our history. Where it began. Where it ended. Our first game together. Our last, just now.

And as I stare out the window at the overcast sky, I can't say which of us won.

OPEN BOOK

Kit Mayquist

Johnson's fist collides with the side of the archivist's jaw, arriving with a sickening crack. A pop where the joint surrenders to the force. It is a late-night hour, two, maybe three in the morning, and the sound of shuffling echoes between the ancient wood-paneled walls of the university's lower library. Down to where the door to the archive has been left open, a single light peering out its ghostly, amber glow upon his desk.

It's scarcely enough to show the young student's face.

"I'm sorry!"

Hands raised, wrists shaking, the archivist, James Carrington, barely a man in his own right and younger than most anyone at the old college would expect, releases a panting breath that fills the air between them as it falls, but it's too late. His attacker reaches down, and with trembling hands of his own, grabs him by the shirt collar and hoists the archivist up as if intending another blow.

It isn't like him.

Every muscle in Johnson's body protests the motion, and the archivist stares, unable to understand what is going on. How they got here; why in the world he would try and attack him like this, but no answer comes. It's late. Far too late for anything good, and sleep still clings to his eyes. "What are you *doing*, Adam?"

The boy flinches; doesn't let go. Won't even look him in the eye and so James has no choice but to brace for another impact.

And he's ready. Cheekbone burning, throbbing with the anticipation of what's to come.

Only instead of a second hit, there is something else.

The smallest tear gathers at the corner of the young man's lashes, and Adam Johnson, quiet, unassuming sophomore, with moth holes in his jumper, *squeezes* his fist until the knuckles show veins like threads of blue over bone. The motion is vise-like and self-punishing, before he changes course at the last minute and uses all of his strength to throw the archivist to the side, where his shoulder lands heavy on the frayed threads of the old oriental rug.

"Don't—" Adam stops himself.

He wipes his eyes, knuckles becoming pink again, and clings to something hidden under the safety of his suit jacket. It pulls James' eyes to the smallest corner of aged and time-worn leather. Vellum pages, smoke-stained and brittle.

"You never saw me," the student pleads, pulling the jacket tighter. "Alright?"

Briefly Adam looks at the bruise now blooming on his mentor's cheek. A regretful wince follows. He reaches out then, in a shadow of the kind-natured Adam that James knew before. Something pulling him to help, but instead of doing anything decent, Adam stops himself first. Whatever it is that's forcing his hand so desperately to the old book apparently far, far, more important.

"I'll bring it back when it's safe," Adam says.

And before the archivist can stand, the boy slips away again and James Carrington, St. Ambrose University archivist for all of two uneventful years until now, realizes that the worst of his problems have only just begun.

A book can hold many things. Each page is an echo of the time that it was written. From what constructs the ink, to the paper, the leather that binds it, this is what James Carrington has always adored about his profession. For there was nothing in his life as revealing about the world as the texts in the precious St. Ambrose archive. He understood them, and this is why he loved them.

More than the words, or the lessons that could ever hope to be taught in the classroom, these things, these texts – whose ancient hands left the oil from their fingers and the paw prints of wandering animals in the vellum – revealed their true nature. This was the *true* education, if ever there was one, and he had proudly found his purpose in preserving their tales.

But some books were not meant to leave their shelves; not in hands which did not know how to tame them. And James knew the one that young Adam had stolen was precisely of this kind.

But it was not the grimoire *itself* that was dangerous.

Curious an item as it was, James could not be sure he even put stock in much of the superstition surrounding the thing. If you asked him, he would tell you about a small children's book in the

Dean's private collection that warranted more fear after he'd seen it topple items from the man's mahogany shelf late one night while sharing scotch in his office. *That* book had a concerning air to it. But the grimoire, hundreds of years past its prime usage, beyond the desperate hands that forged it, did not seem as bad.

What did strike fear in James, however, were the students in Adam's Latin course. The way their eyes were too brightly drawn to it the day of the lecture. Their focus, a little too devious.

Winter had come with a predicating yawn that year. A stretching of the sky in bitter cold that seemed to swallow up the last of autumn's gentleness even before December. The clouds hung, a heavy sheet of gray, and sent a shiver down James' scrawny limbs as he hurried down the ancient corridor and past the old carved eavesdroppers of Bellview Hall.

It was two weeks after Autumn Break. Mid-November, when a wave of funding news had hit the esteemed faculty of the old college crueler than anyone would have liked. The Great War had hit hard, as wars often do, and as the economy took a downturn across the globe, England had yet to cease licking its wounds and, as a result, it left little in the way for old St. Ambrose. Families lost inheritances, centuries-old estates were swallowed up, and one by one it seemed any bastion of tradition that managed to avoid the conflict was now destined to fall.

Including the St. Ambrose Latin Department, apparently.

It was knowledge that James wished he did not have when he walked into the classroom that morning.

Smiling, youthful energy filled the air when he laid the old book out in the center of the room for a much-anticipated guest lecture.

It was one of his favorite parts of the job. He spent so many hours alone with the leather-bound volumes that there was always a sense of pride when he was able to share the collection. On occasion he would be asked to bring relevant manuscripts to classrooms in order to assist with their lessons for the week. Though there were many manuscripts to choose from for a Latin class (the old books in his care were seldom written in anything else, after all), he had taken a chance. He had *liked* this one, a small grimoire from the library of a Danish scholar who had served under Queen Elizabeth herself. To him, it was quite an efficient, if quiet, star. One who seldom saw light beyond the shelves of the musty old archive, and he thought it might like a bit of fresh air.

The book was a sextodecimo. Roughly the size of a man's hand and smaller than most of the other texts in the college's collection. The leather had been redone at some point to better fit into the post-Elizabethan library of its previous owner, but the original binding remained inside, just behind the mask. Its pages were roughly cut, handmade vellum stained by too much smoke and poorly made ink. James loved it for that. In a sea of manuscripts from monasteries and the careful hands of trained monks, there had been something charming about this one. Like it had been made in the creator's room in a fit of manic inspiration. A cold place, where the ink still wavered from a shivering hand.

What had been more curious about it, though, were the contents inside.

It was Latin, yes, but it was *different*. The grammar was not entirely correct. There were occasional notes written in the margins from alternative scribes in the years that followed (good for an etymology lesson) where they corrected the author (equally good for a grammar lesson). In some ways it gave it the appearance of a school text. A workbook, from curious academics as James saw it. One page even had a drop of wax from a candle.

Of course, as much as James wished it were these more charming, personable qualities that captured the attention of the classroom that November day, it was, unfortunately, something else.

For the book was, after all, a magic text, and in that, nothing else seemed to matter to the hungry-eyed students. They'd just been informed not all of them would make it to Spring term, and competition was a very swift and cruel thing.

The lesson itself had gone fine. The professor, one Lyle Edmonds who had been teaching the course since James himself was a student some five years prior, had thanked him and sent him on his way when it was all said and done. But the gossip had already started. The whispers among the cohort had filled the air like the buzz of a dozen little flies and that evening, before he closed the archive for the night, not one, not two, but six of the students from Edmonds' Latin class took a detour across the snow-covered quad to shiver in the darkened room and ask James if they could perhaps see the text again.

He did not allow it.

Their fingers were cold and damp for starters, and he did not trust there was anything good that they were interested in seeing in the delicate pages. There was something about one of them. One who lingered outside the door, his pants soaked in the melting ice around his ankles. One who met James Carrington's eyes, and swiftly looked away, with snow covering his tracks before he'd made it back to the safety of the halls.

James followed that same path now. Cheek aching, eyes burning from the cruel wind.

He'd been lucky that a mark had not yet formed.

If anyone found out what Adam had done, exams would be the least of the poor boy's concerns, and James' stomach twisted with the knowledge that if he didn't find him soon, both of their reputations at St. Ambrose would be at risk. Whatever magic young Adam sought would hardly be strong enough to save either of them when a school was hungry to cut any disobedience away.

As he approached the hall of residence, the foyer opened into a labyrinth of shadowed halls; a dimly lit welcome cast only by the light of another gray December morning. Outside, flecks of snow still swirled in glistening flurries, piling up until James' path from the main building, too, became little more than a ghost.

The archivist's thin frame trembled beneath his jacket and he gripped the leather strap of his satchel tightly, knuckles stinging as the heels of his shoes clicked against the old stone flooring. He couldn't be sure where to begin, or what he was looking for, but his eyes scanned the space as heat from his cheeks fogged the lenses of his glasses.

The halls were quiet at this time of day.

With only a couple days until exams, most students found better rooms to bide their time in. Classrooms, common rooms, wherever a spare desk could be found. James couldn't be sure Adam would be here at all, but he had to try.

Thankfully it wasn't long until he found him.

In the far end of the eastern corridor, near an alcove at the base of the stairs, Adam stood, his back to him, face-to-face with the bust of an alabaster man.

James hesitated, breath held as unease settled in his stomach.

He waited. Listening. Watching.

And then he swallowed.

"Adam?"

Suddenly the student's body lurched. His arms tightened, squeezing something in his grasp that James could only see as he turned to face him. But there it was. The grimoire, small, treasured, shielded from everything, but it was still there, painting the encounter with hope that this could all be resolved soon.

But when he looked at the boy's face again, something was different.

Adam's usually bright brown eyes had become sunken, rimmed in purple from veins peering through the tired skin. His lips cracked and bled, and he stood there raw with nerves that seemed to vibrate just beneath his coat.

It was as if he hadn't slept a wink since the book came into his possession. He'd been hollowed out, replaced with something jittery and cold.

James knew a book wouldn't do this.

It couldn't.

He refused to believe it.

"Adam," James called again, a cautious foot stepping forward as his voice softened. Adam had nowhere to go but that didn't matter. James still had another eye. He had no reason to think this time Adam would be kind enough to pull the next punch. "Please, wait. I-I just want to talk."

A beat passed, with cold air filling his lungs. Then Adam's head jerked to the side, a sharp and unnatural motion, like a dog being tugged by a leash. His eyes darted to James, then to the empty space behind him, and back to the stone floor at his feet. He didn't run, a mercy, but his grip on the book tightened as he shrunk in on himself further.

Emboldened, James took another step closer, a trail of water left behind from his heel.

"You have to give it back," he urged softly. "It's okay. You're not in trouble. You won't be. We can work this out, it—"

Before he could finish, Adam let out a sound. A hoarse sound that scraped against the cold and uncomfortable silence.

"Not yet," Adam muttered.

James swallowed. Footsteps echoed from down the hall with the sound of someone approaching.

He looked back at Adam's face. "When?" he asked, and then, pressed again. "When, Adam?"

But it was too late. Adam's attention was gone. Instead his eyes bored down the shadows of the long dormitory corridor.

"I-I-I... don't know. I don't know. After," he said, turning away and toward the stairs. "After it's done."

"When what's done?" James wanted to know.

He reached forward then as Adam stepped away, and fearing he may be losing his only chance, grabbed hold of the student's coat. But Adam recoiled, slapping James' hand away with a hiss of rage between his teeth.

"You don't look well," James pleaded, his tone more insistent. "When did you last eat?"

Adam shook his head, his hands twitching over the leather binding. "Earlier this morning," he answered, but his tone carried the weight of a lie.

"You know, that book, Adam, it— You heard my lecture. It's fragile. There's a reason it belongs in the archive."

"It's safe with me."

"Is it?" James asked. "In this weather, in your hand, carrying it like that?"

The student bristled before him. Tongue antsy between his teeth as if he was readying to lash out again, and James' chest tightened. He had seen this kind of obsession before, but never in someone so young. Never over a book. He swallowed, and when he spoke again his voice was laced with quiet urgency.

"Listen to me... whatever you think you've found, it's not helping you. Look at yourself!"

"I'm fine," he snapped. "I'm—" His voice broke, and he clutched the book tighter, as if bracing himself against an invisible weight.

"You're not," James argued, stepping closer. He kept his movements slow, non-threatening, though his own pulse hammered in his ears. "You look *unwell*, like you didn't sleep at all last night. And this... fixation, it's— It's not rational."

Adam's eyes narrowed.

"Who are you to say what's rational?" he said. "This place has given you everything. We all know the story. Shy Mr. Carrington. Too scared for war, too poor for London, too ill-mannered for a wife. You have this place and you didn't even need to *ask*. You don't know what it's like. To be desperate for... for something to make sense. For luck to be on your side for *once*."

James' stomach had grown cold. Bile bubbled between his ribs, bitter and twisting as he fought for something to say.

"I understand more than you think," he said quietly, after a beat. "But this isn't the way. That book— Adam, it's not worth destroying your future over."

"Everything destroys us," he answered. "That's all the world does. Unless you learn to conquer it first."

The footsteps he'd heard before grew closer now. Not one, but a set of them. Three, maybe four, as a group of students entered off the quad and now hurried toward the stairs to return to the warmth of their rooms. Their laughter was grating. A sound that struck James more than he would like to admit, and Adam, all the same.

For a moment, Adam froze, his eyes locked on the approaching classmates. His grip on the book loosened slightly then, his body sagging under the weight of exhaustion.

James knew he could take it. If he wanted to. But there was no time left.

"Tea," James urged. "Meet me for tea. Tomorrow. After your morning lecture."

Adam's lips thinned. "Why?"

"To talk."

"You're not getting the book. I told you. You'll get it—"

"You want to know more about it, right?" James offered, a flash of an idea forming. "I can show you. Translate. I-I know it better than anyone, I can help."

Adam paused, mulling it over far longer than James would have liked. But then, at last, he met the archivist's eyes.

"Where?"

"The Dove's Tail. Near Wilford Hall."

"The pub?"

James nodded, pulse in his throat now as the students quickly approached.

Adam's eyes shifted to them, and the pair listened as their own chatter grew quieter with the new audience.

"Alright," Adam agreed. "Eleven o'clock."

That evening the snow turned to rain, and in the safety of his office James spent every spare hour poring over what he'd seen.

He didn't want to believe there was any truth to the superstitions. The book was just a book. He believed that. There was something in Adam's voice back at the dorm. The change in him over such a short time – he'd seen a similar change in the author's hand. The shaking from the ink. The manic scribbles in the margins.

His cheek throbbed, pain pulsing from the bone, and he brushed his fingers gently over the bruise. And Adam's words earlier still cut deep.

The things people said about James were not often kind. He was skillful, sure. He had been the top of his class academically in most subjects. A favorite of no one's but a man of great promise, they always said.

But a bespectacled and anxious creature of twenty was easy picking for critique. There had been a reason he found solace so young in the university's shelves. A reason the Dean took mercy upon him during graduation and offered employment so he never had to leave.

He wasn't fit for war. Never had been, never would be. Adam had been right about that.

The truth was that his time at St. Ambrose had not been too different from poor Adam's own and in that sense he understood. Or he thought he did. So he reasoned that this might possibly be the best way to reach him.

In the familiar warmth of the oiled oak and leather of his office, James picked up a bottle, popped the topper and sighed.

Brandy poured into the glass, a dark amber ambrosia, and the archivist eased back, knees cracking as he sank into the old desk chair and stared at his evening's work. He had pulled a dozen books. Every mention of the grimoire from the time of its creation in the seventeenth century to twenty years ago, when St. Ambrose first acquired it from the private library of its prior dean.

Carefully, he laid the first text out. He sat the glass down on his desk, and cautiously began his search.

Page by page, James Carrington read a century of obsession, spelled out in delicate hands. For twelve years it had been buried in Dean MacAllister's library. Prior to that, it belonged to an Anders Vestergaard who had journeyed to York in the 1890s. Before that, the Latin documentation was a mix of Nordic languages he could barely make out. Some Danish. Some Swedish. Icelandic even, which he figured would explain the presence of sloppily applied runes in the end pages.

He traced back the provenance as best he could, from library catalogue to catalogue, hoping that in some of them, a clue to what was happening would begin to form. He tried to find comparable texts with similar hands, a tactic that was easier with liturgical scribe hands and not that of commoners, but by the end of the evening, the glass bottle of brandy was empty, and his desk had scarcely an inch of space left to rest his head.

James woke in the morning with a mouth so dry his tongue stuck to the roof of it. Groaning, he pushed a forgotten ledger away with a sigh, pinching the bridge of his nose as a hangover bloomed fresh behind his eyes.

The brandy's dull heat still coursed through him, now far more of a curse than a comfort.

Morning light poured through the slim cut of the upper windows, and the archivist quickly stood to his feet, and at once the room tilted. He stumbled, his hand clutching the edge of the desk to steady himself as the shelves around him spun to the side, and James swallowed to regain his composure before finally finding the grandfather clock in the corner.

At the sight, his stomach sank for an entirely new reason.

It was 10:42 a.m.

He rushed out of the archive as fast as his nausea would allow. The musk of the old room mixing with the sweat of his day-old clothes and greasy mess of his hair as he hurried up the steps toward the main door.

It had snowed again overnight. Recently enough that shovels had yet to carve paths for the students, and so each step was a mix of mud and ice threatening to make him fall. But if he hurried he would still make it to Adam.

There were three main quads in the historic campus. The first, which fell between the main library, the administrative buildings, and the halls, was always busy. If he took it, he'd no doubt be caught up by someone. A professor, a dean, it didn't matter much, all he knew was that he couldn't risk it. But the last of the three, the quad by Wilford Hall, had not been used for half a decade and so he quickly took a left turn toward it.

In the spring the fruit trees would bloom and cover the grass of the old quad in white and pink petals. Overall, it was a charming place, framed in Georgian brick and full of picnics and sunny studying between classes. In winter, however, it was a different beast. The rows of trees were barren, branches twisting and groaning in the unburdened wind, and no one dared cross it if they didn't have to. The only ones foolish enough were those like James that morning, short on time and desperate to make it to the pub.

He hurried onward, feet slipping and skidding in days' worth of half-melted ice, and only stopped at the unexpected sound of footsteps crunching on the other side. That's when he saw them. The same group of students as before.

From the halls.

From the classroom.

A group of five boys circled one another like carrion birds on the far end of the quad. A sea of black wool coats billowing in the wind, leather satchels at their sides and bold laughter hitting the ancient brick walls sharp as a blade.

In the middle of them, Adam's hair was flecked with snow. A wet and melting little crown as another boy's glove was shaken, still sticky with the frozen remnants of the ball he'd thrown only moments ago.

The Adam that James had known before all of this was full of polite smiles. He had never known him to not be warm and offer a toothy half-grin up to the dimples in his cheeks, but now, there was nothing. No response. No joy.

There was just an emptiness as the other boys laughed, and Adam stood, circled and trapped as he held his coat close.

It was obvious to any onlooker that his upbringing didn't come with a built-in social circle the way those surrounding him had. James had naively hoped the friendships he found were genuine. That perhaps there was someone else, other than himself, who would help the poor boy with whatever was troubling him so terribly now.

As they swirled about him, preventing him from stepping forward, James' stomach knotted with the bitter familiarity that sometimes boys laugh along with you.

Sometimes, when their laughter sounds like a bark, you're the victim.

The belltower rang out, a metallic din that filled the frozen air, and James hurried on before the group could look up. He rushed past the St. Ambrose western gate and across the cobblestone street until at last the warmth of the pub awaited him. And at five minutes past, when the door opened again, he watched with a feigned naivety as Adam entered, and brushed the last of the snow from his dampened hair.

He refused to meet James' eyes.

"You made it."

It was the first thing James could think to say. A pot of tea had already been placed on the table, steam rising up to fill the space between them as Adam sat down awkwardly on the opposite side of the booth. His body slumped when he shifted awkwardly on the leather seat.

"Did you think I wouldn't?"

"No, but I saw…" James cleared his throat. Looked to the side and away from where Adam could eye his hesitation. "That Clarence boy. I saw him talking to you earlier."

"Do you make a habit of watching friends commune in the halls?" Adam pressed dryly as a basket of chips were placed down on the table in front of him. He looked down and swallowed, but did not dare to lift a hand to reach for it.

"Are you friends?" James asked, curiously.

"Acquaintances."

"Ah," the archivist offered, fidgeting with his napkin in his lap. "What is this about?"

Adam was getting agitated again. Anxious. The sight of the food appeared to make his stomach turn, judging from the way he swallowed with a new sheen of sweat on his brow. Pouring him a cup of tea barely did anything. He hadn't gone for that either.

"…are they making you do this?" By the time James managed the question, the saliva was thick in his throat. A lump that he had to clear as the peace offering grew cold between them. "Because if they are—"

Adam's voice was a snap that broke the air. "Are you going to tell me about the book or not?"

"I will," James assured. "I would just like you to help me understand."

"Understand what?"

"Why you took it."

The boy retreated in on himself. He twisted his hands. Bounced his leg up and down in a nervous tic.

James sighed.

The conversation was going nowhere.

"...you know, Melinda Cranston said you nearly knocked her head off on the way to the mailroom, but I—"

A sound came from under the table then.

Tap. Tap. Tap.

It was an odd noise. Almost rhythmic, but Adam didn't seem to notice he was doing it. Instead, it was almost like James wasn't even there.

Adam blinked after a moment, looking at him, and folded his hands away, back into his lap. There, he began to chew a nervous sore into his lower lip, grinding down until the skin turned red and chapped lips from the winter peeled beneath the force.

The flakes were pale, translucent, and James pushed the cup of tea closer to him, letting the steam rise up from the mug in the hope it might help.

"I didn't mean to hit her," Adam said softly.

"Her?"

"Melinda."

"Ah."

There was a pause.

"And me?" James asked. "Did you mean to hit me that night?"

Adam looked down. Frowning an answer of guilt even before he could mumble a reply. "It was the only way."

"Was it?" James pushed, fingers burning against the tea in his own mug. "You could have talked to me."

"Wouldn't have done any good."

"Why?"

"You wouldn't have given it to me."

"So you took it."

The door to the pub rang out, a small chime from the little gold bell above, but Adam didn't move. Again, the tapping began, and James lost any appetite he'd managed to build against his hangover.

"Do you even know what's in it?" Adam asked him after a moment, refusing to look him in the eye. "Have you actually looked?"

Tap.

"I know it's a fool's hand," James replied.

"Then I'm a fool," Adam said, finally looking up.

Like any scholar, James knew his favorite scribes, and he knew what it meant to see yourself in a text or smile at a cat's paw on a page, but Adam's words felt different somehow. In a way he couldn't place. There was a desperation in them. And no matter how much he thought back to the grimoire, or the contents of its hand beyond the strange symbols and spells, nothing came to mind.

"What's all this?" A tall boy appeared then, blond hair trimmed short and black coat hanging off his broad, athletic shoulders. His friends gathered behind him as he sauntered over to their table, interrupting the scene. "Having a little tea party?"

Adam stiffened, his already sickly complexion turning ghostly, as if he'd been caught. A field mouse trapped in the corner.

"Just a meeting. None of your concern," James said firmly, a protective surge rising in him at the sight. "Leave us be."

The tall boy smirked. "Touchy, aren't we? Don't tell me you need extra help for exams, Johnson. Worried you won't pass the final tomorrow? Time's ticking, you know."

Adam shot to his feet in a panicked flash, the porcelain cups rattling on the table as he shuffled out of the booth. "This was a bad idea."

"A-Adam wait, what are—"

"I'll see you later," he said, voice shaking, but it was too late. As the snickering of the group built around them James stood to follow, glaring at the Clarence boy as he chased Adam out, back into the cold air, and watched as he disappeared into the snowy street before anyone could stop him.

James Carrington paced the length of his room, the faint glow of his lamp casting shadows across the walls. The snow outside continued its relentless fall, muffling the world beyond his window and despite another dose of brandy warming his stomach his nerves were raw. His thoughts kept circling back to Adam and what the students had said.

Tomorrow.

Exams.

Somehow this was all about exams. And of course it was. He had known that, hadn't he? The cutbacks and competition for a seat in Spring term… was that really what this was all about? Sleep evaded him. The memory of Adam's hollow cheeks and the fire in his sunken eyes gnawed at his conscience. Something was terribly wrong, and if his suspicions were correct, James feared that waiting until morning was not an option.

The clock struck two, and James pulled on his overcoat and gloves, the cold biting through as he stepped into the eerie quiet of night.

St. Ambrose was silent, the kind of silence that belonged only to ancient places and anxious nights and it was all that accompanied him as, one final time, the archivist crossed the snow-covered cobblestones and made his way to Adam's halls.

He pulled out the bit of scrap paper from earlier that same afternoon. A trip to the records office had given him the boy's room number without too much convincing, and as he read it out, he saw the same number etched into a bronze plaque on the door.

James hesitated, his gloved hand hovering over the wood. He could hear faint movement inside, the shuffle of feet, the creak of floorboards.

He knocked more firmly.

"Adam?" he called, his voice steady but insistent. "It's Carrington. Open the door."

For a moment, there was no response. Then, a muffled sound – a chair scraping against the floor. A rattling as it was placed beneath the handle, its back against the door, and at that, James' pulse quickened as he knocked again, harder this time.

"Adam, I know you're in there. Please. We need to talk."

Again, there was no answer. Instead, in the still of the night, James listened to the faintest sound of footsteps retreating on the rug. A knot of dread tightened in his stomach and having had enough, he turned the handle, again and again until it rattled urgently against the hinges but it was locked, and it wasn't budging, and the brandy swirled in his stomach and burned a new kind of fire in his veins.

James leaned against the door, ear pressed to the wood, listening.

From somewhere deeper within the halls, he heard the faint echo of laughter. It was sharp, cruel, and entirely out of place.

It was also terribly familiar.

James' heart sank as a new, sick realization dawned. He listened to the sound of the window opening inside the room, and at that, he turned, and hurried as fast as he could down the stairs and to the cold trail of fresh footsteps leading away from the warm safety of the halls of residence, and out, across campus, through the twisting, darkened trees toward the decrepit, ominous silhouette of Wilford Hall.

The building had been abandoned for years, its once-grand façade now crumbling under the weight of neglect. Much like the St. Ambrose Latin Department, and all that James seemed to love, its time had run out, and it stood as simply a warning. A shadow of wasted potential.

Snow piled in drifts against the old stone steps, and the large oak doors hung ajar, their hinges rusted and frosted over. James hesitated at the threshold, the air inside colder than the night wind, but in it was the smell of candle smoke, and something warm.

Cologne and another scent, left hovering in the air like a ghost.

He stepped in, his boots crunching against the icy floorboards, and followed it.

The whispers reached him first, low and scattered through the web-filled darkness. Then he saw the faint glow of candlelight spilling from a room at the end of the uppermost hall. A trail of ice and snow leading right to the opened door.

James moved toward it, his breath quickening, his pulse a beating burden in his ears.

And that was when he saw it. The scene before him, terrible enough to freeze even a soldier in place.

Adam stood at the center of a crudely drawn circle on the dusty floor, his face pale but defiant, a series of cuts in his skin, and droplets smeared in shapes on the ground below. Around him, the five students James had seen looming like predators above their table at the Dove's Tail stood with their faces twisted in smug cruelty. In their hands they held candles, the flickering light casting grotesque shadows on the peeling wallpaper.

A rope lay coiled on the floor, alongside the blond boy with a gleaming knife in his hand, its blade sharp enough that it caught the dim light like a spark of hellfire. The tip, edged in red.

"Adam..." James breathed, stepping into the room. His voice drew the attention of the students, who turned to him with varying degrees of surprise and irritation.

"What is this?" James demanded, his voice firmer now, though his hands trembled at his sides. Smoke billowed over, stinging his eyes. "Adam— Step away from them!"

The boy stirred and for a moment looked at James, a flicker

of something like regret on his face. But then his expression hardened, his jaw tightening.

"Leave us alone," Adam said, his voice raw but resolute. "This is necessary. I need it to work. We all do."

"Work for what?" James took a cautious step forward, his gaze flickering to the knife still in the other's hand. "Adam, whatever they've told you, it's a lie. This isn't magic. It's bullying, it's cruel."

The tall boy, Clarence, laughed in a sound devoid of humor. "Cruelty?" he said. "We're *helping* him. Isn't that right, Johnson?"

Adam's hands curled into fists at his sides, a new trickle of red ran down to his fingertips.

"They're using you," James pressed, his tone softening even as Adam refused to look at him. He could still see it. The light as it caught his sunken eyes. The way he'd starved himself, hurt himself, abandoned himself not for the demonic messages of a book like he'd naively thought the past few days, but for this. Because of *them*.

"Look at them," he pleaded. "Do they look like people who want to help you?"

Will, a shorter boy, with sharp features and cold eyes, stepped forward. "He's the one who took it," he said. "We didn't do anything. We're just giving him what he wants."

"At what cost?" James shot back. His gaze returned to Adam. "Please. You don't have to do this."

Adam's lips pressed into a thin line, his eyes darting between James and the others as the candles melted down around them.

"I can't fail," he whispered through gritted teeth, the words barely audible. "I can't let them win."

James took another step closer. "You haven't failed, Adam. But if you let them do this to you, they will win. Don't give them that power."

Clarence's smirk faltered, exchanging a glance with the others as the air hung heavy with unspoken words. Adam wavered, his shoulders sagging.

"Enough of this," the shorter boy snapped. "Forget the plan, just finish this. We're running out of time!" He gestured to the others, and two of them moved toward Adam, the rope from the ground now in their hands as they cautiously avoided any of the chalk marks on the old floor.

"Don't touch him!" James shouted, and the students hesitated, the sudden authority in his voice catching them off guard. Adam took a step back, his foot brushing against the edge of the circle.

For a moment, time seemed to stand still. Adam's eyes searched James' face, the anger giving way to something softer, something fragile. Then, with a shuddering breath, he started to step out of the circle.

And suddenly he stopped.

"Coward," Clarence hissed, but Adam ignored him. He looked back at James, and then down, to the lectern at the front of the circle. Where the grimoire sat. Opened, and just out of reach.

"Fuck," James cursed.

The students' eyes followed, and the archivist braced himself. Seizing the only opportunity they'd possibly have, he lunged forward, scuffing the circle and grabbing hold of the grimoire as chaos overtook the room. The leather bent beneath the rough touch but it was there. In his hold again at last, and with his other hand he desperately took Adam by the arm and pulled him toward the lecture hall door to freedom.

The old steps broke beneath their feet as he dragged their bodies down the three stories to the lower floor. Adam was barely conscious. Barely awake enough to run, but it didn't matter. James wasn't going to leave him alone to the wolves. He'd done that enough already.

They didn't stop running until they reached the edge of the quad and Adam's blood had covered James' palm. Tired, the student collapsed onto a bench, his breath coming in ragged gasps as James crouched beside him.

"It's over," he said softly. "You're safe now."

But Adam didn't respond, his gaze fixed on the snow-covered ground.

On the bulge of the book inside the archivist's coat.

Still, the tension in his frame began to ease, and James, for the first time in a week, felt a glimmer of hope as he watched an air-raid warden catch sight of the lights flickering in the windows, and storm into Wilford Hall.

James opened the door to his office, the heavy oak creaking as it swung closed. He shrugged off his coat, clumps of snow falling from the dark fabric, and tossed it over a chair before turning to check on Adam.

The boy stood near the desk, pale and shivering, his hands buried in the pockets of his overcoat.

James' desk was still a mess of books and ledgers from his drunken quest the night before and he shoved it all aside to make room for the grimoire, glancing over his shoulder.

"Take a seat," he said, gesturing to the chair across from him. "It's alright. I'll fetch you a drink. I may even have a biscuit or something in here…"

Adam didn't move immediately. His brown eyes darted around the room, taking in the bookshelves, the cluttered desk, and the small radiator struggling to push back the worst of the winter chill. He stared down at the spot on the rug where all of this began, at an hour not too much later than this one.

The shadows under Adam's eyes seemed deeper now, but that, James believed, would be fixed. Even if it couldn't be resolved before exams in the morning, he would figure something out. He was determined to.

James pulled the grimoire out and set it carefully down on the desk between them.

And then, he realized Adam had moved, and was facing him now.

"Do you know what it means to devour, Mr. Carrington?" Adam said, soft and startling. "To consume until nothing remains?"

James swallowed. Repeating the words in his head.

"…I don't follow, I—"

Adam stepped closer, the smell of candle smoke still wafting off his skin, blending with the iron in his blood. In a flash it was like something had changed. James did not recognize the man who stood in front of him. Whose pale fingers now reached for his face, their tips lifting the frame of his glasses.

"Human beings are creatures of desire," Adam continued, and the archivist's cheek burned beneath the unexpected cool of his touch. "That's what history is, isn't it? We kill because we want something. Money. Land. People."

"Is that... what they wanted?" James asked cautiously. Hopeful.

Adam stared forward. His lips close.

"Possibly," he said simply. "It's what everyone wants, isn't it?"

A smirk edged the cracked corner of his mouth and suddenly Adam pulled away, letting the glasses fall back to James' nose. His cheek left painted with blood like rouge.

James cleared his throat. "...do you?"

"I want to be seen for my worth." Adam smiled, and James watched as his lips twitched into something colder, sharper. "You don't understand, Mr. Carrington. You've never understood."

Adam's gaze fixed on James with an intensity that sent a chill down the archivist's spine.

"Then help me to," James asked.

He glanced at the grimoire. To the way Adam's hand drifted closer to where it lay safely on his desk.

"They didn't manipulate me," Adam said, his voice low. "Do you think I'm that weak? That stupid?"

James blinked, doing his best to follow.

"I wasn't their pawn. I wanted it. I needed it. Convinced them to go through with it and they believed I'd be the poor soul to take the fall. But now I have it," he said, "and they're probably being caught by the wardens, aren't they?"

James' stomach twisted. He was right.

"You and I just freed up five spots for the Spring term," Adam said proudly. "I could fail the exam in the morning and it wouldn't make a difference at all." He leaned against the desk, his body still weak from fasting, still exhausted, but manic with success as he admired the wounds on his arms.

James was suddenly aware of how small the room felt, how close they were. "You can't mean that," he said, his voice barely above a whisper. "The book—"

"It's just a book. You said that yourself, didn't you?" Adam told him. "Just words on a page. The danger isn't in the book, Mr. Carrington. It never was. It's in *people*. It's in what they're willing to do to each other to feel important."

James felt a pang of something – pity, perhaps, or recognition. He'd spent much of his own life trying to escape the shadows cast by others, retreating into the safety of the archive where he could be invisible. But this... this was something else.

"And what happens now?" James asked carefully.

Adam's jaw tightened. "What happens now," he said, his voice steady, "is up to me. Not them. Not you. Not anyone else in this dying old place."

Before James could respond, Adam reached for the grimoire, but James' hand shot out, gripping the edge of the book first.

"Don't," James said, his voice firm. "This ends here."

Adam's eyes narrowed, and for a moment, James thought the boy might strike him again. But then Adam's expression softened, his lips curling into a faint, mocking smile.

"You still think you can save me, don't you?" he asked.

With a sudden, forceful tug, Adam wrenched the grimoire from James' grasp and the archivist stumbled back, his hand striking the edge of the desk with a harsh snap of his knuckles as Adam pressed the book to his chest, turning to leave.

"Thank you for your concern, Mr. Carrington," he said, "but let's be honest. There's a reason you hide yourself away in here. You're far better at reading books than people."

A Short List of Impossible Things

Faridah Àbíké-Íyímídé

Dear Artemis,

    Today I'm writing to you from the vast and temperate hollows of a dragon's stomach – or more accurately its large intestine.

Something that all of the history books by scholars of Dragonology fail to mention is just how *putrid* the inside of a dragon's entrails are. I mean *truly*. I've spent years of my research dedicated to examining the specifics and peculiarities of dragon anatomy; years of studying maps and charts for the geographical borders and flight patterns of the rare and uncommon Sargasso dragon; years spent working out the most careful methods and safest passage into said dragon's digestive tract, and yet not one Dragonologist thought to mention in their writings that its insides smell like an intricate potion gone wrong. I honestly feel betrayed by our forefathers for not mentioning this travesty in their papers.

Despite the fact that I am regretting *every* decision I have ever made in my seven and a half years of being a student of Fine Crafts, and that I am very seriously considering abandoning my post here and coming back home to you, where I'd much rather be, I'm not going to, because I know what you'd tell me.

I know what you'd tell me because it's what you *always* say whenever I have threatened abandon: "One may fall when they fly, but how can they ever truly soar if they never make another attempt to fly again?"

I remember the first time you said that to me, years ago, when I was struggling with a complicated levitation spell and had threatened to quit trying to levitate altogether. It had been a very specific and effective line as I was levitating in no time soon after, but oddly, it still applies to this and every situation I have been in since and always manages to make me feel like trying to fly again.

And I know you'd be right in this instance. You're always so *irksomely* right about things, particularly things pertaining to me. It's why I love you so much. But I *also* love the idea of no longer being encased in this dragon tomb of sorts.

That being said, my research *has* taken me to stranger places... arguably smellier places... On that note, remind me, why did I choose this field again? Why didn't I choose something less exciting and much more sensible like Herbology or Necromancy? The most the Herbology scholars do during their grand research trips is pick wildflowers in the forest. And at least with Necromancy, their subjects are mostly dead.

I, on the other hand, am required to travel across the infinite realms searching for things that shouldn't exist. Whose bright idea was it to be a scholar of *the impossible and the improbable*, anyway?

I can imagine your voice now, as you tell me it was *my* own bright idea to do so. I can hear you reciting my past self's words back to me the night I chose my speciality.

"It would be interesting to write a thesis on the impossible," I'd said.

"The impossible?" you'd replied, tearing your eyes away from your beloved textbooks on Oneiromancy and instead looking up at me through those adorable spectacles of yours, accompanied by your equally adorable look of concentration.

I'd nodded, excited as ever to embark on this impossible thesis of mine.

"More so the improbable. Things that are so rare, so beyond belief, they are almost impossible, or maybe even *actually* impossible. Things beyond our realm, things beyond any of our wildest dreams."

You'd smiled at me then – probably because I used the term *dreams* and, as we both know, you are an Oneiromancy nerd.

"So, impossible things like mythical lands and creatures and such? Or impossible such as the likelihood that Professor Morgause will let any of us miss the Scholars' Assembly tomorrow?" you asked, an eyebrow quirked.

"Both, I suppose... anything impossible should be investigated, but I was thinking more along the lines of the former."

"So, for example, your research would be aiming to prove or disprove the existence of rare and impossible creatures and lands?"

"Yes, like for instance... the baku," I'd said.

As expected, you looked excited then, what with the baku being your favourite mythological creature. I recall you mentioning once, during our first year at the Institute of Fine Crafts, that you were very disappointed with your choice of familiar and wished for a baku instead of the lousy toad (whom we both now love) you'd been stuck with by Professor Morgause. Only *you*, Artemis Arman, would wish for a scary nightmare-devouring creature to be your choice of animal companion.

"So... what do you think? Of my thesis idea," I'd asked, feeling nervous, probably because I was sensing at that point just how much of a great task I was setting myself up for.

"I think it sounds splendid, my dear," you'd said, as bright as ever.

How naïve I was back then, to think of the land's great impossibilities as a fun, leisurely project to undertake and closely study. If I had known that my morbid curiosities would bring me to such dank and rotten conditions, I might've chosen differently.

I know at this point in the letter you'd already be rolling your eyes and muttering about how ridiculous I was being and so I am taking this as my cue to get back to the business of collecting smelly samples from this Sargasso dragon's rectum.

(Seriously, who told me to do this? I have no one but myself to blame.)

Anyway, I guess I should really go now. The rest of the large intestine awaits me!

Yours forever and always,
Isadora Lex

Dear Artemis,

I am writing to you this evening from the Ship of Theseus. *Or am I…?* To be or not to be, that is the age-old question.

I suppose it depends on what you believe about the impossibilities of such a ship both existing and not existing. I got into an argument with the ship's captain about the whole paradoxical debate. He claims that the impossibility of the ship's existence is what makes the Ship of Theseus *The* Ship of Theseus. That the very question of its temporality has become so intertwined with its identity as a ship that, for that very reason, it exists even without truly needing to.

I argued, using this fine analogy, that if the sun kept scorching the sea, eroding its contents slowly over time, and one kept replacing the sea with more of the same sort of matter, the original in its very essence did once exist, yes, but something else, albeit similar in shape and matter, exists in its place now. It can't be the same thing, it can be the same *kind* of thing, but not that *original* thing. Once it is gone, it is an impossibility to have it back.

He contested this using a fine analogy of his own. That if a person is plagued with cancerous cells and is in the latter stages of metastasis, they would essentially undergo a treatment to destroy and repair almost all of their cells. A person whose very constitution has altered them completely as a result of their treatment is still the same person; changed, yes, but still the same.

I argued that if such a person requires *that* much treatment, they are most likely dead by the end of it. He told me I was morbid, uncompromising and unimaginative.

As you would probably predict, the captain and I argued for hours about the improbability of the matter, before agreeing to disagree. It was, however, still a very interesting thought experiment. It begs the question, much like the idea of impossibility at all, is something only impossible if no being has ever set eyes on it? Can it only exist if someone were to touch it, as if to confirm it is not the derivative of hallucinatory desires? Does something have to be seen to exist? Or is wishing for it enough?

As the impossible ship set off on its impossible journey across the infinite realms, gliding impossibly over the turbulent epidermis of the primordial oceans, I couldn't help but silently walk back on my own convictions of what it means to be impossible and thus, indeed, possible.

There is an argument that we are all completely changed, from the moment of our first breath to that of our last. We do not stay the same between those two instants; some may argue that there is nothing of us that remains, every part of us putrefies. That is the fact of life and death – any Necromancy scholar would tell us so.

As the ship sailed towards its final impossible destination (a land situated on the path around the Stream of Oceanus), I sat with those thoughts, considering what in turn this means for all of us. For me. For you. I was thinking about what it means to exist. I mean, who are any of us, really? If we are always changing, who were we before? Who are we now? Who will we be in the future?

All of this is to say that I guess we are all the Ship of Theseus.
And we also aren't.
But also, the Ship of Theseus *is* The Ship of Theseus.
But it also isn't.

I know you'll understand my strange ramblings, you're the only one that ever seems to – which might not bode well with my professors during the written portion of this project. Hopefully I'll come across as more coherent when the time comes to submit my research.

Anyway, despite the ramblings, I promise you I am not as inebriated as I may seem; yes, the captain did give me some whisky but I only had a sip. Really, I'm just *very* sleep-deprived and missing you greatly, my dear Artemis. Thank you once again for letting me bore you to death with updates on my research trip, writing to you is so often the light at the end of so many dark scholarly tunnels.

Yours forever and always,
Isadora Lex

Dear Artemis,
It is nightfall in the land I find myself in, and I have just had an uneventful run-in with what I am most certain was an Arista (colloquially known as a type of weather faerie).

There had been a spell of rain this morning, and I'd been up all night trudging through the enchanted trap-laden mountainous forest that surrounds the coastline, mapping out where I might see the rare creature based on the coordinates provided to me by previous eyewitnesses and scholars of fae. These weather fae are known to reside in deep, dank underground caves at the edges of these forests and so that is where I found myself yesternight, with my academic journals, surrounded by the heat of a few enchanted logs I'd scrummaged together, when I'd made the devastating discovery that the map I had been reading for several days had been upside down, meaning I was on completely the wrong side of the island.

Post-error, I was just about ready to give up on the search when, from the mouth of the dark cave, a small elderly woman wandered in with a sack of flowers and leaves. She noticed me squatting in the centre of the cave, with my books and my fiery logs and just stared at me for several moments, before she started shouting in a language I did not recognise. I had of course learned enough of the local tongue and dialects to get by in the case that I required directions from any locals, or indeed in the case that I managed to track the impossible creature down in the end.

The old woman was persistent with her shouts, and so I began shouting back. This took her by surprise for some reason, maybe she was used to people scurrying off once she began to berate them or something. I could see in her eyes that she was assessing the situation, eyeing me suspiciously.

I decided to give speaking the local language a try, see if it would be a way to bridge our present miscommunication predicament. This didn't work out either, however, as we soon discovered after a few more minutes of awkward back and forth in languages that neither of us quite understood. The old woman eyed me again in that suspicious manner from before and then stood up abruptly and *transformed*.

At this point you might be wondering what in the world I could even mean by she *transformed*, and, my dear Artemis, I mean exactly that. She changed into her true form.

Something you should know about Arista fae is that they often disguise themselves; this is why it is very hard to track them down – they often look nothing like the images you see of them in the textbooks. In fact, they choose a disguise so inconspicuous, there is a high chance that one may pass by an Arista fae without realising it. As I had done.

Her once plain, wizened appearance quickly shifted and metamorphosed into something truly magnificent. Large insect wings sprouted from her back as her ears stretched into pointed coves and the air around her shimmered. She was beautiful.

Once she had shed her own disguise, she pointed at me as if requesting that I do the same. While I was not in disguise as any sort of alternate creature, I had a feeling that she knew just by observing me for those few moments that I would somehow acknowledge her fine nature in a way others might not. And so, I showed her something of my own.

In the end, it appeared that there was a language we both understood succinctly. The language of alchemy.

I'm not quite sure how to put it into words, but we somehow talked for hours, without the burdens or restrictions of spoken language. We started small, with introductions; she told me her name was Arrow and I told her mine. I learned that the cave I had been squatting inside of belonged to her and that the map I'd read in the wrong order had actually been right all along. Turns out that I am not the only scholar with an affinity for rare creatures. She had spent years trying to throw other enthusiasts off the scent, creating illusions that would satisfy them, leading them astray through carefully laid mistruths and inexact clues about her whereabouts.

She had apparently been very surprised to see me here with all of my books. I'd been the first in a long while to find her.

I of course apologised for disturbing her resting place, and said that I meant no harm. She pointed out this poignant truth, that intent does not prevent harm. Arrow told me about how the Arista fae did not used to be an endangered group. They used to populate these areas; hundreds and thousands of them lived in caves much like this one and in valleys across the land. And then explorers, scholars and fanatics came and either captured, killed or chased them away.

The whole thing sent me into a web of questions about the nature of these research trips that we embark on as Scholars of the Fine Crafts and the indirect harm caused by our ethnographies and… I guess, the ethics of it all. It made me question my entire thesis, honestly. I suppose this is something to unpack in my conclusionary paragraphs.

Our conversation devolved into other topics such as our favourite kinds of storm; Arrow loved cyclonic rainstorms, they were her favourite to make. I told her that I wasn't actually all that much a fan of storms, they'd always scared me as a kid, but that you always loved the rain. She was visibly disappointed in my answer, but then seemed to brighten at the mention of you and asked me to speak more of you (which I am always glad to do).

I told her the story of how we met, in that conjuration class in first year – almost a decade ago. How I was immediately swept away by your quiet confidence and how competent you were with very complex spells. I told her the story of how we fell in love, a year later, how you'd sent a message in a glass bottle to my study asking me to meet you after dusk, and then how you'd made me climb the nearest mountain to the Institute so that we would be close to the most northern star when you showed me a difficult spell you'd been working on for weeks. How it involved a very ancient form of celestial magic that required a lot of patience, power and practice. I recounted to her how you'd shot your hand up and plucked the star right out of the sky and gifted it to me and how it was the loveliest thing I had ever received. I showed her the vial of stardust in the small glass valve I always wear around my neck and she smiled and said you seemed like a very tasty creature, which... I'm still not sure is a good thing or a bad thing. I went on, telling this stranger all about you, unable to stop myself from boasting about how my Artemis was a genius. A scholar of dreams, a pioneer in the world of Oneiromancy. I told her all about how your research was literally changing the world, in particular the way we study almost every discipline. Everything from Necromancy to divination and botany. All the papers you've published in the prestigious *Alchemist's Journal*, the awards you've won.

    She smiled even wider and croaked out something that gave me the impression that she would very much like to eat you. I'm afraid now that I might have some fierce competition for your affection. Promise me that you won't leave me for a weather faerie? Even a sophisticated one like Arrow. I wouldn't blame you if you left me for Arrow, I'm not sure *I* could even resist her subtle charms nor her threats of flesh digestion.

    Our conversation ended with me crying all over this poor Arista fae after she'd asked me about my own research. I'd started telling her about my interest in the improbable and then it spiralled into my feelings about how the thesis was going and then Fine Crafts in general and... I guess I didn't realise just how much of a mental toll it had been taking on me. The travel, the sleepless nights, the loneliness. It's been so isolating, Art. I wish I could be with you right now, I'm so sick of my own research at this point, sick of being in my own head, I'd much rather be in yours...

Anyway, Arrow's invited me to stay for a meal she's making us. She said she'd be happy to let me interview her as I also... looked *very tasty*. I should probably go and be a good guest since I did technically invade the poor fae's home.

Yours forever and always,
Isadora Lex

Dear Artemis,
The end is finally in sight.

After a few setbacks in my research, namely a failure to investigate certain impossible entities due to vexatious extenuating circumstances (such as running out of resources, unfavourable climate or just bad timing and luck), I am very nearly done with the data collection portion of my thesis.

I thought I'd give you an update on the list of impossibilities and improbabilities that my research has covered thus far, and so without further ado, here is a short list of impossible things featured in my (probably very bad) thesis:

1. The Chupacabra
2. Atlantis

3. The Sargasso Dragon
4. Niflheim
5. Monoceros
6. The Helm of Malfi
7. Nahuales
8. The Flaming Sword
9. The Ship of Theseus
10. An Arista Fae named Arrow
11. The Philosopher's Stone

This was a lot, no wonder I am so tired. Listing it all out like this is giving me some much needed perspective. Next time, remind me that I should work on a less involved thesis.

As I was writing the list, I kept thinking of what your reaction to it would be. First of all, I think you'd congratulate me for being so ambitious and then I think you'd ask me what my all-time favourite improbability was – I know you'd ask this because I know how much you love to quantify things in such a way. The first thing you ever asked me was what my favourite potions combinations spell was. It had taken me all of Nox term to figure out what my answer would be; as you know, I'm not as decisive as you are. I like too many things to pick a favourite. Even now I can't come up with an answer to the question of my favourite impossibility. Even after so many years, researching and studying this very topic, I don't have an answer. Though, it is possible I just haven't found it yet.

It's probably the sleep deprivation. I haven't slept properly in who knows how many moon cycles. I'll probably have an answer when I'm better rested... but then again maybe not. I find it impossible making my mind up about these things.

I think it's because I get so lost in the infinite possibilities of it all. It reminds me of the time we went sky gazing, a few months before you stole that star and consequently my heart. I remember you asking that very question:

Which one is your favourite?

My favourite? I'd replied, staring up at the sky above us.

Mhm, which star? If you could choose one.

I don't know their names...

You smiled. *Name them and then tell me.*

I raised an eyebrow. *That's a little rude, don't you think? Naming something that probably already has a name. It's like you're saying you know better than their mother or something.*

You laughed, and your laughter came out in wisps of cold air. *I don't think stars have mothers, Iz.*

Of course they do. Everyone does.

I don't, you'd said. *Never have.*

Never? I asked, confuddled.

You nodded, hands behind your head as you gazed up at the world longingly and then looked over at me with the same regard. I didn't pry that night, nor did you offer up any explanation, but one day you'd let me into your mind and your heart, you'd tell me everything there is to know about you, and I'd eventually do the same. We'd become scholars of each other's souls; I'd become an expert in the field of Artemis, so much so that we'd become that irksome couple who finish one another's spells, practising the unique divination of knowing exactly what the other is thinking and will be thinking in the future, too. But that expertise would come with time, and in that moment, under the weight of the stars, we were novices on the path to becoming experts in each other.

I suppose you're right then, I'd said.

Right about what?

Stars. Maybe they don't have mothers. I mean I think you're a star and you don't have one and so it appears you are right about something – for once.

You smiled so widely then but said nothing, your brown skin illuminated in the paleness of the moonlight. I remember thinking how beautiful you were.

A comfortable silence settled over us as we lay side by side with nothing but the blanket of night to shelter us. You eventually coerced me into naming several stars and choosing a favourite, and while I was against it at first, I grew to love naming stars with you.

As I write this I am lying on a patch of moss in a dark wood, looking up at the sky, lost in the stars, lost in thinking about you and how you always named each and every star before you eventually tired yourself to sleep. I tried doing that too tonight, but I think my brain is broken, it must be the toll of this endless research trip of mine…

I miss you so very much, Art. I could cry.

Maybe I'm already crying. Maybe I've never stopped.

I'm looking at the stars right now as I write, Art. I'm naming them all after you.

Yours forever and always,
Isadora Lex

Dear Artemis,
There was something I failed to mention in my last letter. I have been keeping a terrible secret from you.

Terrible only in the sense that it is something you would have wished to know sooner, not terrible in the actuality of it all.

The thing I have been keeping from you, the terrible not-terrible thing is... that there was a 12th impossible thing that I was researching on my list. I didn't want to mention it to you before because I wanted to tell you about it only if it was indeed something that proved to be an improbable success – which so much of my research hasn't been.

And I can now reveal to you that it indeed has been.

Thesis item number 12: The Baku

This was the first impossible creature I'd put on my list the moment I knew I was actually going through with this research project. I didn't want to tell you and have you be disappointed if nothing came of it, and so I did my research in private, plotting out my travel paths and methodology for months and months without uttering a single word about it to you – which was one of the hardest things I've ever had to do.

I almost told you before you left on your own scholarly excursion, but I knew how equally stressed and excited you were about the trip, so I thought it could wait until we both got back.

But I guess I'm telling you now, Art, because why not?

I made contact with a baku – or more accurately, *it* made contact with me a few nights ago. I've been camping out inside various bamboo groves and forests across the land of Miyako for a few weeks, hoping to set my sights on the baku. I was not having much luck with it at all, which was to be expected given that the literature on the creature is sparse and few and far between. But with the little scholarship that exists, I created my own maps and theories for how I might go about making contact.

I know what you're thinking at this point, that it was dangerous of me to do so, knowing even a little about the capabilities of such a creature, but as you are very aware, I am incredibly smart and thought ahead of all possible and impossible contingencies. I put up strong wards around my camping sites, as well as a spell of protection on my mind so that if a baku did come, it would not completely ravish more than just my dreams.

I know it is an odd thing to say, but I have never been happier to have my mind feasted upon. It sounds a lot more terrifying in theory than it is in practice. There is almost something... peaceful about the process. Having something take away all of the grief and pain that bleeds into your mind when you are at rest and at your most vulnerable, emptying you out and freeing you from the true demons that reside inside.

I almost wish for a baku to feast on my dreams and nightmares every night... maybe then I'd sleep more easily. Maybe then when I wake it won't be in a pool of my own sweat, or with me clutching my chest as an involuntary cry rattles through me.

Maybe a baku might break this cycle and devour the nightmares that plague me even as I exist in the waking world. The nightmares that are mostly about you...

Maybe I shouldn't be writing any of this. I'm sorry, Artemis. I truly, truly am.

When you read this letter, I hope you understand me in the way you always do.

Yours forever and always,
Isadora Lex

Dear Artemis,
I'm sorry about my last letter, I haven't been doing well lately. Actually, I haven't been doing well for a long while now.

I've decided that this should be my final letter to you. They are becoming increasingly difficult to write. Professor Morgause said writing them would help with dealing with it all, but they haven't. I think they've made this whole situation much worse.

In my last note I asked you for a favour. I asked that when you read my letters, that you try to understand me the way you always used to. But even in writing it, I knew it would be an impossible thing to ask of you.

The truth is it would be impossible for you to read these letters at all, because I never sent them.

Even addressing this to *you* feels strange, but I don't know how else to write this at all, especially since there is no *you*. Just myself inside the stomach of a dragon, on the Ship of Theseus, in a cave on a high mountain, in the space between bamboo trees. Just me writing to myself in the dark, wanting nothing more than the possibility of you reading a single thing I'd sent you again. But as we just established, that would be impossible.

Art, I've spent years studying the impossible, my thesis is literally an in-depth study into the biggest impossibilities that exist across our infinite realms, and yet the biggest impossibility of them all, the one my thesis fails to examine, is the impossibility of you and me.

I will never see you again, Art, and that knowledge has completely destroyed me. I never thought you were capable of destroying me, but there you are again, doing what once was thought to be impossible. Being without you is the hardest, most impossible thing I have ever been assigned to do. Even harder than these letters that Professor Morgause said might help ease the grief of your dying.

But that's impossible, I should have known it was impossible. Nothing in all the realms will ease my grief other than the impossibility of you being here, *alive*.

I guess I did it to humour her, make her think I was getting better, back on track to finally complete my thesis after my leave of absence following your death last year. I didn't want to tell her that there would be no getting better; I am no longer myself, Artemis. Every part of me, every cell, every atom died with you, and like Theseus there is no telling what I am anymore.

I wanted to be strong, Art. I wanted to be noble like you always were, finish my work and not let this grief drown and consume me. But it seems an impossible creature might before my heartbreak gets the chance to. I think I'd prefer to go out that way, eaten by a basilisk or another impressive creature that would mean all of these sacrifices might have been for something. So that when I am remembered I am remembered like you, someone who took risks for the greater good of Fine Crafts and changed the world while doing so. If anyone knows about the risks and rewards of scholarly prowess... it's you.

You are the noble hero; they are literally building a sculpture of you to be resurrected at the Institute. You died for your work, you chose your work over everything else... over me, and I know why you did, because I know everything about you, but I don't know if I can forgive it. I don't know if I can ever forgive you for dying.

What you did was so impossibly foolish, Artemis. Planning an excursion to the fabled Land of Dreams, a land that has only ever been written about in theory, a land with zero scholarship that could have given you safe passage. *You* had to be the one to find a loophole in all of the theories that told you that there is no current way out of the land once an entity enters its gates. But you foolishly thought you'd be the one to beat the odds, do the impossible, visit the land of dreams and return with a groundbreaking paper to show for it, but this place was not even rare, it was entirely improbable, a very *clearly* impossible thing – a topic I happen to know a thing or two about – and yet you went anyway. You should've listened to me, I could have helped, or maybe talked you out of it... you didn't have to do this alone. And now you're dead, and so am I.

In one of my letters, I pondered on what my favourite impossibility would be. It should've been obvious, but at the time my mind was blocked by this immovable dam of grief. I know, now that my mind feels clearer, that my favourite impossibility would of course be the impossibility that we could someday be together again. I would do *anything* to make that impossibility real.

Anything.

While drowning in the well of my own grief these past few

weeks, I thought that maybe there was something… a last resort, and most possibly a deadly one.

You might recall from the impossible Ship of Theseus, the captain and his journey, to the impossible land that lies beyond the Stream of Oceanus. That land, as you would know if you were able to read this, is the land of dreams, *Demos Oneiroi*. It is the place where you went and never returned, the place I plan to head to soon, on that paradoxical ship once again.

If among the infinite realms, there is a dangerous realm where dreams do reside, maybe I'll find you there, maybe we'll be together then, Artemis. Maybe we can be impossible together.

I'll see you soon, my love.

Yours *impossibly*, forever and always,
Isadora Lex

The Harrowing of Lucas Mortier

M. K. Lobb

*"The mind is its own place,
and in itself can make a heaven of hell, a hell of heaven."*
— John Milton, *Paradise Lost*

Lucas Mortier is, above all else, a creature of habit.

He wakes every morning at six forty-five. He eats two-thirds of a cup of oatmeal, drinks a black coffee in his blue mug, and ensures the temperature in his apartment is set to nineteen point five degrees Celsius. He's at the campus gymnasium half an hour later, where he exercises until he needs to get ready for class. He rarely speaks to anyone unless they initiate conversation; he focuses on his studies. Every night he prays for absolution, goes to bed at a reasonable time, then wakes up and does it all over again. Reliability comes from patterns; following patterns means control.

And Lucas is all about control. It was the only thing he had to cling to as the rest of his life spiralled into chaos, and he can't seem to let it go. Relinquishing control was what had got him into this mess in the first place. A boy like him ought to have known better – after all, he cut his teeth on Sunday School stories and faded colouring sheets. On lambs and shepherds and smile-padded warnings of a steep descent.

It's too late now, of course. Here is another fact about Lucas Mortier: He's destined for Hell. He knows it in the inherent way that other people know when they're falling in love, and it terrifies him.

He knows it because he's already been there.

The memories exist in fragments. A dark road, headlights in the distance. Cold hands on a colder steering wheel. The icy surge of fear in his chest, and that voice in his ear giving way to a scream. The crunch of metal, the squeal of tires. Then nothing.

Nothing.

Nothing.

And then... *something*. A fear unlike anything Lucas had ever known. A darkness threading along his bones. A presence at his back, a prickling up his neck, his body somehow everywhere and nowhere, a simultaneous expanding and condensing. He saw, and he felt, but he did not exist. Not in any way he was accustomed to.

That, Lucas figures, was Hell. A place even more terrible than his world in the aftermath of the accident – a world in which he existed and Delilah did not. His first serious girlfriend, frozen forever at eighteen. Now he skirts through his borrowed life with the Devil on his shoulder, a stifling presence waiting to collect his due.

Perhaps Lucas deserves eternal damnation. What else could possibly await someone like him? He'd seen the car coming as time slowed, his existence suddenly precarious, pendulous. It hadn't been an automatic decision – a choice made out of the inherent human need to preserve one's own life first – but an informed one. Had Lucas stayed his course, it would surely have been him. Instead, he'd swerved, and it had been her.

It was his fault in more ways than one. Waking to the assaultive fluorescence of a sterile room had only driven that fact home. He'd been a pious boy turned principled young adult, at least to begin with. He'd known better than to give in to those human urges until they were bound in eternal union. Him to her, her to him. His confessions, although scarce, always elicited the same advice: To feel temptation is not to sin. Acting upon temptation is what lowers one sufficiently into the Devil's reach.

Although born from mutual desire, the choice to take her virtue had been Lucas', sick bastard that he was. But the crash, he knew, had been divine intervention. His punishment on Earth had been losing her; a suffering of the psychological variety. His punishment in death would be so much worse.

Equal parts armed and trapped with this knowledge, he returned to continue his secondary education as intended, recommitting himself to the pursuit of immutable truths – a philosophy major, in less pretentious terms. His grades were passable at first, then good, then excellent. At this point he can't remember the last time he left Catabasia University. And why should he? It's the kind of place that feels alive. More alive than him, the boy who ought to have been dead. The boy who got spat back out of the hellfire.

And if the narrow corridors are the university's veins, the faceless students its lifeblood, then the library is its beating heart.

Lucas spends far too much time there, plucking book after book from the shelves in the humanities wing. It's enormous, Catabasia's library, with wide mahogany shelves that seem to stretch into oblivion. The lights are dim, the walls devoid of windows. It smells like dust and wood varnish and things long forgotten. Every hour not spent in his lectures is spent here, devouring facts and theoretical treatises, as if each page yields the barest hit of a drug that keeps him teetering on the periphery of overdose. Lucas can't quite put into words what he's looking for – he simply knows it has to be here. The answer to his problem doesn't lie within the realm of science, he suspects, but that of history, philosophy, metaphysics. He seeks not a biological solution, but a spiritual one.

A third fact about Lucas Mortier is this: He needs to save his soul. It wasn't his seminary courses that sparked his obsession with finding a foolproof way to do just that, but an introductory class on metaphysics. How could he not be transfixed by theories of reality when his conversations with God feel like hollow soliloquies? Lucas would need more assurance of salvation than prayer could ever provide, if indeed he thought salvation still within his grasp. He is no longer naive enough to think he can be saved by the traditional methods of his youth, though. He needs something more. He needs to *become* something more. This is the fascination that presently consumes his entire being.

But then: *Her.*

It's a Wednesday evening when he sees her for the first time. Silhouetted by the dark, her hair a vibrant flame, she's the kind of lovely that deserves a song. This is Lucas' first thought, and he is quick to dismiss it as a foolish one. He lives in that narrow space between romantic and romanticizer, and neither one is appropriate when it comes to a girl he doesn't know.

Lucas' second thought is one of surprise – surprise that he doesn't recognize her. In a place where the sea of faces is little more than an incessant haze, he surely would have remembered hers. There's something tantalizing about her beauty as she approaches his preferred table in the far corner of the library, and Lucas recoils from it. She's tall, willowy, her upturned lips red as blood. Her presence puts him on edge. "Mortier, right?"

She knows his name. He doesn't dare ask why. His instinctive need is to get as far away from her as possible, yet every human part of him clamours for her attention. Preening in the gift of it.

"Lucas is fine." He extends a hand, and she takes it.

"Lorelei," she says. "Lorelei Alastor."

That familiar apprehension has settled around Lucas' shoulders. Maybe because her hair is the same deep red that Delilah's was, her nose pointed in a similar way. He's not even sure how he notices – there's otherwise nothing similar about the woman and his dead girlfriend. Delilah's face was fuller, happier, sprinkled with freckles. Lorelei's is harsh, her cheeks pale and hollowed out. Her eyes are so light a brown they look orange in the library's dim light. The smile on her mouth doesn't quite reach them.

It's been far too long since Lucas looked a woman in the eye, let alone studied their features with this kind of intensity. He's become accomplished in the art of restraint, the success of which hinges heavily on avoidance. Something about Lorelei Alastor, however, gives him the strangest sensation that he's just awoken from a formerly interminable sleep.

He needs her to leave. More critically, he needs her to stay.

He *needs* her.

There's an empty seat across from Lucas, but Lorelei doesn't sit. He wonders if she's waiting for him to extend an invitation. He shouldn't, he *can't*, but he does, indicating the chair. Her smile widens as she sinks into it, the legs screeching as she adjusts. She smells like blackberries and the barest hint of smoke.

"What can I do for you?" he asks, then curses himself for sounding so strangely formal. He's well and truly misplaced his wits.

Lorelei's eyes dart around the library, as though she wants to make sure they're not overheard. It's an unnecessary precaution; by all appearances they are entirely alone. It's a state of being that seems to follow Lucas wherever he goes. Until now, that is. "Do you really need to ask?"

"Yes."

"I heard you're Catabasia's unofficial expert on deification."

"Who told you that?" Lucas demands at once. He's shaken to hear her say it so plainly. As far as he can recall, he's never told anyone about his obsession with achieving godliness. He might as well admit to entertaining heresy. Still, just because he can't recall telling anyone doesn't mean it hasn't happened. Much of the last few years is a blur, each day melting and contorting into the next. Wake up, oatmeal, coffee. Nineteen point five degrees, *ad infinitum*.

Lorelei sidesteps the question. "What I want to know is, do you truly believe it's possible?"

"I don't understand what you mean."

"Don't play with me." She leans across the table, bringing her face closer to his. Her lips are red, red, crocosmia red. "A man like you doesn't take an interest in something like that unless he's trying to achieve it."

Lucas interlaces his fingers. She's not supposed to know this. *Nobody* is supposed to know this. But Lorelei Alastor, he suspects, is the kind of person who understands desire. Everything about her – from her air of confidence to the snake tattoo contorting around her left forearm – screams of a woman undaunted by the relentless press of wanting.

"Whether it's possible or not doesn't matter," he lies. But the very prospect of a shared interest has him mirroring her movements, leaning forward so that his gaze locks with hers, dark brown warring with light. "It's the theory that interests me. The idea that one might be able to work backwards in a sense, to separate from themselves and the material world so completely that they begin to exist as something divine in their own right... How could that *not* be of interest?"

Lorelei's jaw works as she considers his words. "If your interest is purely theoretical, then I must have gotten the wrong impression. I'll excuse myself."

When she makes to rise, though, Lucas lurches forward. He finds his fingers digging into the delicate bones of her wrist, and he releases her just as quickly. The mere touch sparks something deep in his core. Something hungry and unrestrained. For a breath of a moment, control seems to evade him; he hurriedly wrests the shackles of his self-discipline back into place.

"Sorry," he mutters. "I'm— What did you mean by it, when you said *a man like me?*"

He wouldn't have blamed her if she'd left without answering. Instead, Lorelei appears pleased. Almost like she was waiting for him to give in.

"A desperate man, Mortier," she says. "That's what I mean. Everything about you screams of desperation."

"How do you figure?"

"You're thin and pale as hell. You look as though you haven't slept properly in days. Your hair is a mess."

Almost without thinking, Lucas rakes a hand through the overgrown blond strands, trying to rectify his dishevelled appearance. "Sorry."

Lorelei makes a noise of thinly veiled amusement. "You're a philosophy major, right? Is it henosis or apotheosis that you want to achieve? Do you want to become one with God, Lucas Mortier? Or is it that you intend to become a god in your own right?"

"I've considered both options," he says. He's pleased she knows the terms, but panic tightens like a vise around his lungs. If she didn't sound so genuinely intrigued, he might not have answered. After all, he's reached a deadlock, an impasse. How can he proceed until he decides what divinity *is*? Does it describe a single entity, one's notion of God as the only example? Or is it an achievable state of higher existence?

"Which have you settled on?" Lorelei prods.

"That's what I'm still trying to figure out."

The moment stretches between them. Her gaze searches his again, and Lucas has the sense she's looking for something specific and consequential there. "Let me help you."

"Why?"

"Because we want the same thing."

"I only want to save my soul. Why would someone like you need saving?" Lucas can't help but tack on the question as Lorelei slides back into a seat, this time opting for the one beside him. He promptly leans away, putting distance between them. It's no use; her mere proximity is like an electrical conduit running beneath his skin, perpetual circuits that coalesce deep within his core.

She arches a thin brow. "Same reason you do, I expect."

"I doubt that."

"What, do you think a woman like me isn't capable of terrible things?"

Lucas gives a tight-lipped smile, eyes dropping to her black-tipped nails. The snake tattoo bold against her skin. "I think you want people to *believe* you're capable of terrible things."

That makes her laugh. He likes the way she laughs – breathily and with abandon, her chin tilting up, her thin shoulders shaking. But there's a hard edge to the sound, a sort of self-deprecation that makes Lucas feel as though he's missing part of the joke. "You don't seem all that terrible yourself, Mortier. What do you need saving from?"

"Hell," he answers simply. What else is there to say? For some reason, he imagines that lying to this woman would be futile. Besides, this is the first time in too long that he's felt any kind of connection with another person. Every day, every hour spent in Catabasia University thus far might as well have been solitary confinement.

Lorelei nods as if this makes perfect sense. "I suppose nobody wants to end up there. What makes you think you will?"

Lucas raises a shoulder and lets it drop. Finally, he says, "My actions got someone killed. Someone I cared about."

"Is that it?"

"Is that not enough?"

"Killing someone isn't the same as letting them die. I should know."

Lucas reacts without meaning to, brows ascending his forehead now. "Did you—?" He lowers his voice, glancing around the same way Lorelei did before. They're still alone, the rest of the library deserted, though anthropomorphic shadows congregate around the stacks of dusty tomes. "I mean, have you killed someone?"

A wry smile is Lorelei's only response. It's vague, but then again, so was he. If he doesn't plan to tell her about Delilah, he figures he can't very well expect her to reveal all her secrets. How strange, though, that she sought him out. Something about the university seems to draw people like them: people who couldn't possibly belong anywhere else but here, reward-driven rodents in an experimental maze of endless corridors and infinite knowledge.

"I have a better question," she says, "so humour me. If you decide to take the route of henosis, which theory compels you more? That of Plotinus or Iamblichus?"

Lucas doesn't have to ask what she means this time. There are two prevailing schools of thought when it comes to mystical unification, at least where Western philosophy is concerned. The first, Plotinus, makes Lucas wrinkle his nose. He doesn't care for the Platonist philosopher, whose principal idea – *the One* – is perplexing on account of being nearly indescribable. To Lucas, Plotinus is the worst type of thinker, relying on Plato's Theory of Forms. Just as Plato contended that the visible, physical world was a mere imitation of the non-physical, the One goes beyond the concept of existence and non-existence. It is the source of existence itself, yet is more emanation than creation, and remains insentient, unchanging, indistinct. It's an experience. A potentiality.

It is absurdity.

"I'm not convinced anything can be achieved through contemplation alone," is his stiff reply. "I think that if anyone wants to incite change within themselves, they ought to rely on something more actionable."

Lorelei's smile grows, and he's mesmerized by it. "So you lean more towards ritual theurgy. You believe in magic."

Does he dare admit it? That in his bid to avoid Hell, his research has him delving into such things? This, he thinks, is the only area of his life in which control feels like a hard-won thing. He yearns to prove himself virtuous once more; he secretly suspects it will never be enough. For a regular person, sins can be forgiven. For Lucas, who has previewed his foul eternity just long enough to fear it, hope is lost. He careens back and forth between these two truths. Wanting to believe in redemption pushes up against the immutable fact of his damnation – the implication of each so enormous, it feels like two tectonic plates converging along his mental fault line.

"You could say that," he says finally. His voice is hoarse, and he hurries to clarify. "Only because I find myself not knowing what else to call it. I agree with Iamblichus that the soul is intertwined with the body. Did you know he believed what sets the divine apart from everything else is that they aren't bound by fate? That's what I need – to escape my fate. But no one book, no one philosopher, lays out the steps to be followed in sufficient precision. I'm hoping if I can read enough of their theories, maybe I'll be able to find the commonalities and work it out myself."

"And how much progress have you made?" Lorelei asks, wicked amusement dancing across her face.

"Not enough." Lucas doesn't mind admitting it. He can tell by her expression that she already knew the answer, so voicing it aloud doesn't feel quite so humiliating. Why he's admitting anything at all, though, he can't say. Something about Lorelei Alastor seems uniquely posed to draw out honesty. She was not here, and then suddenly she was, and it feels like she was created just for him. Her knowledge is alluring. Her appeal is stifling.

She leans close, bringing her lips to his ear, her hair tickling his cheek. Lucas doesn't so much as inhale. He's a man hewn from stone as she says softly, "I think I can help you. Meet me here again tomorrow. Same time."

His heart is no longer a pulse, but a throb. Blood being carried away from the muscle, flooding his extremities, panic saturating every cell. He hasn't felt this way in some time. It wasn't always accompanied by the panic, but Lucas is no longer a foolish boy. He pulls at the collar of his shirt. His cheeks are flushed, his skin warm. Out of habit, he glances to the ceiling, wordlessly begging forgiveness. But Lorelei demands his undivided attention; she rests a hand on his thigh as she pulls away, and Lucas nearly convulses.

Her lashes flutter. Her eyes are wide and perplexed. "Are you going to answer me, Mortier?"

He swallows. He nods.

Then she's gone, heels clicking on the wooden floor. Her absence leaves him inexplicably bereft.

Lucas returns his books and goes home. He lives on campus, so as always, his walk takes between seven and eight minutes. As he showers, he thinks about Lorelei's offer. Despite her intriguing claim, despite his silent nod, he doesn't have to meet her again. He shouldn't, he *can't*, but he will. Not because of the way she makes him feel, but what she has to offer.

As always, he says his prayers and goes to bed at a reasonable time. Unlike always, he doesn't close his eyes and will sleep to find him. Instead, he stares blindly into the dark, feeling more awake than he has in ages. That feeling of apprehension only grows, swelling and elongating, threatening to consume him alive. He cannot let himself be distracted by Lorelei. A man in pursuit of godliness would never divert his attention to such a thing. If he hopes to achieve deification, he knows he'll need to prove himself. His record is not clean, but he's remained pure ever since. Surely that ought to count for something.

But the thoughts that continue to plague him are not pure by any stretch of the imagination. Even when he squeezes his eyes shut, trying to think of something, *anything* else, they're determined to persist. His body responds in kind, and he lurches up to sit. His skin is hot, hot, hot. He crosses to his wardrobe and blindly runs his hands along the surface, knocking various items down in the process. If he cannot control his thoughts, then he will punish himself for them.

Before desperation has him heading to the kitchen, however, he remembers that mortification of the flesh is not always so severe. Head spinning, thoughts churning, he falls to his knees in the centre of the room. He stays like that until every part of him aches with something other than desire.

Lucas doesn't know what time he finally drags himself to bed, but when he wakes at six forty-five the next morning, it feels far earlier than usual. He forgoes his oatmeal as he drinks his black coffee in his blue mug. He ensures the temperature in his apartment is set to nineteen point five degrees Celsius. When he arrives at the campus gymnasium half an hour later, his daily exercise fatigues him more than it normally does. His classes, too, fail to hold his interest. He doesn't hear a word the professor says as the old man rambles on about Dante's *Inferno*. He knows it's because he's keen to meet with Lorelei again, and balks from the fact. By the time he makes his way to the library that evening, his stomach is growling in protest, his nerve endings frayed and raw. He sits at his preferred table in the far corner to wait for her.

When Lorelei appears, everything else fades away. Lucas forgets his oatmeal-less morning, his less-than-comfortable hours spent kneeling on the floor. He's not certain what compels him more: her, or the book she has tucked under her arm.

Her grin is sly as she settles beside him, flipping it open. It's not old in the way of most books in the library, their spines cracked and taped, but *old* old, with yellowing pages and a nondescript cover that might be vellum. Lucas would be hesitant to even lay a finger on it, but Lorelei thumbs through the tome with no indication of concern.

"Apotheosis," she advises without glancing up. "Ancient Greek religion was big on it. There are so many myths about people becoming divine. Think of Hercules, for example."

"Those are just stories."

"Every system of belief starts and ends as a story. It's up to us to decide which we think are true."

Lucas peers skeptically at the page Lorelei indicates, a feat made difficult by his attempt to stay an arm's length away from her. He frowns at what he sees. "I can't read it."

"Like I said – Ancient Greek."

"You understand it?"

"Yes." At first Lorelei offers no explanation. Then she sighs and says, "The important bits, anyway. I'm majoring in classical linguistics. I came across this book ages ago and assumed it was full of nonsense. As I paged through it, though, I realized it was full of rituals, some of them with deification as the end goal. When I started asking around, I was told to seek you out."

"By *who*?" Lucas presses, but Lorelei acts as though she doesn't hear him. Oh, he's spoken to people during his time at Catabasia, but none of them matter. None of them stuck. His mind is a black hole where names and faces go to die. Anytime he begins to think too hard about his isolation, his brain seems to shy away from it, perhaps in unconscious self-preservation. And so, he's long resigned himself to his lonely, predictable life.

"It sort of combines the ideas of Plotinus and Iamblichus," Lorelei says unprompted. "If you're pursuing divinity, you have to extricate yourself from human distractions and temptations. You have to become a blank slate."

It's the common theme in all literature on the subject, Lucas has found – that the first step in becoming something more is reverting to your basest form. "So, in other words, it's about sacrifice."

"Isn't it always?" There's a note of teasing in her voice. She's turned to face him fully, which means he can't ignore the treacherously low cut of her shirt. "What tempts you, Lucas?"

You, he might have said, might have screamed, but he is nothing if not controlled. He forces himself to think of Delilah. Not the sweet softness of her most intimate flesh, or the way she gave herself to him so fully, so beautifully. No – he thinks of her trusting eyes. Her warm smile. The fervour of her faith, and how easy it was to convince her that it couldn't possibly be a sin if they were truly in love. The real sin, Lucas insisted, was lack of commitment. And that, of course, didn't apply to them.

What could be more sinful than claiming to know better than God? Lucas did just that, and he paid the price. He tastes divine justice like blood in his mouth.

Knowing it, though, is not enough. Not with Lorelei's face inches from his. If he wanted to, he could count each of her black-coated eyelashes. Instead, he lurches to his feet, clarity hitting him with breathtaking force. She doesn't object. Doesn't even question him. This time, Lucas is the first to leave the library.

He doesn't eat. He remains in one spot, knees pressed to the cold floorboards, and wills his thoughts away. He does not sleep until his body physically and vehemently demands it. Perhaps there is something to be said for contemplation after all. Because when he rises at six forty-five the next morning, he knows one thing with abject certainty: Lorelei is a test.

How could she not be? Why else would he yearn for her this way, knowing as little about her as he does? Lucas wonders if she truly is a murderer. He wonders if she drives men to madness. He resolves to stay away from her – the temptation of her body, the temptation of her book with its promised answers. If Delilah was his first test, he failed miserably. If Lorelei is to be his second, he will not let history repeat itself.

Once again Lucas eschews his oatmeal. He makes his coffee, then forgets to drink it, letting the bottom of the pot blacken as the kitchen air grows increasingly acrid. He ensures the thermostat is set to nineteen point five degrees. Despite his light-headedness, he heads for the campus gymnasium at the usual time, clad in his usual outfit. When he arrives, though, *she* is there.

Lorelei, waiting outside the main entrance, auburn hair vibrant in the dawn light. Even from a distance Lucas can see her red, red lips.

His heartbeat crashes in his ears. He pivots on a heel and makes for the location of his first class, not caring that he's more than an hour early. He sits outside the locked lecture hall, foot tap-tap-tapping. It earns him an odd look from his professor when he finally arrives, but Lucas barely notices. He makes a beeline for his usual seat at the back of the room. He's resigned to another day hearing about Dante's *Inferno*, and does his best to pay attention as they enter the Seventh Circle of Hell: Violence. But his mind wanders, and he glances down one of the rows only to spot Lorelei seated at the very end.

She's not in this class. She can't be. Lucas would have remembered her – he's certain of it. Yet she doesn't look out of place. She has her notebook open, a pen poised between two of her fingers. Every so often she gnaws on the end of it, and he finds himself enraptured by her mouth. Her teeth. The movement of her jaw. He has to get out of there. And so he does just that, gathering his books and darting out of the lecture hall long before the hour is up. He skips the rest of the day's classes, opting to go home instead. When he arrives, the thermostat on the wall reads twelve degrees Celsius. Too cold. Nonsensically cold.

Something is wrong. *Everything* is wrong. He feels it in his bones, in the pit of his stomach, in the pressure behind his too-heavy eyes. How much longer can he keep doing this? He has spent years crying out for forgiveness, and God does not answer.

Lucas remembers, in the days following the accident, how the colours around him were muted. So, too, were his emotions. He felt like an automated character in a black-and-white rendering of a world he no longer recognized. There was only the fear, only the guilt, only two-thirds of a cup of oatmeal in the morning. Now Lorelei Alastor has knocked him from his reliable, boring orbit. She has infiltrated his mind and compromised his thoughts. She has reignited Lucas' forbidden connection with his body, and hers is all he can see as he unzips his trousers. His breaths are hot and rapid, his grip unyielding, his need for release suddenly insatiable. His hand becomes Lorelei's, too, and for a collision of moments he feels close to Heaven again.

Then it all comes crashing down on him, ecstasy distorting into shame. He needs to unshackle himself from temptation. The first time, he thinks, God removed it for him. Reclaimed Delilah in the spray of glass and the crunch of metal and the blaring wail of sirens.

This time, Lucas will do it himself.

He doesn't eat. He doesn't sleep. He doesn't know the temperature in his apartment – he only knows that it's cold, cold, cold. The blue-green veins in the backs of his hands are too prominent. Gooseflesh breaks out along his limbs. He kneels, and he prays, and he seeks guidance. His teeth chatter. He's given everything up, has he not? Everything that tethers him, everything that makes him human. Food. Water. Sleep. Love. He'll never achieve divinity, however, if he can't overcome temptation. He thinks of Virgil leading Dante into the vestibule of Hell; he thinks of Lorelei's voice saying *You have to become a blank slate.* What is humanity's basest form? He suspects he knows.

When his alarm cries out six forty-five, Lucas is already wide awake.

He follows none of his usual routines. Instead, he walks dreamlike into the kitchen and yanks a knife from its wooden block on the counter. He presses the tapered point to his own skin, feeling the cool kiss of metal that turns quickly to heat. It's sharp enough, so he pockets it, then makes his way to the library once more.

The air outside is frigid, the streets deserted. The sky overhead is black. If Lucas hadn't known better, he might have thought it still nighttime. His confusion is only compounded by the fact that, when he arrives at the library, the doors are locked. They're glass, but he can see nothing in the room beyond. He curses, pivoting to scan his surroundings, then half-heartedly tries again.

This time, the doors open.

The library looks the same as it always has. His legs are leaden as he makes his way to his preferred table, frowning in the familiar dim light. He's alone; each step echoes throughout the cavernous space. He has the strangest sensation that time isn't operating the way it normally does. In fact, he has no sense of time at all.

Still, some part of Lucas knows Lorelei will come. It feels as if everything has been leading up to this very moment. She is temptation, placed in his path to test him. He knows what he has to do. He's gripped by the gravity of it, resigned to the necessity of it.

Here is a final fact about Lucas Mortier: He believes humanity's basest nature is one of violence.

"I wasn't sure you'd come."

When he whirls around, he's not at all shocked to see Lorelei standing behind him, ghostly pale and silhouetted by shadows. Her mouth is arranged in a smile, her lips painted the vibrant red of freshly spilled blood. Crocosmia red. She's the kind of lovely that makes him want to throttle her.

"What do you mean?" he asks, his voice hoarse from hours of disuse.

Lorelei shrugs. "You don't always come. Sometimes it takes longer." She's wearing the same shoes as every other time he's seen her. The heels are delicate points, causing each of her steps to reverberate crisply down the length of shelving. She's circling him like a predator, and Lucas realizes he's gone motionless, slack-jawed as he watches her progress.

He clears his throat. "I have no idea what you're talking about."

She ignores that and comes to a halt. Her dark leather jacket is zipped up to the throat, and she begins to undo it, separating the teeth. Lucas quickly redirects his gaze to the ceiling as she bares the slender curve of her collarbone.

"Oh, relax." Lorelei's lips are at his ear, her voice teasing. "You're always so uptight."

He doesn't understand any of this, least of all why she speaks as though she knows him so well. His head feels stuffed with wool from days of malnutrition and little sleep. He clings to that one simple thought: He needs to remove temptation. He needs to become better, become more. He wonders if God wept when he drowned the world. If transcendence always feels like slow, agonizing decay.

Lorelei is too close. She's lust and warmth and the scent of blackberries, and Lucas feels that incorrigible monster at his core stir. He draws her in even closer, his lashes shuttering as his eyes roll back in his head. One hand drifts down to the curve of her waist. Her mouth moves to the slope of his neck. Teeth meet skin, blood rushes downward, and that is when Lucas strikes.

It takes more effort than he might have thought. The kitchen knife is hard to grip, harder still to thrust. There's a guttural scream – he thinks it might be him. He's covered in sweat, covered in blood, covered in tears. He drives the blade in again and again and again. The panic chokes him, blinds him, spurs him onward. He wonders, briefly, how such a thing can be holy. Has he gotten it wrong? Has he somehow misunderstood? But there's a sort of detached mindlessness to it after a while, and when he falls to his knees to catch his breath, he feels certain he must have carved out everything human within himself. He's sick, sick, sick.

"I'm sorry," he gasps, nausea threatening to overwhelm him.

Black spots congregate at the edges of his vision. "Oh God, I'm so sorry." He crawls forward on hands and knees, shaking, babbling, forcing himself to look at what he's done. His eyes drift up to Lorelei's pallid face.

Except he's not looking at Lorelei.

The face he stares into is his own.

His eyes are partially open, unseeing, the sclera laced with red. His face is the grey-white of a body deep in the throes of pallor mortis, and his clothes are covered in dried blood. Lucas chokes out a curse, scrambling back from himself. Despite the blood, the wounds to his torso are quite clearly from something other than a knife. The angle of his spine is crooked, distorted, both of his legs facing a way they ought not to. One of his arms is mostly severed, holding on by a bit of skin and sinew.

"Rather unpleasant, isn't it?"

Lucas turns fast enough to give himself whiplash. Lorelei stands by his side, staring at the body – *his* body – with an expression of unbridled disgust on her beautiful face. He gapes at her, unable to comprehend what he's seeing. "I don't – you're supposed to be—"

"Dead," she finishes dryly, and it isn't a question. She sounds tired, almost bored, as if they're playing a game she's long grown weary of. "Yes, that's the conclusion you keep coming to. I'll admit, I keep expecting you to do better. I don't know why." Lorelei blinks, and abruptly her face shifts to Delilah's. The unexpected familiarity of it has Lucas breaking out in a cold sweat. Bile rises in the back of his throat. "Did you really think crashing your car was the answer? Did you really think killing her would keep your families from finding out?"

Lucas swallows past a dry throat as the pieces start flooding back and fitting into place, one by one, the way they always do. The fragments of memory warp and change. A dark road, headlights in the distance. The stark white stick in Delilah's lap, two pink lines on the screen. Cold hands on a colder steering wheel, the numbers on the corner of the dashboard deeming the outside temperature to be twelve degrees. Delilah's face hidden behind shaking fingers. The icy surge of fear in his chest, and that voice in his ear telling him to end it, to save them both from ruin, to make it all go away. He'd swerved left, the passenger-side door directly in the path of the oncoming transport truck.

He hadn't necessarily intended to die alongside her. But he had, his body flung from the vehicle like a discarded rag doll.

"I don't know what I thought," he moans belatedly, the words almost inaudible. "I suppose death seemed better than whatever might come next."

"And how about now, Lucas Mortier? How do you like death now?"

He glances around wildly, but Lorelei – Delilah – is gone, her disembodied voice the only evidence that he wasn't alone. The library floor tilts beneath him, the walls narrowing in. Lucas begins to cry, all laboured breaths and fat tears, the way he always does when he realizes. "I don't like it. *I don't like it.* Please, don't make me do it again. I can't do it again."

There is no response. The dread within him has reached its apex, twisting and pulling and scratching. He tries to scream, but he has no voice. He tries to claw at the cage of his chest, but all control eludes him. There is only the darkness threading along his bones, the presence at his back, the prickling up his neck. His body is somehow everywhere and nowhere, a simultaneous expanding and condensing. The library contorts around him, the ringing in his ears growing and amplifying to a scream.

The scream gives way to silence.

The silence gives way to an alarm, blaring its daily acknowledgement of six forty-five in the morning. Lucas sighs, quieting it and dragging himself from the comfort of his bed. He eats two-thirds of a cup of oatmeal, drinks a black coffee in his blue mug, and ensures the temperature in his apartment is set to nineteen point five degrees Celsius.

He is, above all else, a creature of habit.

The Coventry School for the Arts

Ariel Djanikian

Naturally, because he was a painter, we mostly saw my father from the back. He was loud and youthful then, in my earliest memories of him, and jolting back and forth in front of a canvas as if in a lurching, cursed dance. Before he left us to teach at The Coventry School for the Arts, before I joined him there, he and my mother and I lived as a family – or some approximation of that – in the main living area of a tiny apartment in Boston. It was a shadowy place, saturated with the smells of oil paint and turpentine, and overfilled with my father's personality, which bullied and blotted out everything else. The single bedroom was not a bedroom for us, but a cordoned-off studio, from which the bangs and scrapes and sighs of activity were carried out at relentless intervals, and shied away from no nighttime hour. When you looked into the room – let's assume you would dare to – it was never the painter's front that met yours, never his eyes: instead it was those of his creations. They were women, mostly, and girls too. I used to think, in some bizarre homage to me and my mother. Bizarre, I say, because I didn't want to see myself in those images. They were tortured and desperate and surrounded by wide brushstrokes of danger. The colors were stormy green and vituperous gray, with notes of inauspicious orange and red. You could almost compare the figures with the one in *The Scream*, except that they were in modern clothing, entrenched by woodlands, and enwrapped with distinctly female torrents of hair. I'll also say, which I suppose is a testament to my father's skill: the figures peered out from the canvases as if they were imploring the viewer to reach inside their swirling worlds, and unlock that which bound them, and set them free.

Around the time I started at the public middle school, my parents' marriage began to shift from cold stasis to deterioration. My father developed the habit of taking his meals in his studio; and his conversations with us dwindled to nothing. When my mother protested, when she reminded him it was her salary as a nurse that was keeping us all afloat, he attached a lock to the door, as in, an actual chain and padlock, a gesture to which my mother, understandably, took offense. She gave him an ultimatum and experienced a nasty surprise when he took the wrong end of it, and abruptly announced that he couldn't stand living with us, that we were impeding his work, and that he'd asked to return to his job at the boarding school where he'd held a prestigious teaching position just before and after meeting my mother. Within days, he had moved his painting supplies and paltry collection of other belongings out of our home. As my father had taken no role in caring for me – had never once put me to bed, walked me to school, prepared so much as a slice of toast – my sense of abandonment was not too much to bear. With him gone, we had more space. We dragged the mattresses into the bedroom and slept there like normal people would. My mother's mood in the face of these changes was at first morose, then thoughtful, then by the following springtime, I'd say she was giddy. By the next year, she'd begun neglecting her nursing shifts, which for most of my childhood had been our sun and moon, the clock by which we organized everything. Also, in opposition to her former exactitude – and this was the greatest surprise to me – she began to laugh it off, those lazy mornings when she'd realize, with a cartoonish, forehead-slapping gesture, that it was in fact a Monday, or a Wednesday, and that I'd slept in again and neglected to go off to school.

People began passing through our once-hermetic home in the evenings. "Friends," she called them, though I could easily sniff out the rot in the word. Her gatherings became uproarious. The months muddled on in a permanent haze of smoke. The downstairs neighbor would bang with something – a broom, perhaps – which my mother would respond to by marching over to the same spot, planting herself on one foot, and stomping. Most of the time, I did my best to avoid my mother's strange gatherings. In fact, in an echo of my father, I would lock myself in the bedroom, where stray papers and charcoal pencils that he'd left behind provided me the opportunity of new, artistic experiments, so that soon I was losing myself to the world of my own fledgling drawings, and with a growing obsessiveness that, even I could sense, with quiet humor, was the right of my blood. Eventually, I stopped going to school. I stopped interacting with my mother, who had become a stranger to me, though I still liked to recreate her by drawing her face on a sheet of giant paper plumed with black charcoal dust. That's what I was doing, actually, the night the hard thuds fell on our door.

There were two cops. They spied the powder and pipes. They spied the pills in orange bottles that crowded the tabletops like buildings in a miniature city. Possibly even more damning, they spied me, wan and cautious, peering out from the bedroom like a starving sidewalk artist or a grievously neglected child, depending on who was doing the looking.

In most respects, I was an easy case. I had a father still living. Not only that, but he was a faculty member at a prestigious all-girls boarding school, with students in residence only slightly older than me. "You're going to have a fresh start," the social workers assigned to my case liked to tell me. And, knowing about my drawings: "Maybe you'll be an artist one day." But I did not want to go. And most of the time, to this blurred merry-go-round of assurances, I would reply: "I don't want to leave Boston. I don't like my father." My language was direct, the meaning plain. But if anyone valued my stance on the matter, they gave no sign beyond a second or two of mute, blinking hesitation, before carrying on with the paperwork.

The Coventry School for the Arts, veiled among the green hills of Northen Vermont, comprised a collection of four large brick buildings, the center one boasting a tall triangle point. The severe architecture was in contrast to the soft lawns, undulating like waves, as well as to the dizzying, magisterial forest of pine trees that stood at the back of the campus. My father – after a three-year absence, even at a distance, he was very much recognizable – stood at the top of the arched driveway, gaunt and hunched and sour. He stared a moment, then approached in the long, lopsided strides of a man impatient with even the act of walking. "Katherine," he said in greeting, as I slipped from the car, throwing my backpack over my shoulder. The social worker passed him a clipboard: fat with the forms that would render me the exclusive bane of my father. He signed where he was meant to sign, grunting, and passed them back. Then he began walking away.

"You go with him," the social worker had to tell me. Then, as if to give me a boost: "This is supposed to be a really good school."

On the current of this small endorsement, I followed my father's off-kilter strides across the gravel driveway and up the steps of the center brick building. Inside was a vast, empty reception hall. A great, iron lighting fixture hung from the ceiling. For a moment, I stood in awe. The school could not have struck more of a contrast to the cinderblock claustrophobia and cheap metal desks I was used to. Then I realized that my father had moved through the doors to our left, into a dining hall lined with long wooden tables and benches, and I trailed him through. At a far corner were a trio of girls, maybe fifteen, all in their uniforms, the khaki skirts and white tops and blue ties that I'd received from the school. The group took one quick look at us, then jumped from their seats and absconded. My father seemed neither to notice nor care. He went to the large buffet – the great steel trays empty and cleaned, it must have been long after dinner – and came back to me with a single apple.

"A snack," he said.

We both looked at it as he set it down on the table. "Thank you," I said.

"Are you really twelve?" he grunted. "I was off by a year. I must have done the math wrong. The youngest here are fourteen."

"I'm twelve," I answered. "But I don't mind if I'm younger."

"What's your favorite subject?"

I had not been to my classes for nearly a year. Still, I had at the ready what I hoped was a pleasing answer.

"Language Arts, Geography. But my favorite is Art."

"You like to paint?" He was surprised, maybe even annoyed.

"At home, I was drawing with the charcoals you left. But I draw pretty things," I added, merely for clarification. "Not like what you do."

I had not intended to be so impertinent, though it was clear by the way his expression narrowed that he had taken my comment badly.

"Do you know what state I was born in?"

"Here?" I asked, remembering as I answered his habit for quick changes of subject.

"That's correct," he said. "In Vermont. I've lived here all my life, except for the ten years I was with you and your mother in Boston. Before Boston, I actually taught at this school. I was their big hire when I was thirty. I met your mother when she came to do the vision and hearing exams for the students, and we got married.

She lived with me for six months in the faculty housing. Let's just say she didn't like it. Or maybe, she didn't like *me* as I was here. She thought a change of scene would help me. I indulged her and we shipped ourselves off to Boston around the time she got pregnant with you. That was a mistake." The move, I wondered, or having me? Probably he would have said both. "Turns out, geography has no effect on the state of my mind, so I might as well stick around the place I know best. The farthest I'll drive now is Montpelier." He looked at me; cruelly, I thought. "What are you nodding at? Have you ever heard of Montpelier?"

"Um..." I tilted my head towards the ceiling. "Is it near here?"

"Two hours away. But you should know, shouldn't you? It's the capital city. And here I thought you were a geography buff."

He laughed, and for a second I laughed too, until worry stopped the air in my throat. At the same time, I heard a terrible noise. It was those girls. They were spying on us from the doorway, a mass of pale khaki. One had emitted a shriek of bemusement, causing my father to jump up and rush for the door. Holding the frame, his body but not his head visible to me, he yelled, "Joslyn, Adrienne, Gretchen, that's three demotions I'll be writing tonight!"

He returned to the table, self-satisfied. If he noticed my despair, he showed no sign of it. But the realization had risen high and crashed over me as I sat hunched on the bench that – with my strange circumstances and young age and my father working against me – I had no chance of fitting in at this school.

"Here's what you'll do," my father said, tapping the table. "During the day, you'll attend classes with the freshman students. English. Math. Music. Art. I don't expect you to absorb much, but get what you can. Next year we'll run you through the curriculum again. God knows what else I'm supposed to do with you." He folded his hands and blinked, gazing at me. Then, in a tone perhaps meant to be gentle: "Life is precious, Katherine, it's no good to waste it like your mother was doing. Every minute, every second of the day is precious and we must seize upon it with greed." Then he rose again. "You may come and visit me when you'd like in my classroom. But you are not to enter my studio. That's a stipulation I put into my contract when I took this job. I need a spot to paint away from the students. And 'students' now includes you. Can you swim?"

"Doggy-paddle," I muttered.

"In that case, stay away from the river. It's just through the woods behind the school. Only the upperclassmen are permitted near it. It's not too wide, but the current's strong. After a rain, it could drown a horse."

Our interview ended there and, as he disappeared from the room, a pretty, laconic woman with long brown hair showed up out of nowhere, greeted me with quiet words of welcome, and told me that she was the assistant teacher in Art. She led me up the giant stairs and to a coffin-sized room at the top of the hall. It was after lights-out, and the only sounds were of an occasional flushing toilet and the lonely running of sinks. I unpacked my set of uniforms into the dresser then sat down on the bed. I still had the apple, and the crunching of it was loud in my head. That night, I lay upon a low, narrow bed while the outside changed from gray moonlight to a cloud-covered black, my loneliness coming over me like an ache. I had been separated from every familiar thing:

my home, my mother, even the public school that would have taken me back, if I'd only been allowed to stay in Boston. I cried in sporadic heaves into the pillow, feeling myself to be the most pitiable person in the world – as so many children, and perhaps adults, are too easily willing to believe of themselves.

At the Coventry School, one day did not differ from the others. At seven o'clock the bell rang and I dressed in my khaki skirt and white top and blue tie and walked to the bathroom where I stood in line to brush my teeth and use the toilet in a room so cold that the porcelain was like ice to the flesh. We then walked down the wide stairs for breakfast in the dining hall. The grief I'd felt upon first arriving at the school was only accentuated by the company of eighty teenage girls who – my instincts on that first night were painfully accurate – did not care much for my father, and, by extension, did not care much for me. The classes were far beyond my capacity. Algebra was a mystery. If the answer was printed there, on the right side of the equal sign, then what was the meaning of walking backward, to figure out the earlier numbers? I did not know anything about a pig named Snowball and why he'd run away. I could not outspread my thoughts to perceive political meaning in a story about talking animals who lived on a farm. I'd thought that talking animals were only for babies. The Art classes were their own complication. These might have been my favorite hours – after all, I got to sit alone in front of a canvas, not talk to anyone, and, within the day's parameters, make whatever picture I wished. Except of course that my father happened to be the teacher. He walked around the easels and commented on the other girls' creations, but when he came to me, a kind of spasm of indecision took over his person. I don't know if he liked my drawings or if he was embarrassed by them, and how they failed to reflect his own talent. It was not until the assistant teacher, the woman with long brown hair who'd showed me to my dorm room on the night I'd arrived, commented on my work that I felt his reaction was layered with more than simple distaste.

"You're very good," she said of my picture, a drawing of a swell of land and the overlapping pine trees. "Do you like art?"

"I do."

"Then it's nice that you ended up at this school."

"It's been okay. The other girls are all older than me."

I was expectant. I wanted her to say something nice again. But instead the woman threw her long hair back over her shoulders and frowned.

"The important thing," she said, "is that you keep getting better, and that you learn from the other students here. When an artist goes bad, and I've seen it happen, it's because they become obsessed with themselves. They forget the talents of the people around them."

It was a harsh thing to say to a child, and too strong a rebuke for a small moment of ego. And yet still I was interested in this woman. After all, she was my father's assistant. She followed him during his classes with soft steps around the lawn. She helped him with setting up easels and washing the brushes. Often, I felt jealous of her. My father spent far more time with her than he'd ever condescended to spend with me or my mother. And here, at the Coventry School, he insisted on treating me as just another anonymous student. By the second week, he'd only stopped me once in the hallway to grumble, "Your grades could be better, you could try a bit harder," after I'd received a four out of ten on my first algebra quiz.

Though there *was* one incident that did soften my feelings for my father as those first, difficult weeks rolled on. One evening after dinner I was meandering near my father's studio – alone while the older girls were huddled off in their cliques – when I heard him talking inside. It was public knowledge that no one was allowed to enter his studio, a small wooden shed at the edge of the campus, so the possibility of his having a person with him was startling. I stopped and, taking a risk, crept toward the shed and rested my cheek near the oversized window. By half-inches I rotated my face, until I was looking into the space. Aversion washed over me, for the paintings were in the same style I remembered from Boston: the grays and threatening spots of colors, the women and girls looking desperately out from the canvases. My father was not, in this moment, at work. He was pacing the bare, paint-splattered floor, shaking his fist one moment and crying the next. It was difficult to hear, but finally I was sure I'd parsed out his ramblings. He was saying: "Poor woman, oh my poor darling wife," which made me wonder, in a rush of rare, warm feelings toward him, if he perhaps regretted the cruel insults he would often hurl at my mother, and perhaps – if I dared let hope extend so far – that seeing me had made him wish we were a family again.

It might seem odd for a child to spend her days in a bubble of solitude, without conversation or company, but I don't think I felt that oddness, or the full pain of my social isolation, until one sunny afternoon when we were outside for fresh air after lunch, and a slightly eccentric girl whom I knew was named Abigail actually chose to speak with me. I'd noticed her before, I'd even marked her out as a possible friend, because she was the only girl brave enough to walk around by herself, or eat alone with a book, unlike the others who seemed to need to be touching hands with their friends as a prerequisite for their very existence. We intersected near the edge of the lawn. She was emerging from the trees, a red rope swinging from her hand, so distracted she was inches from colliding with me. Her chin jerked up and she gazed at me with such intensity that my defenses went up.

"You're the Art teacher's daughter."

"I know I am. I wouldn't be at this school if I wasn't."

She gave me a long, thoughtful look. "He's not very popular."

I shrugged. Though it was all very upsetting. "I don't care. That's not my problem."

"That's one of the reasons all the girls hate you. The other reason is that you're not very smart."

"I'm not supposed to be in high school yet!"

"Your paintings are good. You're better than some of the seniors."

Again I shrugged, though my feelings had swung in a new direction. To divert attention from the flush of pride that had come over me, I pointed to the red rope. "What's that for?"

She held up the rope, as if she hadn't realized till then what she was clutching.

"There's a stray dog in the woods. He used to let me pet him, but I haven't seen him for a while. If I find him, I'm going to use this as a leash." The girl's face became so overwhelmingly forlorn that I suddenly harbored nothing but generous feelings toward her.

"I could help you look," I offered. "We could call him."

"His name is Arnie. But he's really skittish. I don't think he'll come when we call."

"Oh."

She was a sad girl, maybe even sadder than me. Now she was looking off into the trees. Meanwhile, the need for a friend was flaring in me, from some once-dormant but now irrepressible source.

"That really is your dad?" she asked, abrupt, "you aren't lying?"

It was such an odd question that it took me aback. "He is. I guess I don't really look like him."

"My mom doesn't want me to talk to you." She saw my confusion at this, and explained: "You aren't the only teacher's kid at this school. You know your dad's assistant? The woman with long brown hair?"

"That's your *mom*?" A mix of surprise and joy bubbled high within me, because this was something big we had in common, enough to build a friendship upon. Then a small disappointment lapped back. I'd thought that the pretty woman had liked me. I guess she didn't like me that much.

"Why shouldn't you talk to me?" I pressed. "Why does your mother say that?"

But in the next moment the answer played itself out for us both. A bang echoed from my father's studio as the door swung open. Abigail's eyes opened wide with terror, though technically we were breaking no rules. Still, she turned and sprinted away toward the clumps of girls lounging around on campus, the unattached makeshift leash swinging and lashing the grass. I was so focused on watching her that I didn't notice the swiftness of my father's approach.

"What are you looking at? This is study hour. Why aren't you studying?"

His cheeks were tense with rage, and I cowered before him.

"I was about to start."

He looked across the lawn. "I don't want you wasting time chatting."

"Fine."

But he was still angry. "What is life, Katherine?" he asked.

I gripped my books. "Life is precious."

"And time?"

"Precious," I said. "More than gold. I was only taking a break for a second."

I turned and began making my way to one of the picnic tables where I could start on my math assignments. I hated being yelled at, but I wasn't too down: the simple reason was that, starting now, I had Abigail to think of.

And yet the next day Abigail ignored me. Then during the ensuing week of study times she did not so much as turn her head in my direction. But one day while I was drawing with my sketch book on my knees, looking off into the trees, she surfaced from across the lawn, so quiet that I was startled.

"I finished my homework, did you? I want to start looking for Arnie." She had the rope wrapped up her arm again, like a livid red thing she was trying to tame. I put down my pencil. "Is your father in his studio?" she asked.

"Yes," I said. "He teaches a morning class today. I bet he's locked himself in there till tomorrow."

She joined me on the grass. "I saw him yell at you that day after we talked."

"I hate him. He's been mean to me my whole life. He was worse to my mother."

"Then why did you come here?"

"It wasn't my choice. My mom lost custody of me so the state sent me here."

For some reason, Abigail seemed pleased by my answer. "Oh," she said. "I thought it was something else. I thought he wanted you here because you're so good at drawing." She stretched luxuriously on the grass then sat up.

"I have an idea. Want me to show you the river? There's a pathway just through those trees."

"I thought we weren't allowed to go?" I remembered my father's warnings on that first night of my arrival.

"We're not. But it's nothing to worry about. A lot of the older girls go there with their easels to paint. I bet you could make a beautiful picture if you tried it. It's just your style of landscape. Like the sketches you draw."

The gentle appeal to my ego had me convinced, and we headed into the shadow of the trees together, grabbing at twigs and ripping their leaves as we passed. We heard the water before we saw it. And soon the ground became damp and sticky under our shoes, and our destination appeared.

The river was wide and fast, and the water deep brown, almost black, from the mud churned up by the current. The air rushed along over it in sweet, cold gusts.

"Can you swim?" Abigail asked.

"Only a little."

"I can't swim at all."

We sat at the place right before the grass turned to mud, throwing stones. Abigail told me about her mother. She was a quiet woman who'd worked here for all of Abigail's life. She didn't paint, but she liked assisting the teachers. She'd been my father's assistant when he'd first worked here, and had resumed the position when he'd returned to the school three years ago.

"At least he's nice to her," I said.

"I wouldn't say that."

Then, before I could think of a way to find out more, Abigail turned to me with a mischievous grin. "Hey," she said, "do you ever play tricks on people, like April Fools'?"

"I hope you don't mean my dad."

"He won't know it's us. Here, take as many rocks as you can."

Despite my misgivings, I followed her lead: we made slings from the fronts of our shirts and filled them up with as many cold river stones as we could. As we walked back on the pathway, Abigail told me the plan: we would throw rocks at the studio walls, on opposite sides, so that my father would be running back and forth all confused. We reached my dad's studio and I stood in position behind a trio of apple trees and a large, gray plastic bin that held the badminton equipment. I can't explain what caused me to do this against my every, screaming instinct, except that I would have done anything to keep this new friendship alive.

I threw a stone and watched it hit: a dull thud on the wood. Then I heard the pound of rock hitting the wall on the far side. I stepped out and threw another stone. This one hit the window, a clanking noise that made me feel slightly sick. My courage failed. I dropped the rest of the stones and ran as fast as I could toward the side of the school. I had just neared the corner of the building when the sound of a fourth stone hitting the studio, and then of shattering, falling glass made me gasp.

The door knocked open and, immediately, my father caught sight of me. He had not seen Abigail in the bushes; at least she might have time to escape.

"What are you *doing*?" he yelled. I did not move, I was too scared. "You broke the window, you monster! They'll expel you for that!"

"I didn't break it." If it hadn't been true, I wouldn't have had the courage to say it.

"Then what, the wind?" He gestured across the empty campus.

"I didn't break it." I was crying now. "I can't throw as hard as that!"

This was absolutely the truth. All the windows at the Coventry School were storm windows: built to survive the worst New England blizzards. I couldn't understand how Abigail had not only cracked the glass but brought down both panes.

"Not as hard as that, eh?"

My father rested his hands on his hips. He contemplated the studio, the wretched, jagged hole in the glass; from this position, the lines in his face had gone slack. I waited for him to ask me again who did it, what older student with a grievance against him had passed this way. But he never asked. He never said, "Who?" If he had, I would have confessed, that was his power. But no, he slunk back into the shadowy interior of his damaged studio, leaving me still. A few minutes later, Abigail burst out of the trees laughing and alight with the thrill of success. She zipped across the lawn, a finger to her lips, and disappeared to the opposite side of the building, apparently headed for the front entrance, on her way into dinner.

We started sneaking to the river two or three times a week after that. I brought my sketch pad and would sit on a dry rock, outlining the moving of water, the labyrinth of branches, the vivacity of the natural world. A few times Abigail tried to get me to play another trick on my father, but I refused, and she mostly resigned herself to constructing little twig-and-moss houses in the roots of trees, which she imagined Arnie finding, and using as a refuge.

    We became careless. We skipped meals. I skipped math, and Abigail skipped whatever class she had during that time. We spent long, uncounted hours by the river, during which I pushed unpleasant thoughts of being caught here, of my father's menacing presence, firmly out of my head. The water rushed with a roar that sounded almost like it came from inside my own head, and we liked to let the dank, sweet and mud-smelling air dampen our flesh, and watch as the shadows of pine branches played games with the earth. Sometimes we'd simply sit transfixed, watching a leaf zooming down the current get caught, turn in dizzying, relentless circles, until it became too saturated, or folded over itself, and sank. On rare occasions, a group of older girls infringed on our privacy, but as far as we could tell they never ratted us out. In fact they seemed to desire only to keep a safe distance from us. So that once when I bumped shoulders with a senior girl accidentally – a girl in purple pompom earrings – she jumped back as if I were disgusting. Abigail, who was bolder than I, often shouted hello to them from upstream, and even called them by name, but not once did they answer her, and they seemed intent on pretending that they couldn't hear her – she, a lowly freshman, and I, even less than a freshman – over the sound of the water. That was fine. I filled a sketch book with nearly twenty drawings. Abigail liked to flip through them – she hated when I acted embarrassed – and she said that they were very good, and that I'd clearly inherited my father's talent. "The river's a perfect subject for you," she stated, so authoritatively that I almost had to laugh.

Of course, it couldn't go on forever. And one afternoon, our luck ran out. I was walking with my sketch book under my arm, and Abigail was close beside me, batting my shoulder and laughing at something, when we emerged from the trail where the Art teacher, my father, was setting up easels. We saw him right away. He stood about halfway between us and his studio: his gray shirt splattered with blues and greens and deep russet-reds – his signature colors – his bald head shining in the sun, and his face blank with shock.

"What are you doing?" He asked me that, though he could barely speak. His bright eyes were fixed upon Abigail.

Abigail looked at me worriedly, but encouragingly too, like she thought this could be my big chance to stand up for myself. Clearly she didn't understand anything. I started to cry.

"We were only down by the river," Abigail said, turning now to my father, taking charge and smiling prettily. "There's a dog that lives there. I was looking for him." She held up her right arm, which, as on most days, had the red rope wrapped around it. "Katherine was helping me."

"What dog?" my father sputtered.

"Arnie," she said. "Do you remember Arnie?"

When my father did not respond, Abigail sighed. Then she did something extremely bizarre: she took the bottom of her tee shirt and rolled it all the way to her neck.

There were pink, angry lines crisscrossed over her thin, pale torso, and across the two nascent lumps of her barely-there breasts. A deep cut slashed diagonally through the center of one pink nipple. I stared, horrified at the scars, at her nakedness, and so did my father.

"Arnie. He got scared while I was holding him. He ran away and I haven't been able to find him. Sometimes I think I see him in the woods. He must live there. But he won't let me catch him."

She smiled again, smug, and lowered her shirt.

"Can you see this?" my father asked suddenly, addressing me.

"A dog did it," I whispered, trying clumsily to apologize or somehow account for what Abigail had just done.

"Can you see a girl standing beside you?"

Now my eyes flashed away from Abigail and fixed upon him. A moment ago, I could only think about the strange behavior of the girl beside me, now my fear and surprise had transferred itself five paces onto my father instead. I was too young to know the many labels for crazy, though I knew enough – especially thanks to the erratic and often foul-smelling men who'd cozied up to my mother – to understand that it existed out there. People who were detached from the shared network of facts and experience.

But I did not have time to think more, for in a flash my father lunged forward, grabbed my arm and began pulling me toward the school with such strength that my feet missed the ground and dragged for several steps before my knees could lock again. The bell rang to mark the end of the fourth period classes, putting me in full view of several crowds of students, who, in my emergency, were mere blurs of khaki and horrified faces. He brought me to the threshold of my coffin-sized dorm room, waited for me to cross inside, then slammed the door. Adult voices arrived into the hallway. I could hear my father arguing with someone, perhaps the headmistress who'd never paid me much mind: "I know I fought to get her here, but I made a mistake. The other students are corrupting her mind!"

So be it. I felt finished with everyone. For several days I hardly left my room, except to use the toilet or to snatch a bit of food from the dining hall during the last ten minutes of mealtimes, when all of the tables were mostly cleared out. As for the students, I heard one girl say loudly in the hallway, "If she's so sick, shouldn't she move to the hospital?" causing me to discern I was the subject of some kind of lie on the part of the teachers. Though by the fourth night I wondered if even the girls were suspicious, for I could hear them at my door, scratching, tapping, cajoling me to speak to them through the wood. But after so long in the coolness of their neglect, I felt no need to satisfy their curiosity. In the dark, I lay curled under my quilt, hating the feeling in my stomach and listening to the sounds of far-off wolves in the forest.

On the fifth night, I was curled up against the far wall, when I heard a sudden twisting of the knob and the door creaking open. I sat up in bed, my heart beating hard. She was there: Abigail. She was hanging her weight upon the knob, her hair almost white in the dim light of the hallway lamp. She wore an old, threadbare jacket over a long nightgown, and sandals strapped over a pair of thick socks. She brought a finger to her lips. "Shhh."

"How'd you get in here?" I whispered. Even in my situation, I was not glad to see her. I was afraid of what kind of help she had come to offer. She ignored this question; she had something more urgent to tell me.

"I think my mom's with your father now. In his studio. Do you want to go see them?"

"He never lets anyone into his studio," I told her, feeling defensive. "He talks to himself. It might sound like someone's there, but they're not."

"Come look if you don't believe me."

With dread a chastising weight in my stomach, I slipped into a pair of loafers and followed Abigail out of the room and down the stairs into the cold night air. We were silent as we walked, lest we raise the other girls out of sleep. The lights were all ablaze in the studio. And as we approached, we could hear my father's voice.

"Don't you know that I'm tortured by it," he was saying thickly, as if caught inside a great emotion. "Every second of my life I think about it. I *regret*. I would do anything to turn back time. To have another chance."

Abigail motioned with one finger for me to look.

I turned my head. One eye closed against the studio wall, one peering through a section of jagged glass. My father kneeled in the middle of the studio, in the warm lamplight, his hands clasped and raised before him as if in prayer. He was not alone. There was his assistant, Abigail's mother. She was standing before the canvases, almost camouflaged by the like-looking figures. She was still and serene, her flesh smooth and luminescent, her eyes as hard and cold as the green-tinted stones you could find at the river. She wore a blue dress with the collar askew at her neck. With a jolt, I realized how much she resembled her company. The women standing behind her in the paintings had her same brown hair, her long arms, her blazing look. They were too similar in appearance to be anything else but a replication of herself: all this time, I realized with grief, despite my long-held assumptions, it must have been this woman, not my mother, forever repeating herself in my father's paintings.

"Please," he said now, shaking his hands at her waist. "I loved you. And Abigail. My beautiful girl, I loved her more than life itself. You want to torture me, but what does it matter? You know I never wanted you to suffer."

"There is only one thing you can do." The assistant teacher's voice was lovely and scary at once. "You understand. Only one thing."

My father's body sank, his hands came up to clutch his face and he sobbed into his palms.

"Please. I'm afraid of the water."

The woman did not move; she stared down at him, sympathetic as a statue. "If I could bear it, so can you."

I could feel Abigail shifting behind me. My muscles had become rigid with terror. A new, more appalling terror, because it was not my father causing this fear. I rose slowly, careful to remain out of sight of the woman and my father. Abigail regarded me with a calm half-smile on her lips. Our eyes were exactly level, we were just the same height. Now I realized something else. It was never me in the painting either. The likeness was close; but even closer was the likeness to Abigail.

"What are you?" I said.

"Those are my parents talking," she answered. "My mother and father."

"No."

"He would have told you about us, when you were older. He thought you were still too young to know."

"What's your mother doing to him?"

"He didn't treat us well," she said, a certain forbiddingness settling onto her face. "Much worse than he ever treated you and your mom. They had me when they were really young and it was a strain on him, but that's no excuse. He wanted to paint – he only wanted to paint – and he resented any second we stole from his work. If it weren't for us, he would have been a recluse, a complete obsessive, locked away with his canvases. But he couldn't do that with a baby and wife. He had to look for teaching jobs, and he hated us for that."

"What happened to you?"

We had switched positions now: Abigail stood with her back to the studio, and I was standing with my back to the school. I was edging backwards, casually, my loose nightgown tapping my legs.

"We were driving to this school," she said. "He'd taken the job and then regretted it and spent the whole week in a rage. He might have been drinking, I don't know. I was only your age when it happened. We were on that road we can see from the river. As we got close to the school, he went into a fit of yelling. He was telling us that his career as an artist was over, how we'd ruined his life. He stopped paying attention and the car veered and he drove right into the deepest part of the river. I was in the backseat with all the suitcases," she said, "with Arnie." She lifted her shirt to show me again the scars on her chest. "He didn't mean to hurt me. He was trying to get away, but I don't think he made it either. Only my dad did. His door opened in the crash and he floated right up to the surface. Me and my mom drowned in the car."

I had managed to move back several steps, toward the looming dining hall outcrop of the building.

"It hurt really bad," she said. "You can't imagine how much it hurts to die."

Her gaze, her stance, everything about her was insistent. But I didn't want to imagine anything; I think she saw that in me, and it made her angry. "My dad didn't know what to do with his life," she continued. "He took the job. He was a mess when it came to teaching his classes, but I guess they took pity on him, and at least he could be near the place where we died. Your mom met him nine years later and fell in love with him. He was so morose – so depressed. She wanted to make him into a rescue case. She knew what had happened and she convinced him that moving to Boston would do him good. But we didn't want him to go. He knew that. At least he came back."

"Has he always been able to see you?"

"Yes, as long as he's here, at the school."

"And the other people, the other students too, or just me?"

"As long as we stay near enough to the river, we can mingle with people as if we were still alive. It's nice to have a School for the Arts right here. It's nice to have people around. Though," she looked askance, thinking deeply, "I don't know how to explain it. We come through more clearly for you and my father. For other people, they tend to ignore us, but for you and your dad, we're fully present."

That was enough for me. As my father's voice began to rise again to a desperate pitch, I whirled around, and began springing toward the back door of the dining hall. I heard my father groan, "Katherine," but I knew he could not come to me, and that, even if he did, there was nothing he could do to help me.

I reached the dining hall door and, tripping over the step, bundled myself inside.

"Katherine," Abigail called from across the lawn. "Katherine, you don't have to be afraid. We aren't mad at you. It wasn't your fault for being born. But you know," she continued, a new edge to her voice, "you shouldn't treat me this way. If anything, you should be thankful to me. If my mom and I hadn't died, you wouldn't exist. Have you thought of that? My dad never would have married again. Do you realize what I'm telling you, Katherine? Because I've been thinking about it since the first day we met."

My body was braced against the door, my socks kicked off to give my feet traction on the wood.

"Okay," she said, a little sad, as if I'd hurt her feelings. "I'll leave you alone."

My father's voice quieted after that, falling to low, barely discernable moans. An hour passed, maybe more, and I never moved from my stance. Then, all of a sudden, I heard the unmistakable slam of the studio door.

The light poured out on the rough green lawn. Then in the bluish moonlight, I saw three figures walking swiftly towards the woods: the woman holding Abigail's hand, and a few feet behind them, my father. They were approaching the gap in the trees that Abigail and I had ducked in and out of so many times: the path that led directly through the woods to the river. My heart leapt, and a thick feeling rose in my throat. For I understood, then, the payment Abigail and her mother demanded of my father and, more, I understood what my father had, after perhaps years of resistance, finally agreed to do. And I knew too, instinctively, as sure as my quick breath on the window glass, that it was my own outrageous presence that had somehow hastened this long standoff to its present conclusion: he had seen Abigail with me, he'd called my name. He was trying to protect me, but he hadn't thought it all the way through: he hadn't realized that, as a result of his protection, I would blame myself for whatever happened to him tonight.

Fear released me from its hold. I burst from the dining hall, across the lawn, and toward the giant, swaying pine trees, black against the night sky. They were long out of sight. But it didn't matter, I knew where to find them. The sharp twigs and matted brush sliced my face and pierced the soles of my feet, but I didn't stop; I didn't slow down until I could hear the rush of the river.

Indeed, they were there, as I'd expected – except that they were not together. Abigail stood holding her mother's hand on a dry, high spot on the opposite bank, at the edge of the road – two ethereal forms that seemed almost to glow from within.

But my father was here, nearer to me, just at the bottom of the sloping bank. I could not see his face but I knew he was looking at them, and that they were, by their mere position and their own steady gazes, demanding that he cross the river to them: a distance of twenty-five feet which he was not meant to traverse alive.

"Father!" I screamed.

He looked at me, shocked. The woman acted as if she had not heard my call, but Abigail cocked her head toward me in a way that said: you again? I thought that we were done with you.

"Katherine," he said, "go home. You shouldn't be here. I don't want you to see this."

"No!" I ran towards him, down the slippery bank. My grasp closed around his freezing arm. I tried to pull him back to the trees. "You can't listen to them, they're trying to kill you."

"I know." He was stooped, resigned. "They're my family too," he said. "They have a right to ask I go with them."

"But you'll die!"

"That's the point," he said. "You'll be all right. You can go back to Boston. Your mother will pull things together. You're much better off without me. If you haven't noticed, I'm not too good at being a father in this world."

"You don't love me." Tears broke their constraints.

"No." In an absentminded gesture, he patted the top of my head. "That's not true."

"Then you love her more," I cried, glancing briefly at Abigail.

"No," he said again. "I love you the same. You and Abigail. You're both my daughters. If you were in her situation, I'd do the same for you."

They were watching us from the opposite bank, cold and tranquil and patient.

"They need me," he said. "And it's important that I go to them, that we be together."

"I don't understand." I was sobbing now. "Be together where?"

"You have no right to know that," Abigail answered for him, her voice impossibly sharp and clear above the rush of the river. "Not unless you're coming with us. Actually," she said, a sly expression lifting her lips, "maybe that's a good idea. I was the same age as you, when I died. I don't see why you should get more life than me."

But her mother touched her shoulder, quieting her.

"Go back to the school, Katherine," my father said. "Call for help. Tell them your father's missing and you don't know where he's gone. I'm an old, sad drunk with a fat file attached to my name. They'll decide for themselves what's happened to me."

And then there was nothing, nothing more I could do. I pulled and pleaded with him until my strength gave out, at which point, at last – with the love of my own life too robust – I released him. He told me again to go, and this time I crawled to the top of the bank, my feet slipping and sinking in the wet, soft earth. I gripped the sharp twigs of the brush at the tree line to hold myself up, then I turned.

"Father!" It was a desperate, futile scream. "Come back here!"

But his tall, slender form – the weight of the water was already pulling down on his clothes – did not twist around to look at me. His attention remained, to the last, fixed on *them*. I never saw his face again: as in my earliest memories of him, the spots of hair at the base of his scalp were the brightest things about him as I looked on. The water rushed around his knees, he stepped, and it covered up to his hips; now, to his waist. He paused there a moment, letting his hands skim the surface of the water, as if permitting them this last sensation. The dark sky was falling, melding into the earth. The two commanding figures waited motionlessly on the opposite bank: confident of meeting their aim. "Please, *please*." The words erupted from my throat in mournful tones, dissipating once they hit the vaporous air, and hardly sturdy enough to reach my own ears.

He stepped again, the water rising to his neck now, another step, and the water had half-subsumed what was left of him; and then, in a motion too horribly quick, the water lapped up over his head, a roof closing over him, and he was gone. By the time I looked up, the greedy and victorious figures on the opposite bank were already beginning to fade: a smug suggestion of ownership was the last of their earthly expressions. Finally I was alone in this night, with a damp breeze numbing my flesh, and the terrible rush of the river overrunning and filling my skull.

As far as child welfare services was concerned, I now became a difficult case. After they found my father – it took them a day, a passing driver noticed the body – no one was sure what to do with me. The school resisted keeping me on. I was too young;

and, apparently, it had only been at my father's insistence that I'd ever been allowed to take classes. Finally, after some weeks, I was, in one swift gesture, permanently removed from the place. For several months afterward I lived with a foster family: an experience which was mercifully free from further terror. Then several surprising things happened. The first was that, far from sinking deeper into a hopeless state at the news of her husband's death, my mother was miraculously buoyed by it; and by the time of the Christmas holiday – it happened so fast I could hardly believe it – I found myself delivered back to her care.

I began at my public school again, this time consistently. My mother reprised her medical work and soon accepted a nurse's assistant job at the university hospital near our apartment. Within the year, she had sold a few of my father's paintings; and we found ourselves with bank accounts boasting an actual excess of cash. We moved into a townhouse with two bedrooms and carpeted stairs. Around this time too, and this was a shock that exceeded the others, my father achieved a boom of fame in the art world. The paintings we'd sold had caused a stir, and sent collectors clamoring after the others. The large, terrifying figures in his canvases – backed by the biographical details of his family tragedy, his teaching job at a prestigious school, and what was thought to be his recent suicide – rendered him into one of those looming embodiments of despair that more contented people find irresistible.

Riding high on the wave of this wealth, now at age seventeen, I accepted an admissions offer from Amherst College, and once again went off to start a new life. I had never planned to talk about my father, or the bizarre episode in my childhood, but the first week of freshman year I found myself in a stranger's dorm room, sitting cross-legged on the floor, and sharing pours from a giant bottle of discount vodka with people I'd known for a matter of hours. We were each of us a little bit nervous, a little bit lonely, and desperate to secure a few friends. I suppose we were all searching out the quickest route toward intimacy, and that is why we started the game.

It went like this: we were to go around the circle, person by person, and answer the question, who were our ghosts? A boy with spiky hair and tinted glasses – the one who'd had the idea for the friendly diversion – volunteered to go first. For the last ten years, he said, he'd experienced regular hauntings from his grandmother. In life she'd been a stout, perpetually silent and unhappy woman who, after her husband died, had brought her family over from the Ukraine, at the height of mass starvations during the Second World War. She'd worked at a deli counter part-time, in addition to raising her children. As an old woman she'd asked to live with the family again, but the boy's father had said no, and the rest of the family had agreed with him, as the siblings had each wanted to keep their own rooms. A year later, the grandmother died from a fall at her nursing home, which turned out, in retrospect, to have been a terrible place. Now he couldn't escape her, and though the whole family regretted what had happened, it was too late to quiet her wrath.

The next person in the circle confessed in quiet and evasive tones that he was haunted by his babysitter, who had sexually abused him, then perished in a skydiving accident, before he'd acted upon a plan to confront her. A girl said tearfully that she was haunted by her family cat – dead five years – because she was the one who'd left the front door open, and therefore allowed the animal to escape and dart out into the road. When it was my turn, I was ready for it, and I spoke at length. I told the story of my father and his first wife and Abigail and the Coventry School for the Arts. I described the girls and the teachers, the mingling of these menacing presences, and, if I say so myself, I had the crowd hooked and maybe even a few of them quaking. We were about to move on to the person beside me – I was treating my throat to a large slug of vodka – when the boy with spiky hair and glasses interrupted.

"But wait," he said. "They don't haunt you anymore, do they? The first wife and the daughter?"

"No." I swallowed and wiped my lips. "They disappeared that night at the river and never came back."

"So in a way," he pressed, in the manner of pursuing a fine, academic detail, "they never really haunted you at all. They were your father's ghosts, not yours. Once they had him, they stopped making trouble."

"I guess that's true," I said slowly, acquiescing the point. "Abigail was jealous of me. But not enough to stay with me and follow me back to Boston."

"Because you had nothing to do with them." His voice was excited. "All the bad stuff happened before you were born."

"That's right," I said. Then, remembering the parameters of the game, I added, "I guess I don't have any ghosts of my own."

He had been making eyes at me all night, this boy. Perhaps you'd even say we'd been flirting. Now once again he picked me out from the group. From across the circle, he raised a plastic cup in my direction.

"That's a good thing," he said. "Cheers."

The Magpies

Kate Alice Marshall

ONE FOR SORROW

The day Addison kills Catherine Martin, the sun casts only a weak and reluctant light. The fall air is cool and damp; midterms are just around the corner. It's always been a good time for the magpies. Stressed students are careless ones, and while normal students might skip breakfast or forget their homework in the library, the legacies leave behind more tempting treasures for Addison and Ellory to poach.

The wind blows in from the northeast as Addison crouches on the sidewalk beside the quad. It carries a hum that vibrates in her bones. Last spring she stole the language of the wind from a frightened boy who scratched strange symbols into his arms, but the understanding has faded over the months. All she can hear now is a faint susurrus of disjointed words. *Intent, intrude, invade*, they whisper.

Addison presses her palm to the concrete. Beside her splayed fingers, a crack spreads brittle arms in four directions. If any of the students striding past her had thoughts beyond their essays and exams, they might see it reflected in her pupils, lines limned in gold.

She's a girl of soft edges: plump lips, smooth milky skin, doe eyes. She's all curves and quiet. Not so Ellory, drawing near – a sprig of a girl, sharp chin and sharper eyes, a buzz of energy about her. She halts and watches Addison's lips move in recitation: prime numbers, perhaps, or the digits of pi, or the Fibonacci sequence.

Addison blinks, sighs, straightens. "What is it?" Ellory asks. Above them, the wind sighs. *Unclaimed, untold, unknown*, it says.

"Not sure. It doesn't want to come yet," Addison says, her lips in a focused frown. "Not for me, at least."

Ellory kneels by the crack, an eager tension in her neck. Addison bites back a rebuke. She can tell at a glance whatever power is trapped in that shape isn't made for Ellory, and surely so can the other girl, but it doesn't stop her tracing it with a fingertip to test.

"El," Addison says. Tilts her head. "We should go."

Ellory pushes herself roughly to her feet. "Just checking. Haven't found anything in a while." Her fingers twitch. Never mind that she teased the trick of seeing in the dark from a lingering echo just last week. Addison knows, but does not say, that Ellory is no longer content with the bits and baubles they scavenge. No longer happy to call herself a magpie. Addison knows, but does not say, that it will get her killed someday.

They walk with brisk steps to the double doors of the dining hall. Like all the buildings at the school, it's old – older than it ought to be, better suited to the old world of Europe than the comparative teenager of the American northeast. The stones that make its walls are unhappy things, grumbling (if you know how to listen) of the way time contorts and angles refuse to remain stable here.

As always, even with so few people up and about, the dining hall has sorted itself into two main groups. The general population students, pulling their hair out over literature finals and Latin declensions, and the legacies. You can tell them apart by their wealth and by their names – which are stamped on buildings and plaques everywhere around campus – but most of all by the look in their eyes. It's one of terror and hunger, slightly unfocused, as if they are seeing something not quite there. They move in groups, sometimes whispering, sometimes eerily silent. They vanish to classes that never appear on the schedule. They are the reason this school exists. The rest of the students, students like Addison and Ellory, are merely cover – and a convenient source of funding.

Do you see Catherine? Ellory asks in Addison's mind as she loads her plate with eggs. She ticks her chin toward the table in the corner where the legacies sit.

Addison risks a glance. Catherine Martin sits at a table with four other legacies. Her plate is full and untouched in front of her, hands resting lax on the table to either side. She stares straight ahead as tears roll down her cheeks. No one else looks. No one else pays any mind at all.

What do you think is wrong with her? Ellory asks. Addison only frowns and pours herself coffee. The door knocks open, letting in a stray tongue of wind.

Rebuke, it whispers. *Repent, refuse, renounce.*

Addison looks away from the girl whose blood will coat her hands before the sun rises again.

TWO FOR BLOOD

The first time Ellory stole a bit of magic was entirely by accident. She saw the legacies flitting around: carrying books with leather bindings, staring up at the stars with rapturous intensity, breaking into quiet weeping in the library stacks. Like everyone else at the school, she hadn't wondered about it, inculcated by whatever magic kept the legacies' work secret. Then came the shadow in the hall, one night when she stole out of her dorm room to use the bathroom. Just a shadow, a smudge of darkness on the wall, but with nothing to cast it. For an instant her mind rebelled, began to blot it out, and then—

The words leaped to her lips. "'Swift as a shadow, short as any dream; Brief as the lightning in the collied night.'" Shakespeare, of all things; she was knuckles-deep in the text that week, picking apart each line for hidden strands of meaning, and with these words the shadow began to fix itself in her mind. She reached for the rest of the line, felt the darkness wobble, and then – "'That, in a spleen, unfolds both heaven and earth, And ere a man hath power to say "Behold!"'"

And behold she did. She saw the shadow. Saw what it was, what it meant, saw its edges and its depths, and for an instant – one blinding instant – she could see something else beyond that, vast and powerful and far away, but then it was gone. It was gone and the shadow was gone, because she was the shadow and it was her.

That's how it works. You don't take the magic, you understand it, and in understanding you make room for it. It's yours. Or it's you. They aren't sure. They aren't legacies; they've never been able to study the laws that govern this world they pick and pluck. They're magpies, that's all. Collecting bright, discarded things that appear as cracks in the sidewalk, the dappled shadows of tree leaves, scraps of birdsong on endless repeat. The uses of such power are small, too. A tiny tongue of flame at the tip of Addison's finger. A bag that never grows too heavy, no matter how many textbooks Ellory packs in it.

Echoes, splinters, remnants. No more.

There are rules to being a magpie. Take only what won't be missed. Never force power to come to you; it will come readily, when it's meant for you.

Never get caught.

Ellory knows the rules. She made them, after all. And she's watched the legacies labor and struggle. She's seen what happens when they fail. She notices when they vanish, even if no one else does. Forcing mastery over magic is dangerous, and the magpies can't afford danger. Not when they know so little.

And yet it's not enough.

It's never been enough.

Ellory is keen-eyed, clever, and hungry. Such girls aren't content with bits of bright thread and crumpled foil to line their nests.

After breakfast they walk past a legacy boy, bent-necked with a book on his lap. Ellory cups her hand and angles it just so, and light glimmers in it like the cool surface of a pond, reflecting the view over his shoulder. The words on the page are almost Greek, but not quite. She recognizes the boy – he hustles in and out of language classes all day, freckles stark against increasingly pale cheeks. Language must be his lens. That's what the legacies call it. To master magic is a process of translation, turning the unknowable into the knowable. You can approach it through any means the human mind has to craft meaning and sense from the world. Language, poetry, art, mathematics. Addison's is numbers. Fractals, orbital equations, and the like. The closer to true power, the less sense they make to anyone else, the more they look like madness.

For Ellory, it's always been poetry. What better way to comprehend what can't be comprehended? A poem is a sly tool, slipping in angled meaning between syllables, making truth from contradiction, irony, guileful metaphor. In the rhymes and meters of sonnets she's heard languages never spoken; in the shivering repetition of a villanelle she's numbered the stars caught in an unseen maw; in a cascade of unrestrained verse she's bound to herself a slant of light that shone on another world entirely.

We should be doing more, she says to Addison, parting her fingers to let her reflected glimpse vanish.

Why? Addison asks. Her look is mournful. She stands bowed by the weight of what she thinks is conscience, but Ellory knows is fear. *I thought this was just for fun.*

There's more out there. I want to find out what it is. The legacies aren't doing all of this for a few party tricks, Ellory says.

Addison's voice is quiet, wary. "How much more will be enough?"

She knows the answer. They both do. It will never be enough.

There's no such thing.

THREE FOR THE CITY

Ellory frightens Addison sometimes. She's grown leaner since they began their collecting, her gaze sharper, holding herself constantly like a hawk watching for a mouse among the grass. When Addison was young, she thought magic would be a wondrous, joyful thing, but she was wrong. It's terrifying. Every piece of it she takes into herself changes the shape of her. She finds bruises on her hips because she can't keep track of where she ends anymore, but Ellory – she revels in it.

Addison cannot help but feel that something terrible is going to happen. Ellory is not content to stick to her own rules anymore. She is going to reach for something too great to contain safely, and they won't have the knowledge or the guidance to survive it. The legacies huddle with their special professors – Gant and Franklin and Singh and the rest, each of them with their specialties and with that silvered look in their eyes – and still they don't all make it. She's tracked them, the ones that fail. Some of them transfer to other schools. Normal schools. Some of them go home for unspecified medical reasons. Some of them vanish completely.

She is thinking of this – of the danger Ellory is in, that she herself has so studiously avoided – as she walks through the halls that night and hears the weeping. Addison does not pause to realize that there is no reason she ought to be in this particular hallway, in the Stephenson Art Building; it does not strike her as strange that she can't remember anything between now and when she left her professor's office earlier this afternoon (*One more thing*, she thinks Professor Franklin might have said, and then—). She only hears someone crying, and thinks she might be able to help.

Her kindness is, perhaps, more dangerous than Ellory's ambition.

She knows the voice, the source of the weeping. She knows who she will find in the art room when she pushes open the door. Catherine Martin. She kneels on the floor. Paper is scattered around her, huge sheets torn from sketch pads and obliterated by violent lines of charcoal. Each image is the same: five concentric circles, each missing fractions of its circumference, each level joined to the next with short, straight lines. It repeats and repeats, and yet she is drawing it again, her palms blackened and her face streaked as if by soot. Her hair hangs wildly around her shoulders, in front of her face. She's stripped off her shirt, leaving her torso bare. Another racking sob shakes her body and makes the skin tighten over her ribs.

"Catherine," Addison says. Catherine looks up. Her eyes are occluded, veiled in silver. The charcoal smearing her cheeks is cut by the tracks of her tears, sorrow in negative space.

"Can you see it?" she asks. "Is it still there?" She claws at her back. Addison steps around her.

The shape she has drawn again and again is echoed on her flesh. *In* her flesh. A geometric oddity composed of absence, gaps in her skin, in her being. Beyond the narrow channels through her skin is not blood or bone or flesh but glimpses of something else that makes Addison feel dizzy, and she gasps, staggering a step she thinks will take her away but only draws her closer to it.

Catherine cranes her neck, looking over her shoulder. "Do you see the city?" she asks, her voice a croak.

"What city?" Addison asks, unable to look away. Her fingers dig into her arms, but the pain doesn't register.

"I dream of it," Catherine says, the tears still flowing in silent synchrony down each ashen cheek. "I dream of red stone and red roads, and of the red sun that hangs in the red sky, and the songs – the songs are red, too, and the king is robed in red, and I see him, Addison, I see him and *he sees me*, he sees me, he sees—"

She curves forward, a knuckle bitten hard between her teeth to stifle a scream. The movement should stretch the pattern on her back but it somehow remains unchanging.

Addison reaches out a hand, not quite meaning to. She only wants to know what it feels like – whether her fingertips will slip inside those indentations. But as her hand grows close, the shape refuses interruption. There is no pain. Only an insistent numbness as the lines of the symbol carve themselves through her existence.

Still bent, hands covering her face, Catherine speaks with disconcerting calm. "We seek it. We did not know. I thought that I could capture it. Chiaroscuro, impasto, texture and shape and absence, the form and the abstraction – what more human thing can there be? We painted beasts on cave walls and put our handprints next to them, and mastered the whole of this world, and I thought I could do the same. I thought it would be the key to the city and it *was* and now I can't stop it turning. I can't get it off."

Addison can barely hear her. She's looking at the shape, part of it now carving through her hand. A pattern. A key. That shape is a key – no. A keyhole. You shape the thing, you are shaped to the thing – it is the lock and *you* are the key.

The tumblers click into place within her.

There is a moment, whenever the magpies claim one of their little scraps. It is the clear and crystalline instant when they know with absolute certainty that they have succeeded. That the thing they are trying to claim has accepted their bid; that if they push only the tiniest bit more, it will become part of them. It's like a shiver in the air. Like the moment before a kiss.

This, though. This is like drowning. Lungs empty, vision blackening, and the surface of the water just above, if she could only lift her face and breathe – but there is something else there, too, above the surface, and maybe it is better to drown.

"Please," Catherine says, her voice now childlike, frightened. "Please take it away from me."

"Hold still."

FOUR FOR THE FLOOD

Oh lovely, timid girl. Back to the nest the wounded bird flies, to her place of safety, and waits. Ellory returns frustrated from a late night prowling the grounds, the shape of the damn sidewalk crack a teasing, itching pulse at the back of her mind. She throws aside her bookbag and opens her mouth to rant about the unfairness of it all and then she sees Addison on the bed. Naked, hunched, cross-legged, hands limp in her lap and colored wrong.

Ellory thinks *paint* and *mud* and *a curious light* before she thinks *blood*, before she sees it splashed across Addison's chest and throat and chin as if she's bitten into a peach and let the juices dribble down.

"Do you see?" Addison asks. She rises, wraith-like, and God

help her but Ellory wants to flee. "Do you see?" she asks again, and turns, but there's only the smooth expanse of her back.

"I don't see anything," Ellory tells her, fearful. "Addison, whose blood is that?"

"I tried to get it free without hurting her," she says. "But she tore."

And then she collapses.

The next minutes are both frantic and oddly calm. There's so much to do, after all, and so little time for panic. There's the blood to clean up and Addison's clothes to find and dispose of. Ellory scrubs the drying blood from beneath her best friend's fingernails and tries not to think *It should be mine.*

Addison doesn't wake for the rest of the night, but dreams fitfully and murmurs of a city and a crown and a great rushing tide. For three days, fevers grip her. She babbles of cobblestones and kings; she vomits up briny liquid in which small, unseemly things flick their cilia. Catherine's absence is at first marked, then swiftly unremarked. Professors Leclerc and Calvin mutter outside the art studio in muted argument; Ellory finds bloodied rags burning in the basement and that's the last hint Catherine ever stepped foot on school grounds.

With every scrap and glimmer of power she's gleaned, she sets herself to two purposes: easing Addison's suffering and finding some kind of answer to what is happening to her. How to stop it.

Ellory can't wake her. Can't remove the magic carving its crater in her skin. Can't forgive her. Addison was always the one who urged caution. *Don't. We shouldn't. It's dangerous.*

Yes, they had the rules, but rules are for children. They're made to be outgrown. Ellory tried to make Addison see that, but

Addison always resisted. And then she was the one to reach in with both hands? To claim a greater power? Ellory isn't sure if she's angrier at the hypocrisy of it or the failure.

Because Addison has failed. That's plain to see. She's burning up and she's drowning and Ellory wouldn't have. *It should have been me, you darling fool,* Ellory thinks, mopping sweat from her best friend's brow. And now Addison will die, and Ellory will have nothing to show for it but her spite.

Professor Franklin finds her on the third day. It's a quiet moment of weakness: fists balled up and vision blurred, hiding – unsuccessfully – in an alcove outside the library where she has just tried and failed to walk into the special collections wing. Legacies wander out with stacks of books, but she's left with only a migraine.

"I haven't seen your roommate lately," Franklin says. He's young. The kind of young that makes things dangerous, with his soft brown eyes and long, nimble fingers. Girls – boys, too – titter over him and contrive ways to brush those elegant hands with their own. But Ellory sees the distaste behind his smile, the simmering disdain in his eyes for those silly young things. He has no interest in them.

Today the top two buttons of his shirt are undone, his sleeves rolled up to show forearms inked with a pair of serpentine beasts. His eyes are sharp and leave no shadows to hide in.

"She isn't feeling well," Ellory says. "I think it might be the flu."

His head tilts, his expression considering. It's the look of a man in a play, features arranged for effect. "Interesting," he says, "that she fell ill the same day poor Catherine met her end."

"Her end?" Echoing him, she sounds dimwitted and

contemptibly dull. The sneer in his smile appears, just a hint at the corner of his mouth, and the effect is both instant and catastrophic. Ellory's stomach twists, heart thuds liquidly, hands grow clammy in the grips of her shame.

"Let's not play games," he suggests. "We are better than that. I know what you do, the two of you. The magpies, isn't that right?"

She stammers. His smile only spreads. Heat flames her cheeks but she finds her voice and her dignity. "If you know so much, why are we standing here talking? Shouldn't I have disappeared? Suffered a tragic accident?"

"Is that what you think we do when one of our shadowless stumbles on a great truth?"

"I—" she begins.

"You," he says, "are correct. The secrets we study are dangerous. Not just the knowledge but the knowing – do you understand?"

"A bit. Not enough," Ellory concedes. The truth feels more important than appearing smart right now. His sharp nod signals approval.

"At the same time, you are not our usual innocent blundering into things beyond them. Some so-called scholar addled by tales of potions and magic spells. You've been careful and canny, and with no training you've accomplished more than some of the coddled scions of old bloodlines we're usually saddled with."

"The legacies," Ellory says.

"Is that what you call them? Apt," he says. "All legacies grow old and flaccid given enough time, and must be revived with fresh blood. I could offer you a place in the endeavor, Ellory. If you can claim a great enough power to impress the others."

The whole time he's speaking, he's growing closer, leaning in. His voice stays soft but the weight of it intensifies until he seems to be whispering directly into her soul – if such a thing exists – and then he is so close she could lean forward and kiss those thin, arrogant lips – but then the last word fades and she blinks, and he is standing no nearer than before, well back and well within the bounds of propriety.

"What kind of power?" she asks. Her voice is hoarse and hungry.

"You know the answer to that."

"Will it save her?"

"You know the answer to that, as well."

She wishes it felt worse. She wishes her heart rebelled even a little at the notion, but she discovers this is a price she is not unwilling to pay.

"Come with me," Franklin says, and she does.

He explains. It takes time; it is not easily comprehended, being at its heart a paradox, a puzzle, an impossibility.

Know this—

There are vast realms incomprehensible by humanity. No part of us is built to interact with them on any level, from the cellular to the spiritual. The barest edge of them seeps into our dreams, but they lie *beyond* dreams. We cannot enter such realms, and they cannot enter here. Thus the legacies seek not transportation, but translation. To turn a piece of our world *into* theirs; and in return, to transpose our world, ourselves, on that other realm. By this transformative process, if it could be engineered and reversed, we could explore the worlds beyond dream. Worlds where our rules do not apply, and the boundaries of the possible may be utterly demolished.

Every mind in this place is turned toward the task. To transmute a vial of water into the brine of a salt sea in which leviathans teem; to tattoo themselves with words from a book written by a nameless monk in the monastery of glass; to chart the stars of skies that stretch over plains of living flesh. But there is one goal that rises above all the rest.

To be the first to enter the city at the center of worlds, to claim its knowledge, and return.

"Do you understand?" Franklin asks, eyes burning with an acolyte's fervor.

"No," Ellory says. "Not yet."

"Good."

FIVE FOR THE TRUTH

Addison dreams. Or perhaps it is more accurate to say that dreams consume her. She is not the actor but acted upon, and this is what she sees: *A city.* The name of it either does not matter or does not exist. While Addison dreams of it (while it dreams of her) Ellory learns from Franklin that it is called by some the Crimson City, and it is the great endeavor at the heart of the school. To Addison, of course, it is not a goal but an affliction.

A king. His station is plain by his raiment, by his throne (a spike of translucent red like tree resin) and by the jagged three-thorned crown that rests on his brutish brow. Beneath the crown she cannot make out his face. (*Do not,* Franklin warns, *look upon the face of the Crimson King. There is no death that can save you from what comes next.*)

An ocean. Within it roil two serpents, one black and one yellow. They twist and writhe and make the seas heave with their movements. Within their coils is grappled something of terrible size and demented geometry. (Ellory cannot help the way her eyes fix on the inked bodies of the ropy beasts, and the musculature that moves and flexes beneath them.)

Catherine. The girl stands hip-deep at the ocean's edge with the city arrayed behind her. *Listen,* she says. *I know now what I didn't then. We were wrong. It is –* (*a key,* says Franklin. *A key which fits a door to at last allow a living being to pass from this world to another. Not by the imprecise and perilous process of translation, but truly, physically. We must*) *– never let them do it. Do you see? It will lead only to disaster.*

Addison wakes in her bed with an ache and an itch between her shoulder blades. She is hungry, and she is alone.

She rises, nude, blood at the roots of her hair where Ellory missed it. Something moves beneath the skin of her back like a pupa shifting in its cocoon. She's so hungry. So empty. So thin a casing over the thing gestating in the space behind her lungs.

No one sees her. She is not a thing they can behold any longer. She staggers down the hall and into a dream of a beautiful young man who has spent three months trying to understand a couplet written by a dying monk. In it, he's sure, is a secret – or a power, or a weapon, or an answer that will impress his professors (but really, his parents). His name is Dorian and it is his misfortune that he can see Addison, see the thing she has become; he sees her and knows her and knows what is about to happen, and all at once his eyes widen.

"I've got it," he says. "I understand." He begins to weep, and whether with fear or relief, even he couldn't say. Addison reaches for him.

"I don't," she says. "I don't understand at all."

She touches his face. There is no malice in her. The same cannot be said for the pupating presence at her back. Like all great works, it requires certain things. Among them raw materials and empty space – the sort of empty space provided by the excision from the world of a beautiful boy who only truly longed to study poetry. Grief will soon pack the wound and time scab it over, but not before the work is done.

She untangles him in the basement and begins.

SIX FOR A LIE

Hours later, Ellory goes to find her friend. The room, of course, is empty, but they have ways of keeping track of one another. She hums a note and its vibration tells her where to go. The note today is sour. Corruption has crept in.

She finds Addison in the basement, tending to her art. The beautiful boy has been deconstructed, abstracted – not even bones and flesh any longer but merely color, shape, texture. From what he was she's built something on the floor that makes Ellory think of magic circles and fairy rings. Addison crouches in the corner, her gore-streaked hands a cage before her face.

Ellory's heart gives another hard thump of love and guilt

and horrible longing. She goes to Addison and kneels before her.

"Do you see?" Addison whispers. (*Why do all this?* Ellory had asked Franklin.)

"You made a door," Ellory says. (*To claim the one power mankind has always sought and never achieved. The power to conquer death itself. Kings and priests and alchemists have all sought immortality. But it doesn't lie in this world. We must find it elsewhere.*)

"If we want to step through the door, the door has to be us," Addison says. "He was so afraid. He was—"

"It's not your fault." Ellory lays her hand gently on Addison's wrist. She aches for her friend. The magic that comes to Addison has always been soft and kind and beautiful, and it wasn't until talking to Franklin that Ellory realized just how rare and astonishing that is. How little kindness makes it through the veil of dreams.

"I was trying to save her," Addison whispers. And then, "I can't stop it."

"It's not your fault. It's too powerful," Ellory tells her. *And you never were.* "Catherine was trying to find the key to the worlds beyond dreams. They've searched for centuries. That kind of power... you couldn't have known."

Addison's hand twists. It seizes Ellory's so tight the bones grind together. Addison looks like she's about to say something, but she only shakes her head. Ellory smiles tremblingly. "It will be all right. We can help you. We have a plan."

When Franklin arrives soon after and sees what Addison has created, his eyes alight with an almost religious awe. The swirls of viscera and sinew, the knotted bone, the delicate stranding of nerves. The shape is not one made for the minds of those who live their lives awake; only the skittering logic of dreams can make sense of it. Across the hideous spill, Addison kneels, hands resting lightly in her lap, blood-soaked hair offering a parody of modesty where it hangs over her breasts. Ellory makes the third part of their triangle, pacing tightly to and fro. Addison watches her. Watches Franklin.

It is important to know that Addison is diminished, but no part of her is gone. It is more that something *else* is taking up space within her soul, like gas forced into a sealed vessel of water. She is not replaced but compressed, and the soft and diffuse girl she was has become concentrated, dense as steel.

"Addison," Franklin says, tone honeyed and solicitous. "Ellory told me what happened. I can help. Don't be afraid."

"I am not afraid," Addison states. "The time for fear has passed."

He blinks, unsure what to make of this. In the end he nods, smiles. "Then shall we begin? Ellory." He beckons Ellory with an outstretched hand. She takes it lightly and, at his touch, shivers. "You can do this," he murmurs. He brushes his thumb across the back of her hand, and when she wets her lips his eyes fix on the movement.

"What do we do?" Ellory asks, dots of color high on her cheeks.

"I'll show you. I'll be with you every step of the way," he promises.

Together, they wash the gore from Addison's skin, only to paint it fresh with their own blood.

The students at the school begin their quest for the worlds

beyond dream by caging the strange with the familiar. They capture small motes of power, comprehending them with known languages, mathematical expressions, artistic techniques, quoted poetry. Most can manage it. Far fewer succeed in going further, in freeing their minds from the laws and structure of this world. Linguistics, chemistry, meter and rhyme – they are the foundation, but we build beyond them. The symbols Franklin paints on Addison's skin come from an alphabet that not only has never been spoken on Earth but never *could* be.

Franklin reaches out one of those lovely long-fingered hands to take Addison's. He guides her to the center of the bloody sigil. He tells Ellory the words to speak. Words to open a door. Words to make a key. Words to unmake a girl.

"That's it?" Ellory asks.

"That's it. Simple," he says. "Then we will have achieved something no one ever has. It will guarantee you a place among us."

Her lip trembles. "I don't know if I can do this," she says. A tear streaks down her face. "I can't— I—"

"Shh," he says. He draws near and cups her cheek. "You can. You want this. You are so close to having everything you longed for."

"I know," Ellory says. There is enough time for the briefest of quizzical looks to cross his face before Addison, moving on swift and silent feet, brings a bit of stray pipe down on the back of his head.

It is all too easy to forget the hard edges of our world and the simplicity of the laws of physics, when you spend all your days defying them.

SEVEN FOR THE DAY TO COME
WHEN EVEN DEATH SHALL DIE

Franklin wakes to what should be a nightmare. A girl with bloodied teeth stands over him. When she turns away, her back is hinged open, ribs splayed out like beetles' wings, baring a hole where something once nested. And when he looks down, that thing – limbless, faceless, yet beholding him just the same – crouches on his chest. He tries to scream, but is no longer something that can do so.

It is the last mercy of his life that there is no reflective surface nearby with which he can see what he has become.

He tries in vain to speak.

Shh, says Ellory's voice in his mind.

It's no use, Addison tells him. They take their places at either side of him and interlock their fingers.

Why are you doing this? he asks, plaintive. *I thought you wanted power. I thought you wanted a place.*

And I will have it. I will claim *it. With your help. Isn't that what you promised?* Her voice is impatient. She's done with him.

Ellory and Addison start to speak. The words begin as half-familiar syllables, but soon twist into sounds no human tongue should be able to produce. Between them, this small and venal man writhes.

Know this.

It is Ellory, it is Addison, it is both and neither.

You are fools. All of you. You seek a key. A door. A passageway. But a door may be walked through in either direction. You have chased after the end of death but found only its certainty.

The wriggling thing that still has Franklin's face goes still.

"Do you see him?" Addison hisses. Franklin's mouth opens. It is not his breath that forces its way through his throat but a wind from elsewhere, one that stinks of brine and rot.

"I see him, and he sees me. He is I, and I am he," he intones, and the last flickers of his humanity show only in the horror in his eyes.

"There are so many worlds. I know that now," Addison says. "You sought those most cruel, and your seeking drew them nearer. What does that say about you and your precious endeavor?"

"He is near. He is near!" cries the corpse of their teacher.

The key is in the lock. They cannot let it open. They cannot let through the being that stands eagerly on the other side. "Wait," Ellory says. "Wait a moment—"

For she longs to see. She longs to catch a glimpse of just the corner of that robe, to spy the shape of that crown. She is certain she could bear it. She is certain she could be quick enough.

With one wrenching gesture, a sound like the severing of a throat, Addison breaks the key – breaks Franklin. The broken key will jam the lock. Will hold the door shut for good (*for a time*).

The glistening heap in the center of the circle gives one last rippling shudder and is still. Ellory lets out a breath, shoulders sagging. She knows it was the right thing to do. She will always harbor some small sliver of hatred for Addison because of it.

But it is done. Slowly, the wound at Addison's back seals itself. The thing that inhabited her is gone and she unfurls into herself.

Ellory stares at the door, the key. Both are dissolving, turning to gray, acrid vapor.

"There are other worlds," Addison says, almost in supplication. "Kinder ones."

"And you can seek them," Ellory replies. She lifts her eyes to Addison's. What burns there is a lust untempered by the horrors she has witnessed. Her hunger has only grown, and what Addison has always thought was a small, restrained part of her is now unleashed entirely.

In that moment, Addison realizes the mistake she's made. She thought she knew her friend's true self, the person she wanted to be. But Ellory has always been this. Has always been one of them, in her heart.

Ellory's chin tips up. "I will claim my place, as promised. I've proven myself. They won't deny me. Or you. We've done what they couldn't."

"You'd join their endeavor, knowing where it leads?" Addison asks. "Three people are dead already."

Ellory looks for a moment as if she's trying to remember who Addison is talking about. To add it up. Which did she forget? Weeping Catherine? The terrified boy? Ellory only waves a hand. "This door wasn't safe. Or we weren't strong enough for it. But there's more power out there, and I mean to find it." Her eyes burn with endless appetite.

The last of the door is gone. All that's left is the two of them.

"Come with me," one of them says, in their voice a note of pleading. It doesn't matter which. The answer is the same.

AND ONE – AGAIN

They speak a few times more, after that, but none of the words spoken signify anything; the end was the basement, and it's that moment they remember. Addison leaves soon after. Ellory stays. She's right about the place she's earned. Here, her betrayal is a sign of her strength. It earns her a welcome, and it earns her enemies, and it's impossible to say which is more dangerous. She doesn't mind. She is more dangerous still.

The endeavor continues.

To Ellory, to all at the school, Addison ceases to be of interest. They think her weak, soft, fearful; they think she is turning away from something, but she is turning toward it. There are other worlds, other roads, other doors, and she cannot believe that they contain only horror. It's just that such worlds were easier for those ambitious minds to comprehend. She longs for kinder magics, and she finds them, in her slow and quiet way. She tells no one. She takes only what is freely given. She is, for a time, happy. And so, for her part, is Ellory.

We should leave them there. We should not linger. We should not stay to witness the morning Addison wakes with Ellory's voice in her mind.

Do you see? Do you see him? The crown – I have – the sea is at the gates – we have done it, Addison, we've—

There is no more.

Addison rises, and sits on her porch, and waits for the sun to rise. She wonders if Ellory is looking up at the sun, too.

She wonders if that sun is red.

ABOUT THE AUTHORS

Erica Waters is a lifelong Southerner who now lives in Salem, Massachusetts. She writes dark fantasy and gothic horror. Her novel *The River Has Teeth* won the Bram Stoker Award® for Superior Achievement in a Young Adult Novel and was also an Indie Next pick and a *Kirkus Reviews* Best Young Adult Book of 2021. Erica's other works include *Ghost Wood Song*, *The Restless Dark*, and *All That Consumes Us*. She is also a contributor to the bestselling folk horror anthology *The Gathering Dark*.

Genevieve Cogman started on Tolkien and Sherlock Holmes at an early age, and has never looked back. She is the author of the Invisible Library series and the Scarlet Revolution series. She has an MSc in Statistics with Medical Applications and has wielded this in an assortment of jobs: clinical coder, data analyst, and classifications specialist. Although *The Invisible Library* was her debut novel, she previously worked as a freelance roleplaying game writer. Genevieve's hobbies include patchwork, knitting, and gaming, and she lives in the north of England. She has far too many books about Goetia.

Jamison Shea (they/them) is the author of dark fantasy I Feed Her to the Beast duology and speculative standalone *Roar of the Lambs*, hailing from Buffalo, NY, and now dwelling in the dark forests of Finland. When they're not writing about monsters, they're drinking milk tea or searching for eldritch horrors in uncanny places.

Elspeth Wilson is a writer interested in exploring the limitations and possibilities of the body. Her pamphlet, *Too Hot to Sleep*, is published by Written Off Publishing. Her debut novel, *These Mortal Bodies*, is forthcoming with Simon & Schuster in 2025. She can often be found in the sea.

Taylor Grothe graduated cum laude with Honors from Duke University (2012), and is a 2024 Nonfiction MFA graduate of Fairfield University's Creative Writing Program. Their shorts can be found in *Coffin Bell*, Bag of Bones Press, *Haven Speculative*, *Shortwave* magazine, and various other places. Taylor was a Round 9 Author Mentor Match adult mentor, the graduate Assistant Managing Editor of *Brevity* magazine for 2022–23, and one of the founding members and the 2023–24 program coordinator of Round Table Mentor. Their debut YA horror novel, *Hollow*, comes out with Peachtree Teen in fall 2025, with another book to follow in 2026. Taylor is represented by Victoria Marini of High Line Literary Collective.

Olivie Blake is the *New York Times* bestselling author of *The Atlas Six*, *Alone With You in the Ether*, *Masters of Death*, and other works of adult contemporary sci-fi and fantasy, including the short stories "Pythia" from the anthology *In These Hallowed Halls*, and "The Fall Guy" from the anthology *The Secret Romantic's Book of Magic*. As Alexene Farol Follmuth, she is also the author of the young adult rom-coms *My Mechanical Romance* and *Twelfth Knight*. She lives in Los Angeles with her husband and goblin prince/toddler.

De Elizabeth (she/her) is a horror and dark fantasy author writing haunted, romantic books. She is passionate about telling emotionally resonant dark stories that feature messy main characters and bisexual representation. She is the author of *This Raging Sea*, an upper YA dark fantasy, and *A Shared Haunting*, a dark academia horror novel. In addition to writing fiction, De is a journalist specialising in pop culture, mental health, and LGBTQ+ issues. Her articles have been featured in *Teen Vogue*, *HuffPost*, MTV News, and more. You can find her online at deelizabeth.com and on Instagram @WordsByDe.

Kit Mayquist is a queer mystery author living in New England where he loves finding new ways to explore the dark and beautiful side of nature. He has a Master's degree in Medieval History from the University of Iceland and remains an active student for all things strange and bizarre. His debut novel, *Tripping Arcadia* (Dutton), has been featured in *Cosmopolitan*, *BuzzFeed*, and Belletrist.

Faridah Àbíké-Íyímídé is the instant *New York Times* international bestselling and award-winning author of *Ace of Spades*, *Where Sleeping Girls Lie*, and *Four Eids and a Funeral*. She has also written stories for Marvel's *Spider-Verse* and the BBC's *Doctor Who*. Faridah is a graduate from a university in Scotland where she received a BA in English Literature. She also has an MA in Shakespeare Studies from King's College London.

M. K. Lobb is a fantasy writer with a love of all things dark – be it literature, humour, or general aesthetic. She grew up in small-town Ontario and studied political science at both the University of Western Ontario and the University of Ottawa. She now lives by the lake with her partner and their cats. When not reading or writing, she can be found at the gym or contemplating the harsh realities of existence.

Ariel Djanikian is the author of *The Prospectors* (William Morrow), selected for the Barnes & Noble Book Club, and *The Office of Mercy* (Viking). She holds degrees from the University of Pennsylvania and the University of Michigan, and is the previous recipient of a Fulbright grant, Meijer Fellowship, Cowden Award, and Hopwood Award. Her writing has appeared in *Tin House*, *Alaska Quarterly Review*, *Glimmer Train*, *The Millions*, and *The Rumpus*. Born in Philadelphia, she currently lives near Washington, DC, where she teaches creative writing at Georgetown University.

Kate Alice Marshall is the bestselling author of thrillers and horror for adults and teens. Her books include *What Lies in the*

Woods, *Rules for Vanishing*, *I Am Still Alive*, and *A Killing Cold*, as well as middle grade novels *Thirteens* and *Extra Normal*. She spent her childhood searching for magic and adventure in the woods of the Pacific Northwest, which might explain why she can't seem to keep her characters from straying into the forest.

ABOUT THE EDITORS

Marie O'Regan is a British Fantasy Award and Shirley Jackson Award-nominated author and editor, based in Derbyshire. She was awarded the British Fantasy Society's "Legends of FantasyCon" award in 2022. Her first collection, *Mirror Mere*, was published in 2006 by Rainfall Books; her second, *In Times of Want*, came out in September 2016 from Hersham Horror Books. Her third, *The Last Ghost and Other Stories*, was published by Luna Press early in 2019. Her short fiction has appeared in a number of genre magazines and anthologies in the UK, US, Canada, Italy, and Germany, including *Best British Horror 2014*, *Great British Horror: Dark Satanic Mills* (2017), and *The Mammoth Book of Halloween Stories*. Her novella, *Bury Them Deep*, was published by Hersham Horror Books in September 2017. She was shortlisted for the British Fantasy Society Award for Best Short Story in 2006, and Best Anthology in 2010 (*Hellbound Hearts*) and 2012 (*The Mammoth Book of Ghost Stories by Women*). She was also shortlisted for the

Shirley Jackson Award for Best Anthology in 2020 (*Wonderland*). Her genre journalism has appeared in magazines like *The Dark Side*, *Rue Morgue*, and *Fortean Times*, and her interview book with prominent figures from the horror genre, *Voices in the Dark*, was released in 2011. An essay on *The Changeling* was published in PS Publishing's *Cinema Macabre*, edited by Mark Morris. She is co-editor of the bestselling *Hellbound Hearts*, *The Mammoth Book of Body Horror*, *A Carnivàle of Horror: Dark Tales from the Fairground*, *Exit Wounds*, *Wonderland*, *Cursed*, *Twice Cursed*, *The Other Side of Never*, *In These Hallowed Halls*, *Beyond & Within: Folk Horror Short Stories*, *Death Comes at Christmas*, and *The Secret Romantic's Book of Magic*, as well as the charity anthology *Trickster's Treats #3*, plus editor of the bestselling anthologies *The Mammoth Book of Ghost Stories by Women* and *Phantoms*. Her first novel, the internationally bestselling *Celeste*, was published in February 2022. She is also Managing Editor of PS Publishing's award-winning novella imprint, Absinthe Books. Marie was Chair of the British Fantasy Society from 2004 to 2008, and Co-Chair of the UK Chapter of the Horror Writers Association from 2015 to 2022. She was also Co-Chair of ChillerCon UK in 2022. Visit her website at marieoregan.net. She can be found on X @Marie_O_Regan and Instagram @marieoregan8101.

Paul Kane is the award-winning (including the British Fantasy Society's "Legends of FantasyCon" Award 2022), bestselling author and editor of over a hundred and sixty books – such as the Arrowhead trilogy (gathered together in the sellout *Hooded Man* omnibus, revolving around a post-apocalyptic version of Robin

Hood), *The Butterfly Man and Other Stories*, *Hellbound Hearts*, *Wonderland* (a Shirley Jackson Award finalist), and *Pain Cages* (an Amazon #1 bestseller). His non-fiction books include *The Hellraiser Films and Their Legacy* and *Voices in the Dark*, and his genre journalism has appeared in the likes of *SFX*, *Rue Morgue*, and *DeathRay*. He has been a Guest at Alt.Fiction five times, was a Guest at the first SFX Weekender, at Thought Bubble in 2011, Derbyshire Literary Festival and Off the Shelf in 2012, Monster Mash and Event Horizon in 2013, Edge-Lit in 2014 and 2018, HorrorCon, HorrorFest, and Grimm Up North in 2015, The Dublin Ghost Story Festival and Sledge-Lit in 2016, IMATS Olympia and Celluloid Screams in 2017, Black Library Live and the UK Ghost Story Festival in 2019 and 2023, plus the WordCrafter virtual event in 2021 – where he delivered the keynote speech – as well as being a panellist at FantasyCon and the World Fantasy Convention, and a fiction judge at the Sci-Fi-London festival. A former British Fantasy Society Special Publications Editor, he has also served as Co-Chair for the UK Chapter of The Horror Writers Association and co-chaired ChillerCon UK in May 2022.

His work has been optioned and adapted for the big and small screen, including for US network primetime television, and his novelette "Men of the Cloth" was turned into a feature by Loose Canon/Hydra Films, starring Barbara Crampton (*Re-Animator*, *You're Next*): *Sacrifice*, released by Epic Pictures/101 Films. Paul was also asked to pitch, along with a co-writer, for the remake of *Hellraiser* in the late 2010s. His audio work includes the full cast drama adaptation of *The Hellbound Heart* for Bafflegab, starring Tom Meeten (*The Ghoul*), Neve McIntosh (*Doctor Who*), and

Alice Lowe (*Prevenge*), and the *Robin of Sherwood* adventure *The Red Lord* for Spiteful Puppet/ITV narrated by Ian Ogilvy (*Return of the Saint*), plus his plays have been performed at FantasyCon and by Hideout Theatre in London. He has also contributed to the Warhammer 40k universe for Games Workshop and has been asked to pitch on projects for both DC/Warner Bros. and Marvel. Paul's latest novels are *Lunar* (set to be turned into a feature film), the YA story *The Rainbow Man* (as P. B. Kane), the sequels to *RED – Blood RED* and *Deep RED*, all collected in an omnibus edition – the award-winning hit *Sherlock Holmes and the Servants of Hell*, *Before* (an Amazon Top 5 dark fantasy bestseller), *Arcana*, and *The Storm*. In addition he writes thrillers for HQ/HarperCollins as P. L. Kane, the first of which, *Her Last Secret* and *Her Husband's Grave* (a sellout on Waterstones.com and at The Works), came out in 2020, with *The Family Lie* released the following year (*all three novels were Amazon sellouts*). His books have been translated into many languages, including French, German, Spanish, Ukrainian, Turkish, Czech, Bulgarian, and Polish. Paul lives in Derbyshire, UK, with his wife **Marie O'Regan**. Find out more at his site shadow-writer.co.uk which has featured Guest Writers such as Stephen King, Charlaine Harris, Robert Kirkman, Catriona Ward, Dean Koontz, Sarah Pinborough, and Guillermo del Toro. He can also be found @PaulKaneShadow on X, and @paul.kane.376 on Instagram.

ACKNOWLEDGEMENTS

And now for the important bit – our chance to say a big thank you. Firstly to all the authors for their contributions, to Dan Carpenter for commissioning once again, and to all the wonderful team at Titan. Finally, thanks to our respective families, without whom etc.

For more fantastic fiction, author events,
exclusive excerpts, competitions, limited editions and more

VISIT OUR WEBSITE
titanbooks.com

LIKE US ON FACEBOOK
facebook.com/titanbooks

FOLLOW US ON TWITTER AND INSTAGRAM
@TitanBooks

EMAIL US
readerfeedback@titanemail.com